EVERYMAN'S LIBRARY

EVERYMAN,
I WILL GO WITH THEE,
AND BE THY GUIDE,
IN THY MOST NEED
TO GO BY THY SIDE

JOSEPH CONRAD

Typhoon and Other Stories

with an Introduction by
Martin Seymour-Smith

EVERYMAN'S LIBRARY

4

This book is one of 250 volumes in Everyman's Library
which have been distributed to 4500 state schools
throughout the United Kingdom.
The project has been supported by a grant of £4 million
from the Millennium Commission.

First included in Everyman's Library, 1945
Introduction © Martin Seymour-Smith, 1991
Bibliography and Chronology © David Campbell
Publishers Ltd., 1991
Typography by Peter B. Willberg

ISBN 1-85715-004-X

Published by David Campbell Publishers Ltd.,
Gloucester Mansions, 140A Shaftesbury Avenue,
London WC2H 8HD

Distributed by Random House (UK) Ltd.,
20 Vauxhall Bridge Road, London SW1V 2SA

CONTENTS

———

INTRODUCTION

The three works here collected, *The Nigger of the 'Narcissus'* (1897), 'Typhoon' (1902) and *The Shadow-Line* (1917), have in common only that they were all liked by their author (he frequently, if never quite consistently, expressed his dislike of certain of his works, such as *Lord Jim*), and (happily) that all can, reasonably, be claimed as masterpieces or at least near-masterpieces. The first, *The Nigger*, stands at the very beginning of Conrad's auspicious but exceedingly difficult career as a writer, and is prefaced by a famous artistic credo; this was the work in which he discovered his own voice. The second is one of his few relatively simple works. The third is the outstanding item in a list which, from *Chance* (1913) onwards – even though it was, ironically, *Chance* which brought him freedom from indebtedness and reliance upon loans and grants ('miracles') from the Royal Literary Fund – has been reckoned, and on the whole properly reckoned, as marking a decline from the heights represented by *Nostromo* (1904), *The Secret Agent* (1907) and *Under Western Eyes* (1911). I do not propose to make any further, artificial connection between these three tales. It is sufficient that they are all by the same tortured and unique man: a writer who became a master of English style, but whose first and second languages were Polish and French, and whose first career was as man of action, not man sitting at a desk with pen in hand – Conrad the writer's pen sometimes fell, to his enraged consternation, from his gouty fingers to the ground. It was of the greatest significance, and of the greatest possible benefit to literature, that the first career should have been so far removed from literature: decisions made at sea can't have much to do with books (as MacWhirr says, in 'Typhoon') ... It was from his knowledge of the occasional necessity of this kind of practicality that Conrad was able to tell his readers so much they did not yet quite know. His art not only illuminates, but informs.

It was once influentially but carelessly asserted that Conrad did not 'explore human relationships'! But what more appropriate symbol is there of a human relationship than the seafaring life from the experience of which Conrad so often (if not always) drew? He did not like being called a 'sea novelist'. These three tales, all of the sea, show why. He could point to *Nostromo*, *The Secret Agent* and others to demonstrate the misnomer. But he also had in mind the fact that such works as these, unequivocally drawing upon his seafaring experience, have themes which go far beyond mere sea adventures – are, indeed, and very precisely so, studies in 'human relationships'. Conrad, quite unlike W. Clark Russell – a contemporary author of semi-competent maritime adventures – or even R. H. Dana, in his superior *Two Years Before the Mast* (1840), used the sea, and his experiences of trying to master it, as a grand metaphor. After all, although no one has seriously questioned his mastery of seacraft, Conrad had been incongruous among sailors, a super-literate dandy, with a romantic past, and an attempted suicide at that. If illness drove him into the writer's role, then despair had driven him (before that) into the sailor's. In one of the most striking images he ever used to describe his writer's predicament, Conrad told Marguerite Poradowski (1894), 'Man must drag the ball and chain of his individuality up to the end. It is what we pay for the infernal and divine privilege of thought.'

1 *The Nigger of the 'Narcissus'*

At the age of thirty-two, in 1889, Conrad, a British master mariner (he qualified in November 1886), began work on his first novel, *Almayer's Folly*. He had started to experiment with writing some three years before that, with a 'prentice tale called 'The Black Mate', which he entered for a competition in *Tit Bits*. But he did not leave his service with the British merchant marine. He chose (1890) to go to the Belgian Congo in command of a river steamer (in his narrator Marlow's words, a two-penny river steamer with a penny whistle attached) which carried an exploring expedition. Out of that experience grew one of his finest and most famous tales, 'Heart of Darkness', which appeared first in the February–April editions of *Blackwood's Magazine* (1899) and then in the volume

Youth (1902). He had suffered tropical illnesses, including malaria, from the months he spent in Africa – they left him, on top of his other longer-standing ailments, a virtual semi-invalid – and he discovered, on his two voyages as chief mate of the clipper *Torrens*, plying between Plymouth and Port Adelaide in Australia, that he could not continue in the rough life of a mariner any longer. It was on the second of these two voyages that he met John Galsworthy. His last voyage was an abortive one: he went as far as Rouen as second mate on the steamer *Adowa*, bound for Calcutta; but she never sailed further. So his final decision to turn writer, reluctant because he knew what he was risking in both pride and security, was sharpened into necessity by a breakdown in health – by the idea of himself, as he put it, as a 'Punch ... pathetically droll ... in a corner, spine cracked, nose in the dust ...'; real illness, as well as psychosomatic symptoms, pushed him out from the arena of action into that of creative contemplation. At the same time, he had the nearly completed script of *Almayer's Folly*. He badly wanted to be thus pushed, but he also needed the real fact of the push. And just as he was poised on the edge of his writing career, terrified of whether he could bring it off or not, he was going through the worst time of his life, and was gaining relief only by involving himself in a dubious business deal on behalf of someone else. He saw the people in power in the world as uncommitted to anything more than fine words, to material gain, to personal advantage and to 'satisfied vanity'; he saw himself as uninterested in happiness and as no more 'courageous and independent than the others'. *The Nigger of the 'Narcissus'*, even though *Almayer's Folly* and its successor *An Outcast of the Islands* were necessary to his development, is the work in which he found his own voice and began to resolve the conflict in himself between nihilism and responsibility, between the wildnesses and terrors of the sea and the need to move over it with some mastery and grace.

It can be argued that the artistic success of *The Nigger* was what confirmed Conrad as a writer. He was still, while at work on it, seeking a command – if not seriously. And between *An Outcast of the Islands* and *The Nigger* came an abortive effort, the abandoned novel *The Sisters*, which was not published (and then only in a magazine) until 1928, four years after his death. He would not have approved of its being issued. In this 15,000-word script – set aside mainly because Edward Garnett, Conrad's main mentor at this stage, advised against it – Conrad failed to get away from the derivatively impressionistic, *fin de siècle* manner which marked his first two books, which are by no means devoid of purple passages. H. G. Wells, who perceived Conrad's genius very early on, went so far as to say (of *An Outcast of the Islands*) that 'he writes so as to mask and dishonour his genius'. Wells rightly noted that the workmanship was 'copiously bad'. After abandoning *The Sisters*, Conrad married the uneducated Jessie George, fifteen years younger than he (and whom he found 'no bother at all'), and set to work on 'The Rescuer', the novel which he would not be able to complete until 1919 (as *The Rescue: A Romance of the Shallows*, 1920), and then not successfully. He now needed to carve out the new, more original manner – one truer to his intentions – that is first seen in *The Nigger*. He began to write it – thinking of it as a short story – in June 1896, while he and Jessie were in Brittany on their honeymoon, and she was learning to become, in an offensive but in this case wholly accurate phrase (oft used by well-meaning critics until only recently) a 'genius's helpmeet'.

He did not finish it until the following February. It appeared first, serially, in W. E. Henley's monthly magazine (owned by the publisher Heinemann) *The New Review*, from August to December 1897. A version of the famous Preface also appeared here, with the last instalment. Heinemann put out an edition of eight copies (to secure copyright) in December 1897, without the Preface (significantly, S. S. Pawling, the partner responsible for the publication, refused it – presumably as too strong stuff). The trade edition appeared in 1898. In America it appeared serially in an abridged version in *The Illustrated Buffalo Express* (August–September 1897), and then as a book called *Children of the Sea: A Tale of the Forecastle* (1897), under the imprint of Dodd, Mead.

The Preface was so important to Conrad, as a manifesto of his intentions, that in 1902 he had it issued, from Hythe in Kent, as a pamphlet, *The Nigger of the 'Narcissus'/Preface*, in an edition limited to one hundred copies. The forger and bibliographer T. J. Wise may have had a hand in the arrangements for this publication, but since Conrad himself sent copies of it to various people, Wise's influence cannot have been fatally distorting, and was probably not distorting at all. (Conrad, as a highly prestigious but not best-selling author, had to depend for cash on just such dubious people, although he did not know that Wise was a forger – later he became associated with another purveyor of private editions, C. K. Shorter.) Eventually the Preface was incorporated, together with 'To My Readers in America' (printed here before the Preface), into the Doubleday edition of 1914.

Five questions about *The Nigger* require an answer. First, is it 'racist' (as it has often been called)? Concomitantly, to what extent, if at all, is the book a reflection of what has been described as a 'reactionary' outlook? Thirdly, is the undoubtedly shifting identity of the narrative voice a result of authorial confusion, and is it therefore truly inconsistent and ambiguous – or does it work? In other words, can it be justified? Fourthly, how well does this novella work as an allegory, and what, if it does or tries to, is it allegorical of? Finally, to what extent is it autobiographical? How did Conrad transmogrify his own experiences in it? For he had sailed in a vessel called the *Narcissus*, and for just this once he did not change its name (it is the only case in which he did not). This last matter may be disposed of quite briefly.

Frederick Karl, one of Conrad's biographers, remarks that the 'very name of the ship', *Narcissus*, 'must have penetrated some area of experience in Conrad that lay beyond self-awareness, in those recesses that were already stirring and moving him toward his next and final career. The ship name, like the title of the later book, apparently fitted into his view of art itself, as something based on mirrors, memories and reflections, an indirect, not a mimetic, art.' And of course *The Nigger of the 'Narcissus'* was the book which he himself regarded as the turning-point in his career as a writer.

It was April 1884, and Conrad had just left, at Madras, the ship, the *Riversdale*, upon which he had been serving as second mate, on account of a rift with its captain, whom he believed to be lacking in professionalism (he seems to have been: a few weeks later he stranded the vessel and was relieved of his command). As Karl points out, Conrad would always judge writers, too, on the strength of their professionalism, or lack of it. He was therefore, his own professionalism under fire, in a crisis of nerves special even to one of his neurasthenic temperament. He went from Madras to Bombay, and on 28 April signed on as second officer on the *Narcissus*, which he later described as a 'lovely ship, with all the graces of a yacht ... of 1300 tons, built by a sugar refiner of Greenock nine years before', which was bound for Dunkirk. Towards the end of his life, he told his French biographer and admirer Jean-Aubry:

Most of the personages I have portrayed actually belonged to the crew of the real *Narcissus*, including the admirable Singleton (whose real name was Sullivan), Archie, Belfast and Donkin. I got the two Scandinavians from association with another ship. All this is now quite old, but it was quite present before my mind when I wrote this book. I remember, as it had occurred but yesterday, the last occasion I saw the nigger. That morning I was quarter officer, and about five o'clock I entered the double-bedded cabin where he was lying full length. On the lower bunk, ropes, fids and pieces of cloth had been deposited, so as not to have to take them down into the sail-room if they should be wanted at once. I asked him how he felt, but he hardly made me any answer. A little later a man brought him some coffee in a cup provided with a hook to suspend it on the end of the bunk. At about six o'clock the officer-in-charge came to tell me that he was dead. We had just experienced an awful gale in the vicinity of the Needles, south of the cape ... As to the conclusion of the book, it is taken from other voyages which I made under similar circumstances.

But there was in fact no Sullivan aboard the *Narcissus* – he came from another ship upon which Conrad had sailed – and the fictional James Wait, the nigger, seems to have been based on more than one real person: not only on the thirty-five-year-old Joseph Barron whose death Conrad described to Jean-Aubry, but also on another man, George White, who sailed on the *Duke of Sutherland* – and on other seamen, white as well as black. As Conrad remarked, 'I do not write history, but fiction, and I am therefore entitled to choose as I please.' Thus, although those critics such as Norman Sherry (in particular) who have traced the links between Conrad's experience and his fiction have performed sterling service, they have not established (as they are sometimes taken to have, if not by themselves) that he was an autobiographer rather than a novelist. What they have shown is how history can be turned into art.

The hateful Donkin (not Conrad's representation of the awfulness of socialism, as he has been taken to be by a few critics of this cautious author's allegedly reactionary politics, but just an awful example of a man who is often found preaching socialism or communism, neither of which – or anything else – such a type cares about in the least) may have come, in part, from another *Narcissus* sailor, Charles Dutton, who had been put into gaol when the ship stopped off at Cape Town on the way to Bombay. But he is more likely to be drawn from an aggregation of many self-pitying and cowardly bolshie types encountered by Conrad at sea, to which many such men go. Donkin has been taken by some readers to be over-exaggerated, but it is hard to point to a more successful representation of such a type: Conrad seems to have pitched it just right, even to the numerous aspirates. That he had learned from Dickens is clear; but he really learned – he did not merely imitate.

Other sailors known to Conrad, some from the *Narcissus*, gave their names or their characteristics to people in *The Nigger*, including Belfast and Archibald MacLean. Conrad also served on the *Duke of Sutherland* with a mate called Baker. But it is already clear enough that there is little attempt at accurate autobiography, as such, in any of Conrad's fiction. The invaluable researches undertaken by Jerry Allen in her *The Sea Years of Joseph Conrad* (1965), and then by Sherry, show unequivocally that for Conrad the transforming powers of the imagination were all-important. In certain respects *The Nigger* is nearer to a poem than to a novel, both in its deliberately heightened language (sometimes this goes just over the top) and in its fabulous qualities. It owes much, and hardly obliquely, to the most famous literary ballad ever written, Coleridge's 'Rime of the Ancient Mariner'. That influence persists, and becomes even more specific almost twenty years later, in *The Shadow-Line.*

The Nigger has been accused of being 'racist', and an excellent editor of it, Professor Cedric Watts, feels so troubled by its 'reactionary' political implications that he is constrained to announce: 'I think that the prestige of this vivid novel is now, partly for good reasons, in decline.' But he does then add that it has 'outlived many judges' and 'may well outlive more'. As the first work in which Conrad found a voice adequate to his majestic imaginative needs, and one of very great power, one may feel confident that it will. After all, a world without *The Nigger* is a world without Conrad, and for the man of good will, that is not one worth living in. As Karl says, and no one can fail to agree, here Conrad 'found the right rhythms for his fiction'.

As to its 'racist' and 'reactionary' qualities. Watts makes much of what he chooses to call Conrad's advocacy of 'hard primitivism', his 'attacks' on the highly emotional supporter of sailors' rights, the MP Samuel Plimsoll, and his use of the phrase 'the repulsive mask of a nigger's soul' in his initial description of the 'calm, towering, superb' James Wait.

As readers of the note to his American audience will gather, Conrad held the decision by W. E. Henley to include *The Nigger* in his *New Review* to be the 'most gratifying recollection of my writer's life!' But he was not there retrospectively acknowledging the joy of having had an editor accept a set of 'reactionary' and 'racist' ideas! The truth is more complicated.

The courageous, crippled Henley, like Rudyard Kipling, was a jingoist, an extreme imperialist. A more than merely capable editor, and the writer of some impressionistic poetry of real charm and delicacy, he was also given to over-aggressive speciousness (as in the famous 'Invictus'), to provoking violent quarrels, and to the vain notion that the British were superior to other races of men. All that was anathema to Conrad, however much he may have kept it to himself so far as Henley was concerned: the essential humanity, which he expressed in 'Heart of Darkness' (written in 1899 and published in *Youth* in 1902), based on his recent African experiences, was already confirmed. It is less certainly expressed in *The Nigger*, but it is never denied. The mention of Plimsoll (who did sometimes exaggerate the badness of conditions on ships, as no doubt he had to do, to be effective) cannot be taken as critical. Later Conrad did pay him tribute for his work in ensuring better conditions. One cannot purge the speech of an author's characters because it might seem embarrassing in the context of a contemporary town-hall meeting.

Later in life Conrad was to allude, with his habitually fierce irony, in the 1920 note to his novel *The Secret Agent* (1907), of his 'business' as a writer (the book brought him in little in the way of money), to which (he said) he was 'simply attending'. He was talking about the objectifying faculty of his imagination, to the fact that a writer – about whose role he was always assailed, in common with other writers, with the gravest and most tormenting doubts – wherever his personal sympathies may lie, necessarily transcends them in the act of creation. He had been reading Flaubert while writing *The Nigger*, and Flaubert, who believed in the author as a kind of priest, remained his master. When his socialist-anarchist friend R. B. Cunninghame Graham, an ex-MP and disturber of the peace (he had been in gaol for it) and a splendidly effective public nuisance, published his sarcastic and anti-racist article 'Bloody Niggers' in the Marxist magazine *The Social Democrat*, Conrad had finished *The Nigger*, and knew very well just what he had intended. He wrote to Graham: 'very good, very telling'. What then can Watts, who most scrupulously quotes this, think that the 'racist' Conrad had in mind? His friendship with Graham, which could do him no good in terms of career – the flamboy-ant Scot had little influence on the literary establishment – became very close. He used Graham, with whom he had real affinities, to salve his conscience, while he clung to the decent and sincere but essentially conservative Galsworthy as a kind of guarantee that the respectable world would not reject him. To his great irritation, he depended on this world for his sales. The nominally Tory (and lapsed Catholic) Ford, who would come into his life very shortly, was the one who was really going to share his view of the politicians, bankers and million-aires (the real anarchists, Conrad called them) who run the world. But he took so much from Ford that he would eventually have to quarrel with him on dubious grounds (except that Jessie, not a literary woman, resented his influence over her husband, as well as the way he dried his hat in her oven).

The narrator of *The Nigger* writes of James Wait

He held his head up in the glare of the lamp – a head vigorously modelled into deep shadows and shining lights – a head powerful and misshapen with a tormented and flattened face – a face pathetic and brutal: the tragic, the mysterious, the repulsive mask of a nigger's soul.

Watts comments: 'the racism of this passage can be mitigated by noting that it is the mask, rather than the soul, which is declared "repulsive"; but the declaration remains irremediably racist'.

Well, Conrad is dealing with the world of what Watts calls 'common and casual prejudice', and as a highly self-conscious artist he has got to be realistic rather than prissy about it. This is the world itself, rough and nasty and common and prejudiced. No looking askance at colleagues who ought to know better here. Such gestures, including those of slight mitigation, won't wash here. And the real point of Watts' (and others') charge is that Conrad has got no 'business' (I use the word advisedly, in his own special sense) to depict such shocking verbal illiberalism. For such critics there are subjects fit for discussion, and there are subjects that are not. The shifting narrator says at one point: 'The latent egoism of the tenderness to [Wait's] suffering appeared in the developing anxiety not to see him die.' Watts interprets this and other remarks as a straightforward expression of what he calls the 'philosophy' of 'hard primitivism', which he thus summarizes:

... the crew's sympathy with the dying Jimmy is partly a vicarious self-pity ... Those that are apparently ruthless ... are thus the true altruists, because their unsentimental concern for work and duty sustains solidarity and helps to preserve the ship and her voyagers; while those who seem most sympathetic to Jimmy are neglecting their duties and weakening the hierarchic order on which the general good depends.

But none of this is implicit in the text, as an ethical basis for living, and it is of no use to add that its 'metaphysical' import – to which we shall come – 'offers mystical reinforcement to the tale's conservative elements'. Conrad's 'tough-minded' inference (not ethic), does not operate here as some Kiplingesque work-ethic satisfying to Henley and the jingo-prone readership of his magazine: it is bitterly presented as being uncomfortably true under certain circumstances. It records various actual and all too familiar reactions on the part of the crew, and of certain individuals in it, to James Wait and to his colour. The whole crew's responses to Wait's 'irrational' imperiousness and sickness is traced much as Shakespeare traced the crowd's reactions to Brutus and to Mark Antony. The facts of survival and of Wait's death are there as a challenge not just to hostile critics' professed liberalism and humanity, but to Conrad's own. The *mask* of the nigger's soul is recorded as repulsive because to the crew it seems so.

Conrad might have chosen to be more delicate and careful in presenting this had he not been desperately anxious to please Henley, of the nature of whose more crazy ideas he was well aware. He was certainly by no means reluctant to include the lyrical passage (in V) about the *Narcissus* as England, 'A great ship! ... The great flagship of the race; stronger than the storm! and anchored in the open sea.' But so far as 'race' does not here mean 'water', it means 'human race', and to be a flagship of that race is not to be superior. There is no actually imperialistic implication. The crew has survived a terrible storm, they are going into the Port of London, and that is how they would express themselves if they were articulate. The words do reflect Conrad's personal feelings about his chosen country and nationality; but they are somewhat intrusive into the primary, 'metaphysical' meaning of the book, and it is hard to escape the conclusion that Conrad did not somewhat gratuitously include them as a sly appeal to Henley, who had previously seen only a part of the script, and who had said that he wanted the rest to be up to par. That is not the same as *being* racist or imperialistic, and of course everyone knows that Conrad was not. He has been claimed as both a reactionary and as a Marxist; the truth is that he can satisfy neither party. He has his 'business' to attend to, and his business is truth. At the very worst Conrad is guilty of imperfect craftsmanship in presenting the crew's image of Wait as he does (but I doubt if he is), rather than of any intrinsic racism. Perhaps he would have expressed himself more delicately in some modern committee room where pseudo-liberal purity of language takes precedence over action, or foulness of secret inner conviction. But here he was being exactly what he guiltily was: a man, not a spokesperson for a league of linguistic purity. Such a storm as threatened the *Narcissus* is not the equivalent of a dressing-down from a tenured radical who does not believe in authors because he envies them: liberalism, justice, tolerance, identity, humanity itself, are all under actual and severe threat. Conrad shows how they fare, how they vanish, how they survive. In the account of the sea burial of Jimmy, which is moving and above all real, Conrad makes his reader do exactly what – as he writes in the Preface – he intended him to do: to *see*, which meant, for him, not only to evoke clear images, but also 'to dispense insight and understanding'. The notion of his 'racism' (as distinct from his strategy of presentation, which is at least arguably misjudged) is made irrelevant by the context not just of all his work, but by the context of *The Nigger*, when we consider the function of the loathsome Donkin. Singleton is an unimaginative, 'admirable' man (we shall encounter him again, at a rather higher level, as MacWhirr in 'Typhoon') who states the obvious; what Singleton says is in no way whatever racist. Only Donkin is racist, and he steals Jimmy's money...

But although *The Nigger* is realistic on its surface – even deliberately impressionistic, borrowing from Stephen Crane's *The Red Badge of Courage* as it borrows from Maupassant's *Bel Ami* for some details of Wait's death – it is above all poetic and allegorical. Where Conrad is not quite mature is in his handling of the narrative line. The distinctions between the various voices have been noted: there are, at least, an 'I', an individual crewman, a 'we' (the voice of the whole crew), a voice using 'they' of the crew, but not exactly definable; and there is perhaps an 'omniscient' author of some lyrical and analytical passages. While we must agree with Ian Watt (not a critic anxious to pick holes in the interests of making common-room points) that Conrad 'is at liberty to use his pretended narrator in whatever way will best serve his purpose', we also have, I think, to acknowledge that there is sometimes an actual confusion: that the function of each voice has not been fully worked out by Conrad. Hence, almost immediately, the invention of Marlow as narrative device: the introduction of a definite point of view, not Conrad's own, but consistent. For much of the time the narrative of *The Nigger* does work. In particular, a valuable distinction may be made between an individual crewman's point of view, and the 'we' of the crew as a whole. Within a very few years, in France, Jules Romains and others (Duhamel amongst them) would invent 'unanimism', a method by which the crowd itself (as inhabitants of blocks of flats, of barracks, even of cities and countries) would be given the voice these theorists felt it deserved. Zola had been working towards such a method, and so had authors of other countries. The unanimists had a rather rosy view of human nature (it was to be corrected by their war experiences), and Conrad did not. But his view was not wholly pessimistic; it was, rather, very strictly realistic. This frightening phenomenon is shown (exposed?) by Shakespeare in *Julius Caesar*, famously studied in Canetti's *Crowds and Power* and, more brilliantly, in Norman Cohn's chilling *The Pursuit of the Millennium*. It is the football mob that kills and is killed by itself. It is the crew of the *Narcissus*. But had Conrad revised this text, later in his life when he had attained the confidence of a master (*The Nigger* announces a master, but its author is only on the verge of mastery), he might have made fruitful changes, and separated the 'we' more clearly from the multiform 'I'. But he was far too fond of it, and of its Preface, to be inclined to fiddle with it. The lyrical passages may fairly be taken as the articulated voice of the crew as a whole. 'We' were going to mutiny on behalf of James Wait. 'We' found him 'repulsive'. 'We' refused to mutiny. 'We' acclaimed England (it was how the crew felt, whether that pleased Henley or not) as we sailed up the Thames. 'We' are not consistent. And what crowd is? It is the individuals who are variously merciful to, or betray, Wait. Donkin abuses him and steals his money. Belfast gives him aid. Singleton is indifferent. That is how it would be, and has been, in 'real life'. Conrad is not *preaching* irrationalism or 'hard primitivism' (a concept uninvented when he wrote). He is preaching nothing. There is no reason in the mob, which is as pervious to Donkin's whining as it would be impervious to a lecture on correctly liberal speech habits from a deconstructivist professor. But there is a vitality that needs to survive a terrible storm, and which is superstitious about its causes ... The storm is the same one, as Conrad himself actually said, as the one worked out at a more realistic level in 'Typhoon'. Here it serves a more allegorical purpose, for all the very fine and authentic description of it.

We are on a ship of fools here. Twice Conrad specifically refers to *folly*. Each character is a different sort of fool, in the old medieval sense of the fool as presented in Sebastian Brant's *Der Narrenschiff*, a work much adapted and imitated throughout the Middle Ages: a tradition known of course to all literatures, including English and Polish. Erasmus' *In Praise of Folly* is in it. Conrad must have been aware of this tradition. However, I do not claim that he was deliberately making use of some work in it as a model for *The Nigger*. No more needs to be said than that there are wise fools (Singleton?) and stupid fools (Donkin?). The ass upon which Christ rode into Jerusalem was celebrated as a fool.

But the text underlying *The Nigger* is Coleridge's 'Ancient Mariner' (it is to underlie *The Shadow-Line* even more specifically). Wait's strangeness and his nearness to the possession of the secret of death (which he wants to deny) works both ways: Singleton and the boatswain both regard him as bad luck. His name suggests that he is a *weight*, a burden, and that he holds back the ship. The crew 'commenced to believe Singleton, but with unshaken fidelity dissembled to Jimmy', 'our Jimmy', the 'tormentor of all our moments'. 'What makes mankind tragic is not that they are the victims of nature, but that they are conscious of it,' Conrad wrote to Cunninghame Graham. And one thinks in that connection of the moving passage about the gallant ship's cat, Tom, who

...came out from somewhere. He had an ovation. They snatched him from hand to hand, caressed him in a murmur of pet names. They wondered whether he had 'weathered it out'; disputed about it. A squabbling argument began. Two men came in with a bucket of fresh water, and all crowded round it; but Tom, lean and mewing, came up with every hair astir and had the first drink.

Tom, who is not 'conscious of it', is the unequivocal, ironic, untragic hero. And it is as an account of storm and trial that *The Nigger* functions most naturally and perfectly.

The Nigger, then, is an imperfect masterpiece: Conrad has not yet quite reached the top of his narrative bent. There are some confusions. Although the writing is not short of magnificent, it is also occasionally a bit over the top. But it rises so far above the concerns of 'racism' as to deal very firmly with them, and to demonstrate their abject and all-too-human pettiness. 'It is the book by which ... as an artist striving for the utmost sincerity of expressing, I am willing to stand or fall,' Conrad wrote in a copy he gave to a friend. We all know that he stands. As to the Preface: this speaks for itself. Influenced though it is by Flaubert, by Pater, by French *symboliste* doctrine, it too stands as a credo.

2 *'Typhoon'*

Very much less needs to be said about 'Typhoon', which represents Conrad at his most simple. It has been underrated, for it is beautifully written, beautifully worked out, and remains one of its author's finest achievements. If it has not been allowed as work of top quality, then I think this is in part because it lacks the sort of high complexity so over-welcomed by critics. But it is top quality – by virtue of this very simplicity! Conrad finished it in January 1901, and it appeared serially in the January–March 1902 numbers of the *Pall Mall Gazette*. It was published in volume form as the title story of *Typhoon* (1903). He told his friend Richard Curle, long afterwards, that it had been 'meant as a pendant to the storm in *The Nigger*, the ship in this case being a steamship'. It is based on an anecdote Conrad heard, and on a captain called

John MacWhirr under whom he had once sailed. But it is nearer to pure fiction than most of his works.

Conrad had by now met Ford Madox Ford (at that time Ford Madox Hueffer), and had taken him on – after discussing the wisdom of the enterprise with various people – as collaborator. Each man brought out the best from the other. Ford in particular acted as a catalyst for Conrad's genius. He was to support him as collaborator (in the two books *The Inheritors*, 1901, and *Romance*, 1903), as writer (he wrote parts of *Nostromo*, of *The Mirror of the Sea*, and of other books), as friend, as financier. Conrad helped him grow up as a writer (he had written nothing mature). He gave Conrad that Englishness and that irony of style which he required to achieve his major work. Of course the older man had in the end to reject the younger. He had been altogether too much in his life. He was, too, ungenerous to poor Ford, who was, alas, while made of gold, a very convenient figure upon whom to dump feelings of resentment, guilt and hatred. But the true story, the essence of which is told in 'The Secret Sharer' (1902), is much more generous – and that is what really counts, and what counted for Ford, who, very impure himself – but with the impurities running grossly and quite separately from the pure gold of which he was made, and never hopelessly mixed into it, as is so often the case with his insensitive detractors – well understood the necessity of human failings.

Karl thinks that 'Typhoon' shows a 'desire to escape momentarily from the arty world represented by Ford and to move back to a purer and simpler time'. In Conrad's perception that may have been the case, although it is to be doubted. Few critics can resist the temptation to belittle Ford, and fewer still appreciate his own genius. It is as if the critic's usual sense of his own creative shortcomings found some joyful balance in Ford's lack of respectability, and bad luck. Such critics forget *The Good Soldier*, and much other work, and, not least, Conrad's debt to his understanding. But certainly, after *Lord Jim*, Conrad had to demonstrate to himself and to his readers that he could tell a straight story, and tell it well and without many trimmings. Yet 'Typhoon' on every page demonstrates the change that had come about in Conrad since he met Ford, most especially in the confident manner with which he now characterized people. Curiously, or perhaps it is not so curious, he was now doing what Ford himself would not be able to do consistently until *The Good Soldier* (1916), and the Tietjens tetralogy written after the end of World War I. He was revelling in Fordian irony and humour. One cannot imagine his not having talked MacWhirr over, at length, with Ford. He had learned the tone from Ford's conversation. But they had also evolved it together. The opening characterization of MacWhirr, a very fine piece of writing, simply cannot be conceived outside this context. Few similar passages of English prose combine genuinely amazed humane respect with kindly irony in so incisive a manner. I would not want to claim that Ford wrote this, although it happens that, logistically, he could have done; but Conrad trusted him (and only him, ever) to write for him, to write under his name. But such a hypothesis is unnecessary. When these two met they meshed in their attitudes, each offering his particular observations from his own experience, in a perfect symbiosis of which (alas) they had only to 'become conscious' for it to become 'tragic'.

And so, in 'Typhoon', the storm is the storm run through by the *Narcissus*, and MacWhirr is Singleton, but a Singleton given more ability, and born rather higher up the human order. MacWhirr is an astonishingly unimaginative man. Too unimaginative, really, to be a hero, a character with whom the intelligent reader can identify. He appears comically, at first, even to Jukes, that deliberately commonplacely named grand hero. One is reminded of some lines by Laura Riding that are not perhaps quite as famous as they should be:

> It falls to an idiot to talk wisely.
> It falls to a sot to wear beauty.
> It falls to many to be blessed
> In their shortcomings,
> As to the common brute it falls
> To see real miracle
> And howl with irksome joy.
>
> Many are the confusions that fall,
> Many are the inspired ones,

> Much is there indeed contrary,
> Much is there indeed wonderful.
> A most improbable one it takes
> To tell what is so,
> And the strangest of all
> To be natural.

Few will demur at what is said here, and few will fail to see the immediate relevance to 'Typhoon': to MacWhirr, whose illogical and perhaps even stupid decision not to change course blessed him in a shortcoming. The man embodies just the paradoxes mentioned in the poem:

Yet the uninteresting lives of men so entirely given to the actuality of the bare existence have their mysterious side. It was impossible in Captain MacWhirr's case, for instance, to understand what under heaven could have induced that perfectly satisfactory son of a petty grocer in Belfast to run away to sea. And yet he had done that very thing at the age of fifteen. It was enough, when you thought it over, to give you the idea of an immense, potent and invisible hand thrust into the antheap of the earth, laying hold of shoulders, knocking heads together, and setting the unconscious faces of the multitude towards inconceivable goals and undreamt-of directions.

So the end of it is that MacWhirr muddles through, or perhaps even just gets through without even exactly muddling it (as Conrad–Ford might have put it). Jukes can write: 'The skipper remarked to me the other day, "There are things you find nothing about in books". I think that he got out of it very well for such a stupid man.' We are reminded yet again of Conrad's words to Graham about the tragic consequences of 'consciousness', as well as of Hamlet's 'nothing's good nor bad but thinking makes it so' – and of his phrase 'sicklied o'er with the pale cast of thought'. MacWhirr, very emphatically *not* an imaginative writer (we are given amusing examples of his amazing letters home – they are just like a child's, and yet he is hardly a child, and he has children of his own), manages to be so strange as almost to be 'natural'. Yet he is 'fortunate', 'ignorant of life to the last', 'disdained by destiny or by the sea'. It is Conrad the writer's tribute to the tough virtues of that unartistic world which his own creative imagination so painfully transmutes: the world that gives him the strength and courage to exercise that terrible 'consciousness' of the 'tragedy' of existence.

3 *The Shadow-Line*

The Shadow-Line came late in Conrad's writing life. A version of it was published ('dragged out' was how Conrad thought of it, as he believed the instalments ought to have been longer) in the *English Review* during 1916; the definitive version appeared as a single volume – Conrad did not want it to appear with other stories – in 1917.

By the time of the publication of *Victory* (1915) Conrad's powers were in decline, although he was by no means written out. He was ill and tired, and he had lived for too long between the extremes of a highly self-conscious artistic integrity – for he simply could not help himself in that respect – and a fear of collapse into penury. One can make a rather formidable defence of *Victory*, in which he expressed his feelings about money and sex; but whether such a defence can hold or not (it is harder to argue for the success of this novel than it is for that of *The Nigger*; but Conradians will never find much in it to dislike), he was exhausted at the end of it. Although what he wrote after that is of the greatest biographical interest, and is at the least good reading, it cannot stand by his best fiction without suffering from the comparison. The single exception is *The Shadow-Line*, although there has been disagreement about it. Some critics find much of it 'disastrously weak', while others have hailed it as a masterful allegory of the disintegration of Europe cast in terms of a sea voyage. This last it certainly is not, but it is a work of many meanings, and one which is more likely than not to survive as one of Conrad's best shorter works.

He had had it in his mind since 1899, under the tentative title of 'The First Command'. In it he wanted to try to discover the full meaning of his own first command, in early 1888, of the *Otago* (at £14 a month, it is worth recalling). But by 1915 (he wrote the tale between February and December of that year: the '1916' in the 'Author's Note' is a mistake) his intentions had changed. Inspired by the heroic plight of his seventeen-year-old son Borys (and the others like him), who had just been sent to France, Conrad now wanted to write an elaborate allegory in which his own most testing experience would provide a commentary – if only an oblique one – on the meaning of war. It became the most exactly autobiographical of his works of fiction, for his narrative, while it does deviate from the facts in the matter of the states of mind of some of the characters, does not do so in any very marked degree. Fidelity to fact in a work of fiction does not matter half as much as some moralistically or perhaps only sensationally inclined critics like to think, especially since it is not even possible (as has now become commonplace) to tell the exact truth even in so-called non-fiction. But in this case the essential truth, the faithfulness to his own perception, naturally hyperbolic (but not manipulative, as begins to happen in *The Arrow of Gold*) though this might sometimes be, was especially precious to him, because of his feelings about his son and about the disaster of the war.

Like any father, he felt for his son, and through him he felt, as he put it in a letter, for 'the Others'. They, for him, were victims of more than just nature. Jacques Berthoud, whose interpretation of this work is the most sensitive and sensible, is right when he claims that, in effect, Conrad wanted 'to do his bit'. He chose to do it by the act of re-living his own experiences when he crossed the twilit 'shadow-line' between youth and adulthood. So it was the very act of writing that supplied the parallel to what Borys and the others were going through. By the art of hyperbole he saw into the very hearts of those men with whom, twenty-seven years earlier, he had served. The book is in part dedicated to them, in a moving phrase: 'Worthy of my undying-regard.' He saw into their essential souls: into the madness and weakness and confusion of the steward, into the conceit of Hamilton, into the courtesy and heroism of the unforgettable Ransome, and, above all, into his own sincerity of purpose – something about which, now, to feel thankful relief.

One of Conrad's most persistent themes, besides that of the details of his own painful consciousness of being a 'victim of nature', is intimately connected with it: the question of a person's destiny, which he sees as a matter of what 'nature' is going to do to him. Can people avoid their destiny? The answer for Conrad, as for his near contemporary Thomas Hardy, is that they cannot. But they can choose between the cowardice of an attempted avoidance of it, and a courageous and graceful acceptance of it. So *The Shadow-Line* is, at one level, the account of a rite of passage: the young captain passes his test.

A physician called Willis had written to Conrad in February 1888 telling him:

I think it is not out of place on my part that I should state, although not asked by you to do so, to prevent any misapprehension thereafter, that the crew of the sailing-ship *Otago* has suffered severely whilst in Bangkok from tropical diseases, dysentery and cholera; and I can speak of my own knowledge that you have done all in your power in the trying and responsible position of Master of the Ship to hasten the departure of your vessel from this unhealthy place and at the same time to save the lives of the men under your command.

The former master, a John Snedden, now dead, really had been half-mad, and had allowed the ship to wander the seas ('loaf at sea for inscrutable reasons') while he kept to his cabin or sawed away at his violin. The young captain was (much later) described by someone as 'dressed like a dandy' in 'fancy trousers', and as 'neurasthenic'. Before he took up the command Conrad had been bored, seekingly aimlessly for some kind of adventure. Hence the epigram from Baudelaire: 'D'autre fois calme plat, grand miroir/De mon désespoir' ('At other times, flat calm, great mirror of my despair'). This is a perfect image for the bored young dandy, a Narcissus, looking for meaning in his reflection. But in the events which took place just after he took over the command, Conrad found himself as a man.

As he writes in the 'Author's Note', Conrad was anxious to dispel all notion of the 'supernatural'. But he was by no means seeking to secularize, so to say, such elements of the supernatural as are in the Ancient Mariner or the Flying Dutchman legend. He was instead seeking to interpret them properly: to transform them from superstition (that is how his character Burns perceives things) into something *not* 'beyond the confines of this world'; into a real 'marvel and mystery', an 'effect of the tangible and visible world'. It is from reality, however 'inexplicable', that the marvellous arises.

Another of Conrad's concerns, of course – it is seen in both *The Nigger* and 'Typhoon' – is the need for reciprocity between men, if they are to survive. Durkheim, the French sociologist who was more or less contemporary with Conrad and whose work he may or may not have known (probably not), following Comte, explored the same kind of territory. He was subtler than Comte, and a superior thinker. A convinced atheist, he wanted to take the 'collective' element out of religion and put it to secular use. He spent his life trying to establish the real existence of the 'collective conscience'. Conrad does not go so far. He allows (as a very careful reading of the 'Author's Note' confirms) for an element of mystery, although not of superstition. He is content to demonstrate that no 'effects' arise from any forces or powers separate from mankind, and in need of appeasement from it. But he does seek, as Durkheim did, for some real reciprocity between men. In *The Shadow-Line* he demonstrates its possibility – and I think he does this successfully. He was tired, he was exhausted, his powers were on the wane; but sheer emotion, memory of his own initiation, love for his son, and the comparative brevity of his narrative, saw him through. It has been suggested that the affirmation of the ending of *The Shadow-Line* is a false affirmation. But this is so movingly and convincingly qualified by illness and death that it will seem to most readers to be an unfair judgement. In particular, the poignant 'blue funk' of Ransome, about his heart, qualifies it sufficiently to rob it of any note of insincere glibness – to make it, rather, into a true representation of the extent to which the positive can reach without recourse to false rhetoric. Conrad, who was peculiarly averse to the lush and specious patriotism of anti-German propaganda, and to all such popular rhetoric, did not want to evolve any *theory* of the existence of reciprocity; had he wanted to, he could not have done it. But it was not his 'business'. Nor did he, like Durkheim, want merely to discover possible examples of it in historical or anthropological records. But here and now his son was risking his life – and wanting to – against an enemy which threatened life itself. For Conrad the universe was always temptingly meaningless – it was not at all so for the more firmly secular Durkheim – however tainted and guilty he felt about possessing such feelings. But, like a surprising number of other writers who shared the same pessimism, he was spurred into something like optimism and affirmation by the spectacle of German militarism and its terrible implications. 'We are fighting for life first, for freedom of thought and development in whatever form we need,' he wrote. And he, too, as a bored and dandyish young man, had once discovered that he was fighting for life, in order to be free to develop – into, ironically, a giver of real, non-rhetorical, wrested-out-of-experience meaning, to the world.

One critic has found Conrad's treatment of supernaturalism in *The Shadow-Line* 'ambiguous'. But such a critic is simple-minded, for it is hardly possible for a writer of Conrad's stature to treat such a theme honestly without some sort of 'ambiguity'. What this critic really means is that his own mind irritably reaches out for certainties which do not exist except falsely, as in popular and ephemeral works, or in the speeches of politicians. Conrad's treatment, surely, with its studious restraint – its refusal to retreat into the complete rationalization of a Mac-Whirr – comes as near as anyone has come, in a century characterized at one extreme by a callous atheistic scientism which blasphemes against Nature by its attribution to mankind of the means of self-creation (no less), and at the other by a specious and thoughtless piety, to a definition of man's true and uncertain state. This arises in the first place from a piece of pure and sincere, and affirmatory, recollection. The narrator has recorded his 'spiritual drowsiness', his conceited feeling that there was 'no wisdom to acquire' (later he would know that 'one has to learn everything'), 'no fun to enjoy'. But then a 'strange sense of exultation began to creep into' him; and later a

sudden passion of impatience rushed through my veins, and gave me a sense of the intensity of existence as I have never felt before or since. I discovered how much of a seaman I was, in heart, in mind, and, as it were, physically – a man exclusively of the sea and ships; the sea the only world that counted, and the ships the test of manliness, of temperament, of courage and fidelity – and love.

This is completely convincing, and nothing further in the story spoils it. What would have spoiled it, and what too many critics have tried to do, is to link its episodes up too firmly (and therefore too artificially) into various over-elaborate allegorical schemes. There is no need for this. The echoes from *Hamlet*, from Coleridge, from the Flying Dutchman legend, are explicit enough. The links between the immediate European situation and the events related are also explicit enough, and are not made so only by the dedication to Borys. I do not think that much 'envy' of Borys is evident, as has been posulated. This is simply a father who has been through his initiation offering a salute to one who is about to go through his; as such, it is moving enough, and it really is Conrad's swansong, the final nearly perfect work after *Under Western Eyes*. It was, as an admirer said, 'truly worthy of him'.

Martin Seymour-Smith

SELECT BIBLIOGRAPHY

BIOGRAPHIES
BAINES, JOCELYN, *Joseph Conrad: A Critical Biography*, Weidenfeld & Nicolson, 1960.
SHERRY, NORMAN, *Conrad and His World*, Thames & Hudson, 1972. Useful short illustrated introductory biography.
KARL, FREDERICK, *Joseph Conrad: The Three Lives*, Farrar, Straus & Giroux, New York, 1978, and Faber, 1979.
NAJDER, ZDZISLAW, *Joseph Conrad: A Chronicle*, Cambridge University Press, 1983, Generally reckoned to be the best full life.
MEYER, BERNARD, *Joseph Conrad: A Psychoanalytic Biography*, Princeton University Press, Princeton, N.J., 1967. By a psychoanalyst; an interesting and intelligent investigation, quite out of the general run of such studies.

LETTERS
JEAN-AUBRY, G., ed., *Joseph Conrad: Life and Letters*, Doubleday, New York, 1927.
KARL, FREDERICK, AND DAVIES, LAURENCE, eds., *The Collected Letters*, Cambridge University Press, 1983—. Will print every known letter when complete.

CRITICISM
BERTHOUD, JACQUES, *Joseph Conrad: The Major Phase*, Cambridge University Press, 1978. One of the most important critical studies.
FORD, FORD MADOX, *Joseph Conrad: A Personal Remembrance*, Little, Brown, Boston, 1924. Must be read critically, but absolutely essential for an understanding of Conrad.
FLEISHMAN, AVROM, *Conrad's Politics*, Johns Hopkins Press, Baltimore, 1967.
GEDDES, GARY, *Conrad's Later Novels*, McGill-Queen's University Press, Montreal, 1980. Stimulating discussions of the later novels.
GUERARD, ALBERT, *Conrad the Novelist*, Harvard University Press, Cambridge, Mass., 1958. A useful study along psychoanalytical lines.
HAY, ELOISE KNAPP, *The Political Novels of Joseph Conrad*, Chicago University Press, Chicago, 1963.
KIRSCHNER, PAUL, *Conrad: The Psychologist as Artist*, Oliver & Boyd, 1968.

MOSER, THOMAS, *Conrad: Achievement and Decline*, Harvard University Press, Cambridge, Mass., 1957. An influential study.
SCHWARTZ, D. R., *Conrad: The Later Fiction*, Macmillan, 1982.
SHERRY, NORMAN, *Conrad's Eastern World*, Routledge, 1966.
SHERRY, NORMAN, *Conrad's Western World*, Routledge, 1971. Both the Sherry books are essential for their revelation of Conrad's sources.
STALLMAN, R. W., ed., *The Art of Joseph Conrad: A Critical Symposium*, Michigan State University Press, East Lansing, 1960.

CHRONOLOGY

DATE	AUTHOR'S LIFE	LITERARY CONTEXT
1853		Charlotte Brontë: *Villette*.
1856	Marriage of Apollo Korzeniowski to Ewelina Bobrowska in Oratów.	Bernard Shaw born.
1857	December 3: birth of their son, Józef Teodor Konrad Korzeniowski (later to be known as Joseph Conrad).	Flaubert: *Madame Bovary*. Baudelaire: *Fleurs du mal*.
1859	Family moves to Żytomierz.	Dickens: *A Tale of Two Cities*.
1861	Apollo Korzeniowski arrested in Warsaw for patriotic conspiracy.	Dickens: *Great Expectations*.
1862	Conrad's parents exiled to Vologda, Russia: he accompanies them.	Turgenev: *Fathers and Sons*. Ruskin: *Unto This Last*.
1863	Family moved to Chernikhov.	Thackeray dies.
1865	Death of Conrad's mother.	Birth of Kipling and Yeats.
1866	Stays with uncle at Nowochwastów.	Dostoevsky: *Crime and Punishment*.
1869	Death of Apollo Korzeniowski; Conrad becomes ward of relatives.	Tolstoy: *War and Peace*.
1870	Taught by Adam Pulman in Kraków.	Charles Dickens dies.
1871	Also taught by Isydor Kopernicki.	Dostoevsky: *The Devils*.
1872	Resolves to go to sea.	George Eliot: *Middlemarch*.
1874	Leaves Poland for Marseille to join French merchant navy.	Hardy: *Far from the Madding Crowd*.
1875	Sails Atlantic on *Mont-Blanc*.	Thomas Mann born.
1876	Serves as steward on *Saint-Antoine*.	Death of George Sand.
1877	Possibly involved in smuggling arms to Spanish royalists.	Tolstoy: *Anna Karenina*.
1878	Shoots himself in chest, recovers, and joins British ship *Mavis*.	Hardy: *The Return of the Native*.
1879	Serves on clipper *Duke of Sutherland*.	Ibsen: *A Doll's House*.
1880	Sails to Australia on *Loch Etive*.	Dostoevsky: *The Brothers Karamazov*.
1881	Second mate of *Palestine*.	Death of Dostoevsky and Carlyle.

HISTORICAL EVENTS

Crimean War begins.
Crimean War ends. Freud born.

Indian Mutiny.

Darwin's *Origin of Species*.
Emancipation of Russian serfs.
American Civil War begins.
Bismarck gains power in Prussia.

American slaves freed. Polish uprising.
American Civil War ends.

Gandhi born. Suez Canal opens.

Franco-Prussian War. Lenin born.

Paris Commune.

Mazzini dies. Bertrand Russell born.
Winston Churchill born.

Bakunin dies.

Russia declares war on Turkey.

Afghan War. Congress of Berlin.

Zulu War. Einstein and Stalin born.

Tsar Alexander II assassinated.

DATE	AUTHOR'S LIFE	LITERARY CONTEXT
1882	Storm-damaged *Palestine* repaired.	Birth of Virginia Woolf and James Joyce.
1883	Shipwrecked when *Palestine* sinks.	Nietzsche: *Thus Spake Zarathustra*.
1885	Sails to Calcutta on *Tilkhurst*.	Birth of D. H. Lawrence.
1886	Takes British nationality; qualifies as captain.	Stevenson: *Dr Jekyll and Mr Hyde*.
1887	Sails to Java on *Highland Forest*.	Birth of Marianne Moore.
1888	Master of the ship *Otago*.	Birth of T. S. Eliot.
1889	Resigns from *Otago* and settles in London, writing *Almayer's Folly*.	Death of Robert Browning.
1890	Works in Belgian Congo.	Ibsen: *Hedda Gabler*.
1891	Officer of *Torrens* until 1893.	Hardy: *Tess of the D'Urbervilles*.
1894	*Almayer's Folly* accepted by Unwin. Meets Edward Garnett and Jessie George.	R. L. Stevenson dies; Aldous Huxley born. Kipling: *The Jungle Book*.
1895	*Almayer's Folly* published.	Crane: *The Red Badge of Courage*. Hardy: *Jude the Obscure*.
1896	*An Outcast of the Islands*. Marries Jessie George. Meets H. G. Wells.	William Morris dies; Scott Fitzgerald born.
1897	Corresponds with Cunninghame Graham. *The Nigger of the 'Narcissus'*.	Kipling: *Captains Courageous*.
1898	*Tales of Unrest*. Enters collaboration with Ford Madox Hueffer (later known as Ford Madox Ford). First son, Borys, born.	Wilde: 'Ballad of Reading Gaol'. Wells: *War of the Worlds*. Rilke: *Advent*.
1899	*Heart of Darkness* serialized. Serialization of *Lord Jim* begins.	Birth of Hemingway.
1900	*Lord Jim* (book). J. B. Pinker becomes Conrad's agent.	Death of Ruskin, Nietzsche, Oscar Wilde and Stephen Crane.
1901	*The Inheritors* (co-author Hueffer).	Kipling: *Kim*.
1902	*Youth* volume.	Gorky: *The Lower Depths*.
1903	*Typhoon* volume. *Romance* (co-author Hueffer).	James: *The Ambassadors*. Birth of George Orwell.
1904	*Nostromo*.	Chekhov: *The Cherry Orchard*.
1905	*One Day More* (play) fails.	Wells: *Kipps*.
1906	*The Mirror of the Sea* (with Hueffer). Second son, John, born.	Samuel Beckett born. Ibsen dies.
1907	*The Secret Agent*.	Birth of W. H. Auden.
1908	*A Set of Six* (tales).	Bennett: *The Old Wives' Tale*.

CHRONOLOGY

DATE	AUTHOR'S LIFE	LITERARY CONTEXT
1909	Quarrels with Hueffer.	Death of Swinburne.
1910	Moves to Capel House, near Ashford.	Yeats: *The Green Helmet.*
1911	*Under Western Eyes.*	William Golding born.
1912	*A Personal Record. 'Twixt Land and Sea* (tales). *Chance* serialized in *New York Herald.*	Patrick White born. Pound: *Ripostes.*
1913	Meets Bertrand Russell.	Lawrence: *Sons and Lovers.*
1914	Book of *Chance* has large sales. Conrad becomes prosperous at last.	Joyce: *Dubliners.* Birth of Dylan Thomas.
1915	*Within the Tides* (tales); *Victory.*	Lawrence: *The Rainbow.*
1916	*The Shadow-Line* serialized.	Henry James dies.
1917	*The Shadow-Line* (book).	Anthony Burgess born.
1918	Borys Conrad wounded in war.	Death of Wilfred Owen.
1919	*The Arrow of Gold.*	Woolf: *Night and Day.*
1920	*The Rescue.*	Lawrence: *Women in Love.* Katherine Mansfield: *Bliss.*
1921	*Notes on Life and Letters.*	Huxley: *Crome Yellow.*
1922	*The Secret Agent* (play) fails.	Eliot: *The Waste Land.* Joyce: *Ulysses.*
1923	Visits USA to acclamation. *The Rover.*	Yeats wins Nobel Prize. Huxley: *Antic Hay.*
1924	Declines knighthood. Dies of heart attack; buried at Canterbury.	Forster: *A Passage to India.* Shaw: *Saint Joan.*
1925	Publication of *Tales of Hearsay* and the unfinished *Suspense.*	Eliot: *Poems 1909–25.* Shaw wins Nobel Prize.
1926	*Last Essays.*	Kafka: *The Castle.*
1927	*Joseph Conrad: Life & Letters,* written and edited by G. Jean-Aubry.	Woolf: *To the Lighthouse.*

CHRONOLOGY

THE NIGGER OF THE 'NARCISSUS'
A TALE OF THE SEA

TO
EDWARD GARNETT
This tale
about my friends
of the sea

PREFACE

A WORK that aspires, however humbly, to the condition of art should carry its justification in every line. And art itself may be defined as a single-minded attempt to render the highest kind of justice to the visible universe, by bringing to light the truth, manifold and one, underlying its every aspect. It is an attempt to find in its forms, in its colours, in its light, in its shadows, in the aspects of matter and in the facts of life what of each is fundamental, what is enduring and essential – their one illuminating and convincing quality – the very truth of their existence. The artist, then, like the thinker or the scientist, seeks the truth and makes his appeal. Impressed by the aspect of the world the thinker plunges into ideas, the scientist into facts – whence, presently, emerging they make their appeal to those qualities of our being that fit us best for the hazardous enterprise of living. They speak authoritatively to our common sense, to our intelligence, to our desire of peace or to our desire of unrest; not seldom to our prejudices, sometimes to our fears, often to our egoism – but always to our credulity. And their words are heard with reverence, for their concern is with weighty matters: with the cultivation of our minds and the proper care of our bodies, with the attainment of our ambitions, with the perfection of the means and the glorification of our precious aims.

It is otherwise with the artist.

Confronted by the same enigmatical spectacle the artist descends within himself, and in that lonely region of stress and strife, if he be deserving and fortunate, he finds the terms of his appeal. His appeal is made to our less obvious

3

capacities: to that part of our nature which, because of the warlike conditions of existence, is necessarily kept out of sight within the more resisting and hard qualities – like the vulnerable body within a steel armour. His appeal is less loud, more profound, less distinct, more stirring – and sooner forgotten. Yet its effect endures for ever. The changing wisdom of successive generations discards ideas, questions facts, demolished theories. But the artist appeals to that part of our being which is not dependent on wisdom; to that in us which is a gift and not an acquisition – and, therefore, more permanently enduring. He speaks to our capacity for delight and wonder, to the sense of mystery surrounding our lives; to our sense of pity, and beauty, and pain; to the latent feeling of fellowship with all creation – and to the subtle but invincible conviction of solidarity that knits together the loneliness of innumerable hearts, to the solidarity in dreams, in joy, in sorrow, in aspirations, in illusions, in hope, in fear, which binds men to each other, which binds together all humanity – the dead to the living and the living to the unborn.

It is only some such train of thought, or rather of feeling, that can in a measure explain the aim of the attempt, made in the tale which follows, to present an unrestful episode in the obscure lives of a few individuals out of all the disregarded multitude of the bewildered, the simple and the voiceless. For, if any part of truth dwells in the belief confessed above, it becomes evident that there is not a place of splendour or a dark corner of the earth that does not deserve, if only a passing glance of wonder and pity. The motive then, may be held to justify the matter of the work; but this preface, which is simply an avowal of endeavour, cannot end here – for the avowal is not yet complete.

Fiction – if it at all aspires to be art – appeals to temperament. And in truth it must be, like painting, like music, like all art, the appeal of one temperament to all the other innumerable temperaments, whose subtle and resistless power endows passing events with their true meaning, and creates the moral, the emotional atmosphere of the place and time. Such an appeal to be effective must be an impression conveyed through the senses; and, in fact, it cannot be made in any other way, because temperament, whether individual or collective, is not amenable to persuasion. All art, therefore, appeals primarily to the senses, and the artistic aim when expressing itself in written words must also make its appeal through the senses, if its high desire is to reach the secret spring of responsive emotions. It must strenuously aspire to the plasticity of sculpture, to the colour of painting, and to the magic suggestiveness of music – which is the art of arts. And it is only through complete, unswerving devotion to the perfect blending of form and substance; it is only through an unremitting never-discouraged care for the shape and ring of sentences that an approach can be made to plasticity, to colour, and that the light of magic suggestiveness may be brought to play for an evanescent instant over the common-place surface of words: of the old, old words, worn thin, defaced by ages of careless usage.

The sincere endeavour to accomplish that creative task, to go as far on that road as his strength will carry him, to go undeterred by faltering, weariness or reproach, is the only valid justification for the worker in prose. And if his conscience is clear, his answer to those who in the fulness of a wisdom which looks for immediate profit, demand specifically to be edified, consoled, amused; who demand to be promptly improved, or encouraged, or frightened, or shocked, or charmed, must run thus: My task which I am trying to achieve is, by the power of the written word to make you hear, to make you feel – it is, before all, to make you *see*. That – and no more, and it is everything. If I succeed, you shall find there according to your deserts: encouragement, consolation, fear, charm – all you demand – and, perhaps, also that glimpse of truth for which you have forgotten to ask.

To snatch in a moment of courage, from the remorseless rush of time, a passing phase of life, is only the beginning of the task. The task approached in tenderness and faith is to hold up unquestioningly, without choice and without fear, the rescued fragment before all eyes in the light of a sincere mood. It is to show its vibration, its colour, its form; and through its movement, its form, and its colour, reveal the substance of its truth – disclose its inspiring secret: the stress and passion within the core of each convincing moment. In a single-minded attempt of that kind, if one be deserving and fortunate, one may perchance attain to such clearness of sincerity that at last the presented vision of regret or pity, of terror or mirth, shall awaken in the hearts of the beholders that feeling of unavoidable solidarity; of the solidarity in mysterious origin, in toil, in joy, in hope, in uncertain fate, which binds men to each other and all mankind to the visible world.

It is evident that he who, rightly or wrongly, holds by the convictions expressed above cannot be faithful to any one of the temporary formulas of his craft. The enduring part of them – the truth which each only imperfectly veils – should abide with him as the most precious of his possessions, but they all: Realism, Romanticism, Naturalism, even the unofficial sentimentalism (which like the poor, is exceedingly difficult to get rid of), all these gods must, after a short period of fellowship, abandon him – even on the very threshold of the temple – to the stammerings of his conscience and to the outspoken consciousness of the difficulties of his work. In that uneasy solitude the supreme cry of Art for Art, itself, loses the exciting ring of its apparent immorality. It sounds far off. It has ceased to be a cry, and is heard only as a whisper, often incomprehensible, but at times and faintly encouraging.

Sometimes, stretched at ease in the shade of a road-side tree, we watch the motions of a labourer in a distant field, and after a time, begin to wonder languidly as to what the fellow may be at. We watch the movements of his body, the waving of his arms, we see him bend down, stand up, hesitate, begin again. It may add to the charm of an idle hour to be told the purpose of his exertions. If we know he is trying to lift a stone, to dig a ditch, to uproot a stump, we look with a more real interest at his efforts; we are disposed to condone the jar of his agitation upon the restfulness of the landscape; and even, if in a brotherly frame of mind, we may bring ourselves to forgive his failure. We understood his object, and, after all, the fellow has tried, and perhaps he had not the strength – and perhaps he had not the knowledge. We forgive, go on our way – and forget.

And so it is with the workman of art. Art is long and life is short, and success is very far off. And thus, doubtful of strength to travel so far, we talk a little about the aim – the aim of art, which, like life itself, is inspiring, difficult – obscured by mists. It is not in the clear logic of a triumphant conclusion; it is not in the unveiling of one of those heartless secrets which are called the Laws of Nature. It is not less great, but only more difficult.

To arrest, for the space of a breath, the hands busy about the work of the earth, and compel men entranced by the sight of distant goals to glance for a moment at the surrounding vision of form and colour, of sunshine and shadows; to make them pause for a look, for a sigh, for a smile – such is the aim, difficult and evanescent, and reserved only for a very few to achieve. But sometimes, by the deserving and the fortunate, even that task is accomplished. And when it is accomplished – behold! – all the truth of life is there: a moment of vision, a sigh, a smile – and the return to an eternal rest.

1897.   J. C.

THE NIGGER OF THE 'NARCISSUS'

I

MR BAKER, chief mate of the ship 'Narcissus,' stepped in one stride out of his lighted cabin into the darkness of the quarter-deck. Above his head, on the break of the poop, the night-watchman rang a double stroke. It was nine o'clock. Mr Baker, speaking up to the man above him, asked: – 'Are all the hands aboard, Knowles?'

The man limped down the ladder, then said reflectively: 'I think so, sir. All our chaps are there, and a lot of new men has come.... They must be all there.'

'Tell the boatswain to send all hands aft,' went on Mr Baker; 'and tell one of the youngsters to bring a good lamp here. I want to muster our crowd.'

The main deck was dark aft, but half-way from forward, through the open doors of the forecastle, two streaks of brilliant light cut the shadow of the quiet night that lay upon the ship. A hum of voices was heard there, while port and starboard, in the illuminated doorways, silhouettes of moving men appeared for a moment, very black, without relief, like figures cut out of sheet tin. The ship was ready for sea. The carpenter had driven in the last wedge of the main-hatch battens, and, throwing down his maul, had wiped his face with great deliberation, just on the stroke of five. The decks had been swept, the windlass oiled and made ready to heave up the anchor; the big tow-rope lay in long bights along one side of the main deck, with one end carried up and hung over the bows, in readiness for the tug that would come paddling and hissing noisily, hot and smoky, in the limpid, cool quietness of the early morning. The captain was ashore, where he had been engaging some new hands to make up his full crew; and, the work of the

9

day over, the ship's officers had kept out of the way, glad of
a little breathing-time. Soon after dark the few liberty-men
and the new hands began to arrive in shore-boats rowed by
white-clad Asiatics, who clamoured fiercely for payment
before coming alongside the gangway-ladder. The feverish
and shrill babble of Eastern language struggled against the
masterful tones of tipsy seamen, who argued against brazen
claims and dishonest hopes by profane shouts. The
resplendent and bestarred peace of the East was torn into
squalid tatters by howls of rage and shrieks of lament raised
over sums ranging from five annas to half a rupee; and every
soul afloat in Bombay Harbour became aware that the new
hands were joining the 'Narcissus.'

Gradually the distracting noise had subsided. The boats
came no longer in splashing clusters of three or four
together, but dropped alongside singly, in a subdued buzz
of expostulation cut short by a 'Not a pice more! You go to
the devil!' from some man staggering up the accommoda-
tion-ladder – a dark figure, with a long bag poised on the
shoulder. In the forecastle the newcomers, upright and
swaying amongst corded boxes and bundles of bedding,
made friends with the old hands, who sat one above
another in the two tiers of bunks, gazing at their future
shipmates with glances critical but friendly. The two forecastle lamps were turned up high, and shed an intense hard
glare; shore-going round hats were pushed far on the backs
of heads, or rolled about on the deck amongst the chain-
cables; white collars, undone, stuck out on each side of red
faces; big arms in white sleeves gesticulated; the growling
voices hummed steady amongst bursts of laughter and
hoarse calls. 'Here, sonny, take that bunk!... Don't you
do it!... What's your last ship?... I know her.... Three
years ago, in Puget Sound.... This here berth leaks, I tell
you!... Come on; give us a chance to swing that
chest!... Did you bring a bottle, any of you shore
toffs?... Give us a bit of 'baccy.... I know her; her skipper
drank himself to death.... He was a dandy boy!... Liked

his lotion inside, he did!...No!...Hold your row, you chaps!...I tell you, you came on board a hooker, where they get their money's worth out of poor Jack, by ——!...'

A little fellow, called Craik and nicknamed Belfast, abused the ship violently, romancing on principle, just to give the new hands something to think over. Archie, sitting aslant on his sea-chest, kept his knees out of the way, and pushed the needle steadily through a white patch in a blue pair of trousers. Men in black jackets and stand-up collars, mixed with men bare-footed, bare-armed, with coloured shirts open on hairy chests, pushed against one another in the middle of the forecastle. The group swayed, reeled, turning upon itself with the motion of a scrimmage, in a haze of tobacco smoke. All were speaking together, swearing at every second word. A Russian Finn, wearing a yellow shirt with pink stripes, stared upwards, dreamy-eyed, from under a mop of tumbled hair. Two young giants with smooth, baby faces – two Scandinavians – helped each other to spread their bedding, silent, and smiling placidly at the tempest of good-humoured and meaningless curses. Old Singleton, the oldest able seaman in the ship, sat apart on the deck right under the lamps, stripped to the waist, tattooed like a cannibal chief all over his powerful chest and enormous biceps. Between the blue and red patterns his white skin gleamed like satin; his bare back was propped against the heel of the bowsprit, and he held a book at arm's length before his big, sunburnt face. With his spectacles and a venerable white beard, he resembled a learned and savage patriarch, the incarnation of barbarian wisdom serene in the blasphemous turmoil of the world. He was intensely absorbed, and as he turned the pages an expression of grave surprise would pass over his rugged features. He was reading *Pelham*. The popularity of Bulwer Lytton in the forecastles of Southern-going ships is a wonderful and bizarre phenomenon. What ideas do his polished and so curiously insincere sentences awaken in the simple minds of the big children who people those dark and wandering places of the earth? What meaning their rough, inexperienced souls can find in the elegant verbiage of his pages? What excitement? – what forgetfulness? – what appeasement? Mystery! Is it the fascination of the incomprehensible? – is it the charm of the impossible? Or are those beings who exist beyond the pale of life stirred by his tales as by an enigmatical disclosure of a resplendent world that exists within the frontier of infamy and filth, within that border of dirt and hunger, of misery and dissipation, that comes down on all sides to the water's edge of the incorruptible ocean, and is the only thing they know of life, the only thing they see of surrounding land – those life-long prisoners of the sea? Mystery!

Singleton, who had sailed to the southward since the age of twelve, who in the last forty-five years had lived (as we had calculated from his papers) no more than forty months ashore – old Singleton, who boasted, with the mild composure of long years well spent, that generally from the day he was paid off from one ship till the day he shipped in another he seldom was in a condition to distinguish daylight – old Singleton sat unmoved in the clash of voices and cries, spelling through *Pelham* with slow labour, and lost in an absorption profound enough to resemble a trance. He breathed regularly. Every time he turned the book in his enormous and blackened hands the muscles of his big white arms rolled slightly under the smooth skin. Hidden by the white moustache, his lips, stained with tobacco-juice that trickled down the long beard, moved in inward whisper. His bleared eyes gazed fixedly from behind the glitter of black-rimmed glasses. Opposite to him, and on a level with his face, the ship's cat sat on the barrel of the windlass in the pose of a crouching chimera, blinking its green eyes at its old friend. It seemed to meditate a leap on to the old man's lap over the bent back of the ordinary seaman who sat at Singleton's feet. Young Charley was lean and long-necked. The ridge of his backbone made a chain of small hills under the old shirt. His face of a street-boy – a face precocious, sagacious, and ironic, with deep downward folds on each side of the thin, wide mouth – hung low over his bony knees. He was learning to make a lanyard knot with a bit of an old rope. Small drops of perspiration stood out on his bulging forehead; he sniffed from time to time, glancing out of the corners of his restless eyes at the old seaman, who took no notice of the puzzled youngster muttering at his work.

The noise increased. Little Belfast seemed, in the heavy heat of the forecastle, to boil with facetious fury. His eyes danced; in the crimson of his face, comical as a mask, the mouth yawned black, with strange grimaces. Facing him, a half-undressed man held his sides, and, throwing his head back, laughed with wet eyelashes. Others stared with amazed eyes. Men sitting doubled up in the upper bunks smoked short pipes, swinging bare brown feet above the heads of those who, sprawling below on sea-chests, listened, smiling stupidly or scornfully. Over the white rims of berths stuck out heads with blinking eyes; but the bodies were lost in the gloom of those places, that resembled narrow niches for coffins in a whitewashed and lighted mortuary. Voices buzzed louder. Archie, with compressed lips, drew himself in, seemed to shrink into a smaller space, and sewed steadily, industrious and dumb. Belfast shrieked like an inspired Dervish: '... So I seez to him, boys, seez I, "Beggin' yer pardon, sorr," seez I to that second mate of that steamer – "beggin' your-r-r pardon, sorr, the Board of Trade must 'ave been drunk when they granted you your certificate!" – "What do you say, you——!" seez he, comin' at me like a mad bull ... all in his white clothes; and I up with my tar-pot and capsizes it all over his blamed lovely face and his lovely jacket.... "Take that!" seez I. "I am a sailor, anyhow, you nosing, skipper-licking, useless, sooperfloos bridge-stanchion, you!" – "That's the kind of man I am!" shouts I.... You should have seed him skip, boys! Drowned, blind with tar, he was! So...'

'Don't 'ee believe him! He never upset no tar; I was there!' shouted somebody. The two Norwegians sat on a chest side by side, alike and placid, resembling a pair of lovebirds on a perch, and with round eyes stared innocently; but the Russian Finn, in the racket of explosive shouts and rolling laughter, remained motionless, limp and dull, like a deaf man without a backbone. Near him Archie smiled at his needle. A broad-chested, slow-eyed newcomer spoke deliberately to Belfast during an exhausted lull in the noise: 'I wonder any of the mates here are alive yet with such a chap as you on board! I concloode they ain't that bad now, if you had the taming of them, sonny.'

'Not bad! Not bad!' screamed Belfast. 'If it wasn't for us sticking together.... Not bad! They ain't never bad when they ain't got a chawnce, blast their black 'arts....' He foamed, whirling his arms, then suddenly grinned and, taking a tablet of black tobacco out of his pocket, bit a piece off with a funny show of ferocity. Another new hand – a man with shifty eyes and a yellow hatchet face, who had been listening open-mouthed in the shadow of the midship locker – observed in a squeaky voice: 'Well, it's a 'omeward trip, anyhow. Bad or good, I can do it on my 'ed – s'long as I get 'ome. And I can look after my rights! I will show 'em!' All the heads turned towards him. Only the ordinary seaman and the cat took no notice. He stood with arms akimbo, a little fellow with white eyelashes. He looked as if he had known all the degradations and all the furies. He looked as if he had been cuffed, kicked, rolled in the mud; he looked as if he had been scratched, spat upon, pelted with unmentionable filth... and he smiled with a sense of security at the faces around. His ears were bending down under the weight of his battered felt hat. The torn tails of his black coat flapped in fringes about the calves of his legs. He unbuttoned the only two buttons that remained and every one saw that he had no shirt under it. It was his deserved misfortune that those rags which nobody could possibly be supposed to own looked on him as if they had been stolen. His neck was long and thin; his eyelids were red; rare hairs hung about his jaws; his shoulders were peaked and drooped like the broken wings of a bird; all his left side was caked with mud which showed that he had lately slept in a wet ditch. He had saved his inefficient carcass from violent destruction by running away from an American ship where, in a moment of forgetful folly, he had dared to engage himself; and he had knocked about for a fortnight ashore in the native quarter, cadging for drinks, starving, sleeping on rubbish-heaps, wandering in sunshine: a startling visitor from a world of nightmares. He stood repulsive and smiling in the sudden silence. This clean white forecastle was his refuge; the place where he could be lazy; where he could wallow, and lie and eat – and curse the food he ate; where he could display his talents for shirking work, for cheating, for cadging; where he could surely find some one to wheedle and some one to bully – and where he would be paid for doing all this. They all knew him. Is there a spot on earth where such a man is unknown, an ominous survival testifying to the eternal fitness of lies and impudence? A taciturn long-armed shellback, with hooked fingers, who had been lying on his back smoking, turned in his bed to examine him dispassionately, then, over his head, sent a long jet of clear saliva towards the door. They all knew him! He was the man that cannot steer, that cannot splice, that dodges the work on dark nights; that, aloft, holds on frantically with both arms and legs, and swears at the wind, the sleet, the darkness; the man who curses the sea while others work. The man who is the last out and the first in when all hands are called. The man who can't do most things and won't do the rest. The pet of philanthropists and self-seeking landlubbers. The sympathetic and deserving creature that knows all about his rights, but knows nothing of courage, of endurance, and of the unexpressed faith, of the unspoken loyalty that knits together a ship's company. The

independent offspring of the ignoble freedom of the slums
full of disdain and hate for the austere servitude of the sea.

Some one cried at him: 'What's your name?' – 'Donkin,'
he said, looking round with cheerful effrontery. – 'What
are you?' asked another voice. – 'Why, a sailor like you, old
man,' he replied, in a tone that meant to be hearty but was
impudent. – 'Blamme if you don't look a blamed sight
worse than a broken-down fireman,' was the comment in
a convinced mutter. Charley lifted his head and piped in a
cheeky voice: 'He is a man and a sailor' – then wiping his
nose with the back of his hand bent down industriously
over his bit of rope. A few laughed. Others stared doubt-
fully. The ragged newcomer was indignant – 'That's a fine
way to welcome a chap into a fo'c'sle,' he snarled. 'Are you
men or a lot of 'artles scannybals?' – 'Don't take your shirt
off for a word, shipmate,' called out Belfast, jumping up in
front, fiery, menacing, and friendly at the same time. – 'Is
that 'ere bloke blind?' asked the indomitable scarecrow,
looking right and left with affected surprise. 'Can't 'ee see
I 'aven't got no shirt?'

He held both his arms out crosswise and shook the rags
that hung over his bones with dramatic effect.

''Cos why?' he continued very loud. 'The bloody
Yankees been tryin' to jump my guts out 'cos I stood up
for my rights like a good 'un. I am an Englishman, I am.
They set upon me an' I 'ad to run. That's why. Ain't yer
never seed a man 'ard up? Yah! What kind of blamed ship is
this? I'm dead broke. I 'aven't got nothink. No bag, no bed,
no blanket, no shirt – not a bloomin' rag but what I stand
in. But I 'ad the 'art to stand up agin' them Yankees. 'As any
of you 'art enough to spare a pair of old pants for a chum?'

He knew how to conquer the naïve instincts of that
crowd. In a moment they gave him their compassion,
jocularly, contemptuously, or surlily; and at first it took
the shape of a blanket thrown at him as he stood there
with the white skin of his limbs showing his human kinship
through the black fantasy of his rags. Then a pair of old

shoes fell at his muddy feet. With a cry: 'From under,' a rolled-up pair of canvas trousers, heavy with tar stains, struck him on the shoulder. The gust of their benevolence sent a wave of sentimental pity through their doubting hearts. They were touched by their own readiness to alleviate a shipmate's misery. Voices cried: 'We will fit you out, old man.' Murmurs: 'Never seed seech a hard case.... Poor beggar.... I've got an old singlet.... Will that be of any use to you?... Take it, matey....' Those friendly murmurs filled the forecastle. He pawed around with his naked foot, gathering the things in a heap and looked about for more. Unemotional Archie perfunctorily contributed to the pile an old cloth cap with the peak torn off. Old Singleton, lost in the serene regions of fiction, read on unheeding. Charley, pitiless with the wisdom of youth, squeaked: 'If you want brass buttons for your new unyforms I've got two for you.' The filthy object of universal charity shook his fist at the youngster. – 'I'll make you keep this 'ere fo'c'sle clean, young feller,' he snarled viciously. 'Never you fear. I will learn you to be civil to an able seaman, you ignerant ass.' He glared harmfully, but saw Singleton shut his book, and his little beady eyes began to roam from berth to berth. – 'Take that bunk by the door there – it's pretty fair,' suggested Belfast. So advised, he gathered the gifts at his feet, pressed them in a bundle against his breast, then looked cautiously at the Russian Finn, who stood on one side with an unconscious gaze, contemplating, perhaps, one of those weird visions that haunt the men of his race. – 'Get out of my road, Dutchy,' said the victim of Yankee brutality. The Finn did not move – did not hear. – 'Get out, blast ye,' shouted the other, shoving him aside with his elbow. 'Get out, you blanked deaf and dumb fool. Get out.' The man staggered, recovered himself, and gazed at the speaker in silence. – 'Those damned furriners should be kept under,' opined the amiable Donkin to the forecastle. 'If you don't teach 'em their place they put on you like anythink.' He flung all his worldly possessions into the

empty bed-place, gauged with another shrewd look the
risks of the proceeding, then leaped up to the Finn, who
stood pensive and dull. – 'I'll teach you to swell around,' he
yelled. 'I'll plug your eyes for you, you blooming square-
head.' Most of the men were now in their bunks and the
two had the forecastle clear to themselves. The development of the destitute Donkin aroused interest. He danced
all in tatters before the amazed Finn, squaring from a
distance at the heavy, unmoved face. One or two men
cried encouragingly: 'Go it, Whitechapel!' settling themselves luxuriously in their beds to survey the fight. Others
shouted: 'Shut yer row! . . . Go an' put yer 'ed in a bag! . . .'
The hubbub was recommencing. Suddenly many heavy
blows struck with a handspike on the deck above boomed
like discharges of small cannon through the forecastle.
Then the boatswain's voice rose outside the door with an
authoritative note in its drawl: – 'D'ye hear, below there?
Lay aft! Lay aft to muster all hands!'

There was a moment of surprised stillness. Then the
forecastle floor disappeared under men whose bare feet
flopped on the planks as they sprang clear out of their
berths. Caps were rooted for amongst tumbled blankets.
Some, yawning, buttoned waistbands. Half-smoked pipes
were knocked hurriedly against woodwork and stuffed
under pillows. Voices growled: 'What's up? . . . Is there no
rest for us?' Donkin yelped: 'If that's the way of this ship,
we'll 'ave to change all that. . . . You leave me alone. . . . I will
soon. . . .' None of the crowd noticed him. They were
lurching in twos and threes through the doors, after the
manner of merchant Jacks who cannot go out of a door
fairly, like mere landsmen. The votary of change followed
them. Singleton, struggling into his jacket, came last, tall
and fatherly, bearing high his head of a weather-beaten
sage on the body of an old athlete. Only Charley remained
alone in the white glare of the empty place, sitting between
two rows of iron links that stretched into the narrow gloom
forward. He pulled hard at the strands in a hurried

endeavour to finish his knot. Suddenly he started up, flung the rope at the cat, and skipped after the black tom which went off leaping sedately over chain compressors, with its tail carried stiff and upright, like a small flag-pole.

Outside the glare of the steaming forecastle the serene purity of the night enveloped the seamen with its soothing breath, with its tepid breath flowing under the stars that hung countless above the mastheads in a thin cloud of luminous dust. On the town side the blackness of the water was streaked with trails of light which undulated gently on slight ripples, similar to filaments that float rooted to the shore. Rows of other lights stood away in straight lines as if drawn up on parade between towering buildings; but on the other side of the harbour sombre hills arched high their black spines, on which, here and there, the point of a star resembled a spark fallen from the sky. Far off, Byculla way, the electric lamps at the dock gates shone on the end of lofty standards with a glow blinding and frigid like captive ghosts of some evil moons. Scattered all over the dark polish of the roadstead, the ships at anchor floated in perfect stillness under the feeble gleam of their riding-lights, looming up, opaque and bulky, like strange and monumental structures abandoned by men to an ever-lasting repose.

Before the cabin door Mr Baker was mustering the crew. As they stumbled and lurched along past the mainmast, they could see aft his round, broad face with a white paper before it, and beside his shoulder the sleepy head, with dropped eyelids, of the boy, who held, suspended at the end of his raised arm, the luminous globe of a lamp. Even before the shuffle of naked soles had ceased along the decks, the mate began to call over the names. He called distinctly in a serious tone befitting this roll-call to unquiet loneliness, to inglorious and obscure struggle, or to the more trying endurance of small privations and wearisome duties. As the chief mate read out a name, one of the men would answer: 'Yes, sir!' or 'Here!' and, detaching himself

from the shadowy mob of heads visible above the blackness
of starboard bulwarks, would step bare-footed into the
circle of light, and in two noiseless strides pass into the
shadows on the port side of the quarter-deck. They
answered in divers tones: in thick mutters, in clear, ringing
voices; and some, as if the whole thing had been an outrage
on their feelings, used an injured intonation: for discipline
is not ceremonious in merchant ships, where the sense of
hierarchy is weak, and where all feel themselves equal
before the unconcerned immensity of the sea and the
exacting appeal of the work.

Mr Baker read on steadily: 'Hansen – Campbell – Smith
– Wamibo. Now, then, Wamibo. Why don't you answer?
Always got to call your name twice.' The Finn emitted at
last an uncouth grunt, and, stepping out, passed through
the patch of light, weird and gaudy, with the face of a man
marching through a dream. The mate went on faster:
'Craik – Singleton – Donkin. . . . O Lord!' he involuntarily
ejaculated as the incredibly dilapidated figure appeared in
the light. It stopped; it uncovered pale gums and long,
upper teeth in a malevolent grin. – 'Is there anythink
wrong with me, Mister Mate?' it asked, with a flavour of
insolence in the forced simplicity of its tone. On both sides
of the deck subdued titters were heard. – 'That'll do. Go
over,' growled Mr Baker, fixing the new hand with steady
blue eyes. And Donkin vanished suddenly out of the light
into the dark group of mustered men, to be slapped on the
back and to hear flattering whispers: 'He ain't afeard, he'll
give sport to 'em, see if he don't. . . . Reg'lar Punch and Judy
show. . . . Did ye see the mate start at him? . . . Well!
Damme, if I ever! . . .'

The last man had gone over, and there was a moment of
silence while the mate peered at his list. 'Sixteen, seventeen,' he muttered. 'I am one hand short, bo'sen,' he said
aloud. The big west-countryman at his elbow, swarthy and
bearded like a gigantic Spaniard, said in a rumbling bass:
'There's no one left forward, sir. I had a look round. He

ain't aboard, but he may turn up before daylight.' – 'Ay. He may or he may not,' commented the mate, 'can't make out that last name. It's all a smudge.... That will do, men. Go below.'

The distinct and motionless group stirred, broke up, began to move forward.

'Wait!' cried a deep, ringing voice.

All stood still. Mr Baker, who had turned away yawning, spun round open-mouthed. At last, furious, he blurted out: 'What's this? Who said "Wait"? What...'

But he saw a tall figure standing on the rail. It came down and pushed through the crowd, marching with a heavy tread towards the light on the quarter-deck. Then again the sonorous voice said with insistence: 'Wait!' The lamplight lit up the man's body. He was tall. His head was away up in the shadows of lifeboats that stood on skids above the deck. The whites of his eyes and his teeth gleamed distinctly, but the face was indistinguishable. His hands were big and seemed gloved.

Mr Baker advanced intrepidly. 'Who are you? How dare you...' he began.

The boy, amazed like the rest, raised the light to the man's face. It was black. A surprised hum – a faint hum that sounded like the suppressed mutter of the word 'Nigger' – ran along the deck and escaped out into the night. The nigger seemed not to hear. He balanced himself where he stood in a swagger that marked time. After a moment he said calmly: 'My name is Wait – James Wait.'

'Oh!' said Mr Baker. Then, after a few seconds of smouldering silence, his temper blazed out. 'Ah! Your name is Wait. What of that? What do you want? What do you mean, coming shouting here?'

The nigger was calm, cool, towering, superb. The men had approached and stood behind him in a body. He overtopped the tallest by half a head. He said: 'I belong to the ship.' He enunciated distinctly, with soft precision. The deep rolling, tones of his voice filled the deck without effort. He was naturally scornful, unaffectedly condescending, as if from his height of six foot three he had surveyed all the vastness of human folly and had made up his mind not to be too hard on it. He went on: 'The captain shipped me this morning. I couldn't get aboard sooner. I saw you all aft as I came up the ladder, and could see directly you were mustering the crew. Naturally I called out my name. I thought you had it in your list, and would understand. You misapprehended.' He stopped short. The folly around him was confounded. He was right as ever, and as ever ready to forgive. The disdainful tones had ceased, and, breathing heavily, he stood still, surrounded by all these white men. He held his head up in the glare of the lamp – a head vigorously modelled into deep shadows and shining lights – a head powerful and misshapen with a tormented and flattened face – a face pathetic and brutal: the tragic, the mysterious, the repulsive mask of a nigger's soul.

Mr Baker, recovering his composure, looked at the paper close. 'Oh, yes; that's so. All right, Wait. Take your gear forward,' he said.

Suddenly the nigger's eyes rolled wildly, became all whites. He put his hand to his side and coughed twice, a cough metallic, hollow, and tremendously loud; it resounded like two explosions in a vault; the dome of the sky rang to it, and the iron plates of the ship's bulwarks seemed to vibrate in unison, then he marched off forward with the others. The officers lingering by the cabin door could hear him say: 'Won't some of you chaps lend a hand with my dunnage? I've got a chest and a bag.' The words, spoken sonorously, with an even intonation, were heard all over the ship, and the question was put in a manner that made refusal impossible. The short, quick shuffle of men carrying something heavy went away forward, but the tall figure of the nigger lingered by the main hatch in a knot of smaller shapes. Again he was heard asking: 'Is your cook a coloured gentleman?' Then a disappointed and disapproving 'Ah! h'm!' was his comment upon the information that the cook happened to be a mere white man. Yet, as they went all together towards the forecastle, he condescended to put his head through the galley door and boom out inside a magnificent 'Good evening, Doctor!' that made all the saucepans ring. In the dim light the cook dozed on the coal locker in front of the captain's supper. He jumped up as if he had been cut with a whip, and dashed wildly on deck to see the backs of several men going away laughing. Afterwards, when talking about that voyage, he used to say: 'The poor fellow had scared me. I thought I had seen the devil.' The cook had been seven years in the ship with the same captain. He was a serious-minded man with a wife and three children, whose society he enjoyed on an average one month out of twelve. When on shore he took his family to church twice every Sunday. At sea he went to sleep every evening with his lamp turned up full, a pipe in his mouth, and an open Bible in his hand. Some one had always to go during the night to put out the light, take the book from his hand, and the pipe from between his teeth. 'For' – Belfast used to say, irritated and complaining – 'some night, you stupid cookie, you'll swallow your ould clay, and we will have no cook.' – 'Ah! sonny, I am ready for my Maker's call . . . wish you all were,' the other would answer with a benign serenity that was altogether imbecile and touching. Belfast outside the galley door danced with vexation. 'You holy fool! I don't want you to die,' he howled, looking up with furious, quivering face and tender eyes. 'What's the hurry? You blessed wooden-headed ould heretic, the divvle will have you soon enough. Think of Us . . . of Us . . . of Us!' And he would go away, stamping, spitting aside, disgusted and worried; while the other, step-ping out, saucepan in hand, hot, begrimed and placid, watched with a superior, cock-sure smile the back of his 'queer little man' reeling in a rage. They were great friends.

Mr Baker, lounging over the after-hatch, sniffed the humid night in the company of the second mate. – 'Those West India niggers run fine and large – some of them ... Ough! ... Don't they? A fine, big man that, Mr Creighton. Feel him on a rope. Hey? Ough! I will take him into my watch, I think.' The second mate, a fair, gentlemanly young fellow, with a resolute face and a splendid physique, observed quietly that it was just about what he had expected. There could be felt in his tone some slight bitterness which Mr Baker very kindly set himself to argue away. 'Come, come, young man,' he said, grunting between the words. 'Come! Don't be too greedy. You had that big Finn in your watch all the voyage. I will do what's fair. You may have those two young Scandinavians and I ... Ough! ... I get the nigger, and will take that ... Ough! that cheeky costermonger chap in a black frock-coat. I'll make him ... Ough! ... make him toe the mark, or my ... Ough! ... name isn't Baker. Ough! Ough! Ough!'

He grunted thrice – ferociously. He had that trick of grunting so between his words and at the end of sentences. It was a fine, effective grunt that went well with his menacing utterance, with his heavy, bullnecked frame, his jerky, rolling gait; with his big, seamed face, his steady eyes, and sardonic mouth. But its effect had been long ago discounted by the men. They liked him; Belfast – who was a favourite, and knew it – mimicked him, not quite behind his back. Charley – but with greater caution – imitated his rolling gait. Some of his sayings became established, daily quotations in the forecastle. Popularity can go no farther! Besides, all hands were ready to admit that on a fitting occasion the mate could 'jump down a fellow's throat in a reg'lar Western Ocean style.'

Now he was giving his last orders. 'Ough! ... You, Knowles! Call all hands at four. I want ... Ough! ... to heave short before the tug comes. Look out for the captain. I am going to lie down in my clothes. ... Ough! ... Call me when you see the boat coming. Ough! Ough! ... The old man is sure to have something to say when he gets aboard,' he remarked to Creighton. 'Well, good night. ... Ough! A long day before us to-morrow.... Ough!... Better turn in now. Ough! Ough!'

Upon the deck a band of light flashed, then a door slammed, and Mr Baker was gone into his neat cabin. Young Creighton stood leaning over the rail, and looked dreamily into the night of the East. And he saw in it a long country lane, a lane of waving leaves and dancing sunshine. He saw stirring boughs of old trees outspread, and framing in their arch the tender, the caressing blueness of an English sky. And through the arch a girl in a light dress, smiling under a sunshade, seemed to be stepping out of the tender sky.

At the other end of the ship the forecastle, with only one lamp burning now, was going to sleep in a dim emptiness traversed by loud breathings, by sudden short sighs. The double row of berths yawned black, like graves tenanted by uneasy corpses. Here and there a curtain of gaudy chintz, half drawn, marked the resting-place of a sybarite. A leg hung over the edge very white and lifeless. An arm stuck straight out with a dark palm turned up, and thick fingers half closed. Two light snores, that did not synchronize, quarrelled in funny dialogue. Singleton stripped again – the old man suffered much from prickly heat – stood cooling his back in the doorway, with his arms crossed on his bare and adorned chest. His head touched the beam of the deck above. The nigger, half undressed, was busy casting adrift the lashing of his box, and spreading his bedding in an upper berth. He moved about in his socks, tall and noiseless, with a pair of braces beating about his calves. Amongst the shadows of stanchions and bowsprit, Donkin munched a piece of hard ship's bread, sitting on the deck with upturned feet and restless eyes; he held the biscuit up before his mouth in the whole fist and snapped his jaws at it with a raging face. Crumbs fell between his outspread legs. Then he got up.

'Where's our water-cask?' he asked in a contained voice.

Singleton, without a word, pointed with a big hand that held a short smouldering pipe. Donkin bent over the cask, drank out of the tin, splashing the water, turned round and noticed the nigger looking at him over the shoulder with calm loftiness. He moved up sideways.

'There's a blooming supper for a man,' he whispered bitterly. 'My dorg at 'ome wouldn't 'ave it. It's fit enouf for you an' me. 'Ere's a big ship's fo'c'sle!...Not a blooming scrap of meat in the kids. I've looked in all the lockers....'

The nigger stared like a man addressed unexpectedly in a foreign language. Donkin changed his tone: 'Giv' us a bit of 'baccy, mate,' he breathed out confidentially, 'I 'aven't 'ad smoke or chew for the last month. I am rampin' mad for it. Come on, old man!'

'Don't be familiar,' said the nigger. Donkin started and sat down on a chest near by, out of sheer surprise. 'We haven't kept pigs together,' continued James Wait in a deep undertone. 'Here's your tobacco.' Then, after a pause, he inquired: 'What ship?' – "Golden State," muttered Donkin indistinctly, biting the tobacco. The nigger whistled low. – 'Ran?' he said curtly. Donkin nodded: one of his cheeks bulged out. 'In course I ran,' he mumbled. 'They booted the life hout of one Dago chap on the passage 'ere, then started on me. I cleared hout 'ere.' – 'Left your dunnage behind?' – 'Yes, dunnage and money,' answered Donkin, raising his voice a little; 'I got nothink. No clothes, no bed. A bandy-legged little Hirish chap 'ere 'as give me a blanket....Think I'll go an' sleep in the fore topmast staysail to-night.'

He went on deck trailing behind his back a corner of the blanket. Singleton, without a glance, moved slightly aside to let him pass. The nigger put away his shore togs and sat in clean working clothes on his box, one arm stretched over his knees. After staring at Singleton for some time he asked without emphasis: 'What kind of ship is this? Pretty fair? Eh?'

Singleton didn't stir. A long while after he said, with unmoved face: 'Ship! . . . Ships are all right. It is the men in them!'

He went on smoking in the profound silence. The wisdom of half a century spent in listening to the thunder of the waves had spoken unconsciously through his old lips. The cat purred on the windlass. Then James Wait had a fit of roaring, rattling cough, that shook him, tossed him like a hurricane, and flung him panting with staring eyes headlong on his sea-chest. Several men woke up. One said sleepily out of his bunk: ''Struth! what a blamed row!' – 'I have a cold on my chest,' gasped Wait. – 'Cold! you call it,' grumbled the man; 'should think 'twas something more. . . .' – 'Oh! you think so,' said the nigger upright and loftily scornful again. He climbed into his berth and began coughing persistently while he put his head out to glare all round the forecastle. There was no further protest. He fell back on the pillow, and could be heard there wheezing regularly like a man oppressed in his sleep.

Singleton stood at the door with his face to the light and his back to the darkness. And alone in the dim emptiness of the sleeping forecastle he appeared bigger, colossal, very old; old as Father Time himself, who should have come there into this place as quiet as a sepulchre to contemplate with patient eyes the short victory of sleep, the consoler. Yet he was only a child of time, a lonely relic of a devoured and forgotten generation. He stood, still strong, as ever unthinking; a ready man with a vast empty past and with no future, with his childlike impulses and his man's passions already dead within his tattooed breast. The men who could understand his silence were gone – those men who knew how to exist beyond the pale of life and within sight of eternity. They had been strong, as those are strong who know neither doubts nor hopes. They had been impatient and enduring, turbulent and devoted, unruly and faithful. Well-meaning people had tried to represent those men as whining over every mouthful of their food; as going about their work in fear of their lives. But in truth they had been men who knew toil, privation, violence, debauchery – but knew not fear, and had no desire of spite in their hearts. Men hard to manage, but easy to inspire; voiceless men – but men enough to scorn in their hearts the sentimental voices that bewailed the hardness of their fate. It was a fate unique and their own; the capacity to bear it appeared to them the privilege of the chosen! Their generation lived inarticulate and indispensable, without knowing the sweetness of affections or the refuge of a home – and died free from the dark menace of a narrow grave. They were the everlasting children of the mysterious sea. Their successors are the grown-up children of a discontented earth. They are less naughty, but less innocent; less profane, but perhaps also less believing; and if they had learned how to speak they have also learned how to whine. But the others were strong and mute; they were effaced, bowed and enduring, like stone caryatides that hold up in the night the lighted halls of a resplendent and glorious edifice. They are gone now – and it does not matter. The sea and the earth are unfaithful to their children: a truth, a faith, a generation of men goes – and is forgotten, and it does not matter! Except, perhaps, to the few of those who believed the truth, confessed the faith – or loved the men.

A breeze was coming. The ship that had been lying tide-rode swung to a heavier puff; and suddenly the slack of the chain cable between the windlass and the hawse-pipe clinked, slipped forward an inch, and rose gently off the deck with a startling suggestion as of unsuspected life that had been lurking stealthily in the iron. In the hawse-pipe the grinding links sent through the ship a sound like a low groan of a man sighing under a burden. The strain came on the windlass, the chain tautened like a string, vibrated – and the handle of the screw-brake moved in slight jerks. Singleton stepped forward.

Till then he had been standing meditative and unthinking, reposeful and hopeless, with a face grim and blank – a sixty-year-old child of the mysterious sea. The thoughts of all his lifetime could have been expressed in six words, but the stir of those things that were as much part of his existence as his beating heart called up a gleam of alert understanding upon the sternness of his aged face. The flame of the lamp swayed, and the old man, with knitted and bushy eyebrows, stood over the brake, watchful and motionless in the wild saraband of dancing shadows. Then the ship, obedient to the call of her anchor, forged ahead slightly and eased the strain. The cable relieved, hung down, and after swaying imperceptibly to and fro dropped with a loud tap on the hard wood planks. Singleton seized the high lever, and, by a violent throw forward of his body, wrung out another half-turn from the brake. He recovered himself, breathed largely, and remained for awhile glaring down at the powerful and compact engine that squatted on the deck at his feet like some quiet monster – a creature amazing and tame.

'You . . . hold!' he growled at it masterfully, in the incult tangle of his white beard.

II

NEXT morning, at daylight, the 'Narcissus' went to sea.

A slight haze blurred the horizon. Outside the harbour the measureless expanse of smooth water lay sparkling like a floor of jewels, and as empty as the sky. The short black tug gave a pluck to windward, in the usual way, then let go the rope, and hovered for a moment on the quarter with her engines stopped; while the slim, long hull of the ship moved ahead slowly under lower topsails. The loose upper canvas blew out in the breeze with soft round contours, resembling small white clouds snared in the maze of ropes. Then the sheets were hauled home, the yards hoisted, and the ship became a high and lonely pyramid, gliding, all shining and white, through the sunlight mist. The tug turned short round and went away towards the land. Twenty-six pairs of eyes watched her low broad stern crawling languidly over the smooth swell between the two paddle-wheels that turned fast, beating the water with fierce hurry. She resembled an enormous and aquatic black beetle, surprised by the light, overwhelmed by the sunshine, trying to escape with ineffectual effort into the distant gloom of the land. She left a lingering smudge of smoke on the sky, and two vanishing trails of foam on the water. On the place where she had stopped a round black patch of soot remained, undulating on the swell – an unclean mark of the creature's rest.

The 'Narcissus' left alone, heading south, seemed to stand resplendent and still upon the restless sea, under the moving sun. Flakes of foam swept past her sides; the water struck her with flashing blows; the land glided away slowly fading; a few birds screamed on motionless wings over the swaying mastheads. But soon the land disappeared, the birds went away; and to the west the pointed sail of an Arab dhow running for Bombay, rose triangular and upright above the sharp edge of the horizon, lingered and vanished like an illusion. Then the ship's wake, long and straight, stretched itself out through a day of immense solitude. The setting sun, burning on the level of the water, flamed crimson below the blackness of heavy rain clouds. The sunset squall, coming up from behind, dissolved itself into the short deluge of a hissing shower. It left the ship glistening from trucks to waterline, and with darkened sails. She ran easily before a fair monsoon, with her decks cleared for the night; and, moving along with her, was heard the sustained and monotonous swishing of the waves, mingled with the low whispers of men mustered aft for the setting of watches; the short plaint of some block aloft; or, now and then, a loud sigh of wind.

Mr Baker, coming out of his cabin, called out the first name sharply before closing the door behind him. He was going to take charge of the deck. On the homeward trip, according to an old custom of the sea, the chief officer takes the first night-watch – from eight till midnight. So Mr Baker, after he had heard the last 'Yes, sir!' said moodily, 'Relieve the wheel and look-out'; and climbed with heavy feet the poop ladder to windward. Soon after Mr Creighton came down, whistling softly, and went into the cabin. On the doorstep the steward lounged, in slippers, meditative, and with his shirt-sleeves rolled up to the armpits. On the main deck the cook, locking up the galley doors, had an altercation with young Charley about a pair of socks. He could be heard saying impressively, in the darkness amidships: 'You don't deserve a kindness. I've been drying them for you, and now you complain about the holes – and you swear, too! Right in front of me! If I hadn't been a Christian – which you ain't, you young ruffian – I would give you a clout on the head.... Go away!' Men in couples or threes stood pensive or moved silently along the bulwarks in the waist. The first busy day of a homeward passage was sinking into the dull peace of resumed routine. Aft, on the high poop, Mr Baker walked shuffling and grunted to himself in the pauses of his thoughts. Forward, the look-out man, erect between the flukes of the two anchors, hummed an endless tune, keeping his eyes fixed dutifully ahead in a vacant stare. A multitude of stars coming out into the clear night peopled the emptiness of the sky. They glittered, as if alive above the sea; they surrounded the running ship on all sides; more intense than the eyes of a staring crowd, and as inscrutable as the souls of men.

The passage had begun, and the ship, a fragment detached from the earth, went on lonely and swift like a small planet. Round her the abysses of sky and sea met in an unattainable frontier. A great circular solitude moved with her, ever changing and ever the same, always monotonous and always imposing. Now and then another wandering white speck, burdened with life, appeared far off – disappeared; intent on its own destiny. The sun looked upon her all day, and every morning rose with a burning, round stare of undying curiosity. She had her own future; she was alive with the lives of those beings who trod her decks; like that earth which had given her up to the sea, she had an intolerable load of regrets and hopes. On her lived timid truth and audacious lies; and, like the earth, she was unconscious, fair to see – and condemned by men to an ignoble fate. The august loneliness of her path lent dignity to the sordid inspiration of her pilgrimage. She drove foaming to the southward, as if guided by the courage of a high endeavour. The smiling greatness of the sea dwarfed the extent of time. The days raced after one another, brilliant and quick like the flashes of a lighthouse, and the nights, eventful and short, resembled fleeting dreams.

The men had shaken into their places, and the half-hourly voice of the bells ruled their life of unceasing care. Night and day the head and shoulders of a seaman could be seen aft by the wheel, outlined high against sunshine or starlight, very steady above the stir of revolving spokes. The faces changed, passing in rotation. Youthful faces, bearded faces, dark faces: faces serene, or faces moody, but all akin with the brotherhood of the sea; all with the same attentive expression of eyes, carefully watching the compass or the sails. Captain Allistoun, serious, and with an old red muffler round his throat, all day long pervaded the poop. At night, many times he rose out of the darkness of the companion, such as a phantom above a grave, and stood watchful and mute under the stars, his night-shirt fluttering like a flag – then, without a sound, sank down again. He was born on the shores of the Pentland Firth. In his youth he attained the rank of harpooner in Peterhead whalers. When he spoke of that time his restless grey eyes became still and cold, like the loom of ice. Afterwards he went into the East Indian trade for the sake of change. He had commanded the 'Narcissus' since she was built. He loved his ship, and drove her unmercifully; for his secret ambition was to make her accomplish some day a brilliantly quick passage which would be mentioned in nautical papers. He pronounced his owner's name with a sardonic smile, spoke but seldom to his officers, and reproved errors in a gentle voice, with words that cut to the quick. His hair was iron-grey, his face hard and of the colour of pump-leather. He shaved every morning of his life – at six – but once (being caught in a fierce hurricane eighty miles south-west of Mauritius) he had missed three consecutive days. He feared naught but an unforgiving God, and wished to end his days in a little house, with a plot of ground attached – far in the country – out of sight of the sea.

He, the ruler of that minute world, seldom descended from the Olympian heights of his poop. Below him – at his feet, so to speak – common mortals led their busy and insignificant lives. Along the main deck, Mr Baker grunted in a manner blood-thirsty and innocuous; and kept all our noses to the grindstone, being – as he once remarked – paid for doing that very thing. The men working about the deck were healthy and contented – as most seamen are, when once well out to sea. The true peace of God begins at any spot a thousand miles from the nearest land; and when He sends there the messengers of His might it is not in terrible wrath against crime, presumption, and folly, but paternally, to chasten simple hearts – ignorant hearts that know noth-ing of life, and beat undisturbed by envy or greed.

In the evening the cleared decks had a reposeful aspect, resembling the autumn of the earth. The sun was sinking to rest, wrapped in a mantle of warm clouds. Forward, on the end of the spare spars, the boatswain and the carpenter sat together with crossed arms; two men friendly, powerful, and deep-chested. Beside them the short, dumpy sailmaker – who had been in the Navy – related, between the whiffs of his pipe, impossible stories about Admirals. Couples tramped backwards and forwards, keeping step and balance without effort, in a confined space. Pigs grunted in the big pig-stye. Belfast, leaning thoughtfully on his elbow, above the bars, communed with them through the silence of his meditation. Fellows with shirts open wide on sunburnt breasts sat upon the mooring bits, and all up the steps of the forecastle ladders. By the foremast a few discussed in a circle the characteristics of a gentleman. One said: 'It's money as does it.' Another maintained: 'No, it's the way they speak.' Lame Knowles stumped up with an unwashed face (he had the distinction of being the dirty man of the forecastle), and showing a few yellow fangs in a shrewd smile, explained craftily that he 'had seen some of their pants.' The backsides of them – he had observed – were thinner than paper from constant sitting down in offices, yet otherwise they looked first-rate and would last for years. It was all appearance. 'It was,' he said, 'bloomin' easy to be a gentleman when you had a clean job for life.' They disputed endlessly, obstinate and childish; they repeated in shouts and with inflamed faces their amazing arguments; while the soft breeze, eddying down the enormous cavity of the foresail, distended above their bare heads, stirred the tumbled hair with a touch passing and light like an indulgent caress.

They were forgetting their toil, they were forgetting themselves. The cook approached to hear, and stood by, beaming with the inward consciousness of his faith, like a conceited saint unable to forget his glorious reward; Donkin, solitary and brooding over his wrongs on the forecastle-head, moved closer to catch the drift of the discussion below him; he turned his sallow face to the sea, and his thin nostrils moved, sniffing the breeze, as he lounged negligently by the rail. In the glow of sunset faces shone with interest, teeth flashed, eyes sparkled. The walking couples stood still suddenly, with broad grins; a man, bending over a washtub, sat up, entranced, with the soapsuds flecking his wet arms. Even the three petty officers listened leaning back, comfortably propped, and with superior smiles. Belfast left off scratching the ear of his favourite pig, and, open-mouthed, tried with eager eyes to have his say. He lifted his arms, grimacing and baffled. From a distance Charley screamed at the ring: 'I

know about gentlemen morn'n any of you. I've been inter-
mit with 'em. . . . I've blacked their boots.' The cook, cran-
ing his neck to hear better, was scandalized. 'Keep your
mouth shut when your elders speak, you impudent young
heathen – you.' – 'All right, old Hallelujah, I'm done,'
answered Charley, soothingly. At some opinion of dirty
Knowles, delivered with an air of supernatural cunning, a
ripple of laughter ran along, rose like a wave, burst with a
startling roar. They stamped with both feet; they turned
their shouting faces to the sky; many, spluttering, slapped
their thighs; while one or two, bent double, gasped, hugging themselves with both arms like men in pain. The
carpenter and the boatswain, without changing their attitude, shook with laughter where they sat; the sailmaker,
charged with an anecdote about a Commodore, looked
sulky; the cook was wiping his eyes with a greasy rag; and
lame Knowles, astonished at his own success, stood in their
midst showing a slow smile.

Suddenly the face of Donkin leaning high-shouldered
over the after-rail became grave. Something like a weak
rattle was heard through the forecastle door. It became a
murmur; it ended in a sighing groan. The washerman
plunged both his arms into the tub abruptly; the cook
became more crestfallen than an exposed backslider; the
boatswain moved his shoulders uneasily; the carpenter got
up with a spring and walked away – while the sailmaker
seemed mentally to give his story up, and began to puff at
his pipe with sombre determination. In the blackness of the
doorway a pair of eyes glimmered white, and big, and
staring. Then James Wait's head protruding, became visible, as if suspended between the two hands that grasped a
doorpost on each side of the face. The tassel of his blue
woollen nightcap, cocked forward, danced gaily over his
left eyelid. He stepped out in a tottering stride. He looked
powerful as ever, but showed a strange and affected un-
steadiness in his gait; his face was perhaps a trifle thinner,
and his eyes appeared rather startlingly prominent. He

seemed to hasten the retreat of departing light by his very presence; the setting sun dipped sharply, as though fleeing before our nigger; a black mist emanated from him; a subtle and dismal influence; a something cold and gloomy that floated out and settled on all the faces like a mourning veil. The circle broke up. The joy of laughter died on stiffened lips. There was not a smile left among all the ship's company. Not a word was spoken. Many turned their backs, trying to look unconcerned; others, with averted heads, sent half-reluctant glances out of the corners of their eyes. They resembled criminals conscious of misdeeds more than honest men distracted by doubt; only two or three stared frankly, but stupidly, with lips slightly open. All expected James Wait to say something, and, at the same time, had the air of knowing beforehand what he would say. He leaned his back against the doorpost, and with heavy eyes swept over them a glance domineering and pained, like a sick tyrant overawing a crowd of abject but untrustworthy slaves.

No one went away. They waited in fascinated dread. He said ironically, with gasps between the words:

'Thank you ... chaps. You ... are nice ... and ... quiet ... you are! Yelling so ... before ... the door. ... '

He made a longer pause, during which he worked his ribs in an exaggerated labour of breathing. It was intolerable. Feet were shuffled. Belfast let out a groan; but Donkin above blinked his red eyelids with invisible eyelashes, and smiled bitterly over the nigger's head.

The nigger went on again with surprising ease. He gasped no more, and his voice rang, hollow and loud, as though he had been talking in an empty cavern. He was contemptuously angry.

'I tried to get a wink of sleep. You know I can't sleep o' nights. And you come jabbering near the door here like a blooming lot of old women. ... You think yourselves good shipmates. Do you? ... Much you care for a dying man!'

Belfast spun away from the pig-stye. 'Jimmy,' he cried tremulously, 'if you hadn't been sick I would——'

He stopped. The nigger waited awhile, then said, in a gloomy tone: – 'You would. . . . What? Go an' fight another such one as yourself. Leave me alone. It won't be for long. I'll soon die. . . . It's coming right enough!'

Men stood around very still and with exasperated eyes. It was just what they had expected, and hated to hear, that idea of a stalking death, thrust at them many times a day like a boast and like a menace by this obnoxious nigger. He seemed to take a pride in that death which, so far, had attended only upon the ease of his life; he was overbearing about it, as if no one else in the world had ever been intimate with such a companion; he paraded it unceasingly before us with an affectionate persistence that made its presence indubitable, and at the same time incredible. No man could be suspected of such monstrous friendship! Was he a reality – or was he a sham – this ever-expected visitor of Jimmy's? We hesitated between pity and mistrust, while, on the slightest provocation, he shook before our eyes the bones of his bothersome and infamous skeleton. He was for ever trotting him out. He would talk of that coming death as though it had been already there, as if it had been walking the deck outside, as if it would presently come in to sleep in the only empty bunk; as if it had sat by his side at every meal. It interfered daily with our occupations, with our leisure, with our amusements. We had no songs and no music in the evening, because Jimmy (we all lovingly called him Jimmy, to conceal our hate of his accomplice) had managed, with that prospective decease of his, to disturb even Archie's mental balance. Archie was the owner of the concertina; but after a couple of stinging lectures from Jimmy he refused to play any more. He said: 'Yon's an uncanny joker. I dinna ken what's wrang wi' him, but there's something verra wrang, verra wrang. It's nae manner of use asking me. I won't play.' Our singers became mute because Jimmy was a dying man. For the same reason

no chap – as Knowles remarked – could 'drive in a nail to
hang his few poor rags upon,' without being made aware of
the enormity he committed in disturbing Jimmy's interminable last moments. At night, instead of the cheerful
yell, 'One bell! Turn out! Do you hear there? Hey! hey! hey!
Show leg!' the watches were called man by man, in whispers, so as not to interfere with Jimmy's, possibly, last
slumber on earth. True, he was always awake, and managed, as we sneaked out on deck, to plant in our backs some
cutting remark that, for the moment, made us feel as if we
had been brutes, and afterwards made us suspect ourselves
of being fools. We spoke in low tones within that fo'c'sle as
though it had been a church. We ate our meals in silence
and dread, for Jimmy was capricious with his food, and
railed bitterly at the salt meat, at the biscuits, at the tea, as
at articles unfit for human consumption – 'let alone for a
dying man!' He would say: 'Can't you find a better slice of
meat for a sick man who's trying to get home to be cured –
or buried? But there! If I had a chance, you fellows would
do away with it. You would poison me. Look at what you
have given me!' We served him in his bed with rage and
humility, as though we had been the base courtiers of a
hated prince; and he rewarded us by his unconciliating
criticism. He had found the secret of keeping for ever on
the run the fundamental imbecility of mankind; he had the
secret of life, that confounded dying man, and he made
himself master of every moment of our existence. We grew
desperate, and remained submissive. Emotional little
Belfast was for ever on the verge of assault or on the verge
of tears. One evening he confided to Archie: 'For a
ha'penny I would knock his ugly black head off – the
skulking dodger!' And the straightforward Archie pretended to be shocked! Such was the infernal spell which
that casual St Kitt's nigger had cast upon our guileless
manhood! But the same night Belfast stole from the galley
the officers' Sunday fruit-pie, to tempt the fastidious
appetite of Jimmy. He endangered not only his long

friendship with the cook but also – as it appeared – his eternal welfare. The cook was overwhelmed with grief; he did not know the culprit but he knew that wickedness flourished; he knew that Satan was abroad amongst those men, whom he looked upon as in some way under his spiritual care. Whenever he saw three or four of us standing together he would leave his stove, to run out and preach. We fled from him; and only Charley (who knew the thief) affronted the cook with a candid gaze which irritated the good man. 'It's you, I believe,' he groaned, sorrowful and with a patch of soot on his chin. 'It's you. You are a brand for the burning! No more of YOUR socks in my galley.' Soon, unofficially, the information was spread about that, should there be another case of stealing, our marmalade (an extra allowance: half a pound per man) would be stopped. Mr Baker ceased to heap jocular abuse upon his favourites, and grunted suspiciously at all. The captain's cold eyes, high up on the poop, glittered mistrustful, as he surveyed us trooping in a small mob from halyards to braces for the usual evening pull at all the ropes. Such stealing in a merchant ship is difficult to check, and may be taken as a declaration by men of their dislike for their officers. It is a bad symptom. It may end in God knows what trouble. The 'Narcissus' was still a peaceful ship, but mutual confidence was shaken. Donkin did not conceal his delight. We were dismayed.

Then illogical Belfast reproached our nigger with great fury. James Wait, with his elbow on the pillow, choked, gasped out: 'Did I ask you to bone the dratted thing? Blow your blamed pie. It has made me worse – you little Irish lunatic, you!' Belfast, with scarlet face and trembling lips, made a dash at him. Every man in the forecastle rose with a shout. There was a moment of wild tumult. Some one shrieked piercingly: 'Easy, Belfast! Easy!...' We expected Belfast to strangle Wait without more ado. Dust flew. We heard through it the nigger's cough, metallic and explosive like a gong. Next moment we saw Belfast hanging over him. He was saying plaintively: 'Don't, Jimmy! Don't be like that. An angel couldn't put up with ye – sick as ye are.' He looked round at us from Jimmy's bedside, his comical mouth twitching, and through tearful eyes; then he tried to put straight the disarranged blankets. The unceasing whisper of the sea filled the forecastle. Was James Wait frightened, or touched, or repentant? He lay on his back with his hand to his side, and as motionless as if his expected visitor had come at last. Belfast fumbled about his feet, repeating with emotion: 'Yes. We know. Ye are bad, but.... Just say what ye want done, and.... We all know ye are bad – very bad....' No! Decidedly James Wait was not touched or repentant. Truth to say, he seemed rather startled. He sat up with incredible suddenness and ease. 'Ah! You think I am bad, do you?' he said gloomily, in his clearest baritone voice (to hear him speak sometimes you would never think there was anything wrong with that man). 'Do you?... Well, act according! Some of you haven't sense enough to put a blanket shipshape over a sick man. There! Leave it alone! I can die anyhow!' Belfast turned away limply with a gesture of discouragement. In the silence of the forecastle, full of interested men, Donkin pronounced distinctly: – 'Well, I'm blowed!' and sniggered. Wait looked at him. He looked at him in a quite friendly manner. Nobody could tell what would please our incomprehensible invalid: but for us the scorn of that snigger was hard to bear.

Donkin's position in the forecastle was distinguished but unsafe. He stood on the bad eminence of a general dislike. He was left alone; and in his isolation he could do nothing but think of the gales of the Cape of Good Hope and envy us the possession of warm clothing and waterproofs. Our sea-boots, our oilskin coats, our well-filled sea-chests, were to him so many causes for bitter meditation: he had none of these things, and he felt instinctively that no man, when the need arose, would offer to share them with him. He was impudently cringing to us and systematically insolent to the officers. He anticipated the best results, for himself, from such a line of conduct – and was mistaken. Such natures forget that under extreme provocation men will be just – whether they want to be so or not. Donkin's insolence to long-suffering Mr Baker became at last intolerable to us, and we rejoiced when the mate, one dark night, tamed him for good. It was done neatly, with great decency and decorum, and with little noise. We had been called – just before midnight – to trim the yards, and Donkin – as usual – made insulting remarks. We stood sleepily in a row with the forebrace in our hands waiting for the next order, and heard in the darkness a scuffly tramping of feet, an exclamation of surprise sounds of cuffs and slaps, suppressed, hissing whispers: 'Ah! Will you!' . . . 'Don't! . . . . Don't!' . . . 'Then behave.' . . . 'Oh! Oh! . . .' Afterwards there were soft thuds mixed with the rattle of iron things as if a man's body had been tumbling helplessly among the main-pump rods. Before we could realize the situation, Mr Baker's voice was heard very near and a little impatient: 'Haul away, men! Lay back on that rope!' And we did lay back on the rope with great alacrity. As if nothing had happened, the chief mate went on trimming the yards with his usual and exasperating fastidiousness. We didn't at the time see anything of Donkin, and did not care. Had the chief officer thrown him overboard, no man would have said as much as 'Hallo! he's gone!' But, in truth, no great harm was done – even if Donkin did lose one of his front teeth. We perceived this in the morning, and preserved a ceremonious silence: the etiquette of the forecastle commanded us to be blind and dumb in such a case, and we cherished the decencies of our life more than ordinary landsmen respect theirs. Charley, with unpardonable want of *savoir vivre*, yelled out: ''Ave you been to your dentyst? . . . Hurt ye, didn't it?' He got a box on the ear from one of his best friends. The boy was surprised, and remained plunged in grief for at least three hours. We were sorry for him, but youth requires even more discipline

than age. Donkin grinned venomously. From that day he
became pitiless; told Jimmy that he was a 'black fraud';
hinted to us that we were an imbecile lot, daily taken in
by a vulgar nigger. And Jimmy seemed to like the fellow!

Singleton lived untouched by human emotions.
Taciturn and unsmiling, he breathed amongst us in that
alone resembling the rest of the crowd. We were trying to
be decent chaps, and found it jolly difficult; we oscillated
between the desire of virtue and the fear of ridicule; we
wished to save ourselves from the pain of remorse, but did
not want to be made the contemptible dupes of our sentiment. Jimmy's hateful accomplice seemed to have blown
with his impure breath undreamt-of subtleties into our
hearts. We were disturbed and cowardly. That we knew.
Singleton seemed to know nothing, understand nothing.
We had thought him till then as wise as he looked, but now
we dared, at times, suspect him of being stupid – from old
age. One day, however, at dinner, as we sat on our boxes
round a tin dish that stood on the deck within the circle of
our feet, Jimmy expressed his general disgust with men and
things in words that were particularly disgusting. Singleton
lifted his head. We became mute. The old man, addressing
Jimmy, asked: 'Are you dying?' Thus interrogated, James
Wait appeared horribly startled and confused. We all were
startled. Mouths remained open; hearts thumped, eyes
blinked; a dropped tin fork rattled in the dish; a man rose
as if to go out, and stood still. In less than a minute Jimmy
pulled himself together: 'Why? Can't you see I am?' he
answered shakily. Singleton lifted a piece of soaked biscuit
('his teeth' – he declared – 'had no edge on them now') to
his lips. – 'Well, get on with your dying,' he said with
venerable mildness; 'don't raise a blamed fuss with us over
that job. We can't help you.' Jimmy fell back in his bunk,
and for a long time lay very still wiping the perspiration off
his chin. The dinner-tins were put away quickly. On deck
we discussed the incident in whispers. Some showed a
chuckling exultation. Many looked grave. Wamibo, after

long periods of staring dreaminess, attempted abortive smiles; and one of the young Scandinavians, much tormented by doubt, ventured in the second dog-watch to approach Singleton (the old man did not encourage us much to speak to him) and ask sheepishly: 'You think he will die?' Singleton looked up. – 'Why, of course he will die,' he said deliberately. This seemed decisive. It was promptly imparted to every one by him who had consulted the oracle. Shy and eager, he would step up and with averted gaze recite his formula: 'Old Singleton says he will die.' It was a relief! At last we knew that our compassion would not be misplaced, and we could again smile without misgivings – but we reckoned without Donkin. Donkin 'didn't want to 'ave no truck with 'em dirty furriners.' When Nilsen came to him with the news: 'Singleton says he will die,' he answered him by a spiteful 'And so will you – you fat-headed Dutchman. Wish you Dutchmen were all dead – 'stead comin' takin' our money inter your starvin' country.' We were appalled. We perceived that after all Singleton's answer meant nothing. We began to hate him for making fun of us. All our certitudes were going; we were on doubtful terms with our officers; the cook had given us up for lost; we had overheard the boatswain's opinion that 'we were a crowd of softies.' We suspected Jimmy, one another, and even our very selves. We did not know what to do. At every insignificant turn of our humble life we met Jimmy over-bearing and blocking the way arm-in-arm with his awful and veiled familiar. It was a weird servitude.

It began a week after leaving Bombay and came on us stealthily like any other great misfortune. Every one had remarked that Jimmy from the first was very slack at his work; but we thought it simply the outcome of his philosophy of life. Donkin said: 'You put no more weight on a rope than a bloody sparrer.' He disdained him. Belfast, ready for a fight, exclaimed provokingly: 'You don't kill yourself, old man!' – 'Would you?' he retorted with extreme scorn – and Belfast retired. One morning, as we were washing decks, Mr Baker called to him: 'Bring your broom over here, Wait.' He strolled languidly. 'Move yourself! Ough!' grunted Mr Baker; 'what's the matter with your hind legs?' He stopped dead short. He gazed slowly with eyes that bulged out with an expression audacious and sad. – 'It isn't my legs,' he said, 'it's my lungs.' Everybody listened. – 'What's … Ough! … What's wrong with them?' inquired Mr Baker. All the watch stood around on the wet deck, grinning, and with brooms or buckets in their hands. He said mournfully: 'Going – or gone. Can't you see I'm a dying man? I know it!' Mr Baker was disgusted. – 'Then why the devil did you ship aboard here?' – 'I must live till I die – mustn't I?' he replied. The grins became audible. – 'Go off the deck – get out of my sight.' said Mr Baker. He was nonplussed. It was a unique experience. James Wait, obedient, dropped his broom, and walked slowly forward. A burst of laughter followed him. It was too funny. All hands laughed…. They laughed! … Alas!

He became the tormenter of all our moments; he was worse than a nightmare. You couldn't see that there was anything wrong with him: a nigger does not show. He was not very fat – certainly – but then he was no leaner than other niggers we had known. He coughed often, but the most prejudiced person could perceive that, mostly, he coughed when it suited his purpose. He wouldn't, or couldn't, do his work – and he wouldn't lie-up. One day he would skip aloft with the best of them, and next time we would be obliged to risk our lives to get his limp body down. He was reported, he was examined; he was remonstrated with, threatened, cajoled, lectured. He was called into the cabin to interview the captain. There were wild rumours. It was said he had cheeked the old man; it was said he had frightened him. Charley maintained that the 'skipper, weepin', 'as giv' 'im 'is blessin' an' a pot of jam.' Knowles had it from the steward that the unspeakable Jimmy had been reeling against the cabin furniture; that he had groaned; that he had complained of general brutality and disbelief; and had ended by coughing all over the old man's meteorological journals which were then spread on the table. At any rate, Wait returned forward supported by the steward, who, in a pained and shocked voice, entreated us: 'Here! Catch hold of him, one of you. He is to lie-up.' Jimmy drank a tin mugful of coffee, and, after bullying first one and then another, went to bed. He remained there most of the time, but when it suited him would come on deck and appear amongst us. He was scornful and brooding; he looked ahead upon the sea, and no one could tell what was the meaning of that black man sitting apart in a meditative attitude and as motionless as a carving.

He refused steadily all medicine; he threw sago and cornflour overboard till the steward got tired of bringing it to him. He asked for paregoric. They sent him a big bottle; enough to poison a wilderness of babies. He kept it between his mattress and the deal lining of the ship's side; and nobody ever saw him take a dose. Donkin abused him to his face, jeered at him while he gasped; and the same day Wait would lend him a warm jersey. Once Donkin reviled him for half an hour; reproached him with the extra work his malingering gave to the watch; and ended by calling him 'a black-faced swine.' Under the spell of our accursed perversity we were horror-struck. But Jimmy positively seemed to revel in that abuse. It made him look cheerful – and Donkin had a pair of old sea boots thrown at him. 'Here, you East-end trash,' boomed Wait, 'you may have that.'

At last Mr Baker had to tell the captain that James Wait was disturbing the peace of the ship. 'Knock discipline on the head – he will, Ough,' grunted Mr Baker. As a matter of fact, the starboard watch came as near as possible to refusing duty, when ordered one morning by the boatswain to wash out their forecastle. It appears Jimmy objected to a wet floor – and that morning we were in a compassionate mood. We thought the boatswain a brute, and, practically, told him so. Only Mr Baker's delicate tact prevented an all-fired row: he refused to take us seriously. He came bustling forward, and called us many unpolite names but in such a hearty and seamanlike manner that we began to feel ashamed of ourselves. In truth, we thought him much too good a sailor to annoy him willingly: and after all Jimmy might have been a fraud – probably was! The forecastle got a clean-up that morning; but in the afternoon a sick-bay was fitted up in the deck-house. It was a nice little cabin opening on deck, and with two berths. Jimmy's belongings were transported there, and then – notwithstanding his protests – Jimmy himself. He said he couldn't walk. Four men carried him on a blanket. He complained that he would have to die there alone, like a dog. We grieved for him, and were delighted to have him removed from the forecastle. We attended him as before. The galley was next door, and the cook looked in many times a day. Wait became a little more cheerful. Knowles affirmed having heard him laugh to himself in peals one day. Others had seen him walking about on deck at night. His little place, with the door ajar on a long hook, was always full of tobacco smoke. We spoke through the crack cheerfully, sometimes abusively, as we passed by, intent on our work. He fascinated us. He would never let doubt die. He over-shadowed the ship. Invulnerable in his promise of speedy corruption he trampled on our self-respect, he demon-strated to us daily our want of moral courage; he tainted our lives. Had we been a miserable gang of wretched immortals, unhallowed alike by hope and fear, he could not have lorded it over us with a more pitiless assertion of his sublime privilege.

III

MEANTIME the 'Narcissus,' with square yards, ran out of the fair monsoon. She drifted slowly, swinging round and round the compass, through a few days of baffling light airs. Under the patter of short warm showers, grumbling men whirled the heavy yards from side to side; they caught hold of the soaked ropes with groans and sighs, while their officers, sulky and dripping with rain water, unceasingly ordered them about in wearied voices. During the short respites they looked with disgust into the smarting palms of their stiff hands, and asked one another bitterly: 'Who would be a sailor if he could be a farmer?' All the tempers were spoilt, and no man cared what he said. One black night, when the watch, panting in the heat and half-drowned with rain, had been through four mortal hours hunted from brace to brace, Belfast declared that he would 'chuck the sea for ever and go in a steamer.' This was excessive, no doubt. Captain Allistoun, with great self-control, would mutter sadly to Mr Baker: 'It is not so bad – not so bad,' when he had managed to shove, and dodge, and manœuvre his smart ship through sixty miles in twenty-four hours. From the doorstep of the little cabin, Jimmy, chin in hand, watched our distasteful labours with insolent and melancholy eyes. We spoke to him gently – and out of his sight exchanged sour smiles.

Then, again, with a fair wind and under a clear sky, the ship went on piling up the South Latitude. She passed outside Madagascar and Mauritius without a glimpse of the land. Extra lashings were put on the spare spars. Hatches were looked to. The steward in his leisure moments and with a worried air tried to fit washboards to the cabin doors. Stout canvas was bent with care. Anxious eyes looked to the westward, towards the cape of storms. The ship began to dip into a south-west swell, and the softly luminous sky of low latitudes took on a harder sheen from day to day above our heads: it arched high above the ship vibrating and pale, like an immense dome of steel, resonant with the deep voice of freshening gales. The sunshine gleamed cold on the white curls of black waves. Before the strong breath of westerly squalls the ship, with reduced sail, lay slowly over, obstinate and yielding. She drove to and fro in the unceasing endeavour to fight her way through the invisible violence of the winds: she pitched headlong into dark smooth hollows; she struggled upwards over the snowy ridges of great running seas; she rolled, restless, from side to side, like a thing in pain. Enduring and valiant, she answered to the call of men; and her slim spars waving for ever in abrupt semicircles, seemed to beckon in vain for help towards the stormy sky.

It was a bad winter off the Cape that year. The relieved helmsmen came off flapping their arms, or ran stamping hard and blowing into swollen, red fingers. The watch on deck dodged the sting of cold sprays or, crouching in sheltered corners, watched dismally the high and merciless seas boarding the ship time after time in unappeasable fury. Water tumbled in cataracts over the forecastle doors. You had to dash through a waterfall to get into your damp bed. The men turned in wet and turned out stiff to face the redeeming and ruthless exactions of their glorious and obscure fate. Far aft, and peering watchfully to windward, the officers could be seen through the mist of squalls. They stood by the weather-rail, holding on grimly, straight and glistening in their long coats; and in the disordered plunges of the hard-driven ship, they appeared high up, attentive, tossing violently above the grey line of a clouded horizon in motionless attitudes.

They watched the weather and the ship as men on shore watch the momentous chances of fortune. Captain Allistoun never left the deck, as though he had been part of the ship's fittings. Now and then the steward, shivering, but always in shirtsleeves, would struggle towards him with some hot coffee, half of which the gale blew out of the cup before it reached the master's lips. He drank what was left gravely in one long gulp, while heavy sprays pattered loudly on his oilskin coat, the seas swishing broke about his high boots; and he never took his eyes off the ship. He kept his gaze riveted upon her as a loving man watches the unselfish toil of a delicate woman upon the slender thread of whose existence is hung the whole meaning and joy of the world. We all watched her. She was beautiful and had a weakness. We loved her no less for that. We admired her qualities aloud, we boasted of them to one another, as though they had been our own, and the consciousness of her only fault we kept buried in the silence of our profound affection. She was born in the thundering peal of hammers beating upon iron, in black eddies of smoke, under a grey sky, on the banks of the Clyde. The clamorous and sombre stream gives birth to things of beauty that float away into the sunshine of the world to be loved by men. The 'Narcissus' was one of that perfect brood. Less perfect than many perhaps, but she was ours, and, consequently, incomparable. We were proud of her. In Bombay, ignorant land-lubbers alluded to her as that 'pretty grey ship.' Pretty! A scurvy meed of commendation! We knew she was the most magnificent sea-boat ever launched. We tried to forget that, like many good sea-boats, she was at times rather crank. She was exacting. She wanted care in loading and handling, and no one knew exactly how much care would be enough. Such are the imperfections of mere men! The ship knew, and sometimes would correct the presumptuous human ignorance by the wholesome discipline of fear. We had heard ominous stories about past voyages. The cook (technically a seaman, but in reality no sailor) – the cook, when unstrung by some misfortune, such as the rolling over of a saucepan, would mutter gloomily while he wiped the floor: 'There! Look at what she has done! Some voy'ge she will drown all hands! You'll see if she won't.' To which the steward, snatching in the galley a moment to draw breath in the hurry of his worried life, would remark philosophi-cally: 'Those that see won't tell, anyhow. I don't want to see it.' We derided those fears. Our hearts went out to the old man when he pressed her hard so as to make her hold her own, hold to every inch gained to windward; when he made her, under reefed sails, leap obliquely at enormous waves.

The men, knitted together aft into a ready group by the first sharp order of an officer coming to take charge of the deck in bad weather: 'Keep handy the watch,' stood admiring her valiance. Their eyes blinked in the wind; their dark faces were wet with drops of water more salt and bitter than human tears; beards and moustaches, soaked, hung straight and dripping like fine sea-weed. They were fantastically misshapen; in high boots, in hats like helmets, and swaying clumsily, stiff and bulky in glistening oilskins, they resembled men strangely equipped for some fabulous adventure. Whenever she rose easily to a towering green sea, elbows dug ribs, faces brightened, lips murmured: 'Didn't she do it cleverly,' and all the heads turning like one watched with sardonic grins the foiled wave go roaring to leeward, white with the foam of a monstrous rage. But when she had not been quick enough and, struck heavily, lay over trembling under the blow, we clutched at ropes, and looking up at the narrow bands of drenched and strained sails waving desperately aloft, we thought in our hearts: 'No wonder. Poor thing!'

The thirty-second day out of Bombay began inauspiciously. In the morning a sea smashed one of the galley doors. We dashed in through lots of steam and found the cook very wet and indignant with the ship: 'She's getting worse every day. She's trying to drown me in front of my own stove!' He was very angry. We pacified him, and the carpenter, though washed away twice from there, managed to repair the door. Through that accident our dinner was not ready till late, but it didn't matter in the end because Knowles, who went to fetch it, got knocked down by a sea and the dinner went over the side. Captain Allistoun, looking more hard and thin-lipped than ever, hung on to full topsail and foresail, and would not notice that the ship, asked to do too much, appeared to lose heart altogether for the first time since we knew her. She refused to rise, and bored her way sullenly through the seas. Twice running, as though she had been blind or weary of life, she put her nose deliberately into a big wave and swept the decks from end to end. As the boatswain observed with marked annoyance, while we were splashing about in a body to try and save a worthless wash-tub: 'Every blooming thing in the ship is going overboard this afternoon.' Venerable Singleton broke his habitual silence and said with a glance aloft: 'The old man's in a temper with the weather, but it's no good bein' angry with the winds of heaven.' Jimmy had shut his door, of course. We knew he was dry and comfortable within his little cabin, and in our absurd way were pleased one moment, exasperated the next, by that certitude. Donkin skulked shamelessly, uneasy and miserable. He grumbled: 'I'm perishin' with cold outside in bloomin' wet rags, an' that 'ere black sojer sits dry on a blamed chest full of bloomin' clothes; blank his black soul!' We took no notice of him; we hardly gave a thought to Jimmy and his bosom friend. There was no leisure for idle probing of hearts. Sails blew adrift. Things broke loose. Cold and wet, we were washed about the deck while trying to repair damages. The ship tossed about, shaken furiously, like a toy in the hand of a lunatic. Just at sunset there was a rush to shorten sail before the menace of a sombre hail cloud. The hard gust of wind came brutal like the blow of a fist. The ship relieved of her canvas in time received it pluckily: she yielded reluctantly to the violent onset; then, coming up with a stately and irresistible motion, brought her spars to windward in the teeth of the screeching squall. Out of the abysmal darkness of the black cloud overhead white hail streamed on her, rattled on the rigging, leaped in handfuls off the yards, rebounded on the deck – round and gleaming in the murky turmoil like a shower of pearls. It passed away. For a moment a livid sun shot horizontally the last rays of sinister light between the hills of steep, rolling waves. Then a wild night rushed in – stamped out in a great howl that dismal remnant of a stormy day.

There was no sleep on board that night. Most seamen remembered in their life one or two such nights of a

culminating gale. Nothing seems left of the whole universe
but darkness, clamour, fury – and the ship. And like the last
vestige of a shattered creation she drifts, bearing an
anguished remnant of sinful mankind, through the distress, tumult, and pain of an avenging terror. No one slept
in the forecastle. The tin oil-lamp suspended on a long
string, smoking, described wide circles; wet clothing made
dark heaps on the glistening floor; a thin layer of water
rushed to and fro. In the bed-places men lay booted, resting
on elbows and with open eyes. Hung-up suits of oil-skin
swung out and in, lively and disquieting like reckless ghosts
of decapitated seamen dancing in a tempest. No one spoke
and all listened. Outside the night moaned and sobbed to
the accompaniment of a continuous loud tremor as of
innumerable drums beating far off. Shrieks passed through
the air. Tremendous dull blows made the ship tremble
while she rolled under the weight of the seas toppling on
her deck. At times she soared up swiftly as if to leave this
earth for ever, then during interminable moments fell
through a void with all the hearts on board of her standing
still, till a frightful shock, expected and sudden, started
them off again with a big thump. After every dislocating
jerk of the ship, Wamibo, stretched full length, his face on
the pillow, groaned slightly with pain of his tormented
universe. Now and then, for the fraction of an intolerable
second, the ship, in the fiercer burst of a terrible uproar,
remained on her side, vibrating and still, with a stillness
more appalling than the wildest motion. Then upon all
those prone bodies a stir would pass, a shiver of suspense. A
man would protrude his anxious head and a pair of eyes
glistened in the sway of light glaring wildly. Some moved
their legs a little as if making ready to jump out. But several,
motionless on their backs and with one hand gripping hard
the edge of the bunk, smoked nervously with quick puffs,
staring upwards; immobilized in a great craving for peace.

At midnight, orders were given to furl the fore and
mizen topsails. With immense efforts men crawled aloft

through a merciless buffeting, saved the canvas and crawled down almost exhausted, to bear in panting silence the cruel battering of the seas. Perhaps for the first time in the history of the merchant service the watch, told to go below, did not leave the deck, as if compelled to remain there by the fascination of a venomous violence. At every heavy gust men, huddled together, whispered to one another: 'It can blow no harder' – and presently the gale would give them the lie with a piercing shriek, and drive their breath back into their throats. A fierce squall seemed to burst asunder the thick mass of sooty vapours; and above the wrack of torn clouds glimpses could be caught of the high moon rushing backwards with frightful speed over the sky, right into the wind's eye. Many hung their heads, muttering that it 'turned their inwards out' to look at it. Soon the clouds closed up and the world again became a raging, blind darkness that howled, flinging at the lonely ship salt sprays and sleet.

About half-past seven the pitchy obscurity round us turned a ghastly grey, and we knew that the sun had risen. This unnatural and threatening daylight, in which we could see one another's wild eyes and drawn faces, was only an added tax on our endurance. The horizon seemed to have come on all sides within arm's length of the ship. Into that narrowed circle furious seas leaped in, struck, and leaped out. A rain of salt, heavy drops flew aslant like mist. The main-topsail had to be goose-winged, and with stolid resignation every one prepared to go aloft once more; but the officers yelled, pushed back, and at last we understood that no more men would be allowed to go on the yard than were absolutely necessary for the work. As at any moment the masts were likely to be jumped out or blown overboard, we concluded that the captain didn't want to see all his crowd go over the side at once. That was reasonable. The watch then on duty, led by Mr Creighton, began to struggle up the rigging. The wind flattened them against the ratlines; then easing a little, would let them ascend a

couple of steps; and again, with a sudden gust, pin all up the
shrouds the whole crawling line in attitudes of crucifixion.
The other watch plunged down on the main deck to haul
up the sail. Men's heads bobbed up as the water flung them
irresistibly from side to side. Mr Baker grunted encouragingly in our midst, spluttering and blowing amongst the
tangled ropes like an energetic porpoise. Favoured by an
ominous and untrustworthy lull, the work was done without any one being lost either off the deck or from the yard.
For the moment the gale seemed to take off, and the ship,
as if grateful for our efforts, plucked up heart and made
better weather of it.

At eight the men off duty, watching their chance, ran
forward over the flooded deck to get some rest. The other
half of the crew remained aft for their turn of 'seeing her
through her trouble,' as they expressed it. The two mates
urged the master to go below. Mr Baker grunted in his ear:
'Ough! surely now...Ough!...confidence in us...noth-
ing more to do...she must lay it out or go. Ough! Ough!'
Tall young Mr Creighton smiled down at him cheerfully:
'...She's as right as a trivet! Take a spell, sir.' He looked at
them stonily with bloodshot, sleepless eyes. The rims of his
eyelids were scarlet, and he moved his jaw unceasingly with
a slow effort, as though he had been masticating a lump of
india-rubber. He shook his head. He repeated: 'Never
mind me. I must see it out – I must see it out,' but he
consented to sit down for a moment on the skylight, with
his hard face turned unflinchingly to windward. The sea
spat at it – and, stoical, it streamed with water as though he
had been weeping. On the weather side of the poop the
watch, hanging on to the mizen rigging and to one another,
tried to exchange encouraging words. Singleton, at the
wheel, yelled out: 'Look out for yourselves!' His voice
reached them in a warning whisper. They were startled.

A big, foaming sea came out of the mist; it made for the
ship, roaring wildly, and in its rush it looked as mischievous
and discomposing as a madman with an axe. One or two,

shouting, scrambled up the rigging; most, with a convulsive catch of the breath, held on where they stood. Singleton dug his knees under the wheel-box, and carefully eased the helm to the head-long pitch of the ship, but without taking his eyes off the coming wave. It towered close-to and high, like a wall of green glass topped with snow. The ship rose to it as though she had soared on wings, and for a moment rested poised upon the foaming crest as if she had been a great sea-bird. Before we could draw breath a heavy gust struck her, another roller took her unfairly under the weather bow, she gave a toppling lurch, and filled her decks. Captain Allistoun leaped up, and fell; Archie rolled over him, screaming: 'She will rise!' She gave another lurch to leeward; the lower deadeyes dipped heavily; the men's feet flew from under them, and they hung kicking above the slanting poop. They could see the ship putting her side in the water, and shouted all together: 'She's going!' Forward the forecastle doors flew open, and the watch below were seen leaping out one after another, throwing their arms up; and, falling on hands and knees, scrambled aft on all fours along the high side of the deck, sloping more than the roof of a house. From leeward the seas rose, pursuing them; they looked wretched in a hopeless struggle, like vermin fleeing before a flood; they fought up the weather ladder of the poop one after another, half naked and staring wildly; and as soon as they got up they shot to leeward in clusters, with closed eyes, till they brought up heavily with their ribs against the iron stanchions of the rail; then, groaning, they rolled in a confused mass. The immense volume of water thrown forward by the last scend of the ship had burst the lee door of the forecastle. They could see their chests, pillows, blankets, clothing, come out floating upon the sea. While they struggled back to windward they looked in dismay. The straw beds swam high, the blankets, spread out, undulated; while the chests, water-logged and with a heavy list, pitched heavily like dismasted hulks, before they sank; Archie's big coat passed with outspread arms, resembling a drowned seaman floating with his head under water. Men were slipping down while trying to dig their fingers into the planks; others, jammed in corners, rolled enormous eyes. They all yelled unceasingly: 'The masts! Cut! Cut!...' A black squall howled low over the ship, that lay on her side with the weather yard-arms pointing to the clouds; while the tall masts, inclined nearly to the horizon, seemed to be of an immeasurable length. The carpenter let go his hold, rolled against the skylight, and began to crawl to the cabin entrance, where a big axe was kept ready for just such an emergency. At that moment the topsail sheet parted, the end of the heavy chain racketed aloft, and sparks of red fire streamed down through the flying sprays. The sail flapped once with a jerk that seemed to tear our hearts out through our teeth, and instantly changed into a bunch of fluttering narrow ribbons that tied themselves into knots and became quiet along the yard. Captain Allistoun struggled, managed to stand up with his face near the deck, upon which men swung on the ends of ropes, like nest robbers upon a cliff. One of his feet was on somebody's chest; his face was purple; his lips moved. He yelled also; he yelled, bending down: 'No! No!' Mr Baker, one leg over the binnacle-stand, roared out: 'Did you say no? Not cut?' He shook his head madly. 'No! No!' Between his legs the crawling carpenter heard, collapsed at once, and lay full length in the angle of the skylight. Voices took up the shout – 'No! No!' Then all became still. They waited for the ship to turn over altogether, and shake them out into the sea; and upon the terrific noise of wind and sea not a murmur of remonstrance came out from those men, who each would have given ever so many years of life to see 'them damned sticks go overboard!' They all believed it their only chance; but a little hard-faced man shook his grey head and shouted 'No!' without giving them as much as a glance. They were silent, and gasped. They gripped rails, they had wound ropes'-ends under their arms; they clutched ringbolts, they crawled in heaps where there was foothold; they held on with both arms, hooked themselves to anything to windward with elbows, with chins, almost with their teeth: and some, unable to crawl away from where they had been flung, felt the sea leap up, striking against their backs as they struggled upwards. Singleton had stuck to the wheel. His hair flew out in the wind; the gale seemed to take its life-long adversary by the beard and shake his old head. He wouldn't let go, and, with his knees forced between the spokes, flew up and down like a man on a bough. As Death appeared unready, they began to look about. Donkin, caught by one foot in a loop of some rope, hung, head down, below us, and yelled, with his face to the deck: 'Cut! Cut!' Two men lowered themselves cautiously to him; others hauled on the rope. They caught him up, shoved him into a safer place, held him. He shouted curses at the master, shook his fist at him with horrible blasphemies, called upon us in filthy words to 'Cut! Don't mind that murdering fool! Cut, some of you!' One of his rescuers struck him a back-handed blow over the mouth; his head banged on the deck, and he became suddenly very quiet, with a white face, breathing hard, and with a few drops of blood trickling from his cut lip. On the lee side another man could be seen stretched out as if stunned; only the washboard prevented him from going over the side. It was the steward. We had to sling him up like a bale, for he was paralysed with fright. He had rushed up out of the pantry when he felt the ship go over, and had rolled down helplessly, clutching a china mug. It was not broken. With difficulty we tore it away from him, and when he saw it in our hands he was amazed. 'Where did you get that thing?' he kept on asking us in a trembling voice. His shirt was blown to shreds; the ripped sleeves flapped like wings. Two men made him fast, and, doubled over the rope that held him, he resembled a bundle of wet rags. Mr Baker crawled along the line of men, asking: 'Are you all there?' and looking them over. Some blinked vacantly, others shook convulsively; Wamibo's head hung over his breast; and in painful attitudes, cut by lashings, exhausted with clutching, screwed up in corners, they breathed heavily. Their lips twitched, and at every sickening heave of the overturned ship they opened them wide as if to shout. The cook, embracing a wooden stanchion, unconsciously repeated a prayer. In every short interval of the fiendish noises around he could be heard there, without cap or slippers, imploring in that storm the Master of our lives not to lead him into temptation. Soon he also became silent. In all that crowd of cold and hungry men, waiting wearily for a violent death, not a voice was heard; they were mute, and in sombre thoughtfulness listened to the horrible imprecations of the gale.

Hours passed. They were sheltered by the heavy inclination of the ship from the wind that rushed in one long unbroken moan above their heads, but cold rain showers fell at times into the uneasy calm of their refuge. Under the torment of that new infliction a pair of shoulders would writhe a little. Teeth chattered. The sky was clearing, and bright sunshine gleamed over the ship. After every burst of battering seas, vivid and fleeting rainbows arched over the drifting hull in the flick of sprays. The gale was ending in a clear blow, which gleamed and cut like a knife. Between two bearded shellbacks Charley, fastened with somebody's long muffler to a deck ring-bolt, wept quietly, with rare tears wrung out by bewilderment, cold, hunger, and general misery. One of his neighbours punched him in the ribs asking roughly: 'What's the matter with your cheek? In fine weather there's no holding you, youngster.' Turning about with prudence he worked himself out of his coat and threw it over the boy. The other man closed up muttering: '"Twill make a bloomin' man of you, sonny.' They flung their arms over and pressed against him. Charley drew his feet up and his eyelids dropped. Sighs were heard, as men, perceiving that they were not to be 'drowned in a hurry,' tried easier positions. Mr Creighton, who had hurt his leg, lay amongst us with compressed lips. Some fellows belonging to his watch set about securing him better. Without a word or a glance he lifted his arms one after another to facilitate the operation, and not a muscle moved in his stern, young face. They asked him with solicitude: 'Easier now, sir?' He answered with a curt: 'That'll do.' He was a hard young officer, but many of his watch used to say they liked him well enough because he had 'such a gentlemanly way of damning us up and down the deck.' Others unable to discern such fine shades of refinement, respected him for his smartness. For the first time since the ship had gone on her beam ends Captain Allistoun gave a short glance down at his men. He was almost upright – one foot against the side of the skylight, one knee on the deck; and with the end of the vang round his waist swung back and forth with his gaze fixed ahead, watchful, like a man looking out for a sign. Before his eyes the ship, with half her deck below water, rose and fell on heavy seas that rushed from under her flashing in the cold sunshine. We began to think she was wonderfully buoyant – considering. Confident voices were heard shouting: 'She'll do, boys!' Belfast exclaimed with fervour: 'I would giv' a month's pay for a draw at a pipe!' One or two, passing dry tongues on their salt lips, muttered something about a 'drink of water.' The cook, as if inspired, scrambled up with his breast against the poop water-cask and looked in. There was a little at the bottom. He yelled, waving his arms, and two men began to crawl backwards and forwards with the mug. We had a good mouthful all round. The master shook his head impatiently, refusing. When it came to Charley one of his neighbours shouted: 'That bloomin' boy's asleep.' He slept as though he had been dosed with narcotics. They let him be. Singleton held to the wheel with one hand while he drank, bending down to shelter his lips from the wind. Wamibo had to be poked and yelled at before he saw the mug held before his eyes. Knowles said sagaciously: 'It's better'n a tot o' rum.' Mr Baker grunted: 'Thank ye.'

Mr Creighton drank and nodded. Donkin gulped greedily, glaring over the rim. Belfast made us laugh when with grimacing mouth he shouted: 'Pass it this way. We're all taytottlers here.' The master, presented with the mug again by a crouching man, who screamed up at him: 'We all had a drink, captain,' groped for it without ceasing to look ahead, and handed it back stiffly as though he could not spare half a glance away from the ship. Faces brightened. We shouted to the cook: 'Well done, doctor!' He sat to leeward, propped by the water-cask and yelled back abundantly, but the seas were breaking in thunder just then, and we only caught snatches that sounded like: 'Providence' and 'born again.' He was at his old game of preaching. We made friendly but derisive gestures at him, and from below he lifted one arm, holding on with the other, moved his lips; he beamed up to us, straining his voice – earnest, and ducking his head before the sprays.

Suddenly some one cried: 'Where's Jimmy?' and we were appalled once more. On the end of the row the boatswain shouted hoarsely: 'Has any one seed him come out?' Voices exclaimed dismally: 'Drowned – is he? . . . No! In his cabin! . . . Good Lord! . . . Caught like a bloomin' rat in a trap. . . . Couldn't open his door . . . Aye! She went over too quick and the water jammed it . . . Poor beggar! . . . No help for 'im. . . . Let's go and see . . .' 'Damn him, who could go?' screamed Donkin. – 'Nobody expects you to,' growled the man next to him: 'you're only a thing.' – 'Is there half a chance to get at 'im?' inquired two or three men together. Belfast untied himself with blind impetuosity, and all at once shot down to leeward quicker than a flash of lightning. We shouted all together with dismay; but with his legs overboard he held and yelled for a rope. In our extremity nothing could be terrible; so we judged him funny kicking there, and with his scared face. Some one began to laugh, and, as if hysterically infected with screaming merriment, all those haggard men went off laughing, wild-eyed, like a lot of maniacs tied up on a wall. Mr

Baker swung off the binnacle-stand and tendered him one leg. He scrambled up rather scared, and consigning us with abominable words to the 'divvle.' 'You are. . . . Ough! You're a foul-mouthed beggar, Craik,' grunted Mr Baker. He answered, stuttering with indignation: 'Look at 'em, sorr. The bloomin' dirty images! laughing at a chum going over-board. Call themselves men too.' But from the break of the poop the boatswain called out: 'Come along,' and Belfast crawled away in a hurry to join him. The five men, poised and gazing over the edge of the poop, looked for the best way to get forward. They seemed to hesitate. The others, twisting in their lashings, turning painfully, stared with open lips. Captain Allistoun saw nothing; he seemed with his eyes to hold the ship up in a superhuman concen-tration of effort. The wind screamed loud in sunshine; columns of spray rose straight up; and in the glitter of rainbows bursting over the trembling hull the men went over cautiously, disappearing from sight with deliberate movements.

They went swinging from belaying pin to cleat above the seas that beat the half-submerged deck. Their toes scraped the planks. Lumps of green cold water toppled over the bulwark and on their heads. They hung for a moment on strained arms, with the breath knocked out of them, and with closed eyes – then, letting go with one hand, balanced with lolling heads, trying to grab some rope or stanchion further forward. The long-armed and athletic boatswain swung quickly, gripping things with a fist hard as iron, and remembering suddenly snatches of the last letter from his 'old woman.' Little Belfast scrambled in a rage spluttering 'cursed nigger.' Wamibo's tongue hung out with excite-ment; and Archie, intrepid and calm, watched his chance to move with intelligent coolness.

When above the side of the house, they let go one after another, and falling heavily, sprawled, pressing their palms to the smooth teak wood. Round them the backwash of waves seethed white and hissing. All the doors had become trapdoors, of course. The first was the galley door. The galley extended from side to side, and they could hear the sea splashing with hollow noises in there. The next door was that of the carpenter's shop. They lifted it, and looked down. The room seemed to have been devastated by an earthquake. Everything in it had tumbled on the bulkhead facing the door, and on the other side of that bulkhead there was Jimmy, dead or alive. The bench, a half-finished meat-safe, saws, chisels, wire rods, axes, crowbars, lay in a heap besprinkled with loose nails. A sharp adze struck up with a shining edge that gleamed dangerously down there like a wicked smile. The men clung to one another peering. A sickening, sly lurch of the ship nearly sent them overboard in a body. Belfast howled 'Here goes!' and leaped down. Archie followed cannily, catching at shelves that gave way with him, and eased himself in a great crash of ripped wood. There was hardly room for three men to move. And in the sunshiny blue square of the door, the boatswain's face, bearded and dark, Wamibo's face, wild and pale, hung over – watching.

Together they shouted: 'Jimmy! Jim!' From above the boatswain contributed a deep growl: 'You . . . Wait!' In a pause, Belfast entreated: 'Jimmy, darlin', are ye aloive?' The boatswain said: 'Again! All together, boys!' All yelled excitedly. Wamibo made noises resembling loud barks. Belfast drummed on the side of the bulkhead with a piece of iron. All ceased suddenly. The sound of screaming and hammering went on thin and distinct – like a solo after a chorus. He was alive. He was screaming and knocking below us with the hurry of a man prematurely shut up in a coffin. We went to work. We attacked with desperation the abominable heap of things heavy, of things sharp, of things clumsy to handle. The boatswain crawled away to find somewhere a flying end of a rope; and Wamibo, held back by shouts: 'Don't jump! . . . Don't come in here, muddlehead!' – remained glaring above us – all shining eyes, gleaming fangs, tumbled hair; resembling an amazed and half-witted

fiend gloating over the extraordinary agitation of the
damned. The boatswain adjured us to 'bear a hand,' and a
rope descended. We made things fast to it and they went up
spinning, never to be seen by man again. A rage to fling
things overboard possessed us. We worked fiercely, cutting
our hands, and speaking brutally to one another. Jimmy
kept up a distracting row; he screamed piercingly, without
drawing breath, like a tortured woman; he banged with
hands and feet. The agony of his fear wrung our hearts so
terribly that we longed to abandon him, to get out of that
place deep as a well and swaying like a tree, to get out of his
hearing, back on the poop where we could wait passively
for death in incomparable repose. We shouted to him to
'shut up, for God's sake.' He redoubled his cries. He must
have fancied we could not hear him. Probably he heard his
own clamour but faintly. We could picture him crouching
on the edge of the upper berth, letting out with both fists at
the wood, in the dark, and with his mouth wide open for
that unceasing cry. Those were loathsome moments. A
cloud driving across the sun would darken the doorway
menacingly. Every movement of the ship was pain. We
scrambled about with no room to breathe, and felt fright-
fully sick. The boatswain yelled down at us: 'Bear a hand!
Bear a hand! We two will be washed away from here
directly if you ain't quick!' Three times a sea leaped over
the high side and flung bucketfuls of water on our heads.
Then Jimmy, startled by the shock, would stop his noise for
a moment – waiting for the ship to sink, perhaps – and
began again, distressingly loud, as if invigorated by the gust
of fear. At the bottom the nails lay in a layer several inches
thick. It was ghastly. Every nail in the world, not driven in
firmly somewhere, seemed to have found its way into that
carpenter's shop. There they were, of all kinds, the rem-
nants of stores from seven voyages. Tin-tacks, copper tacks
(sharp as needles), pump nails, with big heads, like tiny
iron mushrooms; nails without any heads (horrible);
French nails polished and slim. They lay in a solid mass

more inabordable than a hedgehog. We hesitated, yearning for a shovel, while Jimmy below us yelled as though he had been flayed. Groaning, we dug our fingers in, and very much hurt, shook our hands, scattering nails and drops of blood. We passed up our hats full of assorted nails to the boatswain, who, as if performing a mysterious and appeasing rite, cast them wide upon a raging sea.

We got to the bulkhead at last. Those were stout planks. She was a ship, well finished in every detail – the 'Narcissus' was. They were the stoutest planks ever put into a ship's bulkhead – we thought – and then we perceived that, in our hurry, we had sent all the tools overboard. Absurd little Belfast wanted to break it down with his own weight, and with both feet leaped straight up like a springbok, cursing the Clyde shipwrights for not scamping their work. Incidentally he reviled all North Britain, the rest of the earth, the sea – and all his companions. He swore, as he alighted heavily on his heels, that he would never, never any more associate with any fool that 'hadn't savee enough to know his knee from his elbow.' He managed by his thumping to scare the last remnant of wits out of Jimmy. We could hear the object of our exasperated solicitude darting to and fro under the planks. He had cracked his voice at last, and could only squeak miserably. His back or else his head rubbed the planks, now here, now there, in a puzzling manner. He squeaked as he dodged the invisible blows. It was more heartrending even than his yells. Suddenly Archie produced a crowbar. He had kept it back; also a small hatchet. We howled with satisfaction. He struck a mighty blow and small chips flew at our eyes. The boatswain above shouted: 'Look out! Look out there. Don't kill the man. Easy does it!' Wamibo, maddened with excitement, hung head down and insanely urged us: 'Hoo! Strook 'im! Hoo! Hoo!' We were afraid he would fall in and kill one of us and, hurriedly, we entreated the boatswain to 'shove the blamed Finn overboard.' Then, all together, we yelled down at the planks: 'Stand from under! Get forward,' and listened. We only heard the deep hum and moan of the wind above us, the mingled roar and hiss of the seas. The ship, as if overcome with despair, wallowed lifelessly, and our heads swam with that un- natural motion. Belfast clamoured: 'For the love of God, Jimmy, where are ye?...Knock! Jimmy darlint!...Knock! You bloody black beast! Knock!' He was as quiet as a dead man inside a grave; and, like men standing above a grave, we were on the verge of tears – but with vexation, the strain, the fatigue; with the great longing to be done with it, to get away, and lay down to rest somewhere where we could see our danger and breathe. Archie shouted: 'Gi'e me room!' We crouched behind him, guarding our heads, and he struck time after time in the joint of planks. They cracked. Suddenly the crowbar went half-way in through a splin- tered oblong hole. It must have missed Jimmy's head by less than an inch. Archie withdrew it quickly, and that in- famous nigger rushed at the hole, put his lips to it, and whispered 'Help' in an almost extinct voice; he pressed his head to it, trying madly to get out through that opening one inch wide and three inches long. In our disturbed state we were absolutely paralysed by his incredible action. It seemed impossible to drive him away. Even Archie at last lost his composure. 'If ye don't clear oot I'll drive the crowbar thro' your head,' he shouted in a determined voice. He meant what he said, and his earnestness seemed to make an impression on Jimmy. He disappeared sud- denly, and we set to prising and tearing at the planks with the eagerness of men trying to get at a mortal enemy, and spurred by the desire to tear him limb from limb. The wood split, cracked, gave way. Belfast plunged in head and shoulders and groped viciously. 'I've got 'im! Got 'im,' he shouted. 'Oh! There!...He's gone; I've got 'im!...Pull at my legs!...Pull!' Wamibo hooted unceas- ingly. The boatswain shouted directions: 'Catch hold of his hair, Belfast; pull straight up, you two!...Pull fair!' We pulled fair. We pulled Belfast out with a jerk, and dropped him with disgust. In a sitting posture, purple-faced, he sobbed despairingly: 'How can I hold on to 'is blooming short wool?' Suddenly Jimmy's head and shoulders appeared. He stuck half-way, and with rolling eyes foamed at our feet. We flew at him with brutal impatience, we tore the shirt off his back, we tugged at his ears, we panted over him; and all at once he came away in our hands as though somebody had let go his legs. With the same movement, without a pause, we swung him up. His breath whistled, he kicked our upturned faces, he grasped two pairs of arms above his head, and he squirmed up with such precipitation that he seemed positively to escape from our hands like a bladder full of gas. Streaming with perspiration, we swarmed up the rope, and, coming into the blast of cold wind, gasped like men plunged into icy water. With burning faces we shivered to the very marrow of our bones. Never before had the gale seemed to us more furious, the sea more mad, the sunshine more merciless and mocking, and the position of the ship more hopeless and appalling. Every movement of her was ominous of the end of her agony and of the beginning of ours. We staggered away from the door, and, alarmed by a sudden roll, fell down in a bunch. It appeared to us that the side of the house was more smooth than glass and more slippery than ice. There was nothing to hang on to but a long brass hook used sometimes to keep back an open door. Wamibo held on to it and we held on to Wamibo, clutching our Jimmy. He had completely collapsed now. He did not seem to have the strength to close his hand. We stuck to him blindly in our fear. We were not afraid of Wamibo letting go (we remembered that the brute was stronger than any three men in the ship), but we were afraid of the hook giving way, and we also believed that the ship had made up her mind to turn over at last. But she didn't. A sea swept over us. The boatswain spluttered: 'Up and away. There's a lull. Away aft with you, or we will all go to the devil here.' We stood up surrounding Jimmy. We begged him to hold up, to hold on, at least. He glared with his bulging eyes, mute as a fish, and with all the stiffening knocked out of him. He wouldn't stand; he wouldn't even as much as clutch at our necks; he was only a cold black skin loosely stuffed with soft cotton wool; his arms and legs swung jointless and pliable; his head rolled about; the lower lip hung down, enormous and heavy. We pressed round him, bothered and dismayed; sheltering him we swung here and there in a body; and on the very brink of eternity we tottered all together with concealing and absurd gestures, like a lot of drunken men embarrassed with a stolen corpse.

Something had to be done. We had to get him aft. A rope was tied slack under his armpits, and, reaching up at the risk of our lives, we hung him on the foresheet cleet. He emitted no sound; he looked as ridiculously lamentable as a doll that had lost half its sawdust, and we started on our perilous journey over the main deck, dragging along with care that pitiful, that limp, that hateful burden. He was not very heavy, but had he weighed a ton he could not have been more awkward to handle. We literally passed him from hand to hand. Now and then we had to hang him up on a handy belaying-pin, to draw a breath and reform the line. Had the pin broken he would have irretrievably gone into the Southern Ocean, but he had to take his chance of that; and after a little while, becoming apparently aware of it, he groaned slightly, and with a great effort whispered a few words. We listened eagerly. He was reproaching us with our carelessness in letting him run such risks: 'Now, after I got myself out from there,' he breathed out weakly. 'There' was his cabin. And he got himself out. We had nothing to do with it apparently! . . . No matter. . . . We went on and let him take his chances, simply because we could not help it; for though at that time we hated him more than ever – more than anything under heaven – we did not want to lose him. We had so far saved him; and it had become a personal matter between us and the sea. We meant to stick to him. Had we (by an incredible hypothesis) undergone similar toil and trouble for an empty cask, that cask would have become as precious to us as Jimmy was. More precious, in fact, because we would have had no reason to hate the cask. And we hated James Wait. We could not get rid of the monstrous suspicion that this astounding black-man was shamming sick, had been malingering heartlessly in the face of our toil, of our scorn, of our patience – and now was malingering in the face of our devotion – in the face of death. Our vague and imperfect morality rose with disgust at his unmanly lie. But he stuck to it manfully – amazingly. No! It couldn't be. He was at all extremity. His cantankerous temper was only the result of the provoking invincibleness of that death he felt by his side. Any man may be angry with such a masterful chum. But, then, what kind of men were we – with our thoughts! Indignation and doubt grappled within us in a scuffle that trampled upon the finest of our feelings. And we hated him because of the suspicion; we detested him because of the doubt. We could not scorn him safely – neither could we pity him without risk to our dignity. So we hated him, and passed him carefully from hand to hand. We cried, 'Got him?' – 'Yes. All right. Let go.' And he swung from one enemy to another, showing about as much life as an old bolster would do. His eyes made two narrow white slits in the black face. The air escaped through his lips with a noise like the sound of bellows. We reached the poop ladder at last, and it being a comparatively safe place, we lay for a moment in an exhausted heap to rest a little. He began to mutter. We were always incurably anxious to hear what he had to say. This time he mumbled peevishly, 'It took you some time to come. I began to think the whole smart lot of you had been washed overboard. What kept you back? Hey? Funk?' We said nothing. With sighs we started again to drag him up. The secret and ardent desire of our hearts was the desire to beat him viciously with our fists about the head; and we handled him as tenderly as though he had been made of glass. . . .

The return on the poop was like the return of wanderers after many years amongst people marked by the desolation of time. Eyes were turned slowly in their sockets glancing at us. Faint murmurs were heard, 'Have you got 'im after all?' The well-known faces looked strange and familiar; they seemed faded and grimy; they had a mingled expression of fatigue and eagerness. They seemed to have become much thinner during our absence, as if all these men had been starving for a long time in their abandoned attitudes. The captain, with a round turn of a rope on his wrist, and kneeling on one knee, swung with a face cold and stiff; but with living eyes he was still holding the ship up, heeding no one, as if in the unearthly effort of that endeavour. We fastened up James Wait in a safe place. Mr Baker scrambled along to lend a hand. Mr Creighton, on his back, and very pale, muttered, 'Well done,' and gave us, Jimmy and the sky, a scornful glance, then closed his eyes slowly. Here and there a man stirred a little, but most of them remained apathetic, in cramped positions, muttering between shivers. The sun was setting. A sun enormous, unclouded and red, declining low as if bending down to look into their faces. The wind whistled across long sunbeams that, resplendent and cold, struck full on the dilated pupils of staring eyes without making them wink. The wisps of hair and the tangled beards were grey with the salt of the sea. The faces were earthy, and the dark patches under the eyes extended to the ears, smudged into the hollows of sunken cheeks. The lips were livid and thin, and when they moved it was with difficulty, as though they had been glued to the teeth. Some grinned sadly in the sunlight, shaking with cold. Others were sad and still. Charley, subdued by the sudden disclosure of the insignificance of his youth, darted fearful glances. The two smooth-faced Norwegians resembled decrepit children, staring stupidly. To leeward, on the edge of the horizon, black seas leaped up towards the glowing sun. It sank slowly, round and blazing, and the crests of waves splashed on the edge of the luminous circle.

One of the Norwegians appeared to catch sight of it, and, after giving a violent start, began to speak. His voice, startling the others, made them stir. They moved their heads stiffly, or turning with difficulty, looked at him with surprise, with fear, or in grave silence. He chattered at the setting sun, nodding his head, while the big seas began to roll across the crimson disc; and over miles of turbulent waters the shadows of high waves swept with a running darkness the faces of men. A crested roller broke with a loud hissing roar, and the sun, as if put out, disappeared. The chattering voice faltered, went out together with the light. There were sighs. In the sudden lull that follows the crash of a broken sea a man said wearily, 'Here's that blooming Dutchman gone off his chump.' A seaman, lashed by the middle, tapped the deck with his open hand with unceasing quick flaps. In the gathering greyness of twilight a bulky form was seen rising aft, and began marching on all fours with the movements of some big cautious beast. It was Mr Baker passing along the line of men. He grunted encouragingly over every one, felt their fastenings. Some, with half-open eyes, puffed like men oppressed by heat; others mechanically and in dreamy voices answered him, 'Aye! aye! sir!' He went from one to another grunting, 'Ough!...See her through it yet;' and unexpectedly, with loud angry outbursts, blew up Knowles for cutting off a long piece from the fall of the relieving tackle. 'Ough!—— Ashamed of yourself—— Relieving tackle—— Don't you know better!—— Ough!—— Able seaman! Ough!' The lame man was crushed. He muttered, 'Get som'think for a lashing for myself, sir.' – 'Ough! Lashing—— yourself. Are you a tinker or a sailor—— What? Ough!—— May want that tackle directly—— Ough!——More use to the ship than your lame carcass. Ough!——Keep it!——Keep it, now you've done it.' He crawled away slowly, muttering to himself about some men being 'worse than children.' It had been a comforting row. Low exclamations were heard: 'Hallo...Hallo.'...Those who had been painfully dozing

asked with convulsive starts, 'What's up?...What is it?'
The answers came with unexpected cheerfulness: 'The
mate is going bald-headed for lame Jack about something
or other.' – 'No!'...'What 'as he done?' Some one even
chuckled. It was like a whiff of hope, like a reminder of safe
days. Donkin, who had been stupefied with fear, revived
suddenly and began to shout: ''Ear 'im; that's the way they
tawlk to us. Vy donch 'ee 'it 'im – one ov yer? 'It'im! 'It 'im!
Comin' the mate over us. We are as good men as 'ee! We're
all goin' to 'ell now. We 'ave been starved in this rotten ship,
an' now we're goin' to be drowned for them black 'earted
bullies! 'It 'im!' He shrieked in the deepening gloom, he
blubbered and sobbed, screaming: ''It 'im! 'It 'im!' The rage
and fear of his disregarded right to live tried the steadfastness of hearts more than the menacing shadows of the
night that advanced through the unceasing clamour of
the gale. From aft Mr Baker was heard: 'Is one of you
men going to stop him – must I come along?' 'Shut
up!'...'Keep quiet!' cried various voices, exasperated,
trembling with cold. – 'You'll get one across the mug
from me directly,' said an invisible seaman, in a weary
tone, 'I won't let the mate have the trouble.' He ceased
and lay still with the silence of despair. On the black sky the
stars, coming out, gleamed over an inky sea that, speckled
with foam, flashed back at them the evanescent and pale
light of a dazzling whiteness born from the black turmoil of
the waves. Remote in the eternal calm they glittered hard
and cold above the uproar of the earth; they surrounded the
vanquished and tormented ship on all sides: more pitiless
than the eyes of a triumphant mob, and as unapproachable
as the hearts of men.

The icy south wind howled exultingly under the sombre
splendour of the sky. The cold shook the men with a
resistless violence as though it had tried to shake them to
pieces. Short moans were swept unheard off the stiff lips.
Some complained in mutters of 'not feeling themselves
below the waist;' while those who had closed their eyes,

imagined they had a block of ice on their chests. Others, alarmed at not feeling any pain in their fingers, beat the deck feebly with their hands – obstinate and exhausted. Wamibo stared vacant and dreamy. The Scandinavians kept on a meaningless mutter through chattering teeth. The spare Scotchmen, with determined efforts, kept their lower jaws still. The West-country men lay big and stolid in an invulnerable surliness. A man yawned and swore in turns. Another breathed with a rattle in his throat. Two elderly hard-weather shellbacks, fast side by side, whispered dismally to one another about the landlady of a boarding-house in Sunderland, whom they both knew. They extolled her motherliness and her liberality; they tried to talk about the joint of beef and big fire in the downstairs kitchen. The words dying faintly on their lips, ended in light sighs. A sudden voice cried into the cold night, 'Oh Lord!' No one changed his position or took any notice of the cry. One or two passed, with a repeated and vague gesture, their hand over their faces, but most of them kept very still. In the benumbed immobility of their bodies they were excessively wearied by their thoughts, which rushed with the rapidity and vividness of dreams. Now and then, by an abrupt and startling exclamation, they answered the weird hail of some illusion; then, again, in silence contemplated the vision of known faces and familiar things. They recalled the aspect of forgotten shipmates and heard the voice of dead and gone skippers. They remembered the noise of gaslit streets, the steamy heat of taprooms or the scorching sunshine of calm days at sea.

Mr Baker left his insecure place, and crawled, with stoppages, along the poop. In the dark and on all fours he resembled some carnivorous animal prowling amongst corpses. At the break, propped to windward of a stanchion, he looked down on the main deck. It seemed to him that the ship had a tendency to stand up a little more. The wind had eased a little, he thought, but the sea ran as high as ever. The waves foamed viciously, and the lee side of the deck

disappeared under a hissing whiteness as of boiling milk,
while the rigging sang steadily with a deep vibrating note,
and, at every upward swing of the ship, the wind rushed
with a long-drawn clamour amongst the spars. Mr Baker
watched very still. A man near him began to make a blab-
bing noise with his lips, all at once and very loud, as though
the cold had broken brutally through him. He went on: 'Ba
– ba – ba – brrr – brr – ba – ba.' – 'Stop that!' cried Mr Baker,
groping in the dark. 'Stop it!' He went on shaking the leg
he found under his hand. – 'What is it, sir?' called out
Belfast, in the tone of a man awakened suddenly; 'we are
looking after that 'ere Jimmy.' – 'Are you? Ough! Don't
make that row then. Who's that near you?' – 'It's me – the
boatswain, sir,' growled the West-country man; 'we are
trying to keep life in that poor devil.' – 'Aye, aye!' said Mr
Baker. 'Do it quietly, can't you.' – 'He wants us to hold him
up above the rail,' went on the boatswain, with irritation,
'says he can't breathe here under our jackets.' – 'If we lift
'im, we drop 'im overboard,' said another voice, 'we can't
feel our hands with cold.' – 'I don't care. I am choking!'
exclaimed James Wait in a clear tone. – 'Oh, no, my son,'
said the boatswain, desperately, 'you don't go till we all go
on this fine night.' – 'You will see yet many a worse,' said
Mr Baker, cheerfully. – 'It's no child's play, sir!' answered
the boatswain. 'Some of us further aft, here, are in a pretty
bad way.' – 'If the blamed sticks had been cut out of her she
would be running along on her bottom now like any decent
ship, an' giv' us all a chance,' said some one, with a sigh. –
'The old man wouldn't have it . . . much he cares for us,'
whispered another. – 'Care for you!' exclaimed Mr Baker,
angrily. 'Why should he care for you? Are you a lot of
women passengers to be taken care of? We are here to
take care of the ship – and some of you ain't up to that.
Ough! . . . What have you done so very smart to be taken
care of? Ough! . . . Some of you can't stand a bit of a breeze
without crying over it.' – 'Come, sorr. We ain't so bad,'
protested Belfast, in a voice shaken by shivers; 'we

ain't... brrr...' – 'Again,' shouted the mate, grabbing at the
shadowy form; 'again!... Why, you're in your shirt! What
have you done?' – 'I've put my oilskin and jacket over that
half-dead nayggur – and he says he chokes,' said Belfast,
complainingly. – 'You wouldn't call me nigger if I wasn't
half dead, you Irish beggar!' boomed James Wait, vigorously. – 'You... brrr... You wouldn't be white if you were
ever so well... I will fight you... brrrr... in fine weather
... brrr... with one hand tied behind my back... brrrrr...'
– 'I don't want your rags – I want air,' gasped out the other
faintly, as if suddenly exhausted.

   The sprays swept over whistling and pattering. Men
disturbed in their peaceful torpor by the pain of quarrelsome shouts, moaned, muttering curses. Mr Baker crawled
off a little way to leeward where a water-cask loomed up
big, with something white against it. 'Is it you, Podmore?'
asked Mr Baker. He had to repeat the question twice before
the cook turned, coughing feebly. – 'Yes, sir. I've been
praying in my mind for a quick deliverance; for I am
prepared for any call.... I——'. – 'Look here, cook,' interrupted Mr Baker, 'the men are perishing with cold.' –
'Cold!' said the cook, mournfully; 'they will be warm
enough before long.' – 'What?' asked Mr Baker, looking
along the deck into the faint sheen of frothing water. –
'They are a wicked lot,' continued the cook solemnly, but in
an unsteady voice, 'about as wicked as any ship's company
in this sinful world! Now, I' – he trembled so that he could
hardly speak; his was an exposed place, and in a cotton
shirt, a thin pair of trousers, and with his knees under his
nose, he received, quaking, the flicks of stinging, salt drops;
his voice sounded exhausted – 'now, I – any time... My
eldest youngster, Mr Baker... a clever boy... last Sunday
on shore before this voyage he wouldn't go to church, sir.
Says I, "You go and clean yourself, or I'll know the reason
why!" What does he do?... Pond, Mr Baker – fell into the
pond in his best rig, sir!... Accident?... "Nothing will save
you, fine scholar though you are!" says I.... Accident!... I

whopped him, sir, till I couldn't lift my arm. . . .' His voice faltered. 'I whopped 'im!' he repeated, rattling his teeth; then, after a while, let out a mournful sound that was half a groan, half a snore. Mr Baker shook him by the shoulders. 'Hey! Cook! Hold up, Podmore! Tell me – is there any fresh water in the galley tank? The ship is lying along less, I think; I would try to get forward. A little water would do them good. Hallo! Look out! Look out!' The cook struggled. – 'Not you, sir – not you!' He began to scramble to windward. 'Galley! . . . my business!' he shouted. – 'Cook's going crazy now,' said several voices. He yelled: 'Crazy, am I? I am more ready to die than any of you, officers incloosive – there! As long as she swims I will cook! I will get you coffee.' – 'Cook, ye are a gentleman!' cried Belfast. But the cook was already going over the weather-ladder. He stopped for a moment to shout back on the poop: 'As long as she swims I will cook!' and disappeared as though he had gone overboard. The men who had heard sent after him a cheer that sounded like a wail of sick children. An hour or more afterwards some one said distinctly: 'He's gone for good.' – 'Very likely,' assented the boatswain; 'even in fine weather he was as smart about the deck as a milch-cow on her first voyage. We ought to go and see.' Nobody moved. As the hours dragged slowly through the darkness Mr Baker crawled back and forth along the poop several times. Some men fancied they had heard him exchange murmurs with the master, but at that time the memories were incomparably more vivid than anything actual, and they were not certain whether the murmurs were heard now or many years ago. They did not try to find out. A mutter more or less did not matter. It was too cold for curiosity, and almost for hope. They could not spare a moment or a thought from the great mental occupation of wishing to live. And the desire of life kept them alive, apathetic and enduring, under the cruel persistence of wind and cold; while the bestarred black dome of the sky revolved slowly above the ship, that drifted, bearing their patience and their suffering, through the stormy solitude of the sea.

Huddled close to one another, they fancied themselves utterly alone. They heard sustained loud noises, and again bore the pain of existence through long hours of profound silence. In the night they saw sunshine, felt warmth, and suddenly, with a start, thought that the sun would never rise upon a freezing world. Some heard laughter, listened to songs; others, near the end of the poop, could hear loud human shrieks, and opening their eyes, were surprised to hear them still, though very faint, and far away. The boatswain said: 'Why, it's the cook, hailing from forward, I think.' He hardly believed his own words or recognized his own voice. It was a long time before the man next to him gave a sign of life. He punched hard his other neighbour and said: 'The cook's shouting!' Many did not understand, others did not care; the majority further aft did not believe. But the boatswain and another man had the pluck to crawl away forward to see. They seemed to have been gone for hours, and were very soon forgotten. Then suddenly men who had been plunged in a hopeless resignation became as if possessed with a desire to hurt. They belaboured one another with fists. In the darkness they struck persistently anything soft they could feel near, and, with a greater effort than for a shout, whispered excitedly: 'They've got some hot coffee...Boss'en got it....' 'No!...Where?'... 'It's coming! Cook made it.' James Wait moaned. Donkin scrambled viciously, caring not where he kicked, and anxious that the officers should have none of it. It came in a pot, and they drank in turns. It was hot, and while it blistered the greedy palates, it seemed incredible. The men sighed out, parting with the mug: 'How 'as he done it?' Some cried weakly: 'Bully for you, doctor!'

He had done it somehow. Afterwards Archie declared that the thing was 'meeraculous.' For many days we wondered, and it was the one ever-interesting subject of conversation to the end of the voyage. We asked the cook, in fine weather, how he felt when he saw his stove 'reared up on end.' We inquired, in the north-east trade and on serene evenings, whether he had to stand on his head to put things right somewhat. We suggested he had used his bread-board for a raft, and from there comfortably had stoked his grate; and we did our best to conceal our admiration under the wit of fine irony. He affirmed not to know any-thing about it, rebuked our levity, declared himself, with solemn animation, to have been the object of a special mercy for the saving of our unholy lives. Fundamentally he was right, no doubt; but he need not have been so offensively positive about it – he need not have hinted so often that it would have gone hard with us had he not been there, meritorious and pure, to receive the inspiration and the strength for the work of grace. Had we been saved by his recklessness or his agility, we could have at length become reconciled to the fact; but to admit our obligation to anybody's virtue and holiness alone was as difficult for us as for any other handful of mankind. Like many benefac-tors of humanity, the cook took himself too seriously, and reaped the reward of irreverence. We were not ungrateful, however. He remained heroic. His saying – *the* saying of his life – became proverbial in the mouth of men as are the sayings of conquerors or sages. Later, whenever one of us was puzzled by a task and advised to relinquish it, he would express his determination to persevere and to succeed by the words: 'As long as she swims I will cook!'

The hot drink helped us through the bleak hours that precede the dawn. The sky low by the horizon took on the delicate tints of pink and yellow like the inside of a rare shell. And higher, where it glowed with a pearly sheen, a small black cloud appeared, like a forgotten fragment of the night set in a border of dazzling gold. The beams of light skipped on the crests of waves. The eyes of men turned to the eastward. The sunlight flooded their weary faces. They were giving themselves up to fatigue as though they had done for ever with their work. On Singleton's black oilskin

coat the dried salt glistened like hoar frost. He hung on by
the wheel, with open and lifeless eyes. Captain Allistoun,
unblinking, faced the rising sun. His lips stirred, opened
for the first time in twenty-four hours, and with a fresh
firm voice he cried, 'Wear ship!'

The commanding sharp tones made all these torpid men
start like a sudden flick of a whip. Then again, motionless
where they lay, the force of habit made some of them repeat
the order in hardly audible murmurs. Captain Allistoun
glanced down at his crew, and several, with fumbling fingers and hopeless movements, tried to cast themselves
adrift. He repeated impatiently, 'Wear ship. Now then,
Mr Baker, get the men along. What's the matter with
them?' – 'Wear ship. Do you hear there? – Wear ship!'
thundered out the boatswain suddenly. His voice seemed
to break through a deadly spell. Men began to stir and
crawl. – 'I want the foretop-mast stay-sail run up smartly,'
said the master, very loudly; 'if you can't manage it standing
up you must do it lying down – that's all. Bear a hand!' –
'Come along! Let's give the old girl a chance,' urged the
boatswain. – 'Aye! aye! Wear ship!' exclaimed quavering
voices. The forecastle men, with reluctant faces, prepared
to go forward. Mr Baker pushed ahead grunting on all
fours to show the way, and they followed him over the
break. The others lay still with a vile hope in their hearts
of not being required to move till they got saved or
drowned in peace.

After some time they could be seen forward appearing
on the forecastle head, one by one in unsafe attitudes;
hanging on to the rails, clambering over the anchors;
embracing the cross-head of the windlass or hugging the
fore-capstan. They were restless with strange exertions,
waved their arms, knelt, lay flat down, staggered up,
seemed to strive their hardest to go overboard. Suddenly
a small white piece of canvas fluttered amongst them, grew
larger, beating. Its narrow head rose in jerks – and at last it
stood distended and triangular in the sunshine. – 'They

have done it!' cried the voices aft. Captain Allistoun let go
the rope he had round his wrist and rolled to leeward
headlong. He could be seen casting the lee main braces
off the pins while the backwash of waves splashed over him.
– 'Square the main yard!' he shouted up to us – who stared
at him in wonder. We hesitated to stir. 'The main brace,
men. Haul! haul anyhow! Lay on your backs and haul!' he
screeched, half drowned down there. We did not believe we
could move the main yard, but the strongest and the less
discouraged tried to execute the order. Others assisted half-
heartedly. Singleton's eyes blazed suddenly as he took a
fresh grip of the spokes. Captain Allistoun fought his way
up to windward. – 'Haul men! Try to move it! Haul, and
help the ship.' His hard face worked, suffused and furious.
– 'Is she going off, Singleton?' he cried. – 'Not a move yet,
sir,' croaked the old seaman in a horribly hoarse voice. –
'Watch the helm, Singleton,' spluttered the master. 'Haul
men! Have you no more strength than rats? Haul and earn
your salt.' Mr Creighton, on his back, with a swollen leg
and a face as white as a piece of paper, blinked his eyes; his
bluish lips twitched. In the wild scramble men grabbed at
him, crawled over his hurt leg, knelt on his chest. He kept
perfectly still, setting his teeth without a moan, without a
sigh. The master's ardour, the cries of that silent man
inspired us. We hauled and hung in bunches on the rope.
We heard him say with violence to Donkin, who sprawled
abjectly on his stomach, – 'I will brain you with this belaying pin if you don't catch hold of the brace,' and that victim
of men's injustice, cowardly and cheeky, whimpered: 'Are
you goin' to murder us now,' while with sudden desperation
he gripped the rope. Men sighed, shouted, hissed meaningless words, groaned. The yards moved, came slowly
square against the wind, that hummed loudly on the
yard-arms. – 'Going off, sir,' shouted Singleton, 'she's just
started.' – 'Catch a turn with that brace. Catch a turn!'
clamoured the master. Mr Creighton, nearly suffocated
and unable to move, made a mighty effort, and with his

left hand managed to nip the rope. – 'All fast!' cried some one. He closed his eyes as if going off into a swoon, while huddled together about the brace we watched with scared looks what the ship would do now.

She went off slowly as though she had been weary and disheartened like the men she carried. She paid off very gradually, making us hold our breath till we choked, and as soon as she had brought the wind abaft the beam she started to move, and fluttered our hearts. It was awful to see her, nearly overturned, begin to gather way and drag her submerged side through the water. The dead-eyes of the rigging churned the breaking seas. The lower half of the deck was full of mad whirlpools and eddies; and the long line of the lee rail could be seen showing black now and then in the swirls of a field of foam as dazzling and white as a field of snow. The wind sang shrilly amongst the spars; and at every slight lurch we expected her to slip to the bottom sideways from under our backs. When dead before it she made the first distinct attempt to stand up, and we encouraged her with a feeble and discordant howl. A great sea came running up aft and hung for a moment over us with a curling top; then crashed down under the counter and spread out on both sides into a great sheet of bursting froth. Above its fierce hiss we heard Singleton's croak: – 'She is steering!' He had both his feet now planted firmly on the grating, and the wheel spun fast as he eased the helm. – 'Bring the wind on the port quarter and steady her!' called out the master, staggering to his feet, the first man up from amongst our prostrate heap. One or two screamed with excitement: 'She rises!' Far away forward, Mr Baker and three others were seen erect and black on the clear sky, lifting their arms, and with open mouths as though they had been shouting all together. The ship trembled, trying to lift her side, lurched back, seemed to give up with a nerveless dip, and suddenly with an unexpected jerk swung violently to windward, as though she had torn herself out from a deadly grasp. The whole immense volume of water, lifted by her deck, was thrown bodily across to starboard. Loud cracks were heard. Iron ports breaking open thundered with ringing blows. The water topped over the starboard rail with the rush of a river falling over a dam. The sea on deck, and the seas on every side of her, mingled together in a deafening roar. She rolled violently. We got up and were helplessly run or flung about from side to side. Men, rolling over and over, yelled, – 'The house will go!' – 'She clears herself!' Lifted by a towering sea she ran along with it for a moment, spouting thick streams of water through every opening of her wounded sides. The lee braces having been carried away or washed off the pins, all the ponderous yards in the fore swung from side to side and with appalling rapidity at every roll. The men forward were seen crouching here and there with fearful glances upwards at the enormous spars that whirled about over their heads. The torn canvas and the ends of broken gear streamed in the wind like wisps of hair. Through the clear sunshine, over the flashing turmoil and uproar of the seas, the ship ran blindly, dishevelled and headlong, as if fleeing for her life; and on the poop we spun, we tottered about, distracted and noisy. We all spoke at once in a thin babble: we had the aspect of invalids and the gestures of maniacs. Eyes shone, large and haggard, in smiling, meagre faces that seemed to have been dusted over with powdered chalk. We stamped, clapped our hands, feeling ready to jump and do anything; but in reality hardly able to keep on our feet. Captain Allistoun, hard and slim, gesticulated madly from the poop at Mr Baker: 'Steady these fore-yards! Steady them the best you can!' On the main deck, men excited by his cries, splashed, dashing aimlessly here and there with the foam swirling up to their waists. Apart, far aft, and alone by the helm, old Singleton had deliberately tucked his white beard under the top button of his glistening coat. Swaying upon the din and tumult of the seas, with the whole battered length of the ship launched forward in a rolling rush before his steady old eyes, he stood rigidly still,

forgotten by all, and with an attentive face. In front of his
erect figure only the two arms moved crosswise with a swift
and sudden readiness, to check or urge again the rapid stir
of circling spokes. He steered with care.

IV

ON men reprieved by its disdainful mercy, the immortal
sea confers in its justice the full privilege of desired unrest.
Through the perfect wisdom of its grace they are not
permitted to meditate at ease upon the complicated and
acrid savour of existence. They must without pause justify
their life to the eternal pity that commands toil to be hard
and unceasing, from sunrise to sunset, from sunset to
sunrise; till the weary succession of nights and days tainted
by the obstinate clamour of sages, demanding bliss and an
empty heaven, is redeemed at last by the vast silence of pain
and labour, by the dumb fear and the dumb courage of men
obscure, forgetful, and enduring.

   The master and Mr Baker coming face to face stared for
a moment, with the intense and amazed looks of men
meeting unexpectedly after years of trouble. Their voices
were gone, and they whispered desperately at one another.
– 'Any one missing?' asked Captain Allistoun. – 'No. All
there.' – 'Anybody hurt?' – 'Only the second mate.'– 'I will
look after him directly. We're lucky,' – 'Very,' articulated Mr
Baker, faintly. He gripped the rail and rolled bloodshot
eyes. The little grey man made an effort to raise his voice
above a dull mutter, and fixed his chief mate with a cold
gaze, piercing like a dart. – 'Get sail on the ship,' he said,
speaking authoritatively and with an inflexible snap on his
thin lips. 'Get sail on her as soon as you can. This is a fair
wind. At once, sir – Don't give the men time to feel
themselves. They will get done up and stiff, and we will
never...We must get her along now'...He reeled to a
long heavy roll; the rail dipped into the glancing, hissing
water. He caught a shroud, swung helplessly against the

mate ... 'now we have a fair wind at last——Make——
sail.' His head rolled from shoulder to shoulder. His eyelids
began to beat rapidly. 'And the pumps——pumps, Mr
Baker.' He peered as though the face within a foot of his
eyes had been half a mile off. 'Keep the men on the move
to——to get her along,' he mumbled in a drowsy tone, like
a man going off into a doze. He pulled himself together
suddenly. 'Mustn't stand. Won't do,' he said with a painful
attempt at a smile. He let go his hold, and, propelled by the
dip of the ship, ran aft unwillingly, with small steps, till he
brought up against the binnacle stand. Hanging on there
he looked up in an objectless manner at Singleton, who,
unheeding him, watched anxiously the end of the jib-boom
– 'Steering gear works all right?' he asked. There was a
noise in the old seaman's throat, as though the words had
been rattling together before they could come out. –
'Steers ... like a little boat,' he said at last, with hoarse
tenderness, without giving the master as much as half a
glance – then, watchfully, spun the wheel down, steadied,
flung it back again. Captain Allistoun tore himself away
from the delight of leaning against the binnacle, and began
to walk the poop, swaying and reeling to preserve his
balance....

The pump-rods, clanking, stamped in short jumps while
the fly-wheels turned smoothly, with great speed, at the
foot of the mainmast, flinging back and forth with a regular
impetuosity two limp clusters of men clinging to the
handles. They abandoned themselves, swaying from the
hip with twitching faces and stony eyes. The carpenter,
sounding from time to time, exclaimed mechanically:
'Shake her up! Keep her going!' Mr Baker could not speak,
but found his voice to shout; and under the goad of his
objurgations, men looked to the lashings, dragged out new
sails; and thinking themselves unable to move, carried heavy
blocks aloft – overhauled the gear. They went up the rigging
with faltering and desperate efforts. Their heads swam as
they shifted their hold, stepped blindly on the yards like

men in the dark; or trusted themselves to the first rope at
hand with the negligence of exhausted strength. The narrow escapes from falls did not disturb the languid beat of
their hearts; the roar of the seas seething far below them
sounded continuous and faint like an indistinct noise from
another world: the wind filled their eyes with tears, and with
heavy gusts tried to push them off from where they swayed
in insecure positions. With streaming faces and blowing
hair they flew up and down between sky and water, bestrid-
ing the ends of yard-arms, crouching on foot-ropes, embracing lifts to have their hands free, or standing up against
chain ties. Their thoughts floated vaguely between the
desire for rest and the desire of life, while their stiffened
fingers cast off head-earrings, fumbled for knives, or held
with tenacious grip against the violent shocks of beating
canvas. They glared savagely at one another, made frantic
signs with one hand while they held their life in the other,
looked down on the narrow strip of flooded deck, shouted
along to leeward: 'Light-to!' ... 'Haul out!' ... 'Make fast!'
Their lips moved, their eyes started, furious and eager with
the desire to be understood, but the wind tossed their words
unheard upon the disturbed sea. In an unendurable and
unending strain they worked like men driven by a merciless
dream to toil in an atmosphere of ice or flame. They burnt
and shivered in turns. Their eyeballs smarted as if in the
smoke of conflagration; their heads were ready to burst with
every shout. Hard fingers seemed to grip their throats. At
every roll they thought: Now I must let go. It will shake us all
off – and thrown about aloft they cried wildly: 'Look out
there – catch the end.' ... 'Reeve clear' ... 'Turn this
block....' They nodded desperately; shook infuriated
faces, 'No! No! From down up.' They seemed to hate one
another with a deadly hate. The longing to be done with it
all gnawed their breasts, and the wish to do things well was a
burning pain. They cursed their fate, contemned their life,
and wasted their breath in deadly imprecations upon one
another. The sailmaker, with his bald head bared, worked

feverishly, forgetting his intimacy with so many admirals. The boatswain, climbing up with marlinspikes and bunches of spunyarn rovings, or kneeling on the yard and ready to take a turn with the midship-stop, had acute and fleeting visions of his old woman and the youngsters in a moorland village. Mr Baker, feeling very weak, tottered here and there, grunting and inflexible, like a man of iron. He waylaid those who, coming from aloft, stood gasping for breath. He ordered, encouraged, scolded. 'Now then – to the main topsail now! Tally on to that gantline. Don't stand about there!' – 'Is there no rest for us?' muttered voices. He spun round fiercely, with a sinking heart. – 'No! No rest till the work is done. Work till you drop. That's what you're here for.' A bowed seaman at his elbow gave a short laugh. – 'Do or die,' he croaked bitterly, then spat into his broad palms, swung up his long arms, and grasping the rope high above his head sent out a mournful, wailing cry for a pull all together. A sea boarded the quarterdeck and sent the whole lot sprawling to leeward. Caps, handspikes floated. Clenched hands, kicking legs, with here and there a sputtering face, stuck out of the white hiss of foaming water. Mr Baker, knocked down with the rest, screamed – 'Don't let go that rope! Hold on to it! Hold!' And sorely bruised by the brutal fling, they held on to it, as though it had been the fortune of their life. The ship ran, rolling heavily, and the topping crests glanced past port and starboard flashing their white heads. Pumps were freed. Braces were rove. The three topsails and foresails were set. She spurted faster over the water, outpacing the swift rush of waves. The menacing thunder of distant seas rose behind her – filled the air with the tremendous vibrations of its voice. And devastated, battered, and wounded she drove foaming to the northward, as though inspired by the courage of a high endeavour. . . .

The forecastle was a place of damp desolation. They looked at their dwelling with dismay. It was slimy, dripping; it hummed hollow with the wind, and was strewn with shapeless wreckage like a half-tide cavern in a rocky and exposed coast. Many had lost all they had in the world, but most of the starboard watch had preserved their chests; thin streams of water trickled out of them, however. The beds were soaked; the blankets spread out and saved by some nail squashed underfoot. They dragged wet rags from evil-smelling corners, and wringing the water out, recognized their property. Some smiled stiffly. Others looked round blank and mute. There were cries of joy over old waistcoats, and groans of sorrow over shapeless things found among the splinters of smashed bed boards. One lamp was discovered jammed under the bowsprit. Charley whimpered a little. Knowles stumped here and there, sniffing, examining dark places for salvage. He poured dirty water out of a boot, and was concerned to find the owner. Those who, overwhelmed by their losses, sat on the fore-peak hatch, remained elbows on knees, and, with a fist against each cheek, disdained to look up. He pushed it under their noses. 'Here's a good boot. Yours?' They snarled, 'No – get out.' One snapped at him, 'Take it to hell out of this.' He seemed surprised. 'Why? It's a good boot,' but remembering suddenly that he had lost every stitch of his clothing, he dropped his find and began to swear. In the dim light cursing voices clashed. A man came in and, dropping his arms, stood still, repeating from the doorstep, 'Here's a bloomin' old go! Here's a bloomin' old go!' A few rooted anxiously in flooded chests for tobacco. They breathed hard, clamoured with heads down. 'Look at that, Jack!' ... 'Here, Sam! Here's my shore-going rig spoilt for ever.' One blasphemed tearfully holding up a pair of dripping trousers. No one looked at him. The cat came out from somewhere. He had an ovation. They snatched him from hand to hand, caressed him in a murmur of pet names. They wondered where he had 'weathered it out;' disputed about it. A squabbling argument began. Two men brought in a bucket of fresh water, and all crowded round it; but Tom, lean and mewing, came up with every hair astir and had the first drink. A couple of hands went aft for oil and biscuits.

Then in the yellow light and in the intervals of mopping the deck they crunched hard bread, arranging to 'worry through somehow.' Men chummed as to beds. Turns were settled for wearing boots and having the use of oilskin coats. They called one another 'old man' and 'sonny' in cheery voices. Friendly slaps resounded. Jokes were shouted. One or two stretched on the wet deck, slept with heads pillowed on their bent arms, and several, sitting on the hatch, smoked. Their weary faces appeared through a thin blue haze, pacified and with sparkling eyes. The boatswain put his head through the door. 'Relieve the wheel, one of you' – he shouted inside – 'it's six. Blamme if that old Singleton hasn't been there more'n thirty hours. You are a fine lot.' He slammed the door again. 'Mate's watch on deck,' said some one. 'Hey, Donkin, it's your relief!' shouted three or four together. He had crawled into an empty bunk and on wet planks lay still. 'Donkin, your wheel.' He made no sound. 'Donkin's dead,' guffawed some one. 'Sell 'is bloomin' clothes,' shouted another. 'Donkin, if ye don't go to the bloomin' wheel they will sell your clothes – d'ye hear?' jeered a third. He groaned from his dark hole. He complained about pains in all his bones, he whimpered pitifully. 'He won't go,' exclaimed a contemptuous voice, 'your turn, Davis.' The young seaman rose painfully, squaring his shoulders. Donkin stuck his head out, and it appeared in the yellow light, fragile and ghastly. 'I will giv' yer a pound of tobacn' he whined in a conciliating voice, 'so soon as I draw it from aft. I will – s'elp me . . .' Davis swung his arm backhanded and the head vanished. 'I'll go,' he said, 'but you will pay for it.' He walked unsteady but resolute to the door. 'So I will,' yelped Donkin, popping out behind him. 'So I will – s'elp me . . . a pound . . . three bob they chawrge.' Davis flung the door open. 'You will pay my price . . . in fine weather,' he shouted over his shoulder. One of the men unbuttoned his wet coat rapidly, threw it at his head. 'Here, Taffy – take that, you thief!' – 'Thank you!' he cried from the darkness above the swish of rolling water. He could be heard splashing; a sea came on board with a thump. 'He's got his bath already,' remarked a grim shellback. 'Aye, aye!' grunted others. Then, after a long silence, Wamibo made strange noises. 'Hallo, what's up with you?' said some one grumpily. 'He says he would have gone for Davy,' explained Archie, who was the Finn's interpreter generally. 'I believe him!' cried voices.... 'Never mind, Dutchy...You'll do, muddle-head.... Your turn will come soon enough...You don't know when ye're well off.' They ceased, and all together turned their faces to the door. Singleton stepped in, made two paces, and stood swaying slightly. The sea hissed, flowed roaring past the bows, and the forecastle trembled, full of deep murmurs; the lamp flared, swinging like a pendulum. He looked with a dreamy and puzzled stare, as though he could not distinguish the still men from their restless shadows. There were awestruck excla-mations: 'Hallo, hallo'...'How does it look outside now, Singleton?' Those who sat on the hatch lifted their eyes in silence, and the next oldest seaman in the ship (those two understood one another, though they hardly exchanged three words in a day) gazed up at his friend attentively for a moment, then taking a short clay pipe out of his mouth, offered it without a word. Singleton put out his arm towards it, missed, staggered, and suddenly fell forward, crashing down, stiff and headlong like an uprooted tree. There was a swift rush. Men pushed, crying: 'He's done!'...'Turn him over!'...'Stand clear there!' Under a crowd of startled faces bending over him he lay on his back, staring upwards in a continuous and intolerable manner. In the breathless silence of a general consternation, he said in a grating murmur: 'I am all right,' and clutched with his hands. They helped him up. He mumbled despondently: 'I am getting old...old.' – 'Not you,' cried Belfast, with ready tact. Supported on all sides, he hung his head. – 'Are you better?' they asked. He glared at them from under his eyebrows with large black eyes, spreading over his chest the bushy whiteness of a beard long and thick. – 'Old! old!' he repeated sternly. Helped along, he reached his bunk. There was in it a slimy soft heap of something that smelt, as does at dead low water a muddy foreshore. It was his soaked straw bed. With a convulsive effort he pitched himself on it, and in the darkness of the narrow place could be heard growling angrily, like an irritated and savage animal uneasy in its den: 'Bit of a breeze ... small thing ... can't stand up ... old!' He slept at last, high booted, sou'wester on his head, and his oilskin clothes rustled, when with a deep sighing groan he turned over. Men conversed about him in quiet, concerned whispers. 'This will break 'im up' ... 'Strong as a horse' ... 'Aye. But he ain't what he used to be.' ... In sad murmurs they gave him up. Yet at midnight he turned out to duty as if nothing had been the matter, and answered to his name with a mournful 'Here!' He brooded alone more than ever, in an impenetrable silence and with a saddened face. For many years he had heard himself called 'Old Singleton' and had serenely accepted the qualification, taking it as a tribute of respect due to a man who through half a century had measured his strength against the favours and the rages of the sea. He had never given a thought to his mortal self. He lived unscathed, as though he had been indestructible, surrendering to all the temptations, weathering many gales. He had panted in sunshine, shivered in the cold; suffered hunger, thirst, debauch; passed through many trials – known all the furies. Old! It seemed to him he was broken at last. And like a man bound treacherously while he sleeps, he woke up fettered by the long chain of disregarded years. He had to take up at once the burden of all his existence, and found it almost too heavy for his strength. Old! He moved his arms, shook his head, felt his limbs. Getting old ... and then? He looked upon the immortal sea with the awakened and groping perception of its heartless might; he saw it unchanged, black and foaming under the eternal scrutiny of the stars; he heard its impatient voice calling for him out of a pitiless vastness full of unrest, of turmoil, and of terror. He looked afar upon it, and he saw an immensity tormented and blind, moaning and furious, that claimed all his days of his tenacious life, and, when life was over, would claim the worn-out body of its slave....

This was the last of the breeze. It veered quickly, changed to a black south-easter, and blew itself out, giving the ship a famous shove to the northward into the joyous sunshine of the trade. Rapid and white she ran homewards in a straight path, under a blue sky and upon the plain of a blue sea. She carried Singleton's completed wisdom, Donkin's delicate susceptibilities, and the conceited folly of us all. The hours of ineffective turmoil were forgotten; the fear and anguish of these dark moments were never mentioned in the glowing peace of fine days. Yet from that time our life seemed to start afresh as though we had died and had been resuscitated. All the first part of the voyage, the Indian Ocean on the other side of the Cape, all that was lost in a haze, like an ineradicable suspicion of some previous existence. It had ended – then and there were blank hours: a livid blurr – and again we lived! Singleton was possessed of sinister truth; Mr Creighton of a damaged leg; the cook of fame – and shamefully abused the opportunities of his distinction. Donkin had an added grievance. He went about repeating with insistence: ''E said 'e would brain me – did yer 'ear? They are going to murder us now for the least little thing.' We began at last to think it was rather awful. And we were conceited! We boasted of our pluck, of our capacity for work, of our energy. We remembered honourable episodes: our devotion, our indomitable perseverance – and were proud of them as though they had been the outcome of our unaided impulses. We remembered our danger, our toil – and conveniently forgot our horrible scare. We decried our officers – who had done

nothing – and listened to the fascinating Donkin. His care
for our rights, his disinterested concern for our dignity,
were not discouraged by the invariable contumely of our
words, by the disdain of our looks. Our contempt for him
was unbounded – and we could not but listen with interest
to that consummate artist. He told us we were good men –
a 'bloomin' condemned lot of good men.' Who thanked us?
Who took any notice of our wrongs? Didn't we lead a
'dorg's loife for two poun' ten a month?' Did we think
that miserable pay enough to compensate us for the risk
to our lives and for the loss of our clothes? 'We've lost every
rag!' he cried. He made us forget that he, at any rate, had
lost nothing of his own. The younger men listened thinking – this 'ere Donkin's a long-headed chap, though no
kind of man, anyhow. The Scandinavians were frightened
at his audacities; Wamibo did not understand; and the
older seamen thoughtfully nodded their heads making
the thin gold earrings glitter in the fleshy lobes of hairy
ears. Severe, sunburnt faces were propped meditatively on
tattooed forearms. Veined, brown fists held in their
knotted grip the dirty white clay of smouldering pipes.
They listened, impenetrable, broad-backed, with bent
shoulders, and in grim silence. He talked with ardour,
despised and irrefutable. His picturesque and filthy loquacity flowed like a troubled stream from a poisoned source.
His beady eyes danced, glancing right and left, ever on the
watch for the approach of an officer. Sometimes Mr Baker
going forward to take a look at the head sheets would roll
with his uncouth gait through the sudden stillness of the
men; or Mr Creighton limped along, smooth-faced,
youthful, and more stern than ever, piercing our short
silence with a keen glance of his clear eyes. Behind his
back Donkin would begin again darting stealthy, sidelong
looks. ''Ere's one of 'em. Some of yer 'as made 'im fast that
day. Much thanks yer got fer it. Ain't 'ee a-drivin' yer
wusse'n ever? ... Let 'im slip overboard. ... Vy not? It
would 'ave been less trouble. Vy not?' He advanced

confidentially, backed away with great effect; he whispered,
he screamed, waved his miserable arms no thicker than
pipe-stems – stretched his lean neck – spluttered –
squinted. In the pauses of his impassioned orations the
wind sighed quietly aloft, the calm sea unheeded murmured in a warning whisper along the ship's side. We
abominated the creature and could not deny the luminous
truth of his contentions. It was all so obvious. We were
indubitably good men; our deserts were great and our pay
small. Through our exertions we had saved the ship and the
skipper would get the credit of it. What had he done? we
wanted to know. Donkin asked: 'What 'ee could do without hus?' and we could not answer. We were oppressed by
the injustice of the world, surprised to perceive how long
we had lived under its burden without realizing our unfortunate state, annoyed by the uneasy suspicion of our undis-
cerning stupidity. Donkin assured us it was all our 'good
'eartedness,' but we would not be consoled by such shallow
sophistry. We were men enough to courageously admit to
ourselves our intellectual shortcomings; though from that
time we refrained from kicking him, tweaking his nose, or
from accidentally knocking him about, which last, after we
had weathered the Cape, had been rather a popular amusement. Davis ceased to talk to him provokingly about black
eyes and flattened noses. Charley, much subdued since the
gale, did not jeer at him. Knowles deferentially and with a
crafty air propounded questions such as: 'Could we all have
the same grub as the mates? Could we all stop ashore till we
got it? What would be the next thing to try for if we got
that?' He answered readily with contemptuous certitude;
he strutted with assurance in clothes that were much too
big for him as though he had tried to disguise himself.
These were Jimmy's clothes mostly – though he would
accept anything from anybody; but nobody, except Jimmy,
had anything to spare. His devotion to Jimmy was
unbounded. He was for ever dodging in the little cabin,
ministering to Jimmy's wants, humouring his whims,

submitting to his exacting peevishness, often laughing with him. Nothing could keep him away from the pious work of visiting the sick, especially when there was some heavy hauling to be done on deck. Mr Baker had on two occasions jerked him out from there by the scruff of the neck to our inexpressible scandal. Was a sick chap to be left without attendance? Were we to be ill-used for attending a ship-mate? – 'What?' growled Mr Baker, turning menacingly at the mutter, and the whole halfcircle like one man stepped back a pace. 'Set the topmast stunsail. Away aloft, Donkin, overhaul the gear,' ordered the mate inflexibly. 'Fetch the sail along; bend the down-haul clear. Bear a hand.' Then, the sail set, he would go slowly aft and stand looking at the compass for a long time, careworn, pensive, and breathing hard as if stifled by the taint of unaccountable ill-will that pervaded the ship. 'What's up amongst them?' he thought. 'Can't make out this hanging back and growling. A good crowd, too, as they go nowadays.' On deck the men exchanged bitter words, suggested by a silly exasperation against something unjust and irremediable that would not be denied, and would whisper into their ears long after Donkin had ceased speaking. Our little world went on its curved and unswerving path carrying a discontented and aspiring population. They found comfort of a gloomy kind in an interminable and conscientious analysis of their unappreciated worth; and inspired by Donkin's hopeful doctrines they dreamed enthusiastically of the time when every lonely ship would travel over a serene sea, manned by a wealthy and well-fed crew of satisfied skippers.

It looked as if it would be a long passage. The south-east trades, light and unsteady, were left behind; and then, on the equator and under a low grey sky, the ship, in close heat, floated upon a smooth sea that resembled a sheet of ground glass. Thunder squalls hung on the horizon, circled round the ship, far off and growling angrily, like a troop of wild beasts afraid to charge home. The invisible sun, sweeping above the upright masts, made on the clouds a blurred stain of rayless light, and a similar patch of faded radiance kept pace with it from east to west over the unglittering level of the waters. At night, through the impenetrable darkness of earth and heaven, broad sheets of flame waved noiselessly; and for half a second the becalmed craft stood out with its masts and rigging, with every sail and every rope distinct and black in the centre of a fiery outburst, like a charred ship enclosed in a globe of fire. And, again, for long hours she remained lost in a vast universe of night and silence where gentle sighs wandering here and there like forlorn souls, made the still sails flutter as in sudden fear, and the ripple of a beshrouded ocean whisper its compassion afar – in a voice mournful, immense, and faint....

When the lamp was put out, and through the door thrown wide open, Jimmy, turning on his pillow, could see vanishing beyond the straight line of top-gallant rail, the quick, repeated visions of a fabulous world made up of leaping fire and sleeping water. The lightning gleamed in his big sad eyes that seemed in a red flicker to burn themselves out in his black face, and then he would lie blinded and invisible in the midst of an intense darkness. He could hear on the quiet deck soft footfalls, the breathing of some man lounging on the doorstep; the low creak of swaying masts; or the calm voice of the watch-officer reverberating aloft, hard and loud, amongst the unstirring sails. He listened with avidity, taking a rest in the attentive perception of the slightest sound from the fatiguing wanderings of his sleeplessness. He was cheered by the rattling of blocks, reassured by the stir and murmur of the watch, soothed by the slow yawn of some sleepy and weary seaman settling himself deliberately for a snooze on the planks. Life seemed an indestructible thing. It went on in darkness, in sunshine, in sleep; tireless, it hovered affectionately round the imposture of his ready death. It was bright, like the twisted flare of lightning, and more full of surprises than the dark night. It made him safe, and the calm of its

overpowering darkness was as precious as its restless and
dangerous light.

But in the evening, in the dog-watches, and even far into
the first night-watch, a knot of men could always be seen
congregated before Jimmy's cabin. They leaned on each
side of the door peacefully interested and with crossed legs;
they stood astride the doorstep discoursing, or sat in silent
couples on his sea-chest; while against the bulwark along
the spare topmast, three or four in a row stared meditatively; with their simple faces lit up by the projected glare of
Jimmy's lamp. The little place, repainted white, had, in the
night, the brilliance of a silver shrine where a black idol,
reclining stiffly under a blanket, blinked its weary eyes and
received our homage. Donkin officiated. He had the air of
a demonstrator showing a phenomenon, a manifestation
bizarre, simple, and meritorious that, to the beholders,
should be a profound and an everlasting lesson. 'Just look
at 'im, 'ee knows what's what – never fear!' he exclaimed
now and then, flourishing a hand hard and fleshless like the
claw of a snipe. Jimmy, on his back, smiled with reserve and
without moving a limb. He affected the languor of extreme
weakness, so as to make it manifest to us that our delay in
hauling him out from his horrible confinement, and then
that night spent on the poop among our selfish neglect of
his needs, had 'done for him.' He rather liked to talk about
it, and of course we were always interested. He spoke
spasmodically, in fast rushes with long pauses between, as
a tipsy man walks. . . . 'Cook had just given me a pannikin
of hot coffee. . . . Slapped it down there, on my chest –
banged the door to. . . . I felt a heavy roll coming; tried to
save my coffee, burnt my fingers . . . and fell out of my
bunk. . . . She went over so quick. . . . Water came in
through the ventilator. . . . I couldn't move the door . . . dark
as a grave . . . tried to scramble up into the upper
berth. . . . Rats . . . a rat bit my finger as I got up. . . . I could
hear him swimming below me. . . . I thought you would
never come. . . . I thought you were all gone overboard . . . of

course ... Could hear nothing but the wind. ... Then you
came ... to look for the corpse, I suppose. A little more
and ...'

'Man! But ye made a rare lot of noise in here,' observed
Archie, thoughtfully.

'You chaps kicked up such a confounded row
above. ... Enough to scare any one. ... I didn't know what
you were up to. ... Bash in the blamed planks ... my
head. ... Just what a silly, scary gang of fools would
do. ... Not much good to me anyhow. ... Just as
well ... drown. ... Pah.'

He groaned, snapped his big white teeth, and gazed
with scorn. Belfast lifted a pair of dolorous eyes, with a
broken-hearted smile, clenched his fists stealthily; blue-
eyed Archie caressed his red whiskers with a hesitating
hand; the boatswain at the door stared a moment, and
brusquely went away with a loud guffaw. Wamibo
dreamed. ... Donkin felt all over his sterile chin for the
few rare hairs, and said, triumphantly, with a sidelong
glance at Jimmy: – 'Look at 'im! Wish I was 'arf as 'ealthy
as 'ee is – I do.' He jerked a short thumb over his shoulder
towards the after end of the ship. 'That's the blooming way
to do 'em!' he yelped, with forced heartiness. Jimmy said: –
'Don't be a dam' fool,' in a pleasant voice. Knowles, rubbing
his shoulder against the doorpost, remarked shrewdly: –
'We can't all go an' be took sick – it would be mutiny.' –
'Mutiny – gawn!' jeered Donkin, 'there's no bloomin' law
against bein' sick.' – 'There's six weeks' hard for refoosing
dooty,' argued Knowles. 'I mind I once seed in Cardiff the
crew of an overloaded ship – leastways she weren't overloaded, only a fatherly old gentleman with a white beard
and an umbreller came along the quay and talked to the
hands. Said as how it was crool hard to be drownded in
winter just for the sake of a few pounds more for the owner
– he said. Nearly cried over them – he did; and he had a
square mainsail coat, and a gaff-topsail hat too – all proper.
So they chaps they said they wouldn't go to be drownded in

winter – depending upon that 'ere Plimsoll man to see 'em through the court. They thought to have a bloomin' lark and two or three days' spree. And the beak giv' 'em six weeks – coss the ship warn't overloaded. Anyways they made it out in court that she wasn't. There wasn't one overloaded ship in Penarth Dock at all. 'Pears that old coon he was only on pay and allowance from some kind people, under orders to look for overloaded ships, and he couldn't see no further than the length of his umbreller. Some of us in the boarding-house, where I live when I'm looking for a ship in Cardiff, stood by to duck that old weeping spunger in the dock. We kept a good look-out, too – but he topped his boom directly he was outside the court. . . . Yes. They got six weeks' hard. . . .'

They listened, full of curiosity, nodding in the pauses their rough pensive faces. Donkin opened his mouth once or twice, but restrained himself. Jimmy lay still with open eyes and not at all interested. A seaman emitted the opinion that after a verdict of atrocious partiality 'the bloomin' beaks go an' drink at the skipper's expense.' Others assented. It was clear, of course. Donkin said: 'Well, six weeks ain't much trouble. You sleep all night in, reg'lar, in chokey. Do it on my 'ead.' 'You are used to it ainch'ee, Donkin?' asked somebody. Jimmy condescended to laugh. It cheered up every one wonderfully. Knowles, with surprising mental agility, shifted his ground. 'If we all went sick what would become of the ship? eh?' He posed the problem and grinned all round. – 'Let 'er go to 'ell,' sneered Donkin. 'Damn 'er. She ain't yourn.' – 'What? Just let her drift?' insisted Knowles in a tone of unbelief. – 'Aye! Drift, an' be blowed,' affirmed Donkin with fine recklessness. The other did not see it – meditated. – 'The stores would run out,' he muttered, 'and . . . never get anywhere . . . and what about pay-day?' he added with greater assurance. – 'Jack likes a good pay-day,' exclaimed a listener on the doorstep. 'Aye, because then the girls put one arm round his neck an' t'other in his pocket, and call him ducky. Don't

they, Jack?' – 'Jack, you're a terror with the gals.' – 'He takes
three of 'em in tow to once, like one of 'em Watkinses two-
funnel tugs waddling away with three schooners behind.' –
'Jack, you're a lame scamp.' – 'Jack, tell us about that one
with a blue eye and a black eye. Do.' – 'There's plenty of
girls with one black eye along the Highway by...' – 'No,
that's a speshul one – come, Jack.' Donkin looked severe
and disgusted; Jimmy very bored; a grey-haired sea-dog
shook his head slightly, smiling at the bowl of his pipe,
discreetly amused. Knowles turned about bewildered;
stammered first at one, then at another. – 'No!...I
never!...can't talk sensible sense midst you....Always on
the kid.' He retired bashfully – muttering and pleased.
They laughed hooting in the crude light, around Jimmy's
bed, where on a white pillow his hollowed black face moved
to and fro restlessly. A puff of wind came, made the flame
of the lamp leap, and outside, high up, the sails fluttered,
while near by the block of the foresheet struck a ringing
blow on the iron bulwark. A voice far off cried, 'Helm up!'
another, more faint, answered, 'Hard-up, sir!' They became
silent – waited expectantly. The grey-haired seaman
knocked his pipe on the doorstep and stood up. The ship
leaned over gently and the sea seemed to wake up, murmuring drowsily. 'Here's a little wind comin',' said some one
very low. Jimmy turned over slowly to face the breeze. The
voice in the night cried loud and commanding: – 'Haul the
spanker out.' The group before the door vanished out of
the light. They could be heard tramping aft while they
repeated with varied intonations: 'Spanker out!'...'Out
spanker, sir!' Donkin remained alone with Jimmy. There
was a silence. Jimmy opened and shut his lips several times
as if swallowing draughts of fresher air; Donkin moved the
toes of his bare feet and looked at them thoughtfully.

'Ain't you going to give them a hand with the sail?' asked
Jimmy.

'No. If six ov 'em ain't 'nough beef to set that blamed,
rotten spanker, they ain't fit to live,' answered Donkin in a

bored, far-away voice, as though he had been talking from
the bottom of a hole. Jimmy considered the conical, fowl-
like profile with a queer kind of interest; he was leaning out
of his bunk with the calculating, uncertain expression of a
man who reflects how best to lay hold of some strange
creature that looks as though it could sting or bite. But he
said only: 'The mate will miss you – and there will be
ructions.'

Donkin got up to go. 'I will do for 'im some dark night;
see if I don't,' he said over his shoulder.

Jimmy went on quickly: 'You're like a poll-parrot, like a
screechin' poll-parrot.' Donkin stopped and cocked his
head attentively on one side. His big ears stood out, transparent and veined, resembling the thin wings of a bat.

'Yuss?' he said, with his back towards Jimmy.

'Yes! Chatter out all you know – like . . . like a dirty white
cockatoo.'

Donkin waited. He could hear the other's breathing,
long and slow; the breathing of a man with a hundred-
weight or so on the breastbone. Then he asked calmly: –
'What do I know?'

'What? . . . What I tell you . . . not much. What do you
want . . . to talk about my health so . . .'

'It's a blooming imposyshun. A bloomin', stinkin', first-
class imposyshun – but it don't tyke me in. Not it.'

Jimmy kept still. Donkin put his hands in his pockets,
and in one slouching stride came up to the bunk.

'I talk – what's the odds. They ain't men 'ere – sheep they
are. A driven lot of sheep. I 'old you up . . . Vy not? You're
well orf.'

'I am . . . I don't say anything about that. . . .'

'Well. Let 'em see it. Let 'em larn what a man can do.
I am a man, I know all about yer. . . .' Jimmy threw himself
further away on the pillow; the other stretched out his
skinny neck, jerked his bird face down at him as though
pecking at the eyes. 'I am a man. I've seen the inside of
every chokey in the Colonies rather'n give up my rights. . . .'

'You are a jail-prop,' said Jimmy, weakly.

'I am...an' proud of it, too. You! You 'aven't the bloomin' nerve – so you inventyd this 'ere dodge....' He paused; then with marked afterthought accentuated slowly: 'Yer ain't sick – are yer?'

'No,' said Jimmy, firmly. 'Been out of sorts now and again this year,' he mumbled with a sudden drop in his voice.

Donkin closed one eye, amicable and confidential. He whispered: 'Ye 'ave done this afore 'aven'tchee?' Jimmy smiled – then as if unable to hold back he let himself go: 'Last ship – yes. I was out of sorts on the passage. See? It was easy. They paid me off in Calcutta, and the skipper made no bones about it either.... I got my money all right. Laid up fifty-eight days! The fools! O Lord! The fools! Paid right off.' He laughed spasmodically. Donkin chimed in giggling. Then Jimmy coughed violently. 'I am as well as ever,' he said, as soon as he could draw breath.

Donkin made a derisive gesture. 'In course,' he said profoundly, 'any one can see that.' – 'They don't,' said Jimmy, gasping like a fish. – 'They would swallow any yarn,' affirmed Donkin. – 'Don't you let on too much,' admonished Jimmy in an exhausted voice. – 'Your little gyme? Eh?' commented Donkin, jovially. Then with sudden disgust: 'Yer all for yerself, s'long as ye're right....'

So charged with egoism James Wait pulled the blanket up to his chin and lay still for awhile. His heavy lips protruded in an everlasting black pout. 'Why are you so hot on making trouble?' he asked without much interest.

"Cos it's a bloomin' shayme. We are put upon...bad food, bad pay...I want us to kick up a bloomin' row; a blamed 'owling row that would make 'em remember! Knocking people about...brain us...indeed! Ain't we men?' His altruistic indignation blazed. Then he said calmly: – 'I've been airing yer clothes.' – 'All right,' said Jimmy, languidly, 'bring them in.' – 'Giv' us the key of your chest, I'll put 'em away for yer,' said Donkin with friendly eagerness. – 'Bring 'em in, I will put them away myself,' answered James Wait with severity. Donkin looked down, muttering.... 'What d'you say? What d'you say?' inquired Wait anxiously. – 'Nothink. The night's dry, let 'em 'ang out till the morning,' said Donkin, in a strangely trembling voice, as though restraining laughter or rage. Jimmy seemed satisfied. – 'Give me a little water for the night in my mug – there,' he said. Donkin took a stride over the doorstep. – 'Git it yerself,' he replied in a surly tone. 'You can do it, unless you *are* sick.' – 'Of course I can do it,' said Wait, 'only...' – 'Well, then, do it,' said Donkin, viciously, 'if yer can look after yer clothes, yer can look after yerself.' He went on deck without a look back.

Jimmy reached out for the mug. Not a drop. He put it back gently with a faint sigh – and closed his eyes. He thought: – That lunatic Belfast will bring me some water if I ask. Fool. I am very thirsty.... It was very hot in the cabin, and it seemed to turn slowly round, detach itself from the ship, and swing out smoothly into a luminous, arid space where a black sun shone, spinning very fast. A place without any water! No water! A policeman with the face of Donkin drank a glass of beer by the side of an empty well, and flew away flapping vigorously. A ship whose mastheads protruded through the sky and could not be seen, was discharging grain, and the wind whirled the dry husks in spirals along the quay of a dock with no water in it. He whirled along with the husks – very tired and light. All his inside was gone. He felt lighter than the husks – and more dry. He expanded his hollow chest. The air streamed in carrying away in its rush a lot of strange things that resembled houses, trees, people, lamp-posts.... No more! There was no more air – and he had not finished drawing his long breath. But he was in jail! They were locking him up. A door slammed. They turned the key twice, flung a bucket of water over him – Phoo! What for?

He opened his eyes, thinking the fall had been very heavy for an empty man – empty – empty. He was in his

cabin. Ah! All right! His face was streaming with perspiration, his arms heavier than lead. He saw the cook standing
in the doorway, a brass key in one hand and a bright tin
hook-pot in the other.

'I have locked up the galley for the night,' said the cook,
beaming benevolently. 'Eight-bells just gone. I brought
you a pot of cold tea for your night's drinking, Jimmy. I
sweetened it with some white cabin sugar, too. Well – it
won't break the ship.'

He came in, hung the pot on the edge of the bunk, asked
perfunctorily, 'How goes it?' and sat down on the box. –
'H'm,' grunted Wait, inhospitably. The cook wiped his face
with a dirty cotton rag, which, afterwards, he tied round his
neck. – 'That's how them firemen do in steamboats,' he
said, serenely, and much pleased with himself. 'My work is
as heavy as theirs – I'm thinking – and longer hours. Did
you ever see them down the stokehold? Like fiends they
look – firing – firing – firing – down there.'

He pointed his forefinger at the deck. Some gloomy
thought darkened his shining face, fleeting, like the shadow of a travelling cloud over the light of a peaceful sea.
The relieved watch tramped noisily forward, passing in a
body across the sheen of the doorway. Some one cried,
'Good night!' Belfast stopped for a moment and looked at
Jimmy, quivering and speechless with repressed emotion.
He gave the cook a glance charged with dismal foreboding,
and vanished. The cook cleared his throat. Jimmy stared
upwards and kept as still as a man in hiding.

The night was clear, with a gentle breeze. Above the
mastheads the resplendent curve of the Milky Way
spanned the sky like a triumphal arch of eternal light,
thrown over the dark pathway of the earth. On the forecastle head a man whistled with loud precision a lively jig,
while another could be heard faintly, shuffling and stamping in time. There came from forward a confused murmur
of voices, laughter – snatches of song. The cook shook his
head, glanced obliquely at Jimmy, and began to mutter.

'Aye. Dance and sing. That's all they think of. I am surprised that Providence don't get tired. . . . They forget the
day that's sure to come . . . but you. . . .'

Jimmy drank a gulp of tea, hurriedly, as though he had
stolen it, and shrank under his blanket, edging away
towards the bulk-head. The cook got up, closed the door,
then sat down again and said distinctly: –

'Whenever I poke my galley fire I think of you chaps –
swearing, stealing, lying, and worse – as if there was
no such thing as another world. . . . Not bad fellows, either,
in a way,' he conceded, slowly; then, after a pause of
regretful musing, he went on in a resigned tone: 'Well,
well. They will have a hot time of it. Hot! Did I say? The
furnaces of one of them White Star boats ain't nothing to
it.'

He kept very quiet for a while. There was a great stir in
his brain; an addled vision of bright outlines; an exciting
row of rousing songs and groans of pain. He suffered,
enjoyed, admired, approved. He was delighted, frightened,
exalted – as on that evening (the only time in his life –
twenty-seven years ago; he loved to recall the number of
years) when as a young man he had – through keeping bad
company – become intoxicated in an East-end music-hall.
A tide of sudden feeling swept him clean out of his body.
He soared. He contemplated the secret of the hereafter. It
commended itself to him. It was excellent; he loved it,
himself, all hands, and Jimmy. His heart overflowed with
tenderness, with comprehension, with the desire to
meddle, with anxiety for the soul of that black man, with
the pride of possessed eternity, with the feeling of might.
Snatch him up in his arms and pitch him right into the
middle of salvation. . . . The black soul – blacker – body –
rot – Devil. No! Talk – strength – Samson. . . . There was a
great din as of cymbals in his ears; he flashed through an
ecstatic jumble of shining faces, lilies, prayer-books,
unearthly joy, white shirts, gold harps, black coats, wings.
He saw flowing garments, clean shaved faces, a sea of light

– a lake of pitch. There were sweet scents, a smell of sulphur – red tongues of flame licking a white mist. An awesome voice thundered! . . . It lasted three seconds.

'Jimmy!' he cried in an inspired tone. Then he hesitated. A spark of human pity glimmered yet through the infernal fog of his supreme conceit.

'What?' said James Wait, unwillingly. There was a silence. He turned his head just the least bit, and stole a cautious glance. The cook's lips moved without a sound; his face was rapt, his eyes turned up. He seemed to be mentally imploring deck beams, the brass hook of the lamp, two cockroaches.

'Look here,' said Wait, 'I want to go to sleep. I think I could.'

'This is no time for sleep!' exclaimed the cook, very loud. He had prayerfully divested himself of the last vestige of his humanity. He was a voice – a fleshless and sublime thing, as on that memorable night – the night when he went walking over the sea to make coffee for perishing sinners. 'This is no time for sleeping,' he repeated with exaltation. '*I* can't sleep.'

'Don't care damn,' said Wait, with factitious energy. 'I can. Go an' turn in.'

'Swear . . . in the very jaws! . . . In the very jaws! Don't you see the everlasting fire . . . don't you feel it? Blind, chockfull of sin! Repent, repent! I can't bear to think of you. I hear the call to save you. Night and day. Jimmy, let me save you!' The words of entreaty and menace broke out of him in a roaring torrent. The cockroaches ran away. Jimmy perspired, wriggling stealthily under his blanket. The cook yelled. . . . 'Your days are numbered! . . .' – 'Get out of this,' boomed Wait, courageously. – 'Pray with me! . . .' – 'I won't! . . .' The little cabin was as hot as an oven. It contained an immensity of fear and pain; an atmosphere of shrieks and moans; prayers vociferated like blasphemies and whispered curses. Outside, the men called by Charley, who informed them in tones of delight that there was a holy row going on in Jimmy's place, crowded before the closed door, too startled to open it. All hands were there. The watch below had jumped out on deck in their shirts, as after a collision. Men running up, asked: – 'What is it?' Others said: – 'Listen!' The muffled screaming went on: – 'On your knees! On your knees!' – 'Shut up!' – 'Never! You are delivered into my hands.... Your life has been saved.... Purpose.... Mercy.... Repent.' – 'You are a crazy fool!...' – 'Account of you ... you ... Never sleep in this world, if I ...' – 'Leave off.' – 'No!... stokehold... only think!...' Then an impassioned screeching babble where words pattered like hail. – 'No!' shouted Wait. – 'Yes. You are!... No help.... Everybody says so.' – 'You lie!' – 'I see you dying this minnyt...before my eyes...as good as dead already.' – 'Help!' shouted Jimmy, piercingly. – 'Not in this valley.... look upwards,' howled the other. – 'Go away! Murder! Help!' clamoured Jimmy. His voice broke. There were moanings, low mutters, a few sobs.

'What's the matter now?' said a seldom-heard voice. – 'Fall back, men! Fall back, there!' repeated Mr Creighton, sternly, pushing through. – 'Here's the old man,' whispered some. – 'The cook's in there, sir,' exclaimed several, backing away. The door clattered open; a broad stream of light darted out on wondering faces; a warm whiff of vitiated air passed. The two mates towered head and shoulders above the spare, grey-haired man who stood revealed between them, in shabby clothes, stiff and angular, like a small carved figure, and with a thin, composed face. The cook got up from his knees. Jimmy sat high in the bunk, clasping his drawn-up legs. The tassel of the blue night-cap almost imperceptibly trembled over his knees. They gazed astonished at his long, curved back, while the white corner of one eye gleamed blindly at them. He was afraid to turn his head, he shrank within himself; and there was an aspect astounding and animal-like in the perfection of his expectant immobility. A thing of instinct – the unthinking stillness of a scared brute.

'What are you doing here?' asked Mr Baker, sharply. – 'My duty,' said the cook, with ardour. – 'Your...what?' began the mate. Captain Allistoun touched his arm lightly. – 'I know his caper,' he said, in a low voice. 'Come out of that, Podmore,' he ordered, aloud.

The cook wrung his hands, shook his fists above his head, and his arms dropped as if too heavy. For a moment he stood distracted and speechless. – 'Never,' he stammered, 'I...he...I.' – 'What – do – you – say?' pronounced Captain Allistoun. 'Come out at once – or...' – 'I am going,' said the cook, with a hasty and sombre resignation. He strode over the doorstep firmly – hesitated – made a few steps. They looked at him in silence. – 'I make you responsible!' he cried, desperately, turning half round. 'That man is dying. I make you ...' – 'You there yet?' called the master in a threatening tone. – 'No, sir,' he exclaimed, hurriedly, in a startled voice. The boatswain led him away by the arm; some one laughed; Jimmy lifted his head for a stealthy glance, and in one unexpected leap sprang out of his bunk; Mr Baker made a clever catch and felt him very limp in his arms; the group at the door grunted with surprise. – 'He lies,' gasped Wait, 'he talked about black devils – he is a devil – a white devil – I am all right.' He stiffened himself, and Mr Baker, experimentally, let him go. He staggered a pace or two; Captain Allistoun watched him with a quiet and penetrating gaze; Belfast ran to his support. He did not appear to be aware of any one near him; he stood silent for a moment, battling single-handed with a legion of nameless terrors, amidst the eager looks of excited men who watched him far off, utterly alone in the impenetrable solitude of his fear. The sea gurgled through the scuppers as the ship heeled over to a short puff of wind.

'Keep him away from me,' said James Wait at last in his fine baritone voice, and leaning with all his weight on Belfast's neck. 'I've been better this last week...I am well . . . I was going back to duty . . . to-morrow – now if you like – Captain.' Belfast hitched his shoulders to keep him upright.

'No,' said the master, looking at him, fixedly.

Under Jimmy's armpit Belfast's red face moved uneasily. A row of eyes gleaming stared on the edge of light. They pushed one another with elbows, turned their heads, whispered. Wait let his chin fall on his breast and, with lowered eyelids, looked round in a suspicious manner.

'Why not?' cried a voice from the shadows, 'the man's all right, sir.'

'I am all right,' said Wait, with eagerness. 'Been sick . . . better . . . turn-to now.' He sighed. – 'Howly Mother!' exclaimed Belfast with a heave of the shoulders, 'stand up, Jimmy.' – 'Keep away from me then,' said Wait, giving Belfast a petulant push, and reeling fetched against the door-post. His cheekbones glistened as though they had been varnished. He snatched off his night-cap, wiped his perspiring face with it, flung it on the deck. 'I am coming out,' he declared without stirring.

'No. You don't,' said the master, curtly. Bare feet shuffled, disapproving voices murmured all round; he went on as if he had not heard: 'You have been skulking nearly all the passage and now you want to come out. You think you are near enough to the pay-table now. Smell the shore, hey?'

'I've been sick . . . now – better,' mumbled Wait, glaring in the light. – 'You have been shamming sick,' retorted Captain Allistoun with severity; 'Why . . .' he hesitated for less than half a second. 'Why, anybody can see that. There's nothing the matter with you, but you choose to lie-up to please yourself – and now you shall lie up to please me. Mr Baker, my orders are that this man is not to be allowed on deck to the end of the passage.'

There were exclamations of surprise, triumph, indignation. The dark group of men swung across the light. 'What for?' 'Told you so . . .' 'Bloomin' shame . . .' – 'We've got to

say somethink about that,' screeched Donkin from the rear.
– 'Never mind, Jim – we will see you righted,' cried several
together. An elderly seaman stepped to the front. 'D'ye
mean to say, sir,' he asked, ominously, 'that a sick chap
ain't allowed to get well in this 'ere hooker?' Behind him
Donkin whispered excitedly amongst a staring crowd
where no one spared him a glance, but Captain Allistoun
shook a forefinger at the angry bronzed face of the speaker.
– 'You – you hold your tongue,' he said, warningly. – 'This
isn't the way,' clamoured two or three younger men. – 'Are
we bloomin' masheens?' inquired Donkin in a piercing
tone, and dived under the elbow of the front rank. –
'Soon show 'im we ain't boys . . .' – 'The man's a man if he
is black.' – 'We ain't goin' to work this bloomin' ship shorthanded if Snowball's all right . . .' – 'He says he is.' – 'Well
then strike, boys, strike!' – 'That's the bloomin' ticket.'
Captain Allistoun said sharply to the second mate: 'Keep
quiet, Mr Creighton,' and stood composed in the tumult,
listening with profound attention to mixed growls and
screeches, to every exclamation and every curse of the
sudden outbreak. Somebody slammed the cabin door to
with a kick; the darkness full of menacing mutters leaped
with a short clatter over the streak of light, and the men
became gesticulating shadows that growled, hissed,
laughed excitedly. Mr Baker whispered: 'Get away from
them, sir.' The big shape of Mr Creighton hovered silently
about the slight figure of the master. – 'We have been
hymposed upon all this voyage,' said a gruff voice, 'but
this 'ere fancy takes the cake.' – 'That man is a shipmate.'
– 'Are we bloomin' kids?' – 'The port watch will refuse
duty.' Charley carried away by his feeling whistled shrilly,
then yelped: 'Giv' us our Jimmy!' This seemed to cause a
variation in the disturbance. There was a fresh burst of
squabbling uproar. A lot of quarrels were set going at once.
– 'Yes.' – 'No.' – 'Never been sick.' – 'Go for them to once.' –
'Shut yer mouth, youngster – this is men's work.' – 'Is it?'
muttered Captain Allistoun, bitterly. Mr Baker grunted:

'Ough! They're gone silly. They've been simmering for the last month.' – 'I did notice,' said the master. – 'They have started a row amongst themselves now,' said Mr Creighton with disdain, 'better get aft, sir. We will soothe them.' – 'Keep your temper, Creighton,' said the master. And the three men began to move slowly towards the cabin door.

In the shadows of the fore rigging a dark mass stamped, eddied, advanced, retreated. There were words of reproach, encouragement, unbelief, execration. The elder seamen, bewildered and angry, growled their determination to go through with something or other; but the younger school of advanced thought exposed their and Jimmy's wrongs with confused shouts, arguing amongst themselves. They clustered round that moribund carcass, the fit emblem of their aspirations, and encouraging one another they swayed, they tramped on one spot, shouting that they would not be 'put upon.' Inside the cabin, Belfast, helping Jimmy into his bunk, twitched all over in his desire not to miss all the row, and with difficulty restrained the tears of his facile emotion. James Wait, flat on his back under the blanket, gasped complaints. – 'We will back you up, never fear,' assured Belfast, busy about his feet. – 'I'll come out to-morrow morning——take my chance——you fellows must——' mumbled Wait, 'I come out to-morrow——skipper or no skipper.' He lifted one arm with great difficulty, passed the hand over his face; 'Don't you let that cook . . .' he breathed out. – 'No, no,' said Belfast, turning his back on the bunk, 'I will put a head on him if he comes near you.' – 'I will smash his mug!' exclaimed faintly Wait, enraged and weak; 'I don't want to kill a man, but . . .' He panted fast like a dog after a run in sunshine. Some one just outside the door shouted, 'He's as fit as any ov us!' Belfast put his hand on the door-handle. – 'Here!' called James Wait, hurriedly, and in such a clear voice that the other spun round with a start. James Wait, stretched out black and deathlike in the dazzling light, turned his head on the pillow. His eyes stared at

Belfast, appealing and impudent. 'I am rather weak from
lying-up so long,' he said, distinctly. Belfast nodded.
'Getting quite well now,' insisted Wait. – 'Yes. I noticed
you getting better this ... last month,' said Belfast, looking
down. 'Hallo! What's this?' he shouted and ran out.

He was flattened directly against the side of the house by
two men who lurched against him. A lot of disputes
seemed to be going on all round. He got clear and saw
three indistinct figures standing alone in the fainter darkness under the arched foot of the mainsail, that rose above
their heads like a convex wall of a high edifice. Donkin
hissed: 'Go for them ... it's dark!' The crowd took a short
run aft in a body – then there was a check. Donkin, agile
and thin, flitted past with his right arm going like a wind-
mill – and then stood still suddenly with his arm pointing
rigidly above his head. The hurtling flight of some heavy
object was heard; it passed between the heads of the two
mates, bounded heavily along the deck, struck the after
hatch with a ponderous and deadened blow. The bulky
shape of Mr Baker grew distinct. 'Come to your senses,
men!' he cried, advancing at the arrested crowd. 'Come
back, Mr Baker!' called the master's quiet voice. He obeyed
unwillingly. There was a minute of silence, then a deafening hubbub arose. Above it Archie was heard energetic-
ally: 'If ye do oot ageen I wull tell!' There were shouts.
'Don't!' 'Drop it!' – 'We ain't that kind!' The black cluster of
human forms reeled against the bulwark, back again
towards the house. Ringbolts rang under stumbling feet.
– 'Drop it!' 'Let me!' – 'No!' – 'Curse you ... hah!' Then
sounds as of some one's face being slapped; a piece of iron
fell on the deck; a short scuffle, and some one's shadowy
body scuttled rapidly across the main hatch before the
shadow of a kick. A raging voice sobbed out a torrent of
filthy language ... – 'Throwing things – good God!'
grunted Mr Baker in dismay. – 'That was meant for me,'
said the master, quietly; 'I felt the wind of that thing; what
was it – an iron belaying-pin?' – 'By Jove!' muttered Mr

Creighton. The confused voices of men talking amidships mingled with the wash of the sea, ascended between the silent and distended sails – seemed to flow away into the night, further than the horizon, higher than the sky. The stars burned steadily over the inclined mastheads. Trails of light lay on the water, broke before the advancing hull, and, after she had passed, trembled for a long time as if in awe of the murmuring sea.

Meantime the helmsman, anxious to know what the row was about, had let go the wheel, and, bent double, ran with long, stealthy footsteps to the break of the poop. The 'Narcissus,' left to herself, came up gently to the wind without any one being aware of it. She gave a slight roll, and the sleeping sails woke suddenly, coming all together with a mighty flap against the masts, then filled again one after another in a quick succession of loud reports that ran down the lofty spars, till the collapsed mainsail flew out last with a violent jerk. The ship trembled from trucks to keel; the sails kept on rattling like a discharge of musketry; the chain sheets and loose shackles jingled aloft in a thin peal; the gin blocks groaned. It was as if an invisible hand had given the ship an angry shake to recall the men that peopled her decks to the sense of reality, vigilance, and duty. – 'Helm up!' cried the master, sharply. 'Run aft, Mr Creighton, and see what that fool there is up to.' – 'Flatten in the head sheets. Stand by the weather fore-braces,' growled Mr Baker. Startled men ran swiftly repeating the orders. The watch below, abandoned all at once by the watch on deck, drifted towards the forecastle in twos and threes, arguing noisily as they went – 'We shall see to-morrow!' cried a loud voice, as if to cover with a menacing hint an inglorious retreat. And then only orders were heard, the falling of heavy coils of rope, the rattling of blocks. Singleton's white head flitted here and there in the night, high above the deck, like the ghost of a bird. – 'Going off, sir!' shouted Mr Creighton from aft. – 'Full again.' – 'All right...' – 'Ease off the head sheets. That will

do the braces. Coil the ropes up,' grunted Mr Baker, bustling about.

Gradually the tramping noises, the confused sound of
voices, died out, and the officers, coming together on the
poop, discussed the events. Mr Baker was bewildered and
grunted; Mr Creighton was calmly furious; but Captain
Allistoun was composed and thoughtful. He listened to Mr
Baker's growling argumentation, to Creighton's interjected
and severe remarks, while looking down on the deck he
weighed in his hand the iron belaying-pin – that a moment
ago had just missed his head – as if it had been the only
tangible fact of the whole transaction. He was one of those
commanders who speak little, seem to hear nothing, look at
no one – and know everything, hear every whisper, see
every fleeting shadow of their ship's life. His two big
officers towered above his lean, short figure; they talked
over his head; they were dismayed, surprised, and angry,
while between them the little quiet man seemed to have
found his taciturn serenity in the profound depths of a
larger experience. Lights were burning in the forecastle;
now and then a loud gust of babbling chatter came from
forward, swept over the decks, and became faint, as if the
unconscious ship, gliding gently through the great peace of
the sea, had left behind and for ever the foolish noise of
turbulent mankind. But it was renewed again and again.
Gesticulating arms, profiles of heads with open mouths
appeared for a moment in the illuminated squares of doorways; black fists darted – withdrew... 'Yes. It was most
damnable to have such an unprovoked row sprung on one,'
assented the master.... A tumult of yells rose in the light,
abruptly ceased.... He didn't think there would be any
further trouble just then.... A bell was struck aft, another,
forward, answered in a deeper tone, and the clamour of
ringing metal spread round the ship in a circle of wide
vibrations that ebbed away into the immeasurable night
of an empty sea.... Didn't he know them! Didn't he! In
past years. Better men, too. Real men to stand by one in a

tight place. Worse than devils too sometimes – downright, horned devils. Pah! This – nothing. A miss as good as a mile.... The wheel was being relieved in the usual way. – 'Full and by,' said, very loud, the man going off. – 'Full and by,' repeated the other, catching hold of the spokes. – 'This head wind is my trouble,' exclaimed the master, stamping his foot in sudden anger; 'head wind! all the rest is nothing.' He was calm again in a moment. 'Keep them on the move to-night, gentlemen; just to let them feel we've got hold all the time – quietly, you know. Mind you keep your hands off them, Creighton. To-morrow I will talk to them like a Dutch Uncle. A crazy crowd of tinkers! Yes, tinkers! I could count the real sailors amongst them on the fingers of one hand. Nothing will do but a row – if – you – please.' He paused. 'Did you think I had gone wrong there, Mr Baker?' He tapped his forehead, laughed short. 'When I saw him standing there, three parts dead and so scared – black amongst that gaping lot – no grit to face what's coming to us all – the notion came to me all at once, before I could think. Sorry for him – like you would be for a sick brute. If ever creature was in a mortal funk to die!... I thought I would let him go out in his own way. Kind of impulse. It never came into my head, those fools.... H'm! Stand to it now – of course.' He stuck the belaying-pin in his pocket, seemed ashamed of himself, then sharply: 'If you see Podmore at his tricks again tell him I will have him put under the pump. Had to do it once before. The fellow breaks out like that now and then. Good cook tho'.' He walked away quickly, came back to the companion. The two mates followed him through the starlight with amazed eyes. He went down three steps, and changing his tone, spoke with his head near the deck: 'I shan't turn in to-night, in case of anything; just call out if ... Did you see the eyes of that sick nigger, Mr Baker? I fancied he begged me for something. What? Past all help. One lone black beggar amongst the lot of us, and he seemed to look through me into the very hell. Fancy, this wretched Podmore! Well, let him die in peace. I am master here after all. Let him be. He might have been half a man once . . . Keep a good look-out.' He disappeared down below, leaving his mates facing one another, and more impressed than if they had seen a stone image shed a miraculous tear of compassion over the incertitudes of life and death. . . .

In the blue mist spreading from twisted threads that stood upright in the bowls of pipes, the forecastle appeared as vast as a hall. Between the beams a heavy cloud stagnated; and the lamps surrounded by halos burned each at the core of a purple glow in two lifeless flames without rays. Wreaths drifted in denser wisps. Men sprawled about on the deck, sat in negligent poses, or, bending a knee, drooped with one shoulder against a bulkhead. Lips moved, eyes flashed, waving arms made sudden eddies in the smoke. The murmur of voices seemed to pile itself higher and higher as if unable to run out quick enough through the narrow doors. The watch below in their shirts, and striding on long white legs, resembled raving somnambulists; while now and then one of the watch on deck would rush in, looking strangely over-dressed, listen a moment, fling a rapid sentence into the noise and run out again; but a few remained near the door, fascinated, and with one ear turned to the deck. 'Stick together, boys,' roared Davis. Belfast tried to make himself heard. Knowles grinned in a slow, dazed way. A short fellow with a thick clipped beard kept on yelling periodically: 'Who's afeard? Who's afeard?' Another one jumped up, excited, with blazing eyes, sent out a string of unattached curses and sat down quietly. Two men discussed familiarly, striking one another's breast in turn, to clinch arguments. Three others, with their heads in a bunch, spoke all together with a confidential air, and at the top of their voices. It was a stormy chaos of speech where intelligible fragments tossing, struck the ear. One could hear: 'In the last ship' – 'Who cares? Try it on any one of us if——.' 'Knock under' – 'Not a hand's turn' – 'He says he is all right' – 'I always thought' – 'Never mind. . . .'

Donkin, crouching all in a heap against the bowsprit, hunched his shoulderblades as high as his ears, and hanging a peaked nose, resembled a sick vulture with ruffled plumes. Belfast, straddling his legs, had a face red with yelling, and with arms thrown up, figured a Maltese cross. The two Scandinavians, in a corner, had the dumbfounded and distracted aspect of men gazing at a cataclysm. And, beyond the light, Singleton stood in the smoke, monumental, indistinct, with his head touching the beam; like a statue of heroic size in the gloom of a crypt.

He stepped forward, impassive and big. The noise subsided like a broken wave: but Belfast cried once more with uplifted arms: 'The man is dying I tell ye!' then sat down suddenly on the hatch and took his head between his hands. All looked at Singleton, gazing upwards from the deck, staring out of dark corners, or turning their heads with curious glances. They were expectant and appeased as if that old man, who looked at no one, had possessed the secret of their uneasy indignations and desires, a sharper vision, a clearer knowledge. And indeed standing there amongst them, he had the uninterested appearance of one who had seen multitudes of ships, had listened many times to voices such as theirs, had already seen all that could happen on the wide seas. They heard his voice rumble in his broad chest as though the words had been rolling towards them out of a rugged past. 'What do you want to do?' he asked. No one answered. Only Knowles muttered – 'Aye, aye,' and somebody said low: 'It's a bloomin' shame.' He waited, made a contemptuous gesture. – 'I have seen rows aboard ship before some of you were born,' he said, slowly, 'for something or nothing; but never for such a thing.' – 'The man is dying, I tell ye,' repeated Belfast, woefully, sitting at Singleton's feet. – 'And a black fellow, too,' went on the old seaman, 'I have seen them die like flies.' He stopped, thoughtful, as if trying to recollect gruesome things, details of horrors, hecatombs of niggers. They looked at him fascinated. He was old enough to remember slavers, bloody

mutinies, pirates perhaps; who could tell through what
violences and terrors he had lived! What would he say?
He said: 'You can't help him; die he must.' He made another
pause. His moustache and beard stirred. He chewed words,
mumbled behind tangled white hairs; incomprehensible
and exciting, like an oracle behind a veil.... – 'Stop
ashore——sick.——Instead——bringing all this head
wind. Afraid. The sea will have her own.——Die in sight
of land. Always so. They know it——long passage——
more days, more dollars.——You keep quiet.——What
do you want? Can't help him.' He seemed to wake up from
a dream. 'You can't help yourselves,' he said, austerely,
'Skipper's no fool. He has something in his mind. Look
out – I say! I know 'em!' With eyes fixed in front he turned
his head from right to left, from left to right, as if inspecting
a long row of astute skippers. – "Ee said 'ee would brain me!'
cried Donkin in a heartrending tone. Singleton peered
downwards with puzzled attention, as though he couldn't
find him. – 'Damn you!' he said, vaguely, giving it up. He
radiated unspeakable wisdom, hard unconcern, the chilling
air of resignation. Round him all the listeners felt themselves
somehow completely enlightened by their disappointment,
and mute, they lolled about with the careless ease of men
who can discern perfectly the irremediable aspect of their
existence. He, profound and unconscious, waved his arm
once, and strode out on deck without another word.

Belfast was lost in a round-eyed meditation. One or two
vaulted heavily into upper berths, and, once there, sighed;
others dived head first inside lower bunks – swift, and
turning round instantly upon themselves, like animals
going into lairs. The grating of a knife scraping burnt clay
was heard. Knowles grinned no more. Davies said, in a tone
of ardent conviction: 'Then our skipper's looney.' Archie
muttered: 'My faith! we haven't heard the last of it yet!'
Four bells were struck. – 'Half our watch below gone!' cried
Knowles in alarm, then reflected. 'Well, two hours' sleep is
something towards a rest,' he observed, consolingly. Some

already pretended to slumber; and Charley, sound asleep, suddenly said a few slurred words in an arbitrary, blank voice. – 'This blamed boy has worrums!' commented Knowles from under a blanket, in a learned manner. Belfast got up and approached Archie's berth. – 'We pulled him out,' he whispered, sadly. – 'What?' said the other, with sleepy discontent. – 'And now we will have to chuck him overboard,' went on Belfast, whose lower lip trembled. – 'Chuck what?' asked Archie. – 'Poor Jimmy,' breathed out Belfast. – 'He be blowed!' said Archie with untruthful brutality, and sat up in his bunk; 'It's all through him. If it hadn't been for me, there would have been murder on board this ship!' – ''Tain't his fault, is it?' argued Belfast, in a murmur; 'I've put him to bed... an' he ain't no heavier than an empty beef-cask,' he added, with tears in his eyes. Archie looked at him steadily, then turned his nose to the ship's side with determination. Belfast wandered about as though he had lost his way in the dim forecastle, and nearly fell over Donkin. He contemplated him from on high for a while. 'Ain't ye going to turn in?' he asked. Donkin looked up hopelessly. – 'That black'earted Scotch son of a thief kicked me!' he whispered from the floor, in a tone of utter desolation. – 'And a good job, too!' said Belfast, still very depressed; 'You were as near hanging as damn-it to-night, sonny. Don't you play any of your murthering games around my Jimmy! You haven't pulled him out. You just mind! 'Cos if I start to kick you' – he brightened up a bit – 'if I start to kick you, it will be Yankee fashion – to break something!' He tapped lightly with his knuckles the top of the bowed head. 'You moind that, my bhoy!' he concluded, cheerily. Donkin let it pass. – 'Will they split on me?' he asked, with pained anxiety. – 'Who – split?' hissed Belfast, coming back a step. 'I would split your nose this minyt if I hadn't Jimmy to look after! Who d'ye think we are?' Donkin rose and watched Belfast's back lurch through the doorway. On all sides invisible men slept, breathing calmly. He seemed to draw courage and fury from the peace around him. Venomous and thin-faced, he glared from the ample misfit of borrowed clothes as if looking for something he could smash. His heart leaped wildly in his narrow chest. They slept! He wanted to wring necks, gouge eyes, spit on faces. He shook a dirty pair of meagre fists at the smoking lights. 'Ye're no men!' he cried, in a deadened tone. No one moved. 'Yer 'aven't the pluck of a mouse!' His voice rose to a husky screech. Wamibo darted out a dishevelled head, and looked at him wildly. 'Ye're sweepings ov ships! I 'ope you will all rot before you die!' Wamibo blinked, uncomprehending but interested. Donkin sat down heavily; he blew with force through quivering nostrils, he ground and snapped his teeth, and, with the chin pressed hard against the breast, he seemed busy gnawing his way through it, as if to get at the heart within. . . .

In the morning the ship, beginning another day of her wandering life, had an aspect of sumptuous freshness, like the spring-time of the earth. The washed decks glistened in a long clear stretch; the oblique sunlight struck the yellow brasses in dazzling splashes, darted over the polished rods in lines of gold, and the single drops of salt water forgotten here and there along the rail were as limpid as drops of dew, and sparkled more than scattered diamonds. The sails slept, hushed by a gentle breeze. The sun, rising lonely and splendid in the blue sky, saw a solitary ship gliding close-hauled on the blue sea.

The men pressed three deep abreast of the mainmast and opposite the cabin-door. They shuffled, pushed, had an irresolute mien and stolid faces. At every slight movement, Knowles lurched heavily on his short leg. Donkin glided behind backs, restless and anxious, like a man looking for an ambush. Captain Allistoun came out on the quarter-deck suddenly. He walked to and fro before the front. He was grey, slight, alert, shabby in the sunshine, and as hard as adamant. He had his right hand in the side-pocket of his jacket, and also something heavy in there that made folds all down that side. One of the seamen cleared his throat ominously. – 'I haven't till now found fault with you men,' said the master, stopping short. He faced them with his worn, steely gaze, that by a universal illusion looked straight into every individual pair of the twenty pairs of eyes before his face. At his back Mr Baker, gloomy and bull-necked, grunted low; Mr Creighton, fresh as paint, had rosy cheeks and a ready, resolute bearing. 'And I don't now,' continued the master; 'but I am here to drive this ship and keep every man-jack aboard of her up to the mark. If you knew your work as well as I do mine, there would be no trouble. You've been braying in the dark about "See to-morrow morning!" Well, you see me now. What do you want?' He waited, stepping quickly to and fro, giving them searching glances. What did they want? They shifted from foot to foot, they balanced their bodies; some, pushing back their caps, scratched their heads. What did they want? Jimmy was forgotten; no one thought of him, alone forward in his cabin, fighting great shadows, clinging to brazen lies, chuckling painfully over his transparent deceptions. No, not Jimmy; he was more forgotten than if he had been dead. They wanted great things. And suddenly all the simple words they knew seemed to be lost for ever in the immensity of their vague and burning desire. They knew what they wanted, but they could not find anything worth saying. They stirred on one spot, swinging, at the end of muscular arms, big tarry hands with crooked fingers. A murmur died out. – 'What is it – food?' asked the master, 'you know the stores have been spoiled off the Cape.' – 'We know that, sir,' said a bearded shellback in the front rank. – 'Work too hard – eh? Too much for your strength?' he asked again. There was an offended silence. – 'We don't want to go shorthanded, sir,' began at last Davies in a wavering voice, 'and this 'ere black – ...' – 'Enough!' cried the master. He stood scanning them for a moment, then walking a few steps this way and that began to storm at them coldly, in gusts violent and cutting like the gales of

those icy seas that had known his youth. – 'Tell you what's
the matter? Too big for your boots. Think yourselves damn
good men. Know half your work. Do half your duty. Think
it too much. If you did ten times as much it wouldn't be
enough.' – 'We did our best by her, sir,' cried some one with
shaky exasperation. – 'Your best,' stormed on the master:
'You hear a lot on shore, don't you? They don't tell you there
your best isn't much to boast of. I tell you – your best is no
better than bad. You can do no more? No, I know, and say
nothing. But you stop your caper or I will stop it for you. I
am ready for you! Stop it!' He shook a finger at the crowd.
'As to that man,' he raised his voice very much; 'as to that
man, if he puts his nose out on deck without my leave I will
clap him in irons. There!' The cook heard him forward, ran
out of the galley lifting his arms, horrified, unbelieving,
amazed, and ran in again. There was a moment of profound silence during which a bow-legged seaman, stepping
aside, expectorated decorously into the scupper. 'There is
another thing,' said the master, calmly. He made a quick
stride and with a swing took an iron belaying-pin out of his
pocket. 'This!' His movement was so unexpected and sudden that the crowd stepped back. He gazed fixedly at their
faces, and some at once put on a surprised air as though
they had never seen a belaying-pin before. He held it up.
'This is my affair. I don't ask you any questions, but you all
know it; it has got to go where it came from.' His eyes
became angry. The crowd stirred uneasily. They looked
away from the piece of iron, they appeared shy, they were
embarrassed and shocked as though it had been something
horrid, scandalous, or indelicate, that in common decency
should not have been flourished like this in broad daylight.
The master watched them attentively. 'Donkin,' he called
out in a short, sharp tone.

Donkin dodged behind one, then behind another, but
they looked over their shoulders and moved aside. The
ranks kept on opening before him, closing behind, till at
last he appeared alone before the master as though he had

come up through the deck. Captain Allistoun moved close to him. They were much of a size, and at short range the master exchanged a deadly glance with the beady eyes. They wavered. – 'You know this,' asked the master. – 'No, I don't,' answered the other with cheeky trepidation. – 'You are a cur. Take it,' ordered the master. Donkin's arms seemed glued to his thighs; he stood, eyes front, as if drawn on parade. 'Take it,' repeated the master, and stepped closer; they breathed on one another. 'Take it,' said Captain Allistoun again, making a menacing gesture. Donkin tore away one arm from his side. – 'Vy are yer down on me?' he mumbled with effort and as if his mouth had been full of dough. – 'If you don't ...' began the master. Donkin snatched at the pin as though his intention had been to run away with it, and remained stock still holding it like a candle. 'Put it back where you took it from,' said Captain Allistoun, looking at him fiercely. Donkin stepped back opening wide eyes. 'Go, you blackguard, or I will make you,' cried the master, driving him slowly backwards by a menacing advance. He dodged, and with the danger-ous iron tried to guard his head from a threatening fist. Mr Baker ceased grunting for a moment. – 'Good! By Jove,' murmured appreciatively Mr Creighton in the tone of a connoisseur. – 'Don't tech me,' snarled Donkin, backing away. – 'Then go. Go faster.' – 'Don't yer 'it me. ... I will pull yer up afore the magistryt. ... I'll show yer up.' Captain Allistoun made a long stride, and Donkin, turning his back fairly, ran off a little, then stopped and over his shoulder showed yellow teeth. – 'Further on, fore-rigging,' urged the master, pointing with his arm. – 'Are yer goin' to stand by and see me bullied,' screamed Donkin at the silent crowd that watched him. Captain Allistoun walked at him smartly. He started off again with a leap, dashed at the fore-rigging, rammed the pin into its hole violently. 'I'll be even with yer yet,' he screamed at the ship at large and vanished beyond the foremast. Captain Allistoun spun round and walked back aft with a composed face, as though he had already forgotten the scene. Men moved out of his way. He looked at no one. – 'That will do, Mr Baker. Send the watch below,' he said, quietly. 'And you men try to walk straight for the future,' he added in a calm voice. He looked pensively for a while at the backs of the impressed and retreating crowd. 'Breakfast, steward,' he called in a tone of relief through the cabin door. – 'I didn't like to see you – Ough! – give that pin to that chap, sir,' observed Mr Baker; 'he could have bust – Ough! – bust your head like an eggshell with it.' – 'O! he!' muttered the master, absently. 'Queer lot,' he went on in a low voice. 'I suppose it's all right now. Can never tell tho', nowadays, with such a ... Years ago; I was a young master then – one China voyage I had a mutiny; real mutiny, Baker. Different men tho'. I knew what they wanted; they wanted to broach the cargo and get at the liquor. Very simple. ... We knocked them about for two days, and when they had enough – gentle as lambs. Good crew. And a smart trip I made.' He glanced aloft at the yards braced sharp up. 'Head wind day after day,' he exclaimed, bitterly. 'Shall we never get a decent slant this passage?' – 'Ready, sir,' said the steward, appearing before them as if by magic and with a stained napkin in his hand. – 'Ah! All right. Come along, Mr Baker – it's late – with all this nonsense.'

V

A HEAVY atmosphere of oppressive quietude pervaded the ship. In the afternoon men went about washing clothes and hanging them out to dry in the unprosperous breeze with the meditative languor of disenchanted philosophers. Very little was said. The problem of life seemed too voluminous for the narrow limits of human speech, and by common consent it was abandoned to the great sea that had from the beginning enfolded it in its immense grip; to the sea that knew all, and would in time infallibly unveil to each the wisdom hidden in all the errors, the certitude that lurks in doubts, the realm of safety and peace beyond the frontiers of sorrow and fear. And in the confused current of impotent thoughts that set unceasingly this way and that through bodies of men, Jimmy bobbed up upon the surface, compelling attention, like a black buoy chained to the bottom of a muddy stream. Falsehood triumphed. It triumphed through doubt, through stupidity, through pity, through sentimentalism. We set ourselves to bolster it up, from compassion, from recklessness, from a sense of fun. Jimmy's steadfastness to his untruthful attitude in the face of the inevitable truth had the proportions of a colossal enigma – of a manifestation grand and incomprehensible that at times inspired a wondering awe; and there was also, to many, something exquisitely droll in fooling him thus to the top of his bent. The latent egoism of tenderness to suffering appeared in the developing anxiety not to see him die. His obstinate non-recognition of the only certitude whose approach we could watch from day to day was as disquieting as the failure of some law of nature. He was so utterly wrong about himself that one could not but suspect him of having access to some source of supernatural knowledge. He was absurd to the point of inspiration. He was unique, and as fascinating as only something inhuman could be; he seemed to shout his denials already from beyond the awful border. He was becoming immaterial like an apparition; his cheekbones rose, the forehead slanted more; the face was all hollows, patches of shade; and the fleshless head resembled a disinterred black skull, fitted with two restless globes of silver in the sockets of eyes. He was demoralizing. Through him we were becoming highly humanized, tender, complex, excessively decadent: we understood the subtlety of his fear, sympathized with all his repulsions, shrinkings, evasions, delusions – as though we had been overcivilized, and rotten, and without any knowledge of the meaning of life. We had the air of being initiated in some infamous mysteries; we had the profound grimaces of conspirators, exchanged meaning glances, significant short words. We were inexpressibly vile and very much pleased with ourselves. We lied to him with gravity, with emotion, with unction, as if performing some moral trick with a view to an eternal reward. We made a chorus of affirmation to his wildest assertions, as though he had been a millionaire, a politician, or a reformer – and we a crowd of ambitious lubbers. When we ventured to question his statements we did it after the manner of obsequious sycophants, to the end that his glory should be augmented by the flattery of our dissent. He influenced the moral tone of our world as though he had it in his power to distribute honours, treasures, or pain; and he could give us nothing but his contempt. It was immense; it seemed to grow gradually larger, as his body day by day shrank a little more, while we looked. It was the only thing about him – of him – that gave the impression of durability and vigour. It lived within him with an unquenchable life. It spoke through the eternal pout of his black lips; it looked at us through the impertinent mournfulness of his languid and enormous stare. We watched him intently. He seemed unwilling to move, as if distrustful of his own solidity. The slightest gesture must have disclosed to him (it could not surely be otherwise) his bodily weakness, and caused a pang of mental suffering. He was chary of movements. He lay stretched out, chin on blanket, in a kind of sly, cautious immobility. Only his eyes roamed over faces: his eyes disdainful, penetrating and sad.

It was at that time that Belfast's devotion – and also his pugnacity – secured universal respect. He spent every moment of his spare time in Jimmy's cabin. He tended him, talked to him; was as gentle as a woman, as tenderly gay as an old philanthropist, as sentimentally careful of his nigger as a model slave-owner. But outside he was irritable, explosive as gunpowder, sombre, suspicious, and never more brutal than when most sorrowful. With him it was a tear and a blow: a tear for Jimmy, a blow for any one who did not seem to take a scrupulously orthodox view of Jimmy's case. We talked about nothing else. The two Scandinavians, even, discussed the situation – but it was impossible to know in what spirit, because they quarrelled in their own language. Belfast suspected one of them of irreverence, and in this incertitude thought that there was no option but to fight them both. They became very much terrified by his truculence, and henceforth lived amongst us, dejected, like a pair of mutes. Wamibo never spoke intelligibly, but he was as smileless as an animal – seemed to know much less about it all than the cat – and consequently was safe. Moreover, he had belonged to the chosen band of Jimmy's rescuers, and was above suspicion. Archie was silent generally, but often spent an hour or so talking to Jimmy quietly with an air of proprietorship. At any time of the day and often through the night some man could be seen sitting on Jimmy's box. In the evening, between six and eight, the cabin was crowded, and there was an interested group at the door. Every one stared at the nigger.

He basked in the warmth of our interest. His eyes gleamed ironically, and in a weak voice he reproached us with our cowardice. He would say, 'If you fellows had stuck out for me I would be now on deck.' We hung our heads. 'Yes, but if you think I am going to let them put me in irons just to show you sport. . . . Well, no. . . . It ruins my health, this lying-up, it does. You don't care.' We were as abashed as if it had been true. His superb impudence carried all before it. We would not have dared to revolt. We didn't want to, really. We wanted to keep him alive till home – to the end of the voyage.

Singleton as usual held aloof, appearing to scorn the insignificant events of an ended life. Once only he came along, and unexpectedly stopped in the doorway. He peered at Jimmy in profound silence, as if desirous to add that black image to the crowd of Shades that peopled his old memory. We kept very quiet, and for a long time Singleton stood there as though he had come by appointment to call for some one, or to see some important event.

James Wait lay perfectly still, and apparently not aware of the gaze scrutinizing him with a steadiness full of expectation. There was a sense of a contest in the air. We felt the inward strain of men watching a wrestling bout. At last Jimmy with perceptible apprehension turned his head on the pillow. – 'Good evening,' he said in a conciliating tone. – 'H'm,' answered the old seaman, grumpily. For a moment longer he looked at Jimmy with severe fixity, then suddenly went away. It was a long time before any one spoke in the little cabin, though we all breathed more freely as men do after an escape from some dangerous situation. We all knew the old man's ideas about Jimmy, and nobody dared to combat them. They were unsettling, they caused pain; and, what was worse, they might have been true for all we knew. Only once did he condescend to explain them fully, but the impression was lasting. He said that Jimmy was the cause of head winds. Mortally sick men – he maintained – linger till the first sight of land, and then die; and Jimmy knew that the very first land would draw his life from him. It is so in every ship. Didn't we know it? He asked us with austere contempt: what did we know? What would we doubt next? Jimmy's desire encouraged by us and aided by Wamibo's (he was a Finn – wasn't he? Very well!) by Wamibo's spells delayed the ship in the open sea. Only lubberly fools couldn't see it. Whoever heard of such a run of calms and head winds? It wasn't natural.... We could not deny that it was strange. We felt uneasy. The common saying, 'More days, more dollars,' did not give the usual comfort because the stores were running short. Much had been spoiled off the Cape, and we were on half allowance of biscuit. Peas, sugar and tea had been finished long ago. Salt meat was giving out. We had plenty of coffee but very little water to make it with. We took up another hole in our belts and went on scraping, polishing, painting the ship from morning to night. And soon she looked as though she had come out of a band-box; but hunger lived on board of her. Not dead starvation, but steady, living hunger that stalked about the decks, slept in the forecastle; the tormentor of waking moments, the disturber of dreams. We looked to windward for signs of change. Every few hours of night and day we put her round with the hope that she would come up on that tack at last! She didn't. She seemed to have forgotten the way home; she rushed to and fro, heading northwest, heading east; she ran backwards and forwards, distracted, like a timid creature at the foot of a wall. Sometimes, as if tired to death, she would wallow languidly for a day in the smooth swell of an unruffled sea. All up the swinging masts the sails thrashed furiously through the hot stillness of the calm. We were weary, hungry, thirsty; we commenced to believe Singleton, but with unshaken fidelity dissembled to Jimmy. We spoke to him with jocose allusiveness, like cheerful accomplices in a clever plot; but we looked to the westward over the rail with longing eyes for a sign of hope, for a sign of fair wind; even if its first breath should bring death to our reluctant Jimmy. In vain! The universe conspired with James Wait. Light airs from the northward sprang up again; the sky remained clear; and round our weariness the glittering sea, touched by the breeze, basked voluptuously in the great sunshine, as though it had forgotten our life and trouble.

Donkin looked out for a fair wind along with the rest. No one knew the venom of his thoughts now. He was silent, and appeared thinner, as if consumed slowly by an inward rage at the injustice of men and of fate. He was ignored by all and spoke to no one, but his hate for every man dwelt in his furtive eyes. He talked with the cook only, having somehow persuaded the good man that he – Donkin – was a much calumniated and persecuted person. Together they bewailed the immorality of the ship's company. There could be no greater criminals than we, who by our lies conspired to send the unprepared soul of a poor ignorant black man to everlasting perdition. Podmore cooked what there was to cook, remorsefully, and felt all the time that by preparing the food of such sinners he imperilled his own salvation. As to the Captain – he had sailed with him for seven years, now, he said, and would not have believed it possible that such a man... 'Well. Well... There it was... Can't get out of it. Judgment capsized all in a minute... Struck in all his pride... More like a sudden visitation than anything else.' Donkin, perched sullenly on the coal-locker, swung his legs and concurred. He paid in the coin of spurious assent for the privilege to sit in the galley; he was disheartened and scandalized; he agreed with the cook; could find no words severe enough to criticize our conduct; and when in the heat of reprobation he swore at us, Podmore, who would have liked to swear also if it hadn't been for his principles, pretended not to hear. So Donkin, unrebuked, cursed enough for two, cadged for matches, borrowed tobacco, loafed for hours and very much at home before the stove. From there he could hear us on the other side of the bulkhead, talking to Jimmy. The cook knocked the saucepans about, slammed the oven door, muttered prophesies of damnation for all the ship's company; and Donkin, who did not admit of any hereafter (except for purposes of blasphemy) listened, concentrated and angry, gloating fiercely over a called-up image of infinite torment – as men gloat over the accursed images of cruelty and revenge, of greed, and of power....

On clear evenings the silent ship, under the cold sheen of the dead moon, took on a false aspect of passionless repose resembling the winter of the earth. Under her a long band of gold barred the black disc of the sea. Footsteps echoed on her quiet decks. The moonlight clung to her like a frosted mist, and the white sails stood out in dazzling cones as of stainless snow. In the magnificence of the phantom rays the ship appeared pure like a vision of ideal beauty, illusive like a tender dream of serene peace. And nothing in her was real, nothing was distinct and solid but the heavy shadows that filled her decks with their unceasing and noiseless stir: the shadows darker than the night and more restless than the thoughts of men.

Donkin prowled spiteful and alone amongst the shadows, thinking that Jimmy too long delayed to die. That evening land had been reported from aloft, and the master, while adjusting the tubes of the long glass, had observed with quiet bitterness to Mr Baker that, after fighting our way inch by inch to the Western Islands, there was nothing to expect now but a spell of calm. The sky was clear and the barometer high. The light breeze dropped with the sun, and an enormous stillness, forerunner of a night without wind, descended upon the heated waters of the ocean. As long as daylight lasted, the hands collected on the fore-castle-head watched on the eastern sky the island of Flores, that rose above the level expanse of the sea with irregular and broken outlines like a sombre ruin upon a vast and deserted plain. It was the first land seen for nearly four months. Charley was excited, and in the midst of general indulgence took liberties with his betters. Men strangely elated without knowing why, talked in groups, and pointed with bared arms. For the first time that voyage Jimmy's sham existence seemed for a moment forgotten in the face of a solid reality. We had got so far anyhow. Belfast discoursed, quoting imaginary examples of short homeward runs from the Islands. 'Them smart fruit schooners do it in five days,' he affirmed. 'What do you want? – only a good little breeze.' Archie maintained that seven days was the record passage, and they disputed amicably with insulting words. Knowles declared he could already smell home from there, and with a heavy list on his short leg laughed fit to split his sides. A group of grizzled sea-dogs looked out for a time in silence and with grim absorbed faces. One said suddenly – ''Tain't far to London now.' – 'My first night ashore, blamme if I haven't steak and onions for supper... and a pint of bitter,' said another. – 'A barrel ye mean,' shouted someone. – 'Ham an' eggs three times a day. That's the way I live!' cried an excited voice. There was a stir, appreciative murmurs; eyes began to shine; jaws champed; short, nervous laughs were heard. Archie smiled with reserve all to himself. Singleton came up, gave a careless glance, and went down again without saying a word, indifferent, like a man who had seen Flores an incalculable number of times. The night travelling from the East blotted out of the limpid sky the purple stain of the high land. 'Dead calm,' said somebody quietly. The murmur of lively talk suddenly wavered, died out; the clusters broke up; men began to drift away one by one, descending the ladders slowly and with serious faces as if sobered by that reminder of their dependence upon the invisible. And when the big yellow moon ascended gently above the sharp rim of the clear horizon it found the ship wrapped up in a breathless silence; a fearless ship that seemed to sleep profoundly, dreamlessly on the bosom of the sleeping and terrible sea.

Donkin chafed at the peace – at the ship – at the sea that stretching away on all sides merged into the illimitable silence of all creation. He felt himself pulled up sharp by unrecognized grievances. He had been physically cowed, but his injured dignity remained indomitable, and nothing could heal his lacerated feelings. Here was land already – home very soon – a bad pay-day – no clothes – more hard work. How offensive all this was. Land. The land that draws away life from sick sailors. That nigger there had money – clothes – easy times; and would not die. Land draws life away. . . . He felt tempted to go and see whether it did. Perhaps already. . . It would be a bit of luck. There was money in the beggar's chest. He stepped briskly out of the shadows into the moonlight, and, instantly, his craving, hungry face from sallow became livid. He opened the door of the cabin and had a shock. Sure enough, Jimmy was dead! He moved no more than a recumbent figure with clasped hands, carved on the lid of a stone coffin. Donkin glared with avidity. Then Jimmy, without stirring, blinked his eyelids, and Donkin had another shock. Those eyes were rather startling. He shut the door behind his back with gentle care, looking intently the while at James Wait as though he had come in there at a great risk to tell some secret of startling importance. Jimmy did not move but glanced languidly out of the corners of his eyes. – 'Calm?' he asked. – 'Yuss,' said Donkin, very disappointed, and sat down on the box.

Jimmy was used to such visits at all times of night or day. Men succeeded one another. They spoke in clear voices, pronounced cheerful words, repeated old jokes, listened to him; and each, going out, seemed to leave behind a little of his own vitality, surrender some of his own strength, renew the assurance of life – the indestructible thing! He did not like to be alone in his cabin, because, when he was alone, it seemed to him as if he hadn't been there at all. There was nothing. No pain. Not now. Perfectly right – but he couldn't enjoy his healthful repose unless some one was by to see it. This man would do as well as anybody. Donkin watched him stealthily: 'Soon home now,' observed Wait. – 'Vy d'yer whisper?' asked Donkin with interest, 'can't yer speak up?' Jimmy looked annoyed and said nothing for a while; then in a lifeless, unringing voice: 'Why should I shout? You ain't deaf that I know.' – 'Oh! I can 'ear right enough,' answered Donkin in a low tone, and looked down. He was thinking sadly of going out when Jimmy spoke again. – 'Time we did get home ... to get something decent to eat ... I am always hungry.' Donkin felt angry all of a sudden. – 'What about me,' he hissed, 'I am 'ungry too an' got ter work. You, 'ungry!' – 'Your work won't kill you,' commented Wait, feebly; 'there's a couple of biscuits in the lower bunk there – you may have one. I can't eat them.' Donkin dived in, groped in the corner and when he came up again his mouth was full. He munched with ardour. Jimmy seemed to doze with open eyes. Donkin finished his hard bread and got up. – 'You're not going?' asked Jimmy, staring at the ceiling. – 'No,' said Donkin, impulsively, and instead of going out leaned his back against the closed door. He looked at James Wait, and saw him long, lean, dried up, as though all his flesh had shrivelled on his bones in the heat of a white furnace; the meagre fingers of one hand moved lightly upon the edge of the bunk playing an endless tune. To look at him was irritating and fatiguing; he could last like this for days; he was outrageous – belonging wholly neither to death nor life, and perfectly invulnerable in his apparent ignorance of both. Donkin felt tempted to enlighten him. – 'What are yer thinkin' of?' he asked, surlily. James Wait had a grimacing smile that passed over the death-like impassiveness of his bony face, incredible and frightful as would, in a dream, have been the sudden smile of a corpse.

'There is a girl,' whispered Wait.... 'Canton Street girl.——She chucked a third engineer of a Rennie boat——for me. Cooks oysters just as I like...She says——she would chuck——any toff——for a coloured gentleman.... That's me. I am kind to wimmen,' he added a shade louder.

Donkin could hardly believe his ears. He was scandalized. – 'Would she? Yer wouldn't be any good to 'er,' he said with unrestrained disgust. Wait was not there to hear him. He was swaggering up the East India Dock Road; saying kindly, 'Come along for a treat,' pushing glass swing-doors, posing with superb assurance in the gaslight above a mahogany counter. – 'D'yer think yer will ever get ashore?' asked Donkin angrily. Wait came back with a start. 'Ten days,' he said, promptly, and returned at once to the regions of memory that know nothing of time. He felt untired, calm, and safely withdrawn within himself beyond the reach of every grave incertitude. There was something of the immutable quality of eternity in the slow moments of his complete restfulness. He was very quiet and easy amongst his vivid reminiscences which he mistook joyfully for images of an undoubted future. He cared for no one. Donkin felt this vaguely like a blind man feeling in his darkness the fatal antagonism of all the surrounding existences, that to him shall for ever remain irrealizable, unseen and enviable. He had a desire to assert his importance, to break, to crush; to be even with everybody for

everything; to tear the veil, unmask, expose, leave no refuge
– a perfidious desire of truthfulness! He laughed in a
mocking splutter and said:

'Ten days. Strike me blind if I ever! . . . You will be dead
by this time to-morrow p'r'aps. Ten days!' He waited for a
while. 'D'ye 'ear me? Blamme if yer don't look dead already.'

Wait must have been collecting his strength for he said
aloud – 'You're a stinking, cadging liar. Every one knows
you.' And sitting up, against all probability, startled his
visitor horribly. But very soon Donkin recovered himself.
He blustered,

'What? What? Who's a liar? You are – the crowd are –
the skipper – everybody. I ain't! Putting on airs! Who's yer?'
He nearly choked himself with indignation. 'Who's yer to
put on airs,' he repeated, trembling. ''Ave one – 'ave one,
says 'ee – an' cawn't eat 'em 'isself. Now I'll 'ave both. By
Gawd – I will! Yer nobody!'

He plunged into the lower bunk, rooted in there and
brought to light another dusty biscuit. He held it up before
Jimmy – then took a bite defiantly.

'What now?' he asked with feverish impudence. 'Yer
may take one – says yer. Why not giv' me both? No. I'm a
mangy dorg. One fur a mangy dorg. I'll tyke both. Can yer
stop me? Try. Come on. Try.'

Jimmy was clasping his legs and hiding his face on the
knees. His shirt clung to him. Every rib was visible. His
emaciated back was shaken in repeated jerks by the panting
catches of his breath.

'Yer won't? Yer can't! What did I say?' went on Donkin,
fiercely. He swallowed another dry mouthful with a hasty
effort. The other's silent helplessness, his weakness, his
shrinking attitude exasperated him. 'Ye're done!' he cried.
'Who's yer to be lied to; to be waited on 'and an' foot like a
bloomin' ymperor. Yer nobody. Yer no one at all!' he spluttered with such a strength of unerring conviction that it
shook him from head to foot in coming out, and left him
vibrating like a released string.

James Wait rallied again. He lifted his head and turned bravely at Donkin, who saw a strange face, an unknown face, a fantastic and grimacing mask of despair and fury. Its lips moved rapidly; and hollow, moaning, whistling sounds filled the cabin with a vague mutter full of menace, complaint and desolation, like the far-off murmur of a rising wind. Wait shook his head; rolled his eyes; he denied, cursed, threatened – and not a word had the strength to pass beyond the sorrowful pout of those black lips. It was incomprehensible and disturbing; a gibberish of emotions, a frantic dumb show of speech pleading for impossible things, promising a shadowy vengeance. It sobered Donkin into a scrutinizing watchfulness.

'Yer can't oller. See? What did I tell yer?' he said, slowly, after a moment of attentive examination. The other kept on headlong and unheard, nodding passionately, grinning with grotesque and appalling flashes of big white teeth. Donkin, as if fascinated by the dumb eloquence and anger of that black phantom, approached, stretching his neck out with distrustful curiosity; and it seemed to him suddenly that he was looking only at the shadow of a man crouching high in the bunk on the level with his eyes. – 'What? What?' he said. He seemed to catch the shape of some words in the continuous panting hiss. 'Yer will tell Belfast! Will yer? Are yer a bloomin' kid?' He trembled with alarm and rage, 'Tell yer gran'mother! Yer afeard! Who's yer ter be afeard more'n any one?' His passionate sense of his own importance ran away with a last remnant of caution. 'Tell an' be damned! Tell, if yer can!' he cried. 'I've been treated worser'n a dorg by your blooming backlickers. They 'as set me on, only to turn against me. I am the only man 'ere. They clouted me, kicked me – an' yer laffed – yer black, rotten incumbrance, you! You will pay fur it. They giv' yer their grub, their water – yer will pay fur it to me, by Gawd! Who axed me ter 'ave a drink of water? They put their bloomin' rags on yer that night, an' what did they giv' ter me – a clout on the bloomin' mouth – blast their... S'elp me!... Yer will pay for it with yer money. I'm goin' ter 'ave it in a minyte; as soon as ye're dead, yer bloomin' useless fraud. That's the man I am. An' ye're a thing – a bloody thing. Yah – you corpse!'

He flung at Jimmy's head the biscuit he had been all the time clutching hard, but it only grazed, and striking with a loud crack the bulkhead beyond burst like a hand-grenade into flying pieces. James Wait, as if wounded mortally, fell back on the pillow. His lips ceased to move and the rolling eyes became quiet and stared upwards with an intense and steady persistence. Donkin was surprised; he sat suddenly on the chest, and looked down, exhausted and gloomy. After a moment, he began to mutter to himself, 'Die, you beggar – die. Somebody'll come in... I wish I was drunk... Ten days... oysters...' He looked up and spoke louder. 'No... No more for yer... no more bloomin' gals that cook oysters... Who's yer? It's my turn now... I wish I was drunk; I would soon giv' you a leg up. That's where yer bound to go. Feet fust, through a port... Splash! Never see yer any more. Overboard! Good 'nuff fur yer.'

Jimmy's head moved slightly and he turned his eyes to Donkin's face; a gaze unbelieving, desolated and appealing, of a child frightened by the menace of being shut up alone in the dark. Donkin observed him from the chest with hopeful eyes; then, without rising, tried the lid. Locked. 'I wish I was drunk,' he muttered and getting up listened anxiously to the distant sound of footsteps on the deck. They approached – ceased. Some one yawned interminably just outside the door, and the footsteps went away shuffling lazily. Donkin's fluttering heart eased its pace, and when he looked towards the bunk again Jimmy was staring as before at the white beam. – ''Ow d'yer feel now?' he asked. – 'Bad,' breathed out Jimmy.

Donkin sat down patient and purposeful. Every half-hour the bells spoke to one another ringing along the whole length of the ship. Jimmy's respiration was so rapid that it couldn't be counted, so faint that it couldn't be heard. His

eyes were terrified as though he had been looking at
unspeakable horrors; and by his face one could see that he
was thinking of abominable things. Suddenly with an
incredibly strong and heart-breaking voice he sobbed out:

'Overboard! ... I! ... My God!'

Donkin writhed a little on the box. He looked unwillingly. James Wait was mute. His two long bony hands
smoothed the blanket upwards, as though he had wished to
gather it all up under his chin. A tear, a big solitary tear,
escaped from the corner of his eye and, without touching
the hollow cheek, fell on the pillow. His throat rattled
faintly.

And Donkin, watching the end of that hateful nigger,
felt the anguishing grasp of a great sorrow on his heart at
the thought that he himself, some day, would have to go
through it all – just like this – perhaps! His eyes became
moist. 'Poor beggar,' he murmured. The night seemed to
go by in a flash; it seemed to him he could hear the
irremediable rush of precious minutes. How long would
this blooming affair last? Too long surely. No luck. He
could not restrain himself. He got up and approached the
bunk. Wait did not stir. Only his eyes appeared alive and
his hands continued their smoothing movement with a
horrible and tireless industry. Donkin bent over.

'Jimmy,' he called low. There was no answer, but the
rattle stopped. 'D'yer see me?' he asked, trembling. Jimmy's
chest heaved. Donkin, looking away, bent his ear to
Jimmy's lips, and heard a sound like the rustle of a single
dry leaf driven along the smooth sand of a beach. It shaped
itself.

'Light ... the lamp ... and ... go,' breathed out Wait.

Donkin, instinctively, glanced over his shoulder at the
brilliant flame; then, still looking away, felt under the
pillow for a key. He got it at once and for the next few
minutes remained on his knees shakily but swiftly busy
inside the box. When he got up, his face – for the first
time in his life – had a pink flush – perhaps of triumph.

He slipped the key under the pillow again, avoiding to glance at Jimmy, who had not moved. He turned his back squarely from the bunk, and started to the door as though he were going to walk a mile. At his second stride he had his nose against it. He clutched the handle cautiously but at that moment he received the irresistible impression of something happening behind his back. He spun round as though he had been tapped on the shoulder. He was just in time to see Wait's eyes blaze up and go out at once, like two lamps overturned together by a sweeping blow. Something resembling a scarlet thread hung down his chin out of the corner of his lips – and he had ceased to breathe.

Donkin closed the door behind him gently but firmly. Sleeping men, huddled under jackets, made on the lighted deck shapeless dark mounds that had the appearance of neglected graves. Nothing had been done all through the night and he hadn't been missed. He stood motionless and perfectly astounded to find the world outside as he had left it; there was the sea, the ship – sleeping men; and he wondered absurdly at it, as though he had expected to find men dead, familiar things gone for ever: as though, like a wanderer returning after many years, he had expected to see bewildering changes. He shuddered a little in the penetrating freshness of the air, and hugged himself forlornly. The declining moon drooped sadly in the western board as if withered by the cold touch of a pale dawn. The ship slept. And the immortal sea stretched away, immense and hazy, like the image of life, with a glittering surface and lightless depths. Donkin gave it a defiant glance and slunk off noiselessly as if judged and cast out by the august silence of its might.

Jimmy's death, after all, came as a tremendous surprise. We did not know till then how much faith we had put in his delusions. We had taken his chances of life so much at his own valuation that his death, like the death of an old belief, shook the foundations of our society. A common bond was gone; the strong, effective and respectable bond of a

sentimental lie. All that day we mooned at our work, with
suspicious looks and a disabused air. In our hearts we
thought that in the matter of his departure Jimmy had
acted in a perverse and unfriendly manner. He didn't back
us up, as a shipmate should. In going he took away with
himself the gloomy and solemn shadow in which our folly
had posed, with humane satisfaction, as a tender arbiter of
fate. And now we saw it was no such thing. It was just
common foolishness; a silly and ineffectual meddling with
issues of majestic import – that is, if Podmore was right.
Perhaps he was? Doubt survived Jimmy; and, like a community of banded criminals disintegrated by a touch of
grace, we were profoundly scandalized with each other.
Men spoke unkindly to their best chums. Others refused
to speak at all. Singleton only was not surprised. 'Dead – is
he? Of course,' he said, pointing at the island right abeam:
for the calm still held the ship spell-bound within sight of
Flores. Dead – of course. *He* wasn't surprised. Here was the
land, and there, on the forehatch and waiting for the sailmaker – there was that corpse. Cause and effect. And for
the first time that voyage, the old seaman became quite
cheery and garrulous, explaining and illustrating from the
stores of experience how, in sickness, the sight of an island
(even a very small one) is generally more fatal than the view
of a continent. But he couldn't explain why.

Jimmy was to be buried at five, and it was a long day till
then – a day of mental disquiet and even of physical disturbance. We took no interest in our work and, very properly, were rebuked for it. This, in our constant state of
hungry irritation, was exasperating. Donkin worked with
his brow bound in a dirty rag, and looked so ghastly that
Mr Baker was touched with compassion at the sight of this
plucky suffering. – 'Ough! You, Donkin! Put down your
work and go lay-up this watch. You look ill.' – 'I am bad, sir
– in my 'ead,' he said in a subdued voice and vanished
speedily. This annoyed many, and they thought the mate
'bloomin' soft to-day.' Captain Allistoun could be seen on

the poop watching the sky to the south-west, and it soon got to be known about the decks that the barometer had begun to fall in the night, and that a breeze might be expected before long. This, by a subtle association of ideas, led to violent quarrelling as to the exact moment of Jimmy's death. Was it before or after 'that 'ere glass started down'? It was impossible to know, and it caused much contemptuous growling at one another. All of a sudden there was a great tumult forward. Pacific Knowles and good-tempered Davies had come to blows over it. The watch below interfered with spirit, and for ten minutes there was a noisy scrimmage round the hatch, where, in the balancing shade of the sails, Jimmy's body, wrapped up in a white blanket, was watched over by the sorrowful Belfast, who, in his desolation, disdained the fray. When the noise had ceased, and the passions had calmed into surly silence, he stood up at the head of the swathed body, and lifting both arms on high, cried with pained indignation: 'You ought to be ashamed of yourselves!...' We were.

Belfast took his bereavement very hard. He gave proofs of unextinguishable devotion. It was he, and no other man, who would help the sailmaker to prepare what was left of Jimmy for a solemn surrender to the insatiable sea. He arranged the weights carefully at the feet: two holystones, an old anchor-shackle without its pin, some broken links of a worn-out stream cable. He arranged them this way, then that. 'Bless my soul! you aren't afraid he will chafe his heel?' said the sailmaker, who hated the job. He pushed the needle, puffing furiously, with his head in a cloud of tobacco smoke; he turned the flaps over, pulled at the stitches, stretched at the canvas. 'Lift his shoulders.... Pull to you a bit.... So – o – o. Steady.' Belfast obeyed, pulled, lifted, overcome with sorrow, dropping tears on the tarred twine. – 'Don't you drag the canvas too taut over his poor face, Sails,' he entreated, tearfully. – 'What are you fashing yourself for? He will be comfortable enough,' assured the sailmaker, cutting the thread after the last stitch, which came about the middle of Jimmy's forehead. He rolled up the remaining canvas, put away the needles. 'What makes you take on so?' he asked. Belfast looked down at the long package of grey sailcloth. – 'I pulled him out,' he whispered, 'and he did not want to go. If I had sat up with him last night he would have kept alive for me ... but something made me tired.' The sailmaker took vigorous draws at his pipe and mumbled: 'When I ... West India Station ... In the "Blanche" frigate ... Yellow Jack ... sewed in twenty men a week ... Portsmouth-Devonport men ... townies – knew their fathers, mothers, sisters – the whole boiling of 'em. Thought nothing of it. And these niggers like this one – you don't know where it comes from. Got nobody. No use to nobody. Who will miss him?' – 'I do – I pulled him out,' mourned Belfast dismally.

On two planks nailed together and apparently resigned and still under the folds of the Union Jack with a white border, James Wait, carried aft by four men, was deposited slowly, with his feet pointing at an open port. A swell had set in from the westward, and following on the rolling ship, the red ensign, at half-mast, darted out and collapsed again on the grey sky, like a tongue of flickering fire; Charley tolled the bell; and at every swing to starboard the whole vast semicircle of steely waters visible on that side seemed to come up with a rush to the edge of the port, as if impatient to get at our Jimmy. Every one was there but Donkin, who was too ill to come; the Captain and Mr Creighton stood bareheaded on the break of the poop; Mr Baker, directed by the master, who had said to him gravely: 'You know more about the prayer book than I do,' came out of the cabin door quickly and a little embarrassed. All the caps went off. He began to read in a low tone, and with his usual harmlessly menacing utterance, as though he had been for the last time reproving confidentially that dead seaman at his feet. The men listened in scattered groups; they leaned on the fife rail, gazing on the deck;

they held their chins in their hands thoughtfully, or, with crossed arms and one knee slightly bent, hung their heads in an attitude of upright meditation. Wamibo dreamed. Mr Baker read on, grunting reverently at the turn of every page. The words, missing the unsteady hearts of men, rolled out to wander without a home upon the heartless sea; and James Wait, silenced for ever, lay uncritical and passive under the hoarse murmur of despair and hopes.

Two men made ready and waited for those words that send so many of our brothers to their last plunge. Mr Baker began the passage. 'Stand by,' muttered the boatswain. Mr Baker read out: 'To the deep,' and paused. The men lifted the inboard end of the planks, the boatswain snatched off the Union Jack, and James Wait did not move. – 'Higher,' muttered the boatswain angrily. All the heads were raised; every man stirred uneasily, but James Wait gave no sign of going. In death and swathed up for all eternity, he yet seemed to cling to the ship with the grip of an undying fear. 'Higher! Lift!' whispered the boatswain, fiercely. – 'He won't go,' stammered one of the men, shakily, and both appeared ready to drop everything. Mr Baker waited, burying his face in the book, and shuffling his feet nervously. All the men looked profoundly disturbed; from their midst a faint humming noise spread out – growing louder .... 'Jimmy!' cried Belfast in a wailing tone, and there was a second of shuddering dismay.

'Jimmy, be a man!' he shrieked, passionately. Every mouth was wide open, not an eyelid winked. He stared wildly, twitching all over; he bent his body forward like a man peering at a horror. 'Go!' he shouted, and sprang out of the crowd with his arm extended. 'Go, Jimmy! – Jimmy, go! Go!' His fingers touched the head of the body, and the grey package started reluctantly to whizz off the lifted planks all at once, with the suddenness of a flash of lightning. The crowd stepped forward like one man; a deep Ah – h – h! came out vibrating from the broad chests. The ship rolled as if relieved of an unfair burden; the sails flapped. Belfast, supported by Archie, gasped hysterically; and Charley who, anxious to see Jimmy's last dive, leaped headlong on the rail, was too late to see anything but the faint circle of a vanishing ripple.

Mr Baker, perspiring abundantly, read out the last prayer in a deep rumour of excited men and fluttering sails. 'Amen!' he said in an unsteady growl, and closed the book.

'Square the yards!' thundered a voice above his head. All hands gave a jump; one or two dropped their caps; Mr Baker looked up surprised. The master, standing on the break of the poop, pointed to the westward. 'Breeze coming,' he said, 'Man the weather braces.' Mr Baker crammed the book hurriedly into his pocket. – 'Forward, there – let go the foretack!' he hailed joyfully, bareheaded and brisk; 'Square the foreyard, you port-watch!' – 'Fair wind – fair wind,' muttered the men going to the braces. – 'What did I tell you?' mumbled old Singleton, flinging down coil after coil with hasty energy; 'I knowed it – he's gone, and here it comes.'

It came with the sound of a lofty and powerful sigh. The sails filled, the ship gathered way, and the waking sea began to murmur sleepily of home to the ears of men.

That night, while the ship rushed foaming to the northward before a freshening gale, the boatswain unbosomed himself to the petty officers' berth: 'The chap was nothing but trouble,' he said, 'from the moment he came aboard – d'ye remember – that night in Bombay? Been bullying all that softy crowd – cheeked the old man – we had to go fooling all over a half-drowned ship to save him. Dam' nigh a mutiny all for him – and now the mate abused me like a pickpocket for forgetting to dab a lump of grease on them planks. So I did, but you ought to have known better, too, than to leave a nail sticking up, hey, Chips?'

'And you ought to have known better than to chuck all my tools overboard for 'im, like a skeary greenhorn,' retorted the morose carpenter. 'Well – he's gone after 'em now,' he added in an unforgiving tone. 'On the China Station, I remember once, the Admiral he says to me...' began the sailmaker.

A week afterwards the 'Narcissus' entered the chops of the Channel.

Under white wings she skimmed low over the blue sea like a great tired bird speeding to its nest. The clouds raced with her mastheads; they rose astern enormous and white, soared to the zenith, flew past, and, falling down the wide curve of the sky, seemed to dash headlong into the sea – the clouds swifter than the ship, more free, but without a home. The coast to welcome her stepped out of space into the sunshine. The lofty headlands trod masterfully into the sea; the wide bays smiled in the light; the shadows of homeless clouds ran along the sunny plains, leaped over valleys, without a check darted up the hills, rolled down the slopes; and the sunshine pursued them with patches of running brightness. On the brows of dark cliffs white lighthouses shone in pillars of light. The Channel glittered like a blue mantle shot with gold and starred by the silver of the capping seas. The 'Narcissus' rushed past the headlands and the bays. Outward-bound vessels crossed her track, lying over, and with their masts stripped for a slogging fight with the hard sou'wester. And, inshore, a string of smoking steamboats waddled, hugging the coast, like migrating and amphibious monsters, distrustful of the restful waves.

At night the headlands retreated, the bays advanced into one unbroken line of gloom. The lights of the earth mingled with the lights of heaven; and above the tossing lanterns of a trawling fleet a great lighthouse shone steadily, like an enormous riding light burning above a vessel of fabulous dimensions. Below its steady glow, the coast, stretching away straight and black, resembled the high side of an indestructible craft riding motionless upon the immortal and unresting sea. The dark land lay alone in the midst of waters, like a mighty ship bestarred with vigilant lights – a ship carrying the burden of millions of lives – a ship freighted with dross and with jewels, with gold and with steel. She towered up immense and strong, guarding priceless traditions and untold suffering, sheltering glorious memories and base forgetfulness, ignoble virtues and splendid transgressions. A great ship! For ages had the ocean battered in vain her enduring sides; she was there when the world was vaster and darker, when the sea was great and mysterious, and ready to surrender the prize of fame to audacious men. A ship mother of fleets and nations! The great flagship of the race; stronger than the storms! and anchored in the open sea.

The 'Narcissus,' heeling over to off-shore gusts, rounded the South Foreland, passed through the Downs, and, in tow, entered the river. Shorn of the glory of her white wings, she wound obediently after the tug through the maze of invisible channels. As she passed them the red-painted light-vessels, swung at their moorings, seemed for an instant to sail with great speed in the rush of tide, and the next moment were left hopelessly behind. The big buoys on the tails of banks slipped past her sides very low, and, dropping in her wake, tugged at their chains like fierce watch-dogs. The reach narrowed; from both sides the land approached the ship. She went steadily up the river. On the riverside slopes the houses appeared in groups – seemed to stream down the declivities at a run to see her pass, and, checked by the mud of the foreshore, crowded on the banks. Further on, the tall factory chimneys appeared in insolent bands and watched her go by, like a straggling crowd of slim giants, swaggering and upright under the black plummets of smoke, cavalierly aslant. She swept round the bends; an impure breeze shrieked a welcome between her stripped spars; and the land, closing in, stepped between the ship and the sea.

A low cloud hung before her – a great opalescent and tremulous cloud, that seemed to rise from the steaming brows of millions of men. Long drifts of smoky vapours soiled it with livid trails; it throbbed to the beat of millions of hearts, and from it came an immense and lamentable murmur – the murmur of millions of lips praying, cursing, sighing, jeering – the undying murmur of folly, regret, and hope exhaled by the crowds of the anxious earth. The 'Narcissus' entered the cloud; the shadows deepened; on all sides there was the clang of iron, the sound of mighty blows, shrieks, yells. Black barges drifted stealthily on the murky stream. A mad jumble of begrimed walls loomed up vaguely in the smoke, bewildering and mournful, like a vision of disaster. The tugs backed and filled in the stream, to hold the ship steady at the dock-gates; from her bows two lines went through the air whistling, and struck at the land viciously, like a pair of snakes. A bridge broke in two before her, as if by enchantment; big hydraulic capstans began to turn all by themselves, as though animated by a mysterious and unholy spell. She moved through a narrow lane of water between two low walls of granite, and men with check-ropes in their hands kept pace with her, walking on the broad flagstones. A group waited impatiently on each side of the vanished bridge: rough heavy men in caps; sallow-faced men in high hats; two bareheaded women; ragged children, fascinated, and with wide eyes. A cart coming at a jerky trot pulled up sharply. One of the women screamed at the silent ship – 'Hallo, Jack!' without looking at any one in particular, and all hands looked at her from the forecastle head. – 'Stand clear! Stand clear of that rope!' cried the dockmen, bending over stone posts. The crowd murmured, stamped where they stood. – 'Let go your quarter-checks! Let go!' sang out a ruddy-faced old man on the quay. The ropes splashed heavily falling in the water, and the 'Narcissus' entered the dock.

The stony shores ran away right and left in straight lines, enclosing a sombre and rectangular pool. Brick walls rose high above the water – soulless walls, staring through hundreds of windows as troubled and dull as the eyes of over-fed brutes. At their base monstrous iron cranes crouched, with chains hanging from their long necks, balancing cruel-looking hooks over the decks of lifeless ships. A noise of wheels rolling over stones, the thump of heavy things falling, the racket of feverish winches, the grinding of strained chains, floated on the air. Between high buildings the dust of all the continents soared in short flights; and a penetrating smell of perfumes and dirt, of spices and hides, of things costly and of many things filthy, pervaded the space, made for it an atmosphere precious and disgusting. The 'Narcissus' came gently into her berth; the shadows of soulless walls fell upon her, the dust of all the continents leaped upon her deck, and a swarm of strange men, clambering up her sides, took possession of her in the name of the sordid earth. She had ceased to live.

A toff in a black coat and high hat scrambled with agility, came up to the second mate, shook hands, and said: 'Hallo, Herbert.' It was his brother. A lady appeared suddenly. A real lady, in a black dress and with a parasol. She looked extremely elegant in the midst of us, and as strange as if she had fallen there from the sky. Mr Baker touched his cap to her. It was the master's wife. And very soon the Captain, dressed very smartly and in a white shirt, went with her over the side. We didn't recognize him at all till, turning on the quay, he called to Mr Baker: 'Don't forget to wind up the chronometers tomorrow morning.' An underhand lot of seedy-looking chaps with shifty eyes wandered in and out of the forecastle looking for a job, they said. – 'More likely for something to steal,' commented Knowles, cheerfully. Poor beggars. Who cared? Weren't we home! But Mr Baker went for one of them who had given him some cheek, and we were delighted. Everything was delightful. – 'I've finished aft, sir,' called out Mr Creighton. – 'No water in the well, sir,' reported for the last time the carpenter, sounding-rod in hand. Mr Baker glanced along the decks at the expectant group of sailors, glanced aloft at the yards. – 'Ough! That will do, men,' he grunted. The group broke up. The voyage was ended.

Rolled-up beds went flying over the rail; lashed chests went sliding down the gangway – mighty few of both at that. 'The rest is having a cruise off the Cape,' explained Knowles enigmatically to a dock-loafer with whom he had struck a sudden friendship. Men ran, calling to one another, hailing utter strangers to 'lend a hand with the dunnage,' then with sudden decorum approached the mate to shake hands before going ashore. – 'Good-bye, sir,' they repeated in various tones. Mr Baker grasped hard palms, grunted in a friendly manner at every one, his eyes twinkled. – 'Take care of your money, Knowles. Ough! Soon get a nice wife if you do.' The lame man was delighted. – 'Good-bye, sir,' said Belfast, with emotion, wringing the mate's hand, and looked up with swimming eyes. 'I thought I would take 'im ashore with me,' he went on plaintively. Mr Baker did not understand, but said kindly: – 'Take care of yourself, Craik,' and the bereaved Belfast went over the rail, mourning and alone.

Mr Baker, in the sudden peace of the ship, moved about solitary and grunting, trying door-handles, peering into dark places, never done – a model chief mate! No one waited for him ashore. Mother dead; father and two brothers, Yarmouth fisherman, drowned together on the Dogger Bank; sister married and unfriendly. Quite a lady. Married to the leading tailor of a little town, and its leading politician, who did not think his sailor brother-in-law quite respectable enough for him. Quite a lady, quite a lady, he thought, sitting down for a moment's rest on the quarter-hatch. Time enough to go ashore and get a bite and a sup, and a bed somewhere. He didn't like to part with a ship. No one to think about then. The darkness of a misty evening fell, cold and damp, upon the deserted deck; and Mr Baker sat smoking, thinking of all the successive ships to whom, through many long years, he had given the best of a seaman's care. And never a command in sight. Not once! – 'I haven't somehow the cut of a skipper about me,' he meditated, placidly, while the shipkeeper (who had taken possession of the galley), a wizened old man with bleared eyes, cursed him in whispers for 'hanging about so.' – 'Now, Creighton,' he pursued the unenvious train of thought, 'quite a gentleman...swell friends...will get on. Fine young fellow...a little more experience.' He got up and shook himself. 'I'll be back first thing to-morrow morning for the hatches. Don't you let them touch anything before I come, shipkeeper,' he called out. Then, at last, he also went ashore – a model chief mate!

The men scattered by the dissolving contact of the land came together once more in the shipping office. – 'The "Narcissus" pays off,' shouted outside a glazed door a brass-bound old fellow with a crown and the capitals B.T. on his cap. A lot trooped in at once but many were late. The room was large, white-washed, and bare; a counter surmounted by a brass-wire grating fenced off a third of the dusty space, and behind the grating a pasty-faced clerk, with his hair parted in the middle, had the quick, glittering eyes and the vivacious, jerky movements of a caged bird. Poor Captain Allistoun also in there, and sitting before a little table with piles of gold and notes on it, appeared subdued by his captivity. Another Board of Trade bird was perching on a high stool near the door: an old bird that did not mind the chaff of elated sailors. The crew of the 'Narcissus,' broken up into knots, pushed in the corners. They had new shore togs, smart jackets that looked as if they had been shaped with an axe, glossy trousers that seemed made of crumpled sheet-iron, collarless flannel shirts, shiny new boots. They tapped on shoulders, button-holed one another, asked: 'Where did you sleep last night?' whispered gaily, slapped their thighs with bursts of subdued laughter. Most had clean, radiant faces; only one or two turned up dishevelled and sad; the two young Norwegians looked tidy, meek, and altogether of a promising material for the kind ladies who patronize the Scandinavian Home. Wamibo, still in his working clothes, dreamed, upright and burly in the middle of the room, and, when Archie came in, woke up for a smile. But the wide-awake clerk called out a name, and the paying-off business began.

One by one they came up to the pay-table to get the wages of their glorious and obscure toil. They swept the money with care into broad palms, rammed it trustfully into trousers' pockets, or, turning their backs on the table, reckoned with difficulty in the hollow of their stiff hands. – 'Money right? Sign the release. There – there,' repeated the clerk, impatiently. 'How stupid those sailors are!' he thought. Singleton came up, venerable – and uncertain as to daylight; brown drops of tobacco juice hung in his white beard; his hands, that never hesitated in the great light of the open sea, could hardly find the small pile of gold in the profound darkness of the shore. 'Can't write?' said the clerk, shocked. 'Make a mark, then.' Singleton painfully sketched in a heavy cross, blotted the page. 'What a disgusting old brute,' muttered the clerk. Somebody opened the door for him, and the patriarchal seaman passed through unsteadily, without as much as a glance at any of us.

Archie displayed a pocket-book. He was chaffed. Belfast, who looked wild, as though he had already luffed up through a public-house or two, gave signs of emotion and wanted to speak to the Captain privately. The master was surprised. They spoke through the wires, and we could hear the Captain saying: 'I've given it up to the Board of Trade.' 'I should've liked to get something of his,' mumbled Belfast. 'But you can't, my man. It's given up, locked and sealed, to the Marine Office,' expostulated the master; and Belfast stood back, with drooping mouth and troubled eyes. In a pause of the business we heard the master and the clerk talking. We caught: 'James Wait – deceased – found no papers of any kind – no relations – no trace – the Office must hold his wages then.' Donkin entered. He seemed out of breath, was grave, full of business. He went straight to the desk, talked with animation to the clerk, who thought him an intelligent man. They discussed the account, dropping h's against one another as if for a wager – very friendly.

Captain Allistoun paid. 'I give you a bad discharge,' he said, quietly. Donkin raised his voice: – 'I don't want your bloomin' discharge – keep it. I'm goin' ter 'ave a job ashore.' He turned to us. 'No more bloomin' sea fur me,' he said, aloud. All looked at him. He had better clothes, had an easy air, appeared more at home than any of us; he stared with assurance, enjoying the effect of his declaration. 'Yuss. I 'ave friends well off. That's more'n you got. But I am a man. Yer shipmates for all that. Who's comin' fur a drink?'

No one moved. There was a silence; a silence of blank faces and stony looks. He waited a moment, smiled bitterly, and went to the door. There he faced round once more. 'You won't? You bloomin' lot of 'yrpocrits. No? What 'ave I done to yer? Did I bully yer? Did I 'urt yer? Did I? . . . You won't drink? . . . No! . . . Then may ye die of thirst, every mother's son of yer! Not one of yer 'as the sperrit of a bug. Ye're the scum of the world. Work and starve!'

He went out, and slammed the door with such violence that the old Board of Trade bird nearly fell off his perch.

'He's mad,' declared Archie. 'No! No! He's drunk,' insisted Belfast, lurching about, and in a maudlin tone. Captain Allistoun sat smiling thoughtfully at the cleared pay-table.

Outside, on Tower Hill, they blinked, hesitated clumsily, as if blinded by the strange quality of the hazy light, as if discomposed by the view of so many men; and they who could hear one another in the howl of gales seemed deafened and distracted by the dull roar of the busy earth. – 'To the Black Horse! To the Black Horse!' cried some. 'Let us have a drink together before we part.' They crossed the road, clinging to one another. Only Charley and Belfast wandered off alone. As I came up I saw a red-faced, blowsy woman, in a grey shawl, and with dusty, fluffy hair, fall on Charley's neck. It was his mother. She slobbered over him: 'O, my boy! My boy!' – 'Leggo of me,' said Charley, 'Leggo, mother!' I was passing him at the time, and over the untidy head of the blubbering woman he gave me a humorous smile and a glance ironic, courageous, and profound, that seemed to put all my knowledge of life to shame. I nodded and passed on, but heard him say again, good-naturedly: 'If you leggo of me this minyt – ye shall 'ave a bob for a drink out of my pay.' In the next few steps I came upon Belfast. He caught my arm with tremulous enthusiasm. – 'I couldn't go wi''em,' he stammered, indicating by a nod our noisy crowd, that drifted slowly along the side walk. 'When I think of Jimmy... Poor Jim! When I think of him I have no heart for drink. You were his chum, too... but I pulled him out... – didn't I? Short wool he had.... Yes. And I stole the bloom-ing pie.... He wouldn't go.... He wouldn't go for nobody.' He burst into tears. 'I never touched him – never – never!' he sobbed. 'He went for me like... like... a lamb.'

I disengaged myself gently. Belfast's crying fits generally ended in a fight with some one, and I wasn't anxious to stand the brunt of his inconsolable sorrow. Moreover, two bulky policemen stood near by, looking at us with a dis-approving and incorruptible gaze. – 'So long!' I said, and went on my way.

But at the corner I stopped to take my last look at the crew of the 'Narcissus.' They were swaying irresolute and noisy on the broad flagstones before the Mint. They were bound for the Black Horse, where men, in fur caps with brutal faces and in shirt sleeves, dispense out of varnished barrels the illusions of strength, mirth, happiness; the illu-sion of splendour and poetry of life, to the paid-off crews of southern-going ships. From afar I saw them discoursing, with jovial eyes and clumsy gestures, while the sea of life thundered into their ears ceaseless and unheeded. And swaying about there on the white stones, surrounded by the hurry and clamour of men, they appeared to be crea-tures of another kind – lost, alone, forgetful, and doomed; they were like castaways, like reckless and joyous castaways, like mad castaways making merry in the storm and upon an insecure ledge of a treacherous rock. The roar of the town resembled the roar of topping breakers, merciless and strong, with a loud voice and cruel purpose; but overhead the clouds broke; a flood of sunshine streamed down the walls of grimy houses. The dark knot of seamen drifted in sunshine. To the left of them the trees in Tower Gardens sighed, the stones of the Tower gleaming, seemed to stir on the play of light, as if remembering suddenly all the great joys and sorrows of the past, the fighting prototypes of these men; pressgangs; mutinous cries; the wailing of women by the riverside, and the shouts of men welcoming victories. The sunshine of heaven fell like a gift of grace on the mud of the earth, on the remembering and mute stones, on greed, selfishness; on the anxious faces of forgetful men. And to the right of the dark group the stained front of the Mint, cleansed by the flood of light, stood out for a moment dazzling and white like a marble palace in a fairy tale. The crew of the 'Narcissus' drifted out of sight.

I never saw them again. The sea took some, the steamers took others, the graveyards of the earth will account for the rest. Singleton has no doubt taken with him the long record of his faithful work into the peaceful depths of an hospitable sea. And Donkin, who never did a decent day's work in his life, no doubt earns his living by discoursing with filthy eloquence upon the right of labour to live. So be it! Let the earth and the sea each have its own.

A gone shipmate, like any other man, is gone for ever; and I never met one of them again. But at times the spring-flood of memory sets with force up the dark River of the Nine Bends. Then on the waters of the forlorn stream drifts a ship – a shadowy ship manned by a crew of Shades. They pass and make a sign, in a shadowy hail. Haven't we, together and upon the immortal sea, wrung out a meaning from our sinful lives? Good-bye, brothers! You were a good crowd. As good a crowd as ever fisted with wild cries the beating canvas of a heavy foresail; or tossing aloft, invisible in the night, gave back yell for yell to a westerly gale.

TYPHOON

To
R. B. CUNNINGHAME GRAHAM

AUTHOR'S NOTE

I HAD just finished writing *The End of the Tether* and was casting about for some subject which could be developed in a shorter form than the tales in the volume of *Youth* when the instance of a steamship full of returning coolies from Singapore to some port in northern China occurred to my recollection. Years before I had heard it being talked about in the East as a recent occurrence. It was for us merely one subject of conversation amongst many others of the kind. Men earning their bread in any very specialized occupation will talk shop, not only because it is the most vital interest of their lives but also because they have not much knowledge of other subjects. They have never had the time to get acquainted with them. Life, for most of us, is not so much a hard as an exacting taskmaster.

I never met anybody personally concerned in this affair, the interest of which for us was, of course, not the bad weather but the extraordinary complication brought into the ship's life at a moment of exceptional stress by the human element below her deck. Neither was the story itself ever enlarged upon in my hearing. In that company each of us could imagine easily what the whole thing was like. The financial difficulty of it, presenting also a human problem, was solved by a mind much too simple to be perplexed by anything in the world except men's idle talk for which it was not adapted.

From the first the mere anecdote, the mere statement I might say, that such a thing had happened on the high seas, appeared to me a sufficient subject for meditation. Yet it was but a bit of a sea yarn after all. I felt that to bring out its deeper significance which was quite apparent to me, something other, something more was required; a leading motive that would harmonize all these violent noises, and a point of view that would put all that elemental fury into its proper place.

What was needed of course was Captain MacWhirr. Directly I perceived him I could see that he was the man for the situation. I don't mean to say that I ever saw Captain MacWhirr in the flesh, or had ever come in contact with his literal mind and his dauntless temperament. MacWhirr is not an acquaintance of a few hours, or a few weeks, or a few months. He is the product of twenty years of life. My own life. Conscious invention had little to do with him. If it is true that Captain MacWhirr never walked and breathed on this earth (which I find for my part extremely difficult to believe) I can also assure my readers that he is perfectly authentic. I may venture to assert the same of every aspect of the story, while I confess that the particular typhoon of the tale was not a typhoon of my actual experience.

At its first appearance 'Typhoon,' the story, was classed by some critics as a deliberately intended stormpiece. Others picked out MacWhirr, in whom they perceived a definite symbolic intention. Neither was exclusively my intention. Both the typhoon and Captain MacWhirr presented themselves to me as the necessities of the deep conviction with which I approached the subject of the story. It was their opportunity. It was also my opportunity; and it would be vain to discourse about what I made of it in a handful of pages, since the pages themselves are here, between the covers of this volume, to speak for themselves.

1919.   J. C.

TYPHOON

I

CAPTAIN MACWHIRR, of the steamer 'Nan-Shan,' had a physiognomy that, in the order of material appearances, was the exact counterpart of his mind: it presented no marked characteristics of firmness or stupidity; it had no pronounced characteristics whatever; it was simply ordinary, irresponsive, and unruffled.

The only thing his aspect might have been said to suggest, at times, was bashfulness; because he would sit, in business offices ashore, sunburnt and smiling faintly, with downcast eyes. When he raised them, they were perceived to be direct in their glance and of blue colour. His hair was fair and extremely fine, clasping from temple to temple the bald dome of his skull in a clamp as of fluffy silk. The hair of his face, on the contrary, carroty and flaming, resembled a growth of copper wire clipped short to the line of the lip; while, no matter how close he shaved, fiery metallic gleams passed, when he moved his head, over the surface of his cheeks. He was rather below the medium height, a bit round-shouldered, and so sturdy of limb that his clothes always looked a shade too tight for his arms and legs. As if unable to grasp what is due to the difference of latitudes, he wore a brown bowler hat, a complete suit of a brownish hue, and clumsy black boots. These harbour togs gave to his thick figure an air of stiff and uncouth smartness. A thin silver watch-chain looped his waistcoat, and he never left his ship for the shore without clutching in his powerful, hairy fist an elegant umbrella of the very best quality, but generally unrolled. Young Jukes, the chief mate, attending his commander to the gangway, would sometimes venture to say, with the greatest gentleness,

'Allow me, sir' – and possessing himself of the umbrella deferentially, would elevate the ferrule, shake the folds, twirl a neat furl in a jiffy, and hand it back; going through the performance with a face of such portentous gravity, that Mr Solomon Rout, the chief engineer, smoking his morning cigar over the skylight, would turn away his head in order to hide a smile. 'Oh! aye! The blessed gamp.... Thank 'ee, Jukes, thank 'ee,' would mutter Captain MacWhirr, heartily, without looking up.

Having just enough imagination to carry him through each successive day, and no more, he was tranquilly sure of himself; and from the very same cause he was not in the least conceited. It is your imaginative superior who is touchy, overbearing, and difficult to please; but every ship Captain MacWhirr commanded was the floating abode of harmony and peace. It was, in truth, as impossible for him to take a flight of fancy as it would be for a watchmaker to put together a chronometer with nothing except a two-pound hammer and a whip-saw in the way of tools. Yet the uninteresting lives of men so entirely given to the actuality of the bare existence have their mysterious side. It was impossible in Captain MacWhirr's case, for instance, to understand what under heaven could have induced that perfectly satisfactory son of a petty grocer in Belfast to run away to sea. And yet he had done that very thing at the age of fifteen. It was enough, when you thought it over, to give you the idea of an immense, potent, and invisible hand thrust into the ant-heap of the earth, laying hold of shoulders, knocking heads together, and setting the unconscious faces of the multitude towards inconceivable goals and in undreamt-of directions.

His father never really forgave him for this undutiful stupidity. 'We could have got on without him,' he used to say later on, 'but there's the business. And he an only son, too!' His mother wept very much after his disappearance. As it had never occurred to him to leave word behind, he was mourned over for dead till, after eight months, his first letter arrived from Talcahuano. It was short, and contained the statement: 'We had very fine weather on our passage out.' But evidently, in the writer's mind, the only important intelligence was to the effect that his captain had, on the very day of writing, entered him regularly on the ship's articles as Ordinary Seaman. 'Because I can do the work,' he explained. The mother again wept copiously, while the remark, 'Tom's an ass,' expressed the emotions of the father. He was a corpulent man, with a gift for sly chaffing, which to the end of his life he exercised in his intercourse with his son, a little pityingly, as if upon a half-witted person.

MacWhirr's visits to his home were necessarily rare, and in the course of years he despatched other letters to his parents, informing them of his successive promotions and of his movements upon the vast earth. In these missives could be found sentences like this: 'The heat here is very great.' Or: 'On Christmas Day at 4 p.m. we fell in with some icebergs.' The old people ultimately became acquainted with a good many names of ships, and with the names of the skippers who commanded them – with the names of Scots and English shipowners – with the names of seas, oceans, straits, promontories – with out-landish names of lumber-ports, of rice-ports, of cotton-ports – with the names of islands – with the name of their son's young woman. She was called Lucy. It did not suggest itself to him to mention whether he thought the name pretty. And then they died.

The great day of MacWhirr's marriage came in due course, following shortly upon the great day when he got his first command.

All these events had taken place many years before the morning when, in the chart-room of the steamer 'Nan-Shan,' he stood confronted by the fall of a barometer he had no reason to distrust. The fall – taking into account the excellence of the instrument, the time of the year, and the ship's position on the terrestrial globe – was of a nature ominously prophetic; but the red face of the man betrayed no sort of inward disturbance. Omens were as nothing to him, and he was unable to discover the message of a prophecy till the fulfilment had brought it home to his very door. 'That's a fall, and no mistake,' he thought. 'There must be some uncommonly dirty weather knocking about.'

The 'Nan-Shan' was on her way from the southward to the treaty port of Fu-chau, with some cargo in her lower holds, and two hundred Chinese coolies returning to their village homes in the province of Fo-kien, after a few years of work in various tropical colonies. The morning was fine, the oily sea heaved without a sparkle, and there was a queer white misty patch in the sky like a halo of the sun. The fore-deck, packed with Chinamen, was full of sombre clothing, yellow faces, and pigtails, sprinkled over with a good many naked shoulders, for there was no wind, and the heat was close. The coolies lounged, talked, smoked, or stared over the rail; some, drawing water over the side, sluiced each other; a few slept on hatches, while several small parties of six sat on their heels surrounding iron trays with plates of rice and tiny teacups; and every single Celestial of them was carrying with him all he had in the world – a wooden chest with a ringing lock and brass on the corners, containing the savings of his labours: some clothes of ceremony, sticks of incense, a little opium maybe, bits of nameless rubbish of conventional value, and a small hoard of silver dollars, toiled for in coal lighters, won in gambling-houses or in petty trading, grubbed out of earth, sweated out in mines, on railway lines, in deadly jungle, under heavy burdens – amassed patiently, guarded with care, cherished fiercely.

A cross swell had set in from the direction of Formosa Channel about ten o'clock, without disturbing these passengers much, because the 'Nan-Shan,' with her flat bottom, rolling chocks on bilges, and great breadth of beam, had the reputation of an exceptionally steady ship in a seaway. Mr Jukes, in moments of expansion on shore, would proclaim loudly that the 'old girl was as good as she was pretty.' It would never have occurred to Captain MacWhirr to express his favourable opinion so loud or in terms so fanciful.

She was a good ship, undoubtedly, and not old either. She had been built in Dumbarton less than three years before, to the order of a firm of merchants in Siam – Messrs Sigg and Son. When she lay afloat, finished in every detail and ready to take up the work of her life, the builders contemplated her with pride.

'Sigg has asked us for a reliable skipper to take her out,' remarked one of the partners; and the other, after reflecting for a while, said: 'I think MacWhirr is ashore just at present.' 'Is he? Then wire him at once. He's the very man,' declared the senior, without a moment's hesitation.

Next morning MacWhirr stood before them unperturbed, having travelled from London by the midnight express after a sudden but undemonstrative parting with his wife. She was the daughter of a superior couple who had seen better days.

'We had better be going together over the ship, Captain,' said the senior partner; and the three men started to view the perfections of the 'Nan-Shan' from stem to stern, and from her keelson to the trucks of her two stumpy pole-masts.

Captain MacWhirr had begun by taking off his coat, which he hung on the end of a steam windlass embodying all the latest improvements.

'My uncle wrote of you favourably by yesterday's mail to our good friends – Messrs Sigg, you know – and doubtless they'll continue you out there in command,' said the junior partner. 'You'll be able to boast of being in charge of the handiest boat of her size on the coast of China, Captain,' he added.

'Have you? Thank 'ee,' mumbled vaguely MacWhirr, to whom the view of a distant eventuality could appeal no more than the beauty of a wide landscape to a purblind tourist; and his eyes happening at the moment to be at rest upon the lock of the cabin door, he walked up to it, full of purpose, and began to rattle the handle vigorously, while he observed, in his low, earnest voice, 'You can't trust the workmen nowadays. A brand-new lock, and it won't act at all. Stuck fast. See? See?'

As soon as they found themselves alone in their office across the yard: 'You praised that fellow up to Sigg. What is it you see in him?' asked the nephew, with faint contempt.

'I admit he has nothing of your fancy skipper about him, if that's what you mean,' said the elder man, curtly. 'Is the foreman of the joiners on the "Nan-Shan" outside?... Come in, Bates. How is it that you let Tait's people put us off with a defective lock on the cabin door? The Captain could see directly he set eye on it. Have it replaced at once. The little straws, Bates ... the little straws....'

The lock was replaced accordingly, and a few days afterwards the 'Nan-Shan' steamed out to the East, without MacWhirr having offered any further remark as to her fittings, or having been heard to utter a single word hinting at pride in his ship, gratitude for his appointment, or satisfaction at his prospects.

With a temperament neither loquacious nor taciturn he found very little occasion to talk. There were matters of duty, of course – directions, orders, and so on; but the past being to his mind done with, and the future not there yet, the more general actualities of the day required no com-ment – because facts can speak for themselves with overwhelming precision.

Old Mr Sigg liked a man of few words, and one that 'you could be sure would not try to improve upon his instruc-tions.' MacWhirr satisfying these requirements, was con-tinued in command of the 'Nan-Shan,' and applied himself to the careful navigation of his ship in the China seas. She had come out on a British register, but after some time Messrs Sigg judged it expedient to transfer her to the Siamese flag.

At the news of the contemplated transfer Jukes grew restless, as if under a sense of personal affront. He went about grumbling to himself, and uttering short scornful laughs. 'Fancy having a ridiculous Noah's Ark elephant in the ensign of one's ship,' he said once at the engine-room door. 'Dash me if I can stand it: I'll throw up the billet. Don't it make *you* sick, Mr Rout?' The chief engineer only cleared his throat with the air of a man who knows the value of a good billet.

The first morning the new flag floated over the stern of the 'Nan-Shan' Jukes stood looking at it bitterly from the bridge. He struggled with his feelings for a while, and then remarked, 'Queer flag for a man to sail under, sir.'

'What's the matter with the flag?' inquired Captain MacWhirr. 'Seems all right to me.' And he walked across to the end of the bridge to have a good look.

'Well, it looks queer to me,' burst out Jukes, greatly exasperated, and flung off the bridge.

Captain MacWhirr was amazed at these manners. After a while he stepped quietly into the chart-room, and opened his International Signal Code-book at the plate where the flags of all the nations are correctly figured in gaudy rows. He ran his finger over them, and when he came to Siam he contemplated with great attention the red field and the white elephant. Nothing could be more simple; but to make sure he brought the book out on the bridge for the purpose of comparing the coloured drawing with the real thing at the flagstaff astern. When next Jukes, who was carrying on the duty that day with a sort of suppressed fierceness, happened on the bridge, his commander observed:

'There's nothing amiss with that flag.'

'Isn't there?' mumbled Jukes, falling on his knees before a deck-locker and jerking therefrom viciously a spare lead-line.

'No. I looked up the book. Length twice the breadth and the elephant exactly in the middle. I thought the people ashore would know how to make the local flag. Stands to reason. You were wrong, Jukes. . . .'

'Well, sir,' began Jukes, getting up excitedly, 'all I can say —— ' He fumbled for the end of the coil of line with trembling hands.

'That's all right.' Captain MacWhirr soothed him, sitting heavily on a little canvas folding-stool he greatly affected. 'All you have to do is to take care they don't hoist the elephant upside-down before they get quite used to it.'

Jukes flung the new lead-line over on the fore-deck with a loud 'Here you are, bo'ss'en – don't forget to wet it thoroughly,' and turned with immense resolution towards his commander; but Captain MacWhirr spread his elbows on the bridge-rail comfortably.

'Because it would be, I suppose, understood as a signal of distress,' he went on. 'What do you think? That elephant there, I take it, stands for something in the nature of the Union Jack in the flag. . . .'

'Does it!' yelled Jukes, so that every head on the 'Nan-Shan's' decks looked towards the bridge. Then he sighed, and with sudden resignation: 'It would certainly be a dam' distressful sight,' he said, meekly.

Later in the day he accosted the chief engineer with a confidential, 'Here, let me tell you the old man's latest.'

Mr Solomon Rout (frequently alluded to as Long Sol, Old Sol, or Father Rout), from finding himself almost invariably the tallest man on board every ship he joined, had acquired the habit of a stooping, leisurely condescension. His hair was scant and sandy, his flat cheeks were pale, his bony wrists and long scholarly hands were pale, too, as though he had lived all his life in the shade.

He smiled from on high at Jukes, and went on smoking and glancing about quietly, in the manner of a kind uncle lending an ear to the tale of an excited schoolboy. Then, greatly amused but impassive, he asked:

'And did you throw up the billet?'

'No,' cried Jukes, raising a weary, discouraged voice above the harsh buzz of the 'Nan-Shan's' friction winches. All of them were hard at work, snatching slings of cargo, high up, to the end of long derricks, only, as it seemed, to let them rip down recklessly by the run. The cargo chains groaned in the gins, clinked on coamings, rattled over the side; and the whole ship quivered, with her long grey flanks smoking in wreaths of steam. 'No,' cried Jukes, 'I didn't. What's the good? I might just as well fling my resignation at this bulkhead. I don't believe you can make a man like that understand anything. He simply knocks me over.'

At that moment Captain MacWhirr, back from the shore, crossed the deck, umbrella in hand, escorted by a mournful, self-possessed Chinaman, walking behind in paper-soled silk shoes, and who also carried an umbrella.

The master of the 'Nan-Shan,' speaking just audibly and gazing at his boots as his manner was, remarked that it would be necessary to call at Fu-chau this trip, and desired Mr Rout to have steam up to-morrow afternoon at one o'clock sharp. He pushed back his hat to wipe his forehead, observing at the time that he hated going ashore anyhow; while overtopping him Mr Rout, without deigning a word, smoked austerely, nursing his right elbow in the palm of his left hand. Then Jukes was directed in the same subdued voice to keep the forward 'tween-deck clear of cargo. Two hundred coolies were going to be put down there. The Bun Hin Company were sending that lot home. Twenty-five bags of rice would be coming off in a sampan directly, for stores. All seven-years'-men they were, said Captain MacWhirr, with a camphor-wood chest to every man. The carpenter should be set to work nailing three-inch battens along the deck below, fore and aft, to keep these boxes from shifting in a sea-way. Jukes had better look to it at once. 'D'ye hear, Jukes?' This Chinaman here was coming with the ship as far as Fu-chau – a sort of interpreter he would be. Bun Hin's clerk he was, and wanted to have a look at the space. Jukes had better take him forward. 'D'ye hear, Jukes?'

Jukes took care to punctuate these instructions in proper places with the obligatory 'Yes, sir,' ejaculated without enthusiasm. His brusque 'Come along, John; make look see' set the Chinaman in motion at his heels.

'Wanchee look see, all same look see can do,' said Jukes, who having no talent for foreign languages mangled the very pidgin-English cruelly. He pointed at the open hatch. 'Catchee number one piecie place to sleep in. Eh?'

He was gruff, as became his racial superiority, but not unfriendly. The Chinaman, gazing sad and speechless into the darkness of the hatchway, seemed to stand at the head of a yawning grave.

'No catchee rain down there – savee?' pointed out Jukes. 'Suppose all'ee same fine weather, one piecie coolie-man come top-side,' he pursued, warming up imaginatively. 'Make so – Phooooo!' He expanded his chest and blew out his cheeks. 'Savee, John? Breathe – fresh air. Good. Eh? Washee him piecie pants, chow-chow top-side – see, John?'

With his mouth and hands he made exuberant motions of eating rice and washing clothes; and the Chinaman, who concealed his distrust of this pantomime under a collected demeanour tinged by a gentle and refined melancholy, glanced out of his almond eyes from Jukes to the hatch and back again. 'Velly good,' he murmured, in a disconsol-ate undertone, and hastened smoothly along the decks, dodging obstacles in his course. He disappeared, ducking low under a sling of ten dirty gunny-bags full of some costly merchandise and exhaling a repulsive smell.

Captain MacWhirr meantime had gone on the bridge, and into the chart-room, where a letter, commenced two days before, awaited termination. These long letters began with the words, 'My darling wife,' and the steward, between the scrubbing of the floors and the dusting of chronometer-boxes, snatched at every opportunity to read them. They interested him much more than they possibly could the woman for whose eye they were intended; and this for the reason that they related in minute detail each successive trip of the 'Nan-Shan.'

Her master, faithful to facts, which alone his consciousness reflected, would set them down with painstaking care upon many pages. The house in a northern suburb to which these pages were addressed had a bit of garden before the bow-windows, a deep porch of good appearance, coloured glass with imitation lead frame in the front door. He paid five-and-forty pounds a year for it, and did not think the rent too high, because Mrs MacWhirr (a pretentious person with a scraggy neck and a disdainful manner) was admittedly ladylike, and in the neighbourhood considered as 'quite superior.' The only secret of her life was her abject terror of the time when her husband would come home to stay for good. Under the same roof there dwelt also a daughter called Lydia and a son, Tom. These two were but slightly acquainted with their father. Mainly, they knew him as a rare but privileged visitor, who of an evening smoked his pipe in the dining-room and slept in the house. The lanky girl, upon the whole, was rather ashamed of him; the boy was frankly and utterly indifferent in a straightforward, delightful, unaffected way manly boys have.

And Captain MacWhirr wrote home from the coast of China twelve times every year, desiring quaintly to be 'remembered to the children,' and subscribing himself 'your loving husband,' as calmly as if the words so long used by so many men were, apart from their shape, worn-out things, and of a faded meaning.

The China seas north and south are narrow seas. They are seas full of every-day, eloquent facts, such as islands, sandbanks, reefs, swift and changeable currents – tangled facts that nevertheless speak to a seaman in clear and definite language. Their speech appealed to Captain MacWhirr's sense of realities so forcibly that he had given up his state-room below and practically lived all his days on the bridge of his ship, often having his meals sent up, and sleeping at night in the chart-room. And he indited there his home letters. Each of them, without exception, contained the phrase, 'The weather has been very fine this trip,' or some other form of a statement to that effect. And this statement, too, in its wonderful persistence, was of the same perfect accuracy as all the others they contained.

Mr Rout likewise wrote letters; only no one on board knew how chatty he could be, pen in hand, because the chief engineer had enough imagination to keep his desk locked. His wife relished his style greatly. They were a childless couple, and Mrs Rout, a big, high-bosomed, jolly woman of forty, shared with Mr Rout's toothless and venerable mother a little cottage near Teddington. She would run over her correspondence, at breakfast, with lively eyes, and scream out interesting passages in a joyous voice at the deaf old lady, prefacing each extract by the warning shout, 'Solomon says!' She had the trick of firing off Solomon's utterances also upon strangers, astonishing them easily by the unfamiliar text and the unexpectedly jocular vein of these quotations. On the day the new curate called for the first time at the cottage, she found occasion to remark, 'As Solomon says: "the engineers that go down to the sea in ships behold the wonders of sailor nature";' when a change in the visitor's countenance made her stop and stare.

'Solomon...Oh!...Mrs Rout,' stuttered the young man, very red in the face, 'I must say...I don't....'

'He's my husband,' she announced in a great shout, throwing herself back in the chair. Perceiving the joke, she laughed immoderately with a handkerchief to her eyes, while he sat wearing a forced smile, and, from his inexperience of jolly women, fully persuaded that she must be deplorably insane. They were excellent friends afterwards; for, absolving her from irreverent intention, he came to think she was a very worthy person indeed; and he learned in time to receive without flinching other scraps of Solomon's wisdom.

'For my part,' Solomon was reported by his wife to have said once, 'give me the dullest ass for a skipper before a rogue. There is a way to take a fool; but a rogue is smart and slippery.' This was an airy generalization drawn from the particular case of Captain MacWhirr's honesty, which, in itself, had the heavy obviousness of a lump of clay. On the other hand, Mr Jukes, unable to generalize, unmarried, and unengaged, was in the habit of opening his heart after another fashion to an old chum and former shipmate, actually serving as second officer on board an Atlantic liner.

First of all he would insist upon the advantages of the Eastern trade, hinting at its superiority to the Western Ocean service. He extolled the sky, the seas, the ships, and the easy life of the Far East. The 'Nan-Shan,' he affirmed, was second to none as a sea-boat.

'We have no brass-bound uniforms, but then we are like brothers here,' he wrote. 'We all mess together and live like fighting-cocks.... All the chaps of the black-squad are as decent as they made that kind, and old Sol, the Chief, is a dry stick. We are good friends. As to our old man, you could not find a quieter skipper. Sometimes you would think he hadn't sense enough to see anything wrong. And yet it isn't that. Can't be. He has been in command for a good few years now. He doesn't do anything actually foolish, and gets his ship along all right without worrying anybody. I believe he hasn't brains enough to enjoy kicking up a row. I don't take advantage of him. I would scorn it. Outside the routine of duty he doesn't seem to understand more than half of what you tell him. We get a laugh out of this at times; but it is dull, too, to be with a man like this – in the long-run. Old Sol says he hasn't much conversation. Conversation! O Lord! He never talks. The other day I had been yarning under the bridge with one of the engineers, and he must have heard us. When I came up to take my watch, he steps out of the chart-room and has a good look all round, peeps over at the sidelights, glances at the compass, squints upwards at the stars. That's his regular performance. By-and-by he says: "Was that you talking just now in the port alleyway?" "Yes, sir." "With the third engineer?" "Yes, sir." He walks off to starboard, and sits under the dodger on a little campstool of his, and for half an hour perhaps he makes no sound, except that I heard him sneeze once. Then after a while I hear him getting up over there, and he strolls across to port, where I was. "I can't understand what you can find to talk about," says he. "Two solid hours. I am not blaming you. I see people ashore at it all day long, and then in the evening they sit down and keep at it over the drinks. Must be saying the same things over and over again. I can't understand."

'Did you ever hear anything like that? And he was so patient about it. It made me quite sorry for him. But he is exasperating, too, sometimes. Of course one would not do anything to vex him even if it were worth while. But it isn't. He's so jolly innocent that if you were to put your thumb to your nose and wave your fingers at him he would only wonder gravely to himself what got into you. He told me once quite simply that he found it very difficult to make out what made people always act so queerly. He's too dense to trouble about, and that's the truth.'

Thus wrote Mr Jukes to his chum in the Western Ocean trade, out of the fulness of his heart and the liveliness of his fancy.

He had expressed his honest opinion. It was not worth while trying to impress a man of that sort. If the world had been full of such men, life would have probably appeared to Jukes an unentertaining and unprofitable business. He was not alone in his opinion. The sea itself, as if sharing Mr Jukes's good-natured forbearance, had never put itself out to startle the silent man, who seldom looked up, and wandered innocently over the waters with the only visible purpose of getting food, raiment, and house-room for three people ashore. Dirty weather he had known, of course. He had been made wet, uncomfortable, tired in the usual way, felt at the time and presently forgotten. So

that upon the whole he had been justified in reporting fine
weather at home. But he had never been given a glimpse
of immeasurable strength and of immoderate wrath, the
wrath that passes exhausted but never appeased – the wrath
and fury of the passionate sea. He knew it existed, as we
know that crime and abominations exist; he had heard of it
as a peaceable citizen in a town hears of battles, famines,
and floods, and yet knows nothing of what these things
mean – though, indeed, he may have been mixed up in a
street row, have gone without his dinner once, or been
soaked to the skin in a shower. Captain MacWhirr had
sailed over the surface of the oceans as some men go
skimming over the years of existence to sink gently into a
placid grave, ignorant of life to the last, without ever having
been made to see all it may contain of perfidy, of violence,
and of terror. There are on sea and land such men thus
fortunate – or thus disdained by destiny or by the sea.

II

Observing the steady fall of the barometer, Captain
MacWhirr thought, 'There's some dirty weather knocking
about.' This is precisely what he thought. He had had an
experience of moderately dirty weather – the term dirty as
applied to the weather implying only moderate discomfort
to the seaman. Had he been informed by an indisputable
authority that the end of the world was to be finally accomplished by a catastrophic disturbance of the atmosphere, he
would have assimilated the information under the simple
idea of dirty weather, and no other, because he had no
experience of cataclysms, and belief does not necessarily
imply comprehension. The wisdom of his country had
pronounced by means of an Act of Parliament that before
he could be considered as fit to take charge of a ship he
should be able to answer certain simple questions on the
subject of circular storms such as hurricanes, cyclones,
typhoons; and apparently he had answered them, since he

was now in command of the 'Nan-Shan' in the China seas during the season of typhoons. But if he had answered he remembered nothing of it. He was, however, conscious of being made uncomfortable by the clammy heat. He came out on the bridge, and found no relief to this oppression. The air seemed thick. He gasped like a fish, and began to believe himself greatly out of sorts.

The 'Nan-Shan' was ploughing a vanishing furrow upon the circle of the sea that had the surface and the shimmer of an undulating piece of grey silk. The sun, pale and without rays, poured down leaden heat in a strangely indecisive light, and the Chinamen were lying prostrate about the decks. Their bloodless, pinched, yellow faces were like the faces of bilious invalids. Captain MacWhirr noticed two of them especially, stretched out on their backs below the bridge. As soon as they had closed their eyes they seemed dead. Three others, however, were quarrelling barbarously away forward; and one big fellow, half naked, with herculean shoulders, was hanging limply over a winch; another, sitting on the deck, his knees up and his head drooping sideways in a girlish attitude, was plaiting his pigtail with infinite languor depicted in his whole person and in the very movement of his fingers. The smoke struggled with difficulty out of the funnel, and instead of streaming away spread itself out like an infernal sort of cloud, smelling of sulphur and raining soot all over the decks.

'What the devil are you doing there, Mr Jukes?' asked Captain MacWhirr.

This unusual form of address, though mumbled rather than spoken, caused the body of Mr Jukes to start as though it had been probed under the fifth rib. He had had a low bench brought on the bridge, and sitting on it, with a length of rope curled about his feet and a piece of canvas stretched over his knees, was pushing a sail-needle vigorously. He looked up, and his surprise gave to his eyes an expression of innocence and candour.

'I am only roping some of that new set of bags we made last trip for whipping up coals,' he remonstrated, gently. 'We shall want them for the next coaling, sir.'

'What became of the others?'

'Why, worn out, of course, sir.'

Captain MacWhirr, after glaring down irresolutely at his chief mate, disclosed the gloomy and cynical conviction that more than half of them had been lost overboard, 'if only the truth was known,' and retired to the other end of the bridge. Jukes, exasperated by this unprovoked attack, broke the needle at the second stitch, and dropping his work got up and cursed the heat in a violent undertone.

The propeller thumped, the three Chinamen forward had given up squabbling very suddenly, and the one who had been plaiting his tail clasped his legs and stared deject-edly over his knees. The lurid sunshine cast faint and sickly shadows. The swell ran higher and swifter every moment, and the ship lurched heavily in the smooth, deep hollows of the sea.

'I wonder where that beastly swell comes from,' said Jukes aloud, recovering himself after a stagger.

'North-east,' grunted the literal MacWhirr, from his side of the bridge. 'There's some dirty weather knocking about. Go and look at the glass.'

When Jukes came out of the chart-room, the cast of his countenance had changed to thoughtfulness and concern. He caught hold of the bridge-rail and stared ahead.

The temperature in the engine-room had gone up to a hundred and seventeen degrees. Irritated voices were ascending through the skylight and through the fiddle of the stokehold in a harsh and resonant uproar, mingled with angry clangs and scrapes of metal, as if men with limbs of iron and throats of bronze had been quarrelling down there. The second engineer was falling foul of the stokers for letting the steam go down. He was a man with arms like a blacksmith, and generally feared; but that afternoon the stokers were answering him back recklessly, and slammed

the furnace doors with the fury of despair. Then the noise
ceased suddenly, and the second engineer appeared, emerging out of the stokehold streaked with grime and soaking
wet like a chimney-sweep coming out of a well. As soon as
his head was clear of the fiddle he began to scold Jukes for
not trimming properly the stokehold ventilators; and in
answer Jukes made with his hands deprecatory soothing
signs meaning: No wind – can't be helped – you can see for
yourself. But the other wouldn't hear reason. His teeth
flashed angrily in his dirty face. He didn't mind, he said,
the trouble of punching their blanked heads down there,
blank his soul, but did the condemned sailors think you
could keep steam up in the God-forsaken boilers simply by
knocking the blanked stokers about? No, by George! You
had to get some draught, too – may he be everlastingly
blanked for a swab-headed deck-hand if you didn't! And
the chief, too, rampaging before the steam-gauge and
carrying on like a lunatic up and down the engine-room
ever since noon. What did Jukes think he was stuck up
there for, if he couldn't get one of his decayed, good-for-
nothing deck-cripples to turn the ventilators to the wind?

The relations of the 'engine-room' and the 'deck' of the
'Nan-Shan' were, as is known, of a brotherly nature; therefore Jukes leaned over and begged the other in a restrained
tone not to make a disgusting ass of himself; the skipper
was on the other side of the bridge. But the second declared
mutinously that he didn't care a rap who was on the other
side of the bridge, and Jukes, passing in a flash from lofty
disapproval into a state of exaltation, invited him in unflat-
tering terms to come up and twist the beastly things to
please himself, and catch such wind as a donkey of his sort
could find. The second rushed up to the fray. He flung
himself at the port ventilator as though he meant to tear it
out bodily and toss it overboard. All he did was to move the
cowl round a few inches, with an enormous expenditure of
force, and seemed spent in the effort. He leaned against the
back of the wheel-house, and Jukes walked up to him.

'Oh, Heavens!' ejaculated the engineer in a feeble voice. He lifted his eyes to the sky, and then let his glassy stare descend to meet the horizon that, tilting up to an angle of forty degrees, seemed to hang on a slant for a while and settled down slowly. 'Heavens! Phew! What's up, anyhow?'

Jukes, straddling his long legs like a pair of compasses, put on an air of superiority. 'We're going to catch it this time,' he said. 'The barometer is tumbling down like anything, Harry. And you trying to kick up that silly row. . . .'

The word 'barometer' seemed to revive the second engineer's mad animosity. Collecting afresh all his energies, he directed Jukes in a low and brutal tone to shove the unmentionable instrument down his gory throat. Who cared for his crimson barometer? It was the steam – the steam – that was going down; and what between the firemen going faint and the chief going silly, it was worse than a dog's life for him; he didn't care a tinker's curse how soon the whole show was blown out of the water. He seemed on the point of having a cry, but after regaining his breath he muttered darkly, 'I'll faint them,' and dashed off. He stopped upon the fiddle long enough to shake his fist at the unnatural daylight, and dropped into the dark hole with a whoop.

When Jukes turned, his eyes fell upon the rounded back and the big red ears of Captain MacWhirr, who had come across. He did not look at his chief officer, but said at once, 'That's a very violent man, that second engineer.'

'Jolly good second, anyhow,' grunted Jukes. 'They can't keep up steam,' he added, rapidly, and made a grab at the rail against the coming lurch.

Captain MacWhirr, unprepared, took a run and brought himself up with a jerk by an awning stanchion.

'A profane man,' he said, obstinately. 'If this goes on, I'll have to get rid of him the first chance.'

'It's the heat,' said Jukes. 'The weather's awful. It would make a saint swear. Even up here I feel exactly as if I had my head tied up in a woollen blanket.'

Captain MacWhirr looked up. 'D'ye mean to say, Mr Jukes, you ever had your head tied up in a blanket? What was that for?'

'It's a manner of speaking, sir,' said Jukes, stolidly.

'Some of you fellows do go on! What's that about saints swearing? I wish you wouldn't talk so wild. What sort of saint would that be that would swear? No more saint than yourself, I expect. And what's a blanket got to do with it – or the weather either. . . . The heat does not make me swear – does it? It's filthy bad temper. That's what it is. And what's the good of your talking like this?'

Thus Captain MacWhirr expostulated against the use of images in speech, and at the end electrified Jukes by a contemptuous snort, followed by words of passion and resentment: 'Damme! I'll fire him out of the ship if he don't look out.'

And Jukes, incorrigible, thought: 'Goodness me! Somebody's put a new inside to my old man. Here's temper, if you like. Of course it's the weather; what else? It would make an angel quarrelsome – let alone a saint.'

All the Chinamen on deck appeared at their last gasp.

At its setting the sun had a diminished diameter and an expiring brown, rayless glow, as if millions of centuries elapsing since the morning had brought it near its end. A dense bank of cloud became visible to the northward; it had a sinister dark olive tint, and lay low and motionless upon the sea, resembling a solid obstacle in the path of the ship. She went floundering towards it like an exhausted creature driven to its death. The coppery twilight retired slowly, and the darkness brought out overhead a swarm of unsteady, big stars, that, as if blown upon, flickered exceedingly and seemed to hang very near the earth. At eight o'clock Jukes went into the chartroom to write up the ship's log.

He copied neatly out of the rough-book the number of miles, the course of the ship, and in the column for 'wind' scrawled the word 'calm' from top to bottom of the eight hours since noon. He was exasperated by the continuous, monotonous rolling of the ship. The heavy inkstand would slide away in a manner that suggested perverse intelligence in dodging the pen. Having written in the large space under the head of 'Remarks' 'Heat very oppressive,' he stuck the end of the pen-holder in his teeth, pipe fashion, and mopped his face carefully.

'Ship rolling heavily in a high cross swell,' he began again, and commented to himself, 'Heavily is no word for it.' Then he wrote: 'Sunset threatening, with a low bank of clouds to N. and E. Sky clear overhead.'

Sprawling over the table with arrested pen, he glanced out of the door, and in that frame of his vision he saw all the stars flying upwards between the teakwood jambs on a black sky. The whole lot took flight together and disappeared, leaving only a blackness flecked with white flashes, for the sea was as black as the sky and speckled with foam afar. The stars that had flown to the roll came back on the return swing of the ship, rushing downwards in their glittering multitude, not of fiery points, but enlarged to tiny discs brilliant with a clear wet sheen.

Jukes watched the flying big stars for a moment, and then wrote: '8 p.m. Swell increasing. Ship labouring and taking water on her decks. Battened down the coolies for the night. Barometer still falling.' He paused, and thought to himself, 'Perhaps nothing whatever'll come of it.' And then he closed resolutely his entries: 'Every appearance of a typhoon coming on.'

On going out he had to stand aside, and Captain MacWhirr strode over the doorstep without saying a word or making a sign.

'Shut the door, Mr Jukes, will you?' he cried from within.

Jukes turned back to do so, muttering ironically: 'Afraid to catch cold, I suppose.' It was his watch below, but he yearned for communion with his kind; and he remarked cheerily to the second mate: 'Doesn't look so bad, after all – does it?'

The second mate was marching to and fro on the bridge, tripping down with small steps one moment, and the next climbing with difficulty the shifting slope of the deck. At the sound of Jukes's voice he stood still, facing forward, but made no reply.

'Hallo! That's a heavy one,' said Jukes, swaying to meet the long roll till his lowered head touched the planks. This time the second mate made in his throat a noise of an unfriendly nature.

He was an oldish, shabby little fellow, with bad teeth and no hair on his face. He had been shipped in a hurry in Shanghai, that trip when the second officer brought from home had delayed the ship three hours in port by contriving (in some manner Captain MacWhirr could never understand) to fall overboard into an empty coal-lighter lying alongside, and had to be sent ashore to the hospital with concussion of the brain and a broken limb or two.

Jukes was not discouraged by the unsympathetic sound. 'The Chinamen must be having a lovely time of it down there,' he said. 'It's lucky for them the old girl has the easiest roll of any ship I've ever been in. There now! This one wasn't so bad.'

'You wait,' snarled the second mate.

With his sharp nose, red at the tip, and his thin pinched lips he always looked as though he were raging inwardly; and he was concise in his speech to the point of rudeness. All his time off duty he spent in his cabin with the door shut, keeping so still in there that he was supposed to fall asleep as soon as he had disappeared; but the man who came in to wake him for his watch on deck would invariably find him with his eyes wide open, flat on his back in the bunk, and glaring irritably from a soiled pillow. He never wrote any letters, did not seem to hope for news from anywhere; and though he had been heard once to mention West Hartlepool, it was with extreme bitterness, and only in connection with the extortionate charges of a boarding-house. He was one of those men who are picked up at need in the ports of the world. They are competent enough, appear hopelessly hard up, show no evidence of any sort of vice, and carry about them all the signs of manifest failure. They come aboard on an emergency, care for no ship afloat, live in their own atmosphere of casual connection amongst their shipmates who know nothing of them, and make up their minds to leave at inconvenient times. They clear out with no words of leave-taking in some God-forsaken port other men would fear to be stranded in, and go ashore in company of a shabby sea-chest, corded like a treasure-box, and with an air of shaking the ship's dust off their feet.

'You wait,' he repeated, balanced in great swings with his back to Jukes, motionless and implacable.

'Do you mean to say we are going to catch it hot?' asked Jukes with boyish interest.

'Say? . . . I say nothing. You don't catch me,' snapped the little second mate, with a mixture of pride, scorn, and cunning, as if Jukes's question had been a trap cleverly detected. 'Oh, no! None of you here shall make a fool of me if I know it,' he mumbled to himself.

Jukes reflected rapidly that this second mate was a mean little beast, and in his heart he wished poor Jack Allen had never smashed himself up in the coal-lighter. The far-off blackness ahead of the ship was like another night seen through the starry night of the earth – the starless night of the immensities beyond the created universe, revealed in its appalling stillness through a low fissure in the glittering sphere of which the earth is the kernel.

'Whatever there might be about, said Jukes, 'we are steaming straight into it.'

'*You've* said it,' caught up the second mate, always with his back to Jukes. 'You've said it, mind – not I.'

'Oh, go to Jericho!' said Jukes, frankly; and the other emitted a triumphant little chuckle.

'You've said it,' he repeated.

'And what of that?'

'I've known some real good men get into trouble with their skippers for saying a dam' sight less,' answered the second mate feverishly. 'Oh, no! You don't catch me.'

'You seem deucedly anxious not to give yourself away,' said Jukes, completely soured by such absurdity. 'I wouldn't be afraid to say what I think.'

'Aye, to me. That's no great trick. I am nobody, and well I know it.'

The ship, after a pause of comparative steadiness started upon a series of rolls, one worse than the other, and for a time Jukes, preserving his equilibrium, was too busy to open his mouth. As soon as the violent swinging had quieted down somewhat, he said: 'This is a bit too much of a good thing. Whether anything is coming or not I think she ought to be put head on to that swell. The old man is just gone in to lie down. Hang me if I don't speak to him.'

But when he opened the door of the chart-room he saw his captain reading a book. Captain MacWhirr was not lying down: he was standing up with one hand grasping the edge of the bookshelf and the other holding open before his face a thick volume. The lamp wriggled in the gimbals, the loosened books toppled from side to side on the shelf, the long barometer swung in jerky circles, the table altered its slant every moment. In the midst of all this stir and movement Captain MacWhirr, holding on, showed his eyes above the upper edge, and asked, 'What's the matter?'

'Swell getting worse, sir.'

'Noticed that in here,' muttered Captain MacWhirr. 'Anything wrong?'

Jukes, inwardly disconcerted by the seriousness of the eyes looking at him over the top of the book, produced an embarrassed grin.

'Rolling like old boots,' he said, sheepishly.

'Aye! Very heavy – very heavy. What do you want?'

At this Jukes lost his footing and began to flounder.

'I was thinking of our passengers,' he said, in the manner of a man clutching at a straw.

'Passengers?' wondered the Captain, gravely. 'What passengers?'

'Why, the Chinamen, sir,' explained Jukes, very sick of this conversation.

'The Chinamen! Why don't you speak plainly? Couldn't tell what you meant. Never heard a lot of coolies spoken of as passengers before. Passengers, indeed! What's come to you?'

Captain MacWhirr, closing the book on his forefinger, lowered his arm and looked completely mystified. 'Why are you thinking of the Chinamen, Mr Jukes?' he inquired.

Jukes took a plunge, like a man driven to it. 'She's rolling her decks full of water, sir. Thought you might put her head on perhaps – for a while. Till this goes down a bit – very soon, I dare say. Head to the eastward. I never knew a ship roll like this.'

He held on in the doorway, and Captain MacWhirr, feeling his grip on the shelf inadequate, made up his mind to let go in a hurry, and fell heavily on the couch.

'Head to the eastward?' he said, struggling to sit up. 'That's more than four points off her course.'

'Yes, sir. Fifty degrees. . . . Would just bring her head far enough round to meet this. . . .'

Captain MacWhirr was now sitting up. He had not dropped the book, and he had not lost his place.

'To the eastward?' he repeated, with dawning astonishment. 'To the . . . Where do you think we are bound to? You want me to haul a full-powered steamship four points off her course to make the Chinamen comfortable! Now, I've heard more than enough of mad things done in the world – but this. . . . If I didn't know you, Jukes, I would think you were in liquor. Steer four points off. . . . And what afterwards? Steer four points over the other way, I suppose, to make the course good. What put it into your head that I would start to tack a steamer as if she were a sailing-ship?'

'Jolly good thing she isn't,' threw in Jukes, with bitter readiness. 'She would have rolled every blessed stick out of her this afternoon.'

'Aye! And you just would have had to stand and see them go,' said Captain MacWhirr, showing a certain animation. 'It's a dead calm, isn't it?'

'It is, sir. But there's something out of the common coming, for sure.'

'Maybe. I suppose you have a notion I should be getting out of the way of that dirt,' said Captain MacWhirr, speaking with the utmost simplicity of manner and tone, and fixing the oilcloth on the floor with a heavy stare. Thus he noticed neither Jukes's discomfiture nor the mixture of vexation and astonished respect on his face.

'Now, here's this book,' he continued with deliberation, slapping his thigh with the closed volume. 'I've been reading the chapter on the storms there.'

This was true. He had been reading the chapter on the storms. When he had entered the chart-room, it was with no intention of taking the book down. Some influence in the air – the same influence, probably, that caused the steward to bring without orders the Captain's sea-boots and oilskin coat up to the chart-room – had as it were guided his hand to the shelf; and without taking the time to sit down he had waded with a conscious effort into the terminology of the subject. He lost himself amongst advancing semi-circles, left- and right-hand quadrants, the curves of the tracks, the probable bearing of the centre, the shifts of wind and the readings of barometer. He tried to bring all these things into a definite relation to himself, and ended by becoming contemptuously angry with such a lot of words and with so much advice, all head-work and supposition, without a glimmer of certitude.

'It's the damnedest thing, Jukes,' he said. 'If a fellow was to believe all that's in there, he would be running most of his time all over the sea trying to get behind the weather.'

Again he slapped his leg with the book; and Jukes opened his mouth, but said nothing.

'Running to get behind the weather! Do you understand that, Mr Jukes? It's the maddest thing!' ejaculated Captain

MacWhirr, with pauses, gazing at the floor profoundly. 'You would think an old woman had been writing this. It passes me. If that thing means anything useful, then it means that I should at once alter the course away, away to the devil somewhere, and come booming down on Fu-chau from the northward at the tail of this dirty weather that's supposed to be knocking about in our way. From the north! Do you understand, Mr Jukes? Three hundred extra miles to the distance, and a pretty coal bill to show. I couldn't bring myself to do that if every word in there was gospel truth, Mr Jukes. Don't you expect me. . . .'

And Jukes, silent, marvelled at this display of feeling and loquacity.

'But the truth is that you don't know if the fellow is right, anyhow. How can you tell what a gale is made of till you get it? He isn't aboard here, is he? Very well. Here he says that the centre of them things bears eight points off the wind; but we haven't got any wind, for all the barometer falling. Where's his centre now?'

'We will get the wind presently,' mumbled Jukes.

'Let it come, then,' said Captain MacWhirr, with digni-fied indignation. 'It's only to let you see, Mr Jukes, that you don't find everything in books. All these rules for dodging breezes and circumventing the winds of heaven, Mr Jukes, seem to me the maddest thing, when you come to look at it sensibly.'

He raised his eyes, saw Jukes gazing at him dubiously, and tried to illustrate his meaning.

'About as queer as your extraordinary notion of dodging the ship head to sea, for I don't know how long, to make the Chinamen comfortable; whereas all we've got to do is to take them to Fu-chau, being timed to get there before noon on Friday. If the weather delays me – very well. There's your log-book to talk straight about the weather. But suppose I went swinging off my course and came in two days late, and they asked me: "Where have you been all that time, Captain?" What could I say to that? "Went around to

dodge the bad weather," I would say. "It must've been dam'
bad," they would say. "Don't know," I would have to say;
"I've dodged clear of it." See that, Jukes? I have been
thinking it all out this afternoon.'

He looked up again in his unseeing, unimaginative way.
No one had ever heard him say so much at one time. Jukes,
with his arms open in the doorway, was like a man invited
to behold a miracle. Unbounded wonder was the intellectual meaning of his eye, while incredulity was seated in his
whole countenance.

'A gale is a gale, Mr Jukes,' resumed the Captain, 'and a
full-powered steamship has got to face it. There's just so
much dirty weather knocking about the world, and the
proper thing is to go through it with none of what old
Captain Wilson of the "Melita" calls "storm strategy." The
other day ashore I heard him hold forth about it to a lot of
shipmasters who came in and sat at a table next to mine. It
seemed to me the greatest nonsense. He was telling them
how he out-manœuvred, I think he said, a terrific gale, so
that it never came nearer than fifty miles to him. A neat
piece of head-work he called it. How he knew there was a
terrific gale fifty miles off beats me altogether. It was like
listening to a crazy man. I would have thought Captain
Wilson was old enough to know better.'

Captain MacWhirr ceased for a moment, then said, 'It's
your watch below, Mr Jukes?'

Jukes came to himself with a start. 'Yes, sir.'

'Leave orders to call me at the slightest change,' said the
Captain. He reached up to put the book away, and tucked
his legs upon the couch. 'Shut the door so that it don't fly
open, will you? I can't stand a door banging. They've put a
lot of rubbishy locks into this ship, I must say.'

Captain MacWhirr closed his eyes.

He did so to rest himself. He was tired, and he experienced that state of mental vacuity which comes at the end
of an exhaustive discussion that had liberated some belief
matured in the course of meditative years. He had indeed

been making his confession of faith, had he only known it; and its effect was to make Jukes, on the other side of the door, stand scratching his head for a good while.

Captain MacWhirr opened his eyes.

He thought he must have been asleep. What was that loud noise? Wind? Why had he not been called? The lamp wriggled in its gimbals, the barometer swung in circles, the table altered its slant every moment; a pair of limp sea-boots with collapsed tops went sliding past the couch. He put out his hand instantly, and captured one.

Jukes's face appeared in a crack of the door: only his face, very red, with staring eyes. The flame of the lamp leaped, a piece of paper flew up, a rush of air enveloped Captain MacWhirr. Beginning to draw on the boot, he directed an expectant gaze at Jukes's swollen, excited features.

'Came on like this,' shouted Jukes, 'five minutes ago . . . all of a sudden.'

The head disappeared with a bang, and a heavy splash and patter of drops swept past the closed door as if a pailful of melted lead had been flung against the house. A whistling could be heard now upon the deep vibrating noise outside. The stuffy chart-room seemed as full of draughts as a shed. Captain MacWhirr collared the other sea-boot on its violent passage along the floor. He was not flustered, but he could not find at once the opening for inserting his foot. The shoes he had flung off were scurrying from end to end of the cabin, gambolling playfully over each other like puppies. As soon as he stood up he kicked at them viciously, but without effect.

He threw himself into the attitude of a lunging fencer, to reach after his oilskin coat; and afterwards he staggered all over the confined space while he jerked himself into it. Very grave, straddling his legs far apart, and stretching his neck, he started to tie deliberately the strings of his sou'-wester under his chin, with thick fingers that trembled slightly. He went through all the movements of a woman putting on her bonnet before a glass, with a strained, listening attention, as though he had expected every moment to hear the shout of his name in the confused clamour that had suddenly beset his ship. Its increase filled his ears while he was getting ready to go out and confront whatever it might mean. It was tumultuous and very loud – made up of the rush of the wind, the crashes of the sea, with that prolonged deep vibration of the air, like the roll of an immense and remote drum beating the charge of the gale.

He stood for a moment in the light of the lamp, thick, clumsy, shapeless in his panoply of combat, vigilant and red-faced.

'There's a lot of weight in this,' he muttered.

As soon as he attempted to open the door the wind caught it. Clinging to the handle, he was dragged out over the doorstep, and at once found himself engaged with the wind in a sort of personal scuffle whose object was the shutting of that door. At the last moment a tongue of air scurried in and licked out the flame of the lamp.

Ahead of the ship he perceived a great darkness lying upon a multitude of white flashes; on the starboard beam a few amazing stars drooped, dim and fitful, above an immense waste of broken seas, as if seen through a mad drift of smoke.

On the bridge a knot of men, indistinct and toiling, were making great efforts in the light of the wheelhouse windows that shone mistily on their heads and backs. Suddenly darkness closed upon one pane, then on another. The voices of the lost group reached him after the manner of men's voices in a gale, in shreds and fragments of forlorn shouting snatched past the ear. All at once Jukes appeared at his side, yelling, with his head down.

'Watch – put in – wheelhouse shutters – glass – afraid – blow in.'

Jukes heard his commander upbraiding.

'This – come – anything – warning – call me.'

He tried to explain, with the uproar pressing on his lips.

'Light air – remained – bridge – sudden – north-east –
could turn – thought – you – sure – hear.'

They had gained the shelter of the weather-cloth, and
could converse with raised voices, as people quarrel.

'I got the hands along to cover up all the ventilators.
Good job I had remained on deck. I didn't think you would
be asleep, and so . . . What did you say, sir? What?'

'Nothing,' cried Captain MacWhirr. 'I said – all right.'

'By all the powers! We've got it this time,' observed Jukes
in a howl.

'You haven't altered her course?' inquired Captain
MacWhirr, straining his voice.

'No, sir. Certainly not. Wind came out right ahead. And
here comes the head sea.'

A plunge of the ship ended in a shock as if she had
landed her forefoot upon something solid. After a moment
of stillness a lofty flight of sprays drove hard with the wind
upon their faces.

'Keep her at it as long as we can,' shouted Captain
MacWhirr.

Before Jukes had squeezed the salt water out of his eyes
all the stars had disappeared.

III

JUKES was as ready a man as any half-dozen young mates
that may be caught by casting a net upon the waters; and
though he had been somewhat taken aback by the startling
viciousness of the first squall, he had pulled himself
together on the instant, had called out the hands and had
rushed them along to secure such openings about the deck
as had not been already battened down earlier in the
evening. Shouting in his fresh, stentorian voice, 'Jump,
boys, and bear a hand!' he led in the work, telling himself
the while that he had 'just expected this.'

But at the same time he was growing aware that this was
rather more than he had expected. From the first stir of the

air felt on his cheek the gale seemed to take upon itself the accumulated impetus of an avalanche. Heavy sprays enveloped the 'Nan-Shan' from stem to stern, and instantly in the midst of her regular rolling she began to jerk and plunge as though she had gone mad with fright.

Jukes thought, 'This is no joke.' While he was exchanging explanatory yells with his captain, a sudden lowering of the darkness came upon the night, falling before their vision like something palpable. It was as if the masked lights of the world had been turned down. Jukes was uncritically glad to have his captain at hand. It relieved him as though that man had, by simply coming on deck, taken most of the gale's weight upon his shoulders. Such is the prestige, the privilege, and the burden of command.

Captain MacWhirr could expect no relief of that sort from any one on earth. Such is the loneliness of command. He was trying to see, with that watchful manner of a seaman who stares into the wind's eye as if into the eye of an adversary, to penetrate the hidden intention and guess the aim and force of the thrust. The strong wind swept at him out of a vast obscurity; he felt under his feet the uneasiness of his ship, and he could not even discern the shadow of her shape. He wished it were not so; and very still he waited, feeling stricken by a blind man's helplessness.

To be silent was natural to him, dark or shine. Jukes, at his elbow, made himself heard yelling cheerily in the gusts, 'We must have got the worst of it at once, sir.' A faint burst of lightning quivered all round, as if flashed into a cavern – into a black and secret chamber of the sea, with a floor of foaming crests.

It unveiled for a sinister, fluttering moment a ragged mass of clouds hanging low, the lurch of the long outlines of the ship, the black figures of men caught on the bridge, heads forward, as if petrified in the act of butting. The darkness palpitated down upon all this, and then the real thing came at last.

It was something formidable and swift, like the sudden smashing of a vial of wrath. It seemed to explode all round the ship with an overpowering concussion and a rush of great waters, as if an immense dam had been blown up to windward. In an instant the men lost touch of each other. This is the disintegrating power of a great wind: it isolates one from one's kind. An earthquake, a landslip, an avalanche, overtake a man incidentally, as it were – without passion. A furious gale attacks him like a personal enemy, tries to grasp his limbs, fastens upon his mind, seeks to rout his very spirit out of him.

Jukes was driven away from his commander. He fancied himself whirled a great distance through the air. Everything disappeared – even, for a moment, his power of thinking; but his hand had found one of the rail-stanchions. His distress was by no means alleviated by an inclination to disbelieve the reality of this experience. Though young, he had seen some bad weather, and had never doubted his ability to imagine the worst; but this was so much beyond his powers of fancy that it appeared incompatible with the existence of any ship whatever. He would have been incredulous about himself in the same way, perhaps, had he not been so harassed by the necessity of exerting a wrestling effort against a force trying to tear him away from his hold. Moreover, the conviction of not being utterly destroyed returned to him through the sensations of being half-drowned, bestially shaken, and partly choked.

It seemed to him he remained there precariously alone with the stanchion for a long, long time. The rain poured on him, flowed, drove in sheets. He breathed in gasps; and sometimes the water he swallowed was fresh and sometimes it was salt. For the most part he kept his eyes shut tight, as if suspecting his sight might be destroyed in the immense flurry of the elements. When he ventured to blink hastily, he derived some moral support from the green gleam of the starboard light shining feebly upon

the flight of rain and sprays. He was actually looking at it
when its ray fell upon the uprearing sea which put it out.
He saw the head of the wave topple over, adding the mite
of its crash to the tremendous uproar raging around
him, and almost at the same instant the stanchion was
wrenched away from his embracing arms. After a crushing
thump on his back he found himself suddenly afloat and
borne upwards. His first irresistible notion was that the
whole China Sea had climbed on the bridge. Then, more
sanely, he concluded himself gone overboard. All the time
he was being tossed, flung, and rolled in great volumes of
water, he kept on repeating mentally, with the utmost
precipitation, the words: 'My God! My God! My God!
My God!'

All at once, in a revolt of misery and despair, he formed
the crazy resolution to get out of that. And he began to
thresh about with his arms and legs. But as soon as he
commenced his wretched struggles he discovered that he
had become somehow mixed up with a face, an oilskin coat,
somebody's boots. He clawed ferociously all these things in
turn, lost them, found them again, lost them once more,
and finally was himself caught in the firm clasp of a pair of
stout arms. He returned the embrace closely round a thick
solid body. He had found his captain.

They tumbled over and over, tightening their hug.
Suddenly the water let them down with a brutal bang;
and, stranded against the side of the wheelhouse, out of
breath and bruised, they were left to stagger up in the wind
and hold on where they could.

Jukes came out of it rather horrified, as though he had
escaped some unparalleled outrage directed at his feelings.
It weakened his faith in himself. He started shouting aimlessly to the man he could feel near him in that fiendish
blackness, 'Is it you, sir? Is it you, sir?' till his temples
seemed ready to burst. And he heard in answer a voice, as
if crying far away, as if screaming to him fretfully from a
very great distance, the one word 'Yes!' Other seas swept

again over the bridge. He received them defencelessly
right over his bare head, with both his hands engaged in
holding.

The motion of the ship was extravagant. Her lurches
had an appalling helplessness: she pitched as if taking a
header into a void, and seemed to find a wall to hit every
time. When she rolled she fell on her side headlong, and
she would be righted back by such a demolishing blow that
Jukes felt her reeling as a clubbed man reels before he
collapses. The gale howled and scuffled about gigantically
in the darkness, as though the entire world were one black
gully. At certain moments the air streamed against the ship
as if sucked through a tunnel with a concentrated solid
force of impact that seemed to lift her clean out of the water
and keep her up for an instant with only a quiver running
through her from end to end. And then she would begin
her tumbling again as if dropped back into a boiling cauldron. Jukes tried hard to compose his mind and judge
things coolly.

The sea, flattened down in the heavier gusts, would
uprise and overwhelm both ends of the 'Nan-Shan' in
snowy rushes of foam, expanding wide, beyond both rails,
into the night. And on this dazzling sheet, spread under
the blackness of the clouds and emitting a bluish glow,
Captain MacWhirr could catch a desolate glimpse of a
few tiny specks black as ebony, the tops of the hatches,
the battened companions, the heads of the covered
winches, the foot of a mast. This was all he could see of
his ship. Her middle structure, covered by the bridge which
bore him, his mate, the closed wheelhouse where a man
was steering shut up with the fear of being swept overboard
together with the whole thing in one great crash – her
middle structure was like a half-tide rock awash upon a
coast. It was like an outlying rock with the water boiling up,
streaming over, pouring off, beating round – like a rock in
the surf to which shipwrecked people cling before they let
go – only it rose, it sank, it rolled continuously, without

respite and rest, like a rock that should have miraculously struck adrift from a coast and gone wallowing upon the sea.

The 'Nan-Shan' was being looted by the storm with a senseless, destructive fury: trysails torn out of the extra gaskets, double-lashed awnings blown away, bridge swept clean, weather-cloths burst, rails twisted, light-screens smashed – and two of the boats had gone already. They had gone unheard and unseen, melting, as it were, in the shock and smother of the wave. It was only later, when upon the white flash of another high sea hurling itself amidships, Jukes had a vision of two pairs of davits leaping black and empty out of the solid blackness, with one over-hauled fall flying and an iron-bound block capering in the air, that he became aware of what had happened within about three yards of his back.

He poked his head forward, groping for the ear of his commander. His lips touched it – big, fleshy, very wet. He cried in an agitated tone, 'Our boats are going now, sir.'

And again he heard that voice, forced and ringing feebly, but with a penetrating effect of quietness in the enormous discord of noises, as if sent out from some remote spot of peace beyond the black wastes of the gale; again he heard a man's voice – the frail and indomitable sound that can be made to carry an infinity of thought, resolution and purpose, that shall be pronouncing confident words on the last day, when heavens fall, and justice is done – again he heard it, and it was crying to him, as if from very, very far – 'All right.'

He thought he had not managed to make himself understood. 'Our boats – I say boats – the boats, sir! Two gone!'

The same voice, within a foot of him and yet so remote, yelled sensibly, 'Can't be helped.'

Captain MacWhirr had never turned his face, but Jukes caught some more words on the wind.

'What can – expect – when hammering through – such —— Bound to leave – something behind – stands to reason.'

Watchfully Jukes listened for more. No more came. This was all Captain MacWhirr had to say; and Jukes could picture to himself rather than see the broad squat back before him. An impenetrable obscurity pressed down upon the ghostly glimmers of the sea. A dull conviction seized upon Jukes that there was nothing to be done.

If the steering-gear did not give way, if the immense volumes of water did not burst the deck in or smash one of the hatches, if the engines did not give up, if way could be kept on the ship against this terrific wind, and she did not bury herself in one of these awful seas, of whose white crests alone, topping high above her bows, he could now and then get a sickening glimpse – then there was a chance of her coming out of it. Something within him seemed to turn over, bringing uppermost the feeling that the 'Nan-Shan' was lost.

'She's done for,' he said to himself, with a surprising mental agitation, as though he had discovered an unexpected meaning in this thought. One of these things was bound to happen. Nothing could be prevented now, and nothing could be remedied. The men on board did not count, and the ship could not last. This weather was too impossible.

Jukes felt an arm thrown heavily over his shoulders; and to this overture he responded with great intelligence by catching hold of his captain round the waist.

They stood clasped thus in the blind night, bracing each other against the wind, cheek to cheek and lip to ear, in the manner of two hulks lashed stem to stern together.

And Jukes heard the voice of his commander hardly any louder than before, but nearer, as though, starting to march athwart the prodigious rush of the hurricane, it had approached him, bearing that strange effect of quietness like the serene glow of a halo.

'D'ye know where the hands got to?' it asked, vigorous and evanescent at the same time, overcoming the strength of the wind, and swept away from Jukes instantly.

Jukes didn't know. They were all on the bridge when the real force of the hurricane struck the ship. He had no idea where they had crawled to. Under the circumstances they were nowhere, for all the use that could be made of them. Somehow the Captain's wish to know distressed Jukes.

'Want the hands, sir?' he cried, apprehensively.

'Ought to know,' asserted Captain MacWhirr. 'Hold hard.'

They held hard. An outburst of unchained fury, a vicious rush of the wind absolutely steadied the ship; she rocked only, quick and light like a child's cradle, for a terrific moment of suspense, while the whole atmosphere, as it seemed, streamed furiously past her, roaring away from the tenebrous earth.

It suffocated them, and with eyes shut they tightened their grasp. What from the magnitude of the shock might have been a column of water running upright in the dark, butted against the ship, broke short, and fell on her bridge, crushingly, from on high, with a dead burying weight.

A flying fragment of that collapse, a mere splash, enveloped them in one swirl from their feet over their heads, filling violently their ears, mouths and nostrils with salt water. It knocked out their legs, wrenched in haste at their arms, seethed away swiftly under their chins; and opening their eyes, they saw the piled-up masses of foam dashing to and fro amongst what looked like the fragments of a ship. She had given way as if driven straight in. Their panting hearts yielded, too, before the tremendous blow; and all at once she sprang up again to her desperate plunging, as if trying to scramble out from under the ruins.

The seas in the dark seemed to rush from all sides to keep her back where she might perish. There was hate in the way she was handled, and a ferocity in the blows that fell. She was like a living creature thrown to the rage of a mob: hustled terribly, struck at, borne up, flung down, leaped upon. Captain MacWhirr and Jukes kept hold of each other, deafened by the noise, gagged by the wind; and the great physical tumult beating about their bodies, brought, like an unbridled display of passion, a profound trouble to their souls. One of those wild and appalling shrieks that are heard at times passing mysteriously overhead in the steady roar of a hurricane, swooped, as if borne on wings, upon the ship, and Jukes tried to outscream it.

'Will she live through this?'

The cry was wrenched out of his breast. It was as unintentional as the birth of a thought in the head, and he heard nothing of it himself. It all became extinct at once – thought, intention, effort – and of his cry the inaudible vibration added to the tempest waves of the air.

He expected nothing from it. Nothing at all. For indeed what answer could be made? But after a while he heard with amazement the frail and resisting voice in his ear, the dwarf sound, unconquered in the giant tumult.

'She may!'

It was a dull yell, more difficult to seize than a whisper. And presently the voice returned again, half submerged in the vast crashes, like a ship battling against the waves of an ocean.

'Let's hope so!' it cried – small, lonely and unmoved, a stranger to the visions of hope or fear; and it flickered into disconnected words: 'Ship.... This.... Never – Anyhow... for the best.' Jukes gave it up.

Then, as if it had come suddenly upon the one thing fit to withstand the power of a storm, it seemed to gain force and firmness for the last broken shouts:

'Keep on hammering... builders... good men.... And chance it... engines.... Rout... good man.'

Captain MacWhirr removed his arm from Jukes's shoulders, and thereby ceased to exist for his mate, so dark it was; Jukes, after a tense stiffening of every muscle, would let himself go limp all over. The gnawing of profound discomfort existed side by side with an incredible disposition to somnolence, as though he had been buffeted and worried into drowsiness. The wind would get hold of his head and try to shake it off his shoulders; his clothes, full of water, were as heavy as lead, cold and dripping like an armour of melting ice: he shivered – it lasted a long time; and with his hands closed hard on his hold, he was letting himself sink slowly into the depths of bodily misery. His mind became concentrated upon himself in an aimless, idle way, and when something pushed lightly at the back of his knees he nearly, as the saying is, jumped out of his skin.

In the start forward he bumped the back of Captain MacWhirr, who didn't move; and then a hand gripped his thigh. A lull had come, a menacing lull of the wind, the holding of a stormy breath – and he felt himself pawed all over. It was the boatswain. Jukes recognized these hands, so thick and enormous that they seemed to belong to some new species of man.

The boatswain had arrived on the bridge, crawling on all fours against the wind, and had found the chief mate's legs with the top of his head. Immediately he crouched and began to explore Jukes's person upwards with prudent, apologetic touches, as became an inferior.

He was an ill-favoured, undersized, gruff sailor of fifty, coarsely hairy, short-legged, long-armed, resembling an elderly ape. His strength was immense; and in his great lumpy paws, bulging like brown boxing-gloves on the end of furry forearms, the heaviest objects were handled like playthings. Apart from the grizzled pelt on his chest, the menacing demeanour and the hoarse voice, he had none of the classical attributes of his rating. His good nature almost amounted to imbecility: the men did what they liked with him, and he had not an ounce of initiative in his character, which was easy-going and talkative. For these reasons Jukes disliked him; but Captain MacWhirr, to Jukes's scornful disgust, seemed to regard him as a first-rate petty officer.

He pulled himself up by Jukes's coat, taking that liberty with the greatest moderation, and only so far as it was forced upon him by the hurricane.

'What is it, boss'n, what is it?' yelled Jukes, impatiently. What could that fraud of a boss'n want on the bridge? The typhoon had got on Jukes's nerves. The husky bellowings of the other, though unintelligible, seemed to suggest a state of lively satisfaction. There could be no mistake. The old fool was pleased with something.

The boatswain's other hand had found some other body, for in a changed tone he began to inquire: 'Is it you, sir? Is it you, sir?' The wind strangled his howls.

'Yes!' cried Captain MacWhirr.

IV

ALL that the boatswain, out of a superabundance of yells, could make clear to Captain MacWhirr was the bizarre intelligence that 'All them Chinamen in the fore 'tween deck have fetched away, sir.'

Jukes to leeward could hear these two shouting within six inches of his face, as you may hear on a still night half a mile away two men conversing across a field. He heard Captain MacWhirr's exasperated 'What? What?' and the strained pitch of the other's hoarseness. 'In a lump...seen them myself.... Awful sight, sir...thought...tell you.'

Jukes remained indifferent, as if rendered irresponsible by the force of the hurricane, which made the very thought of action utterly vain. Besides, being very young, he had found the occupation of keeping his heart completely steeled against the worst so engrossing that he had come to feel an overpowering dislike towards any other form of activity whatever. He was not scared; he knew this because, firmly believing he would never see another sunrise, he remained calm in that belief.

These are the moments of do-nothing heroics to which even good men surrender at times. Many officers of ships can no doubt recall a case in their experience when just such a trance of confounded stoicism would come all at once over a whole ship's company. Jukes, however, had no wide experience of men or storms. He conceived himself to be calm – inexorably calm; but as a matter of fact he was daunted; not abjectly, but only so far as a decent man may, without becoming loathsome to himself.

It was rather like a forced-on numbness of spirit. The long, long stress of a gale does it; the suspense of the interminably culminating catastrophe; and there is a bodily fatigue in the mere holding on to existence within the excessive tumult; a searching and insidious fatigue that penetrates deep into a man's breast to cast down and sadden his heart, which is incorrigible, and of all the gifts of the earth – even before life itself – aspires to peace.

Jukes was benumbed much more than he supposed. He held on – very wet, very cold, stiff in every limb; and in a momentary hallucination of swift visions (it is said that a drowning man thus reviews all his life) he beheld all sorts of memories altogether unconnected with his present situation. He remembered his father, for instance: a worthy business man, who at an unfortunate crisis in his affairs went quietly to bed and died forthwith in a state of resignation. Jukes did not recall these circumstances, of course, but remaining otherwise unconcerned he seemed to see distinctly the poor man's face; a certain game of nap played when quite a boy in Table Bay on board a ship, since lost with all hands; the thick eyebrows of his first skipper; and without any emotion, as he might years ago have walked listlessly into her room and found her sitting there with a book, he remembered his mother – dead, too, now – the resolute woman, left badly off, who had been very firm in his bringing up.

It could not have lasted more than a second, perhaps not so much. A heavy arm had fallen about his shoulders; Captain MacWhirr's voice was speaking his name into his ear.

'Jukes! Jukes!'

He detected the tone of deep concern. The wind had thrown its weight on the ship, trying to pin her down amongst the seas. They made a clean breach over her, as over a deep-swimming log; and the gathered weight of crashes menaced monstrously from afar. The breakers flung out of the night with a ghostly light on their crests – the light of sea-foam that in a ferocious, boiling-up pale flash showed upon the slender body of the ship the toppling rush, the downfall, and the seething mad scurry of each wave. Never for a moment could she shake herself clear of the water; Jukes, rigid, perceived in her motion the ominous sign of haphazard floundering. She was no longer struggling intelligently. It was the beginning of the end; and the note of busy concern in Captain MacWhirr's voice sickened him like an exhibition of blind and pernicious folly.

The spell of the storm had fallen upon Jukes. He was penetrated by it, absorbed by it; he was rooted in it with a rigour of dumb attention. Captain MacWhirr persisted in his cries, but the wind got between them like a solid wedge. He hung round Jukes's neck as heavy as a millstone, and suddenly the sides of their heads knocked together.

'Jukes! Mr Jukes, I say!'

He had to answer that voice that would not be silenced. He answered in the customary manner: '...Yes, sir.'

And directly, his heart, corrupted by the storm that breeds a craving for peace, rebelled against the tyranny of training and command.

Captain MacWhirr had his mate's head fixed firm in the crook of his elbow, and pressed it to his yelling lips mysteriously. Sometimes Jukes would break in, admonishing hastily: 'Look out, sir!' or Captain MacWhirr would bawl an earnest exhortation to 'Hold hard, there!' and the whole black universe seemed to reel together with the ship. They paused. She floated yet. And Captain MacWhirr would resume his shouts. '...Says...whole lot...fetched away....Ought to see...what's the matter.'

Directly the full force of the hurricane had struck the ship, every part of her deck became untenable; and the sailors, dazed and dismayed, took shelter in the port alley-way under the bridge. It had a door aft, which they shut; it was very black, cold, and dismal. At each heavy fling of the ship they would groan all together in the dark, and tons of water could be heard scuttling about as if trying to get at them from above. The boatswain had been keeping up a gruff talk, but a more unreasonable lot of men, he said afterwards, he had never been with. They were snug enough there, out of harm's way, and not wanted to do anything, either; and yet they did nothing but grumble and complain peevishly like so many sick kids. Finally, one of them said that if there had been at least some light to see each other's noses by, it wouldn't be so bad. It was making him crazy, he declared, to lie there in the dark waiting for the blamed hooker to sink.

'Why don't you step outside, then, and be done with it at once?' the boatswain turned on him.

This called up a shout of execration. The boatswain found himself overwhelmed with reproaches of all sorts. They seemed to take it ill that a lamp was not instantly created for them out of nothing. They would whine after a light to get drowned by – anyhow! And though the unrea-son of their revilings was patent – since no one could hope to reach the lamp-room, which was forward – he became greatly distressed. He did not think it was decent of them to be nagging at him like this. He told them so, and was met by general contumely. He sought refuge, therefore, in an embittered silence. At the same time their grumbling and sighing and muttering worried him greatly, but by-and-by it occurred to him that there were six globe lamps hung in the 'tween-deck, and that there could be no harm in depriving the coolies of one of them.

The 'Nan-Shan' had an athwartship coal-bunker, which, being at times used as cargo space, communicated by an iron door with the fore 'tween-deck. It was empty then, and its manhole was the foremost one in the alleyway. The boatswain could get in, therefore, without coming out on deck at all; but to his great surprise he found he could induce no one to help him in taking off the manhole cover. He groped for it all the same, but one of the crew lying in his way refused to budge.

'Why, I only want to get you that blamed light you are crying for,' he expostulated, almost pitifully.

Somebody told him to go and put his head in a bag. He regretted he could not recognize the voice, and that it was too dark to see, otherwise, as he said, he would have put a head on *that* son of a sea-cook, anyway, sink or swim. Nevertheless, he had made up his mind to show them he could get a light, if he were to die for it.

Through the violence of the ship's rolling, every movement was dangerous. To be lying down seemed labour enough. He nearly broke his neck dropping into the bunker. He fell on his back, and was sent shooting helplessly from side to side in the dangerous company of a heavy iron bar – a coal-trimmer's slice probably – left down there by somebody. This thing made him as nervous as though it had been a wild beast. He could not see it, the inside of the bunker coated with coal-dust being perfectly and impenetrably black; but he heard it sliding and clattering, and striking here and there, always in the neighbourhood of his head. It seemed to make an extraordinary noise, too – to give heavy thumps as though it had been as big as a bridge girder. This was remarkable enough for him to notice while he was flung from port to starboard and back again, and clawing desperately the smooth sides of the bunker in the endeavour to stop himself. The door into the 'tween-deck not fitting quite true, he saw a thread of dim light at the bottom.

Being a sailor, and a still active man, he did not want much of a chance to regain his feet; and as luck would have it, in scrambling up he put his hand on the iron slice, picking it up as he rose. Otherwise he would have been afraid of the thing breaking his legs, or at least knocking him down again. At first he stood still. He felt unsafe in

this darkness that seemed to make the ship's motion unfamiliar, unforeseen, and difficult to counteract. He felt so
much shaken for a moment that he dared not move for fear
of 'taking charge again.' He had no mind to get battered to
pieces in that bunker.

He had struck his head twice; he was dazed a little. He
seemed to hear yet so plainly the clatter and bangs of the
iron slice flying about his ears that he tightened his grip to
prove to himself he had it there safely in his hand. He was
vaguely amazed at the plainness with which down there he
could hear the gale raging. Its howls and shrieks seemed to
take on, in the emptiness of the bunker, something of the
human character, of human rage and pain – being not vast
but infinitely poignant. And there were, with every roll,
thumps, too – profound, ponderous thumps, as if a bulk
object of five-ton weight or so had got play in the hold. But
there was no such thing in the cargo. Something on deck?
Impossible. Or alongside? Couldn't be.

He thought all this quickly, clearly, competently, like a
seaman, and in the end remained puzzled. This noise,
though, came deadened from outside, together with the
washing and pouring of water on deck above his head. Was
it the wind? Must be. It made down there a row like the
shouting of a big lot of crazed men. And he discovered in
himself a desire for a light, too – if only to get drowned by –
and a nervous anxiety to get out of that bunker as quickly as
possible.

He pulled back the bolt: the heavy iron plate turned on
its hinges; and it was as though he had opened the door to
the sounds of the tempest. A gust of hoarse yelling met
him: the air was still; and the rushing of water overhead was
covered by a tumult of strangled, throaty shrieks that
produced an effect of desperate confusion. He straddled
his legs the whole width of the doorway and stretched his
neck. And at first he perceived only what he had come to
seek: six small yellow flames swinging violently on the great
body of the dusk.

It was stayed like the gallery of a mine, with a row of stanchions in the middle, and cross-beams overhead, penetrating into the gloom ahead – indefinitely. And to port there loomed, like the caving in of one of the sides, a bulky mass with a slanting outline. The whole place, with the shadows and the shapes, moved all the time. The boatswain glared: the ship lurched to starboard, and a great howl came from that mass that had the slant of fallen earth.

Pieces of wood whizzed past. Planks, he thought, inexpressibly startled, and flinging back his head. At his feet a man went sliding over, open-eyed, on his back, straining with uplifted arms for nothing: and another came bounding like a detached stone with his head between his legs and his hands clenched. His pigtail whipped in the air; he made a grab at the boatswain's legs, and from his opened hand a bright white disc rolled against the boatswain's foot. He recognized a silver dollar, and yelled at it with astonishment. With a precipitated sound of trampling and shuffling of bare feet, and with guttural cries, the mound of writhing bodies piled up to port detached itself from the ship's side and sliding, inert and struggling, shifted to starboard, with a dull, brutal thump. The cries ceased. The boatswain heard a long moan through the roar and whistling of the wind; he saw an inextricable confusion of heads and shoulders, naked soles kicking upwards, fists raised, tumbling backs, legs, pigtails, faces.

'Good Lord!' he cried, horrified, and banged-to the iron door upon this vision.

This was what he had come on the bridge to tell. He could not keep it to himself; and on board ship there is only one man to whom it is worth while to unburden yourself. On his passage back the hands in the alleyway swore at him for a fool. Why didn't he bring that lamp? What the devil did the coolies matter to anybody? And when he came out, the extremity of the ship made what went on inside of her appear of little moment.

At first he thought he had left the alleyway in the very moment of her sinking. The bridge ladders had been washed away, but an enormous sea filling the after-deck floated him up. After that he had to lie on his stomach for some time, holding to a ring-bolt, getting his breath now and then, and swallowing salt water. He struggled farther on his hands and knees, too frightened and distracted to turn back. In this way he reached the after part of the wheelhouse. In that comparatively sheltered spot he found the second mate. The boatswain was pleasantly surprised – his impression being that everybody on deck must have been washed away a long time ago. He asked eagerly where the captain was.

The second mate was lying low, like a malignant little animal under a hedge.

'Captain? Gone overboard, after getting us into this mess.' The mate, too, for all he knew or cared. Another fool. Didn't matter. Everybody was going by-and-by.

The boatswain crawled out again into the strength of the wind; not because he much expected to find anybody, he said, but just to get away from 'that man.' He crawled out as outcasts go to face an inclement world. Hence his great joy at finding Jukes and the Captain. But what was going on in the 'tween-deck was to him a minor matter by that time. Besides, it was difficult to make yourself heard. But he managed to convey the idea that the Chinamen had broken adrift together with their boxes, and that he had come up on purpose to report this. As to the hands, they were all right. Then, appeased, he subsided on the deck in a sitting posture, hugging with his arms and legs the stand of the engine-room telegraph – an iron casting as thick as a post. When that went, why, he expected he would go, too. He gave no more thought to the coolies.

Captain MacWhirr had made Jukes understand that he wanted him to go down below – to see.

'What am I to do then, sir?' And the trembling of his whole wet body caused Jukes's voice to sound like bleating.

'See first ... Boss'n ... says ... adrift.'

'That boss'n is a confounded fool,' howled Jukes, shakily.

The absurdity of the demand made upon him revolted Jukes. He was as unwilling to go as if the moment he had left the deck the ship were sure to sink.

'I must know ... can't leave. ...'

'They'll settle, sir.'

'Fight ... boss'n says they fight. ... Why? Can't have ... fighting ... board ship. ... Much rather keep you here ... case. ... I should ... washed overboard myself. ... Stop it ... some way. You see and tell me ... through engine-room tube. Don't want you ... come up here ... too often. Dangerous ... moving about ... deck.'

Jukes, held with his head in chancery, had to listen to what seemed horrible suggestions.

'Don't want ... you get lost ... so long ... ship isn't. ... Rout. ... Good man ... Ship ... may ... through this ... all right yet.'

All at once Jukes understood he would have to go.

'Do you think she may?' he screamed.

But the wind devoured the reply, out of which Jukes heard only the one word, pronounced with great energy '... Always. ...'

Captain MacWhirr released Jukes, and bending over the boatswain, yelled 'Get back with the mate.' Jukes only knew that the arm was gone off his shoulders. He was dismissed with his orders – to do what? He was exasperated into letting go his hold carelessly, and on the instant was blown away. It seemed to him that nothing could stop him from being blown right over the stern. He flung himself down hastily, and the boatswain, who was following, fell on him.

'Don't you get up yet, sir,' cried the boatswain. 'No hurry!'

A sea swept over. Jukes understood the boatswain to splutter that the bridge ladders were gone. 'I'll lower you down, sir, by your hands,' he screamed. He shouted also something about the smoke-stack being as likely to go overboard as not. Jukes thought it very possible, and imagined the fires were out, the ship helpless. . . . The boatswain by his side kept on yelling. 'What? What is it?' Jukes cried distressfully; and the other repeated, 'What would my old woman say if she saw me now?'

In the alleyway, where a lot of water had got in and splashed in the dark, the men were still as death, till Jukes stumbled against one of them and cursed him savagely for being in the way. Two or three voices then asked, eager and weak, 'Any chance for us, sir?'

'What's the matter with you fools?' he said, brutally. He felt as though he could throw himself down amongst them and never move any more. But they seemed cheered; and in the midst of obsequious warnings, 'Look out! Mind that manhole lid, sir,' they lowered him into the bunker. The boatswain tumbled down after him, and as soon as he had picked himself up he remarked, 'She would say, "Serve you right, you old fool, for going to sea."'

The boatswain had some means, and made a point of alluding to them frequently. His wife – a fat woman – and two grown-up daughters kept a greengrocer's shop in the East-end of London.

In the dark, Jukes, unsteady on his legs, listened to a faint thunderous patter. A deadened screaming went on steadily at his elbow, as it were; and from above the louder tumult of the storm descended upon these near sounds. His head swam. To him, too, in that bunker, the motion of the ship seemed novel and menacing, sapping his resolution as though he had never been afloat before.

He had half a mind to scramble out again; but the remembrance of Captain MacWhirr's voice made this impossible. His orders were to go and see. What was the good of it? he wanted to know. Enraged, he told himself he would see – of course. But the boatswain, staggering clumsily, warned him to be careful how he opened that door; there was a blamed fight going on. And Jukes, as if in great bodily pain, desired irritably to know what the devil they were fighting for.

'Dollars! Dollars, sir. All their rotten chests got burst open. Blamed money skipping all over the place, and they are tumbling after it head over heels – tearing and biting like anything. A regular little hell in there.'

Jukes convulsively opened the door. The short boat-swain peered under his arm.

One of the lamps had gone out, broken perhaps. Rancorous, guttural cries burst out loudly on their ears, and a strange panting sound, the working of all these straining breasts. A hard blow hit the side of the ship: water fell above with a stunning shock, and in the forefront of the gloom, where the air was reddish and thick, Jukes saw a head bang the deck violently, two thick calves waving on high, muscular arms twined round a naked body, a yellow-face, open-mouthed and with a set wild stare, look up and slide away. An empty chest clattered turning over; a man fell head first with a jump, as if lifted by a kick; and farther off, indistinct, others streamed like a mass of rolling stones down a bank, thumping the deck with their feet and flourishing their arms wildly. The hatchway ladder was loaded with coolies swarming on it like bees on a branch. They hung on the steps in a crawling, stirring cluster, beating madly with their fists the underside of the battened hatch, and the headlong rush of the water above was heard in the intervals of their yelling. The ship heeled over more, and they began to drop off: first one, then two, then all the rest went away together, falling straight off with a great cry.

Jukes was confounded. The boatswain, with gruff anxiety, begged him, 'Don't you go in there, sir.'

The whole place seemed to twist upon itself, jumping incessantly the while; and when the ship rose to a sea Jukes fancied that all these men would be shot upon him in a body. He backed out, swung the door to, and with trembling hands pushed at the bolt. . . .

As soon as his mate had gone Captain MacWhirr, left alone on the bridge, sidled and staggered as far as the wheelhouse. Its door being hinged forward, he had to fight the gale for admittance, and when at last he managed to enter, it was with an instantaneous clatter and a bang, as though he had been fired through the wood. He stood within, holding on to the handle.

The steering-gear leaked steam, and in the confined space the glass of the binnacle made a shiny oval of light in a thin white fog. The wind howled, hummed, whistled, with sudden booming gusts that rattled the doors and shutters in the vicious patter of sprays. Two coils of lead-line and a small canvas bag hung on a long lanyard, swung wide off, and came back clinging to the bulkheads. The gratings underfoot were nearly afloat; with every sweeping blow of a sea, water squirted violently through the cracks all round the door, and the man at the helm had flung down his cap, his coat, and stood propped against the gear-casing in a striped cotton shirt open on his breast. The little brass wheel in his hands had the appearance of a bright and fragile toy. The cords of his neck stood hard and lean, a dark patch lay in the hollow of his throat, and his face was still and sunken as in death.

Captain MacWhirr wiped his eyes. The sea that had nearly taken him overboard had, to his great annoyance, washed his sou'-wester hat off his bald head. The fluffy, fair hair, soaked and darkened, resembled a mean skein of cotton threads festooned round his bare skull. His face, glistening with sea-water, had been made crimson with the wind, with the sting of sprays. He looked as though he had come off sweating from before a furnace.

'You here?' he muttered, heavily.

The second mate had found his way into the wheelhouse some time before. He had fixed himself in a corner with his knees up, a fist pressed against each temple; and this attitude suggested rage, sorrow, resignation, surrender, with a sort of concentrated unforgiveness. He said mournfully and defiantly, 'Well, it's my watch below now: ain't it?'

The steam gear clattered, stopped, clattered again; and the helmsman's eyeballs seemed to project out of a hungry face as if the compass-card behind the binnacle glass had been meat. God knows how long he had been left there to steer, as if forgotten by all his shipmates. The bells had not been struck; there had been no reliefs; the ship's routine had gone down wind; but he was trying to keep her head north-north-east. The rudder might have been gone for all he knew, the fires out, the engines broken down, the ship ready to roll over like a corpse. He was anxious not to get muddled and lose control of her head, because the compass-card swung far both ways, wriggling on the pivot, and sometimes seemed to whirl right round. He suffered from mental stress. He was horribly afraid, also, of the wheel-house going. Mountains of water kept on tumbling against it. When the ship took one of her desperate dives the corners of his lips twitched.

Captain MacWhirr looked up at the wheelhouse clock. Screwed to the bulkhead, it had a white face on which the black hands appeared to stand quite still. It was half-past one in the morning.

'Another day,' he muttered to himself.

The second mate heard him, and lifting his head as one grieving amongst ruins, 'You won't see it break,' he exclaimed. His wrists and his knees could be seen to shake violently. 'No, by God! You won't....'

He took his face again between his fists.

The body of the helmsman had moved slightly, but his head didn't budge on his neck – like a stone head fixed to look one way from a column. During a roll that all but took his booted legs from under him, and in the very stagger to save himself, Captain MacWhirr said austerely, 'Don't you pay any attention to what that man says.' And then with an indefinable change of tone, very grave, he added, 'He isn't on duty.'

The sailor said nothing.

The hurricane boomed, shaking the little place, which seemed air-tight; and the light of the binnacle flickered all the time.

'You haven't been relieved,' Captain MacWhirr went on, looking down. 'I want you to stick to the helm, though, as long as you can. You've got the hang of her. Another man coming here might make a mess of it. Wouldn't do. No child's play. And the hands are probably busy with a job down below.... Think you can?'

The steering-gear leaped into an abrupt short clatter, stopped smouldering like an ember; and the still man, with a motionless gaze, burst out, as if all the passion in him had gone into his lips: 'By Heavens, sir! I can steer for ever if nobody talks to me.'

'Oh! aye! All right....' The Captain lifted his eyes for the first time to the man, '... Hackett.'

And he seemed to dismiss this matter from his mind. He stooped to the engine-room speaking-tube, blew in, and bent his head. Mr Rout below answered, and at once Captain MacWhirr put his lips to the mouthpiece.

With the uproar of the gale around him he applied alternately his lips and his ear, and the engineer's voice mounted to him, harsh and as if out of the heat of an engagement. One of the stokers was disabled, the others had given in, the second engineer and the donkey-man were firing-up. The third engineer was standing by the steam-valve. The engines were being tended by hand. How was it above?

'Bad enough. It mostly rests with you,' said Captain MacWhirr. Was the mate down there yet? No? Well, he would be presently. Would Mr Rout let him talk through the speaking-tube? – through the deck speaking-tube, because he – the Captain – was going out on the bridge directly. There was some trouble among the Chinamen. They were fighting, it seemed. Couldn't allow fighting anyhow....

Mr Rout had gone away, and Captain MacWhirr could feel against his ear the pulsation of the engines, like the beat of the ship's heart. Mr Rout's voice down there shouted something distantly. The ship pitched headlong, the pulsation leaped with a hissing tumult, and stopped dead. Captain MacWhirr's face was impassive, and his eyes were fixed aimlessly on the crouching shape of the second mate. Again Mr Rout's voice cried out in the depths, and the pulsating beats recommenced, with slow strokes – growing swifter.

Mr Rout had returned to the tube. 'It don't matter much what they do,' he said, hastily; and then, with irritation, 'She takes these dives as if she never meant to come up again.'

'Awful sea,' said the Captain's voice from above.

'Don't let me drive her under,' barked Solomon Rout up the pipe.

'Dark and rain. Can't see what's coming,' uttered the voice. 'Must – keep – her – moving – enough to steer – and chance it,' it went on to state distinctly.

'I am doing as much as I dare.'

'We are – getting – smashed up – a good deal up here,' proceeded the voice mildly. 'Doing – fairly well – though. Of course, if the wheelhouse should go . . . .'

Mr Rout, bending an attentive ear, muttered peevishly something under his breath.

But the deliberate voice up there became animated to ask: 'Jukes turned up yet?' Then, after a short wait, 'I wish he would bear a hand. I want him to be done and come up here in case of anything. To look after the ship. I am all alone. The second mate's lost. . . .'

'What?' shouted Mr Rout into the engine-room, taking his head away. Then up the tube he cried, 'Gone overboard?' and clapped his ear to.

'Lost his nerve,' the voice from above continued in a matter-of-fact tone. 'Damned awkward circumstance.'

Mr Rout, listening with bowed neck, opened his eyes wide at this. However, he heard something like the sounds of a scuffle and broken exclamations coming down to him. He strained his hearing; and all the time Beale, the third engineer, with his arms uplifted, held between the palms of his hands the rim of a little black wheel projecting at the side of a big copper pipe. He seemed to be poising it above his head, as though it were a correct attitude in some sort of game.

To steady himself, he pressed his shoulder against the white bulkhead, one knee bent, and a sweat-rag tucked in his belt hanging on his hip. His smooth cheek was begrimed and flushed, and the coal dust on his eyelids, like the black pencilling of a make-up, enhanced the liquid brilliance of the whites, giving to his youthful face something of a feminine, exotic and fascinating aspect. When the ship pitched he would with hasty movements of his hands screw hard at the little wheel.

'Gone crazy,' began the Captain's voice suddenly in the tube. 'Rushed at me...Just now. Had to knock him down....This minute. You heard, Mr Rout?'

'The devil!' muttered Mr Rout. 'Look out, Beale!'

His shout rang out like the blast of a warning trumpet, between the iron walls of the engine-room. Painted white, they rose high into the dusk of the skylight, sloping like a roof; and the whole lofty space resembled the interior of a monument, divided by floors of iron grating, with lights flickering at different levels, and a mass of gloom lingering in the middle, within the columnar stir of machinery under the motionless swelling of the cylinders. A loud and wild resonance, made up of all the noises of the hurricane, dwelt in the still warmth of the air. There was in it the smell of hot metal, of oil, and a slight mist of steam. The blows of the sea seemed to traverse it in an unringing, stunning shock, from side to side.

Gleams, like pale long flames, trembled upon the polish of metal; from the flooring below the enormous crank-heads emerged in their turns with a flash of brass and steel – going over; while the connecting-rods, big-jointed,

like skeleton limbs, seemed to thrust them down and pull
them up again with an irresistible precision. And deep in
the half-light other rods dodged deliberately to and fro,
crossheads nodded, discs of metal rubbed smoothly against
each other, slow and gentle, in a commingling of shadows
and gleams.

Sometimes all those powerful and unerring movements
would slow down simultaneously, as if they had been the
functions of a living organism, stricken suddenly by the
blight of languor; and Mr Rout's eyes would blaze darker in
his long sallow face. He was fighting this fight in a pair of
carpet slippers. A short shiny jacket barely covered his
loins, and his white wrists protruded far out of the tight
sleeves, as though the emergency had added to his stature,
had lengthened his limbs, augmented his pallor, hollowed
his eyes.

He moved, climbing high up, disappearing low down,
with a restless, purposeful industry, and when he stood still,
holding the guard-rail in front of the starting-gear, he
would keep glancing to the right at the steam-gauge, at
the water-gauge, fixed upon the white wall in the light of a
swaying lamp. The mouths of two speaking-tubes gaped
stupidly at his elbow, and the dial of the engine-room
telegraph resembled a clock of large diameter, bearing on
its face curt words instead of figures. The grouped letters
stood out heavily black, around the pivot-head of the
indicator, emphatically symbolic of loud exclamations:
AHEAD, ASTERN, SLOW, HALF, STAND BY; and
the fat black hand pointed downwards to the word FULL,
which, thus singled out, captured the eye as a sharp cry
secures attention.

The wood-encased bulk of the low-pressure cylinder,
frowning portly from above, emitted a faint wheeze at
every thrust, and except for that low hiss the engines
worked their steel limbs headlong or slow with a silent,
determined smoothness. And all this, the white walls, the
moving steel, the floor plates under Solomon Rout's feet,

the floors of iron grating above his head, the dusk and the gleams, uprose and sank continuously, with one accord, upon the harsh wash of the waves against the ship's side. The whole loftiness of the place, booming hollow to the great voice of the wind, swayed at the top like a tree, would go over bodily, as if borne down this way and that by the tremendous blasts.

'You've got to hurry up,' shouted Mr Rout, as soon as he saw Jukes appear in the stokehold doorway.

Jukes's glance was wandering and tipsy; his red face was puffy, as though he had overslept himself. He had had an arduous road, and had travelled over it with immense vivacity, the agitation of his mind corresponding to the exertions of his body. He had rushed up out of the bunker, stumbling in the dark alleyway amongst a lot of bewildered men who, trod upon, asked 'What's up, sir?' in awed mutters all round him; – down the stokehold ladder, missing many iron rungs in his hurry, down into a place deep as a well, black as Tophet, tipping over back and forth like a see-saw. The water in the bilges thundered at each roll, and lumps of coal skipped to and fro, from end to end, rattling like an avalanche of pebbles on a slope of iron.

Somebody in there moaned with pain, and somebody else could be seen crouching over what seemed the prone body of a dead man; a lusty voice blasphemed; and the glow under each fire-door was like a pool of flaming blood radiating quietly in a velvety blackness.

A gust of wind struck upon the nape of Jukes's neck and next moment he felt it streaming about his wet ankles. The stoke-hold ventilators hummed: in front of the six fire-doors two wild figures, stripped to the waist, staggered and stooped, wrestling with two shovels.

'Hallo! Plenty of draught now,' yelled the second engineer at once, as though he had been all the time looking out for Jukes. The donkeyman, a dapper little chap with a dazzling fair skin and a tiny, gingery moustache, worked in a sort of mute transport. They were keeping a full head of steam, and a profound rumbling, as of an empty furniture van trotting over a bridge, made a sustained bass to all the other noises of the place.

'Blowing off all the time,' went on yelling the second. With a sound as of a hundred scoured saucepans, the orifice of a ventilator spat upon his shoulder a sudden gush of salt water, and he volleyed a stream of curses upon all things on earth including his own soul, ripping and raving, and all the time attending to his business. With a sharp clash of metal the ardent pale glare of the fire opened upon his bullet head, showing his spluttering lips, his insolent face, and with another clang closed like the white-hot wink of an iron eye.

'Where's the blooming ship? Can you tell me? blast my eyes! Under water – or what? It's coming down here in tons. Are the condemned cowls gone to Hades? Hey? Don't you know anything – you jolly sailor-man you . . .?'

Jukes, after a bewildered moment, had been helped by a roll to dart through; and as soon as his eyes took in the comparative vastness, peace and brilliance of the engine-room, the ship, setting her stern heavily in the water, sent him charging head down upon Mr Rout.

The chief's arm, long like a tentacle, and straightening as if worked by a spring, went out to meet him, and deflected his rush into a spin towards the speaking-tubes. At the same time Mr Rout repeated earnestly:

'You've got to hurry up, whatever it is.'

Jukes yelled 'Are you there, sir?' and listened. Nothing. Suddenly the roar of the wind fell straight into his ear, but presently a small voice shoved aside the shouting hurricane quietly.

'You, Jukes? – Well?'

Jukes was ready to talk: it was only time that seemed to be wanting. It was easy enough to account for everything. He could perfectly imagine the coolies battened down in the reeking 'tween-deck, lying sick and scared between the rows of chests. Then one of these chests – or perhaps several at once – breaking loose in a roll, knocking out others, sides splitting, lids flying open, and all these clumsy Chinamen rising up in a body to save their property. Afterwards every fling of the ship would hurl that tramping, yelling mob here and there, from side to side, in a whirl of smashed wood, torn clothing, rolling dollars. A struggle once started, they would be unable to stop themselves. Nothing could stop them now except main force. It was a disaster. He had seen it, and that was all he could say. Some of them must be dead, he believed. The rest would go on fighting. . . .

He sent up his words, tripping over each other, crowding the narrow tube. They mounted as if into a silence of an enlightened comprehension dwelling alone up there with a storm. And Jukes wanted to be dismissed from the face of that odious trouble intruding on the great need of the ship.

V

HE waited. Before his eyes the engines turned with slow labour, that in the moment of going off into a mad fling would stop dead at Mr Rout's shout, 'Look out, Beale!' They paused in an intelligent immobility, stilled in midstroke, a heavy crank arrested on the cant, as if conscious of danger and the passage of time. Then, with a 'Now, then!' from the chief, and the sound of a breath expelled through clenched teeth, they would accomplish the interrupted revolution and begin another.

There was the prudent sagacity of wisdom and the deliberation of enormous strength in their movements. This was their work – this patient coaxing of a distracted ship over the fury of the waves and into the very eye of the wind. At times Mr Rout's chin would sink on his breast, and he watched them with knitted eyebrows as if lost in thought.

The voice that kept the hurricane out of Jukes's ear began: 'Take the hands with you . . . ,' and left off unexpectedly.

'What could I do with them, sir?'

A harsh, abrupt, imperious clang exploded suddenly. The three pairs of eyes flew up to the telegraph dial to see the hand jump from FULL to STOP, as if snatched by a devil. And then these three men in the engine-room had the intimate sensation of a check upon the ship, of a strange shrinking, as if she had gathered herself for a desperate leap.

'Stop her!' bellowed Mr Rout.

Nobody – not even Captain MacWhirr, who alone on deck had caught sight of a white line of foam coming on at such a height that he couldn't believe his eyes – nobody was to know the steepness of that sea and the awful depth of the hollow the hurricane had scooped out behind the running wall of water.

It raced to meet the ship, and, with a pause, as of girding the loins, the 'Nan-Shan' lifted her bows and leaped. The flames in all the lamps sank, darkening the engine-room. One went out. With a tearing crash and a swirling, raving tumult, tons of water fell upon the deck, as though the ship had darted under the foot of a cataract.

Down there they looked at each other, stunned.

'Swept from end to end, by God!' bawled Jukes.

She dipped into the hollow straight down, as if going over the edge of the world. The engine-room toppled forward menacingly, like the inside of a tower nodding in an earthquake. An awful racket, of iron things falling, came from the stokehold. She hung on this appalling slant long enough for Beale to drop on his hands and knees and begin to crawl as if he meant to fly on all fours out of the engine-room, and for Mr Rout to turn his head slowly, rigid, cavernous, with the lower jaw dropping. Jukes had shut his eyes, and his face in a moment became hopelessly blank and gentle, like the face of a blind man.

At last she rose slowly, staggering, as if she had to lift a mountain with her bows.

Mr Rout shut his mouth; Jukes blinked; and little Beale stood up hastily.

'Another one like this, and that's the last of her,' cried the chief.

He and Jukes looked at each other, and the same thought came into their heads. The Captain! Everything must have been swept away. Steering-gear gone – ship like a log. All over directly.

'Rush!' ejaculated Mr Rout thickly, glaring with enlarged, doubtful eyes at Jukes, who answered him by an irresolute glance.

The clang of the telegraph gong soothed them instantly. The black hand dropped in a flash from STOP to FULL.

'Now then, Beale!' cried Mr Rout.

The steam hissed low. The piston-rods slid in and out. Jukes put his ear to the tube. The voice was ready for him. It said: 'Pick up all the money. Bear a hand now. I'll want you up here.' And that was all.

'Sir?' called up Jukes. There was no answer.

He staggered away like a defeated man from the field of battle. He had got, in some way or other, a cut above his left eyebrow – a cut to the bone. He was not aware of it in the least: quantities of the China Sea, large enough to break his neck for him, had gone over his head, had cleaned, washed, and salted that wound. It did not bleed, but only gaped red; and this gash over the eye, his dishevelled hair, the disorder of his clothes, gave him the aspect of a man worsted in a fight with fists.

'Got to pick up the dollars.' He appealed to Mr Rout, smiling pitifully at random.

'What's that?' asked Mr Rout, wildly. 'Pick up...? I don't care....' Then, quivering in every muscle, but with an exaggeration of paternal tone, 'Go away now, for God's sake. You deck people'll drive me silly. There's that second mate been going for the old man. Don't you know? You fellows are going wrong for want of something to do....'

At these words Jukes discovered in himself the beginnings of anger. Want of something to do – indeed.... Full of hot scorn against the chief, he turned to go the way he

had come. In the stokehold the plump donkeyman toiled
with his shovel mutely, as if his tongue had been cut out;
but the second was carrying on like a noisy, undaunted
maniac, who had preserved his skill in the art of stoking
under a marine boiler.

'Hallo, you wandering officer! Hey! Can't you get some
of your slush-slingers to wind up a few of them ashes? I am
getting choked with them there. Curse it! Hallo! Hey!
Remember the articles: *Sailors and firemen to assist each
other*. Hey! D'ye hear?'

Jukes was climbing out frantically, and the other,
lifting up his face after him, howled, 'Can't you speak?
What are you poking about here for? What's your game,
anyhow?'

A frenzy possessed Jukes. By the time he was back
amongst the men in the darkness of the alleyway, he felt
ready to wring all their necks at the slightest sign of hanging back. The very thought of it exasperated him. *He*
couldn't hang back. They shouldn't.

The impetuosity with which he came amongst them
carried them along. They had already been excited and
startled at all his comings and goings – by the fierceness
and rapidity of his movements; and more felt than seen in
his rushes, he appeared formidable – busied with matters of
life and death that brooked no delay. At the first word he
heard them drop into the bunker one after another obediently, with heavy thumps.

They were not clear as to what would have to be done.
'What is it? What is it?' they were asking each other. The
boatswain tried to explain; the sounds of a great scuffle
surprised them: and the mighty shocks, reverberating
awfully in the black bunker, kept them in mind of their
danger. When the boatswain threw open the door it
seemed that an eddy of the hurricane, stealing through
the iron sides of the ship, had set all these bodies whirling
like dust: there came to them a confused uproar, a
tempestuous tumult, a fierce mutter, gusts of screams

dying away, and the tramping of feet mingling with the blows of the sea.

For a moment they glared amazed, blocking the doorway. Jukes pushed through them brutally. He said nothing, and simply darted in. Another lot of coolies on the ladder, struggling suicidally to break through the battened hatch to a swamped deck, fell off as before, and he disappeared under them like a man overtaken by a landslide.

The boatswain yelled excitedly: 'Come along. Get the mate out. He'll be trampled to death. Come on.'

They charged in, stamping on breasts, on fingers, on faces, catching their feet in heaps of clothing, kicking broken wood; but before they could get hold of him Jukes emerged waist deep in a multitude of clawing hands. In the instant he had been lost to view, all the buttons of his jacket had gone, its back had got split up to the collar, his waistcoat had been torn open. The central struggling mass of Chinamen went over to the roll, dark, indistinct, helpless, with a wild gleam of many eyes in the dim light of the lamps.

'Leave me alone – damn you. I am all right,' screeched Jukes. 'Drive them forward. Watch your chance when she pitches. Forward with 'em. Drive them against the bulkhead. Jam 'em up.'

The rush of the sailors into the seething 'tween-deck was like a splash of cold water into a boiling cauldron. The commotion sank for a moment.

The bulk of Chinamen were locked in such a compact scrimmage that, linking their arms and aided by an appalling dive of the ship, the seamen sent it forward in one great shove, like a solid block. Behind their backs small clusters and loose bodies tumbled from side to side.

The boatswain performed prodigious feats of strength. With his long arms open, and each great paw clutching at a stanchion, he stopped the rush of seven entwined Chinamen rolling like a boulder. His joints cracked; he said, 'Ha!' and they flew apart. But the carpenter showed the greater intelligence. Without saying a word to anybody he went back into the alleyway, to fetch several coils of cargo gear he had seen there – chain and rope. With these life-lines were rigged.

There was really no resistance. The struggle, however it began, had turned into a scramble of blind panic. If the coolies had started up after their scattered dollars they were by that time fighting only for their footing. They took each other by the throat merely to save themselves from being hurled about. Whoever got a hold anywhere would kick at the others who caught at his legs and hung on, till a roll sent them flying together across the deck.

The coming of the white devils was a terror. Had they come to kill? The individuals torn out of the ruck became very limp in the seamen's hands: some, dragged aside by the heels, were passive, like dead bodies, with open, fixed eyes. Here and there a coolie would fall on his knees as if begging for mercy; several, whom the excess of fear made unruly, were hit with hard fists between the eyes, and cowered; while those who were hurt submitted to rough handling, blinking rapidly without a plaint. Faces streamed with blood; there were raw places on the shaven heads, scratches, bruises, torn wounds, gashes. The broken porcelain out of the chests was mostly responsible for the latter. Here and there a Chinaman, wild-eyed, with his tail unplaited, nursed a bleeding sole.

They had been ranged closely, after having been shaken into submission, cuffed a little to allay excitement, addressed in gruff words of encouragement that sounded like promises of evil. They sat on the deck in ghastly, drooping rows, and at the end the carpenter, with two hands to help him, moved busily from place to place, setting taut and hitching the life-lines. The boatswain, with one leg and one arm embracing a stanchion, struggled with a lamp pressed to his breast, trying to get a light, and growling all the time like an industrious gorilla. The figures of seamen stooped repeatedly, with the movements of gleaners, and everything was being flung into the bunker: clothing, smashed wood, broken china, and the dollars, too, gathered up in men's jackets. Now and then a sailor would stagger towards the doorway with his arms full of rubbish; and dolorous, slanting eyes followed his movements.

With every roll of the ship the long rows of sitting Celestials would sway forward brokenly, and her headlong dives knocked together the line of shaven polls from end to end. When the wash of water rolling on the deck died away for a moment, it seemed to Jukes, yet quivering from his exertions, that in his mad struggle down there he had overcome the wind somehow: that a silence had fallen upon the ship, a silence in which the sea struck thunderously at her sides.

Everything had been cleared out of the 'tween-deck – all the wreckage, as the men said. They stood erect and tottering above the level of heads and drooping shoulders. Here and there a coolie sobbed for his breath. Where the high light fell, Jukes could see the salient ribs of one, the yellow, wistful face of another; bowed necks; or would meet a dull stare directed at his face. He was amazed that there had been no corpses; but the lot of them seemed at their last gasp, and they appeared to him more pitiful than if they had been all dead.

Suddenly one of the coolies began to speak. The light came and went on his lean, straining face; he threw his head up like a baying hound. From the bunker came the sounds of knocking and the tinkle of some dollars rolling loose; he stretched out his arm, his mouth yawned black, and the incomprehensible guttural hooting sounds, that did not seem to belong to a human language, penetrated Jukes with a strange emotion as if a brute had tried to be eloquent.

Two more started mouthing what seemed to Jukes fierce denunciations; the others stirred with grunts and growls. Jukes ordered the hands out of the 'tween-decks hurriedly.

He left last himself, backing through the door, while the grunts rose to a loud murmur and hands were extended after him as after a malefactor. The boatswain shot the bolt, and remarked uneasily, 'Seems as if the wind had dropped, sir.'

The seamen were glad to get back into the alleyway. Secretly each of them thought that at the last moment he could rush out on deck – and that was a comfort. There is something horribly repugnant in the idea of being drowned under a deck. Now they had done with the Chinamen, they again became conscious of the ship's position.

Jukes on coming out of the alleyway found himself up to the neck in the noisy water. He gained the bridge, and discovered he could detect obscure shapes as if his sight had become preternaturally acute. He saw faint outlines. They recalled not the familiar aspect of the 'Nan-Shan,' but something remembered – an old dismantled steamer he had seen years ago rotting on a mudbank. She recalled that wreck.

There was no wind, not a breath, except the faint currents created by the lurches of the ship. The smoke tossed out of the funnel was settling down upon her deck. He breathed it as he passed forward. He felt the deliberate throb of the engines, and heard small sounds that seemed to have survived the great uproar: the knocking of broken fittings, the rapid tumbling of some piece of wreckage on the bridge. He perceived dimly the squat shape of his captain holding on to a twisted bridge-rail, motionless and swaying as if rooted to the planks. The unexpected stillness of the air oppressed Jukes.

'We have done it, sir,' he gasped.

'Thought you would,' said Captain MacWhirr.

'Did you?' murmured Jukes to himself.

'Wind fell all at once,' went on the Captain.

Jukes burst out: 'If you think it was an easy job ——'

But his captain, clinging to the rail, paid no attention. 'According to the books the worst is not over yet.'

'If most of them hadn't been half dead with sea-sickness and fright, not one of us would have come out of that 'tween-deck alive,' said Jukes.

'Had to do what's fair by them,' mumbled MacWhirr, stolidly. 'You don't find everything in books.'

'Why, I believe they would have risen on us if I hadn't ordered the hands out of that pretty quick,' continued Jukes with warmth.

After the whisper of their shouts, their ordinary tones, so distinct, rang out very loud to their ears in the amazing stillness of the air. It seemed to them they were talking in a dark and echoing vault.

Through a jagged aperture in the dome of clouds the light of a few stars fell upon the black sea, rising and falling confusedly. Sometimes the head of a watery cone would topple on board and mingle with the rolling flurry of foam on the swamped deck; and the 'Nan-Shan' wallowed heavily at the bottom of a circular cistern of clouds. This ring of dense vapours, gyrating madly round the calm of the centre, encompassed the ship like a motionless and unbroken wall of an aspect inconceivably sinister. Within, the sea, as if agitated by an internal commotion, leaped in peaked mounds that jostled each other, slapping heavily against her sides; and a low moaning sound, the infinite plaint of the storm's fury, came from beyond the limits of the menacing calm. Captain MacWhirr remained silent, and Jukes's ready ear caught suddenly the faint, long-drawn roar of some immense wave rushing unseen under that thick blackness, which made the appalling boundary of his vision.

'Of course,' he started resentfully, 'they thought we had caught at the chance to plunder them. Of course! You said – pick up the money. Easier said than done. They couldn't tell what was in our heads. We came in, smash – right into the middle of them. Had to do it by a rush.'

'As long as it's done ...,' mumbled the Captain, without attempting to look at Jukes. 'Had to do what's fair.'

'We shall find yet there's the devil to pay when this is over,' said Jukes, feeling very sore. 'Let them only recover a bit, and you'll see. They will fly at our throats, sir. Don't forget, sir, she isn't a British ship now. These brutes know it well, too. The damned Siamese flag.'

'We are on board, all the same,' remarked Captain MacWhirr.

'The trouble's not over yet,' insisted Jukes, prophetically, reeling and catching on. 'She's a wreck,' he added, faintly.

'The trouble's not over yet,' assented Captain MacWhirr, half aloud.... 'Look out for her a minute.'

'Are you going off the deck, sir?' asked Jukes, hurriedly, as if the storm were sure to pounce upon him as soon as he had been left alone with the ship.

He watched her, battered and solitary, labouring heavily in a wild scene of mountainous black waters lit by the gleams of distant worlds. She moved slowly, breathing into the still core of the hurricane the excess of her strength in a white cloud of steam – and the deep-toned vibration of the escape was like the defiant trumpeting of a living creature of the sea impatient for the renewal of the contest. It ceased suddenly. The still air moaned. Above Jukes's head a few stars shone into a pit of black vapours. The inky edge of the cloud-disc frowned upon the ship under the patch of glittering sky. The stars, too, seemed to look at her intently, as if for the last time, and the cluster of their splendour sat like a diadem on a lowering brow.

Captain MacWhirr had gone into the chart-room. There was no light there; but he could feel the disorder of that place where he used to live tidily. His armchair was upset. The books had tumbled out on the floor: he scrunched a piece of glass under his boot. He groped for the matches, and found a box on a shelf with a deep ledge. He struck one, and puckering the corners of his eyes, held out the little flame towards the barometer whose glittering top of glass and metals nodded at him continuously.

It stood very low – incredibly low, so low that Captain MacWhirr grunted. The match went out, and hurriedly he extracted another, with thick, stiff fingers.

Again a little flame flared up before the nodding glass and metal of the top. His eyes looked at it narrowed with attention, as if expecting an imperceptible sign. With his grave face he resembled a booted and misshapen pagan burning incense before the oracle of a Joss. There was no mistake. It was the lowest reading he had ever seen in his life.

Captain MacWhirr emitted a low whistle. He forgot himself till the flame diminished to a blue spark, burnt his fingers and vanished. Perhaps something had gone wrong with the thing!

There was an aneroid glass screwed above the couch. He turned that way, struck another match, and discovered the white face of the other instrument looking at him from the bulkhead, meaningly, not to be gainsaid, as though the wisdom of men were made unerring by the indifference of matter. There was no room for doubt now. Captain MacWhirr pshawed at it, and threw the match down.

The worst was to come, then – and if the books were right this worst would be very bad. The experience of the last six hours had enlarged his conception of what heavy weather could be like. 'It'll be terrific,' he pronounced, mentally. He had not consciously looked at anything by the light of the matches except at the barometer; and yet somehow he had seen that his water-bottle and the two tumblers had been flung out of their stand. It seemed to give him a more intimate knowledge of the tossing the ship had gone through. 'I wouldn't have believed it,' he thought. And his table had been cleared, too; his rulers, his pencils, the inkstand – all the things that had their safe appointed places – they were gone, as if a mischievous hand had plucked them out one by one and flung them on the wet floor. The hurricane had broken in upon the orderly arrangements of his privacy. This had never happened before, and the feeling of dismay reached the very seat of his composure. And the worst was to come yet! He was glad the trouble in the 'tween-deck had been discovered in time. If the ship had to go after all, then, at least, she wouldn't be going to the bottom with a lot of people in her fighting teeth and claw. That would have been odious. And in that feeling there was a humane intention and a vague sense of the fitness of things.

These instantaneous thoughts were yet in their essence heavy and slow, partaking of the nature of the man. He extended his hand to put back the matchbox in its corner of the shelf. There were always matches there – by his order. The steward had his instructions impressed upon him long before. 'A box ... just there, see? Not so very full ... where I can put my hand on it, steward. Might want a light in a hurry. Can't tell on board ship *what* you might want in a hurry. Mind, now.'

And of course on his side he would be careful to put it back in its place scrupulously. He did so now, but before he removed his hand it occurred to him that perhaps he would never have occasion to use that box any more. The vividness of the thought checked him and for an infinitesimal fraction of a second his fingers closed again on the small object as though it had been the symbol of all these little habits that chain us to the weary round of life. He released it at last, and letting himself fall on the settee, listened for the first sounds of returning wind.

Not yet. He heard only the wash of water, the heavy splashes, the dull shocks of the confused seas boarding his ship from all sides. She would never have a chance to clear her decks.

But the quietude of the air was startlingly tense and unsafe, like a slender hair holding a sword suspended over his head. By this awful pause the storm penetrated the defences of the man and unsealed his lips. He spoke out in the solitude and the pitch darkness of the cabin, as if addressing another being awakened within his breast.

'I shouldn't like to lose her,' he said half aloud.

He sat unseen, apart from the sea, from his ship, iso-lated, as if withdrawn from the very current of his own existence, where such freaks as talking to himself surely had no place. His palms reposed on his knees, he bowed his short neck and puffed heavily, surrendering to a strange sensation of weariness he was not enlightened enough to recognize for the fatigue of mental stress.

From where he sat he could reach the door of a wash-stand locker. There should have been a towel there. There was. Good. . . . He took it out, wiped his face, and afterwards went on rubbing his wet head. He towelled himself with energy in the dark, and then remained motionless with the towel on his knees. A moment passed, of a stillness so profound that no one could have guessed there was a man sitting in that cabin. Then a murmur arose.

'She may come out of it yet.'

When Captain MacWhirr came out on deck, which he did brusquely, as though he had suddenly become con-scious of having stayed away too long, the calm had lasted already more than fifteen minutes – long enough to make itself intolerable even to his imagination. Jukes, motionless on the forepart of the bridge, began to speak at once. His voice, blank and forced as though he were talking through hard-set teeth, seemed to flow away on all sides into the darkness, deepening again upon the sea.

'I had the wheel relieved. Hackett began to sing out that he was done. He's lying in there alongside the steering-gear with a face like death. At first I couldn't get anybody to crawl out and relieve the poor devil. That boss'en's worse than no good, I always said. Thought I would have had to go myself and haul out one of them by the neck.'

'Ah, well,' muttered the Captain. He stood watchful by Jukes's side.

'The second mate's in there, too, holding his head. Is he hurt, sir?'

'No – crazy,' said Captain MacWhirr, curtly.

'Looks as if he had a tumble, though.'

'I had to give him a push,' explained the Captain.

Jukes gave an impatient sigh.

'It will come very sudden,' said Captain MacWhirr, 'and from over there, I fancy. God only knows though. These books are only good to muddle your head and make you jumpy. It will be bad, and there's an end. If we only can steam her round in time to meet it . . .'

A minute passed. Some of the stars winked rapidly and vanished.

'You left them pretty safe?' began the Captain abruptly, as though the silence were unbearable.

'Are you thinking of the coolies, sir? I rigged life-lines all ways across that 'tween-deck.'

'Did you? Good idea, Mr Jukes.'

'I didn't . . . think you cared to . . . know,' said Jukes – the lurching of the ship cut his speech as though somebody had been jerking him around while he talked – 'how I got on with . . . that infernal job. We did it. And it may not matter in the end.'

'Had to do what's fair, for all – they are only Chinamen. Give them the same chance with ourselves – hang it all. She isn't lost yet. Bad enough to be shut up below in a gale——'

'That's what I thought when you gave me the job, sir,' interjected Jukes, moodily.

'– without being battered to pieces,' pursued Captain MacWhirr with rising vehemence. 'Couldn't let that go on in my ship, if I knew she hadn't five minutes to live. Couldn't bear it, Mr Jukes.'

A hollow echoing noise, like that of a shout rolling in a rocky chasm, approached the ship and went away again. The last star, blurred, enlarged, as if returning to the fiery mist of its beginning, struggled with the colossal depth of blackness hanging over the ship – and went out.

'Now for it!' muttered Captain MacWhirr. 'Mr Jukes.'

'Here, sir.'

The two men were growing indistinct to each other.

'We must trust her to go through it and come out on the other side. That's plain and straight. There's no room for Captain Wilson's storm-strategy here.'

'No, sir.'

'She will be smothered and swept again for hours,' mumbled the Captain. 'There's not much left by this time above deck for the sea to take away – unless you or me.'

'Both, sir,' whispered Jukes, breathlessly.

'You are always meeting trouble half way, Jukes,' Captain MacWhirr remonstrated quaintly. 'Though it's a fact that the second mate is no good. D'ye hear, Mr Jukes? You would be left alone if . . .'

Captain MacWhirr interrupted himself, and Jukes, glancing on all sides, remained silent.

'Don't you be put out by anything,' the Captain continued, mumbling rather fast. 'Keep her facing it. They may say what they like, but the heaviest seas run with the wind. Facing it – always facing it – that's the way to get through. You are a young sailor. Face it. That's enough for any man. Keep a cool head.'

'Yes, sir,' said Jukes, with a flutter of the heart.

In the next few seconds the Captain spoke to the engine room and got an answer.

For some reason Jukes experienced an access of confidence, a sensation that came from outside like a warm breath, and made him feel equal to every demand. The distant muttering of the darkness stole into his ears. He noted it unmoved, out of that sudden belief in himself, as a man safe in a shirt of mail would watch a point.

The ship laboured without intermission amongst the black hills of water, paying with this hard tumbling the price of her life. She rumbled in her depths, shaking a white plummet of steam into the night, and Jukes's thought skimmed like a bird through the engine-room, where Mr Rout – good man – was ready. When the rumbling ceased it seemed to him that there was a pause of every sound, a dead

pause in which Captain MacWhirr's voice rang out startlingly.

'What's that? A puff of wind?' – it spoke much louder
than Jukes had ever heard if before – 'On the bow. That's
right. She may come out of it yet.'

The mutter of the winds drew near apace. In the forefront could be distinguished a drowsy waking plaint passing on, and far off the growth of a multiple clamour,
marching and expanding. There was the throb as of many
drums in it, a vicious rushing note, and like the chant of a
tramping multitude.

Jukes could no longer see his captain distinctly. The
darkness was absolutely piling itself upon the ship. At
most he made out movements, a hint of elbows spread
out, of a head thrown up.

Captain MacWhirr was trying to do up the top button
of his oilskin coat with unwonted haste. The hurricane,
with its power to madden the seas, to sink ships, to uproot
trees, to overturn strong walls and dash the very birds of the
air to the ground, had found this taciturn man in its path,
and, doing its utmost, had managed to wring out a few
words. Before the renewed wrath of winds swooped on his
ship, Captain MacWhirr was moved to declare, in a tone of
vexation, as it were: 'I wouldn't like to lose her.'

He was spared that annoyance.

VI

ON a bright sunshiny day, with the breeze chasing her
smoke far ahead, the 'Nan-Shan' came into Fu-chau. Her
arrival was at once noticed on shore, and the seamen in
harbour said: 'Look! Look at that steamer. What's that?
Siamese – isn't she? Just look at her!'

She seemed, indeed, to have been used as a running
target for the secondary batteries of a cruiser. A hail of
minor shells could not have given her upper works a more
broken, torn, and devastated aspect: and she had about her

the worn, weary air of ships coming from the far ends of the world – and indeed with truth, for in her short passage she had been very far; sighting, verily, even the coast of the Great Beyond, whence no ship ever returns to give up her crew to the dust of the earth. She was incrusted and grey with salt to the trucks of her masts and to the top of her funnel; as though (as some facetious seaman said) 'the crowd on board had fished her out somewhere from the bottom of the sea and brought her in here for salvage.' And further, excited by the felicity of his own wit, he offered to give five pounds for her – 'as she stands.'

Before she had been quite an hour at rest, a meagre little man, with a red-tipped nose and a face cast in an angry mould, landed from a sampan on the quay of the Foreign Concession, and incontinently turned to shake his fist at her.

A tall individual, with legs much too thin for a rotund stomach, and with watery eyes, strolled up and remarked, 'Just left her – eh? Quick work.'

He wore a soiled suit of blue flannel with a pair of dirty cricketing shoes; a dingy grey moustache drooped from his lip, and daylight could be seen in two places between the rim and the crown of his hat.

'Hallo! what are you doing here?' asked the ex-second-mate of the 'Nan-Shan,' shaking hands hurriedly.

'Standing by for a job – chance worth taking – got a quiet hint,' explained the man with the broken hat, in jerky, apathetic wheezes.

The second shook his fist again at the 'Nan-Shan.' 'There's a fellow there that ain't fit to have the command of a scow,' he declared, quivering with passion, while the other looked about listlessly.

'Is there?'

But he caught sight on the quay of a heavy seaman's chest, painted brown under a fringed sailcloth cover, and lashed with new manila line. He eyed it with awakened interest.

'I would talk and raise trouble if it wasn't for that damned Siamese flag. Nobody to go to – or I would make it hot for him. The fraud! Told his chief engineer – that's another fraud for you – I had lost my nerve. The greatest lot of ignorant fools that ever sailed the seas. No! You can't think...'

'Got your money all right?' inquired his seedy acquaintance suddenly.

'Yes. Paid me off on board,' raged the second mate. '"Get your breakfast on shore," says he.'

'Mean skunk!' commented the tall man, vaguely, and passed his tongue on his lips. 'What about having a drink of some sort?'

'He struck me,' hissed the second mate.

'No! Struck! You don't say?' The man in blue began to bustle about sympathetically. 'Can't possibly talk here. I want to know all about it. Struck – eh? Let's get a fellow to carry your chest. I know a quiet place where they have some bottled beer....'

Mr Jukes, who had been scanning the shore through a pair of glasses, informed the chief engineer afterwards that 'our late second mate hasn't been long in finding a friend. A chap looking uncommonly like a bummer. I saw them walk away together from the quay.'

The hammering and banging of the needful repairs did not disturb Captain MacWhirr. The steward found in the letter he wrote, in a tidy chart-room, passages of such absorbing interest that twice he was nearly caught in the act. But Mrs MacWhirr, in the drawing-room of the forty-pound house, stifled a yawn – perhaps out of self-respect – for she was alone.

She reclined in a plush-bottomed and gilt hammock-chair near a tiled fireplace, with Japanese fans on the mantel and a glow of coals in the grate. Lifting her hands, she glanced wearily here and there into the many pages. It was not her fault they were so prosy, so completely uninteresting – from 'My darling wife' at the beginning, to

'Your loving husband' at the end. She couldn't be really expected to understand all these ship affairs. She was glad, of course, to hear from him, but she had never asked herself why, precisely.

'... They are called typhoons ... The mate did not seem to like it ... Not in books ... Couldn't think of letting it go on....'

The paper rustled sharply. '... A calm that lasted more than twenty minutes,' she read perfunctorily; and the next words her thoughtless eyes caught, on the top of another page, were: 'see you and the children again....' She had a movement of impatience. He was always thinking of coming home. He had never had such a good salary before. What was the matter now?

It did not occur to her to turn back overleaf to look. She would have found it recorded there that between 4 and 6 a.m. on December 25th, Captain MacWhirr did actually think that his ship could not possibly live another hour in such a sea, and that he would never see his wife and children again. Nobody was to know this (his letters got mislaid so quickly) – nobody whatever but the steward, who had been greatly impressed by that disclosure. So much so, that he tried to give the cook some idea of the 'narrow squeak we all had' by saying solemnly, 'The old man himself had a dam' poor opinion of our chance.'

'How do you know?' asked, contemptuously, the cook, an old soldier. 'He hasn't told you, maybe?'

'Well, he did give me a hint to that effect,' the steward brazened it out.

'Get along with you! He will be coming to tell *me* next,' jeered the old cook, over his shoulder.

Mrs MacWhirr glanced farther, on the alert. '... Do what's fair.... Miserable objects ... Only three, with a broken leg each, and one ... Thought had better keep, the matter quiet ... hope to have done the fair thing....'

She let fall her hands. No: there was nothing more about coming home. Must have been merely expressing a pious wish. Mrs MacWhirr's mind was set at ease, and a black marble clock, priced by the local jeweller at £3 18s. 6d., had a discreet stealthy tick.

The door flew open, and a girl in the long-legged, short-frocked period of existence, flung into the room. A lot of colourless, rather lanky hair was scattered over her shoulders. Seeing her mother, she stood still, and directed her pale prying eyes upon the letter.

'From father,' murmured Mrs MacWhirr. 'What have you done with your ribbon?'

The girl put her hands up to her head and pouted.

'He's well,' continued Mrs MacWhirr, languidly. 'At least I think so. He never says.' She had a little laugh. The girl's face expressed a wandering indifference, and Mrs MacWhirr surveyed her with fond pride.

'Go and get your hat,' she said after a while. 'I am going out to do some shopping. There is a sale at Linom's.'

'Oh, how jolly!' uttered the child, impressively, in unexpectedly grave vibrating tones, and bounded out of the room.

It was a fine afternoon, with a grey sky and dry sidewalks. Outside the draper's Mrs MacWhirr smiled upon a woman in a black mantle of generous proportions armoured in jet and crowned with flowers blooming falsely above a bilious matronly countenance. They broke into a swift little babble of greetings and exclamations both together, very hurried, as if the street were ready to yawn open and swallow all that pleasure before it could be expressed.

Behind them the high glass doors were kept on the swing. People couldn't pass, men stood aside waiting patiently, and Lydia was absorbed in poking the end of her parasol between the stone flags. Mrs MacWhirr talked rapidly.

'Thank you very much. He's not coming home yet. Of course it's very sad to have him away, but it's such a comfort to know he keeps so well.' Mrs MacWhirr drew breath.

'The climate there agrees with him,' she added, beamingly, as if poor MacWhirr had been away touring in China for the sake of his health.

Neither was the chief engineer coming home yet. Mr Rout knew too well the value of a good billet.

'Solomon says wonders will never cease,' cried Mrs Rout joyously at the old lady in her armchair by the fire. Mr Rout's mother moved slightly, her withered hands lying in black half-mittens on her lap.

The eyes of the engineer's wife fairly danced on the paper. 'That captain of the ship he is in – a rather simple man, you remember, mother? – has done something rather clever, Solomon says.'

'Yes, my dear,' said the old woman meekly, sitting with bowed silvery head, and that air of inward stillness characteristic of very old people who seem lost in watching the last flickers of life. 'I think I remember.'

Solomon Rout, Old Sol, Father Sol, the Chief, 'Rout, good man' – Mr Rout, the condescending and paternal friend of youth, had been the baby of her many children – all dead by this time. And she remembered him best as a boy of ten – long before he went away to serve his apprenticeship in some great engineering works in the North. She had seen so little of him since, she had gone through so many years, that she had now to retrace her steps very far back to recognize him plainly in the mist of time. Sometimes it seemed that her daughter-in-law was talking of some strange man.

Mrs Rout junior was disappointed. 'H'm. H'm.' She turned the page. 'How provoking! He doesn't say what it is. Says I couldn't understand how much there was in it. Fancy! What could it be so very clever? What a wretched man not to tell us!'

She read on without further remark soberly, and at last sat looking into the fire. The chief wrote just a word or two of the typhoon; but something had moved him to express an increased longing for the companionship of the jolly woman. 'If it hadn't been that mother must be looked after, I would send you your passage-money to-day. You could set up a small house out here. I would have a chance to see you sometimes then. We are not growing younger. . . .'

'He's well, mother,' sighed Mrs Rout, rousing herself.

'He always was a strong healthy boy,' said the old woman, placidly.

But Mr Jukes's account was really animated and very full. His friend in the Western Ocean trade imparted it freely to the other officers of his liner. 'A chap I know writes to me about an extraordinary affair that happened on board his ship in that typhoon – you know – that we read of in the papers two months ago. It's the funniest thing! Just see for yourself what he says. I'll show you his letter.'

There were phrases in it calculated to give the impression of light-hearted, indomitable resolution. Jukes had written them in good faith, for he felt thus when he wrote. He described with lurid effect the scenes in the 'tween-deck. '. . . It struck me in a flash that those confounded Chinamen couldn't tell we weren't a desperate kind of robbers. 'Tisn't good to part the Chinaman from his money if he is the stronger party. We need have been desperate indeed to go thieving in such weather, but what could these beggars know of us? So, without thinking of it twice, I got the hands away in a jiffy. Our work was done – that the old man had set his heart on. We cleared out without staying to inquire how they felt. I am convinced that if they had not been so unmercifully shaken, and afraid – each individual one of them – to stand up, we would have been torn to pieces. Oh! It was pretty complete, I can tell you; and you may run to and fro across the Pond to the end of time before you find yourself with such a job on your hands.'

After this he alluded professionally to the damage done to the ship, and went on thus:

'It was when the weather quieted down that the situation became confoundedly delicate. It wasn't made any better by us having been lately transferred to the Siamese

flag; though the skipper can't see that it makes any difference – "as long as *we* are on board" – he says. There are
feelings that this man simply hasn't got – and there's an end
of it. You might just as well try to make a bedpost understand. But apart from this it is an infernally lonely state for
a ship to be going about the China seas with no proper
consuls, not even a gunboat of her own anywhere, nor a
body to go to in case of some trouble.

'My notion was to keep these Johnnies under hatches for
another fifteen hours or so; as we weren't much farther than
that from Fu-chau. We would find there, most likely, some
sort of a man-of-war, and once under her guns we were safe
enough; for surely any skipper of a man-of-war – English,
French or Dutch – would see white men through as far as
row on board goes. We could get rid of them and their
money afterwards by delivering them to their Mandarin or
Taotai, or whatever they call these chaps in goggles you see
being carried about in sedan-chairs through their stinking
streets.

'The old man wouldn't see it somehow. He wanted to
keep the matter quiet. He got that notion into his head,
and a steam windlass couldn't drag it out of him. He
wanted as little fuss made as possible, for the sake of the
ship's name and for the sake of the owners – "for the sake of
all concerned," says he, looking at me very hard. It made me
angry hot. Of course you couldn't keep a thing like that
quiet; but the chests had been secured in the usual manner
and were safe enough for any earthly gale, while this had
been an altogether fiendish business I couldn't give you
even an idea of.

'Meantime, I could hardly keep on my feet. None of us
had a spell of any sort for nearly thirty hours, and there the
old man sat rubbing his chin, rubbing the top of his head,
and so bothered he didn't even think of pulling his long
boots off.

'"I hope, sir," says I, "you won't be letting them out on
deck before we make ready for them in some shape or

other." Not, mind you, that I felt very sanguine about controlling these beggars if they meant to take charge. A trouble with a cargo of Chinamen is no child's play. I was dam' tired, too. "I wish," said I, "you would let us throw the whole lot of these dollars down to them and leave them to fight it out amongst themselves, while we get a rest."

'"Now you talk wild, Jukes," says he, looking up in his slow way that makes you ache all over, somehow. "We must plan out something that would be fair to all parties."

'I had no end of work on hand, as you may imagine, so I set the hands going, and then I thought I would turn in a bit. I hadn't been asleep in my bunk ten minutes when in rushes the steward and begins to pull at my leg.

'"For God's sake, Mr Jukes, come out! Come on deck quick, sir. Oh, do come out!"

'The fellow scared all the sense out of me. I didn't know what had happened: another hurricane – or what. Could hear no wind.

'"The Captain's letting them out. Oh, he is letting them out! Jump on deck, sir, and save us. The chief engineer has just run below for his revolver."

'That's what I understood the fool to say. However, Father Rout swears he went in there only to get a clean pocket-handkerchief. Anyhow, I made one jump into my trousers and flew on deck aft. There was certainly a good deal of noise going on forward of the bridge. Four of the hands with the boss'en were at work abaft. I passed up to them some of the rifles all the ships on the China coast carry in the cabin and led them on the bridge. On the way I ran against Old Sol, looking startled and sucking at an unlighted cigar.

'"Come along," I shouted to him.

'We charged, the seven of us, up to the chart-room. All was over. There stood the old man with his sea-boots still drawn up to the hips and in shirt-sleeves – got warm thinking it out, I suppose. Bun-hin's dandy clerk at his

elbow as dirty as a sweep, was still green in the face. I could
see directly I was in for something.

'"What the devil are these monkey tricks, Mr Jukes?" asks
the old man, as angry as ever he could be. I tell you frankly it
made me lose my tongue. "For God's sake, Mr Jukes," says
he, "do take away these rifles from the men. Somebody's sure
to get hurt before long if you don't. Damme, if this ship isn't
worse than Bedlam! Look sharp now. I want you up here to
help me and Bun-hin's Chinaman to count that money. You
wouldn't mind lending a hand, too, Mr Rout, now you are
here. The more of us the better."

'He had settled it all in his mind while I was having a
snooze. Had we been an English ship, or only going to land
our cargo of coolies in an English port, like Hong-Kong,
for instance, there would have been no end of inquiries and
bother, claims for damages and so on. But these Chinamen
know their officials better than we do.

'The hatches had been taken off already, and they were
all on deck after a night and a day down below. It made you
feel queer to see so many gaunt, wild faces together. The
beggars stared about at the sky, at the sea, at the ship, as
though they had expected the whole thing to have been
blown to pieces. And no wonder! They had had a doing
that would have shaken the soul out of a white man. But
then they say a Chinaman has no soul. He has, though,
something about him that is deuced tough. There was a
fellow (amongst others of the badly hurt) who had had his
eye all but knocked out. It stood out of his head the size of
half of a hen's egg. This would have laid out a white man on
his back for a month: and yet there was that chap elbowing
here and there in the crowd and talking to the others as if
nothing had been the matter. They made a great hubbub
amongst themselves, and whenever the old man showed his
bald head on the foreside of the bridge, they would all leave
off jawing and look at him from below.

'It seems that after he had done his thinking he made
that Bun-hin's fellow go down and explain to them the only

way they could get their money back. He told me afterwards that, all the coolies having worked in the same place
and for the same length of time, he reckoned he would be
doing the fair thing by them as near as possible if he shared
all the cash we had picked up equally among the lot. You
couldn't tell one man's dollars from another's, he said, and if
you asked each man how much money he brought on board
he was afraid they would lie, and he would find himself a
long way short. I think he was right there. As to giving
up the money to any Chinese official he could scare up in
Fu-chau, he said he might just as well put the lot in his own
pocket at once for all the good it would be to them.
I suppose they thought so, too.

'We finished the distribution before dark. It was rather a
sight: the sea running high, the ship a wreck to look at,
these Chinamen staggering up on the bridge one by one for
their share, and the old man still booted, and in his shirt-
sleeves, busy paying out at the chart-room door, perspiring
like anything, and now and then coming down sharp on
myself or Father Rout about one thing or another not quite
to his mind. He took the share of those who were disabled
himself to them on the No. 2 hatch. There were three
dollars left over, and these went to the three most damaged
coolies, one to each. We turned-to afterwards, and
shovelled out on deck heaps of wet rags, all sorts of fragments of things without shape, and that you couldn't give a
name to, and let them settle the ownership themselves.

'This certainly is coming as near as can be to keeping the
thing quiet for the benefit of all concerned. What's your
opinion, you pampered mail-boat swell? The old chief says
that this was plainly the only thing that could be done. The
skipper remarked to me the other day, "There are things
you find nothing about in books." I think that he got out of
it very well for such a stupid man.'

THE SHADOW-LINE

A CONFESSION
'WORTHY OF MY UNDYING REGARD'

AUTHOR'S NOTE

THIS story, which I admit to be in its brevity a fairly complex piece of work, was not intended to touch on the supernatural. Yet more than one critic has been inclined to take it in that way, seeing in it an attempt on my part to give the fullest scope to my imagination by taking it beyond the confines of the world of the living, suffering humanity. But as a matter of fact my imagination is not made of stuff so elastic as all that. I believe that if I attempted to put the strain of the Supernatural on it it would fail deplorably and exhibit an unlovely gap. But I could never have attempted such a thing, because all my moral and intellectual being is penetrated by an invincible conviction that whatever falls under the dominion of our senses must be in nature and, however exceptional, cannot differ in its essence from all the other effects of the visible and tangible world of which we are a self-conscious part. The world of the living contains enough marvels and mysteries as it is; marvels and mysteries acting upon our emotions and intelligence in ways so inexplicable that it would almost justify the conception of life as an enchanted state. No, I am too firm in my consciousness of the marvellous to be ever fascinated by the mere supernatural, which (take it any way you like) is but a manufactured article, the fabrication of minds insensitive to the intimate delicacies of our relation to the dead and to the living, in their countless multitudes; a desecration of our tenderest memories; an outrage on our dignity.

Whatever my native modesty may be it will never condescend so low as to seek help for my imagination within those vain imaginings common to all ages and that in themselves are enough to fill all lovers of mankind with unutterable sadness. As to the effect of a mental or moral shock on a common mind that is quite a legitimate subject for study and description. Mr Burns's moral being receives a severe shock in his relations with his late captain, and this in his diseased state turns into a mere superstitious fancy compounded of fear and animosity. This fact is one of the elements of the story, but there is nothing supernatural in it, nothing so to speak from beyond the confines of this world, which in all conscience holds enough mystery and terror in itself.

Perhaps if I had published this tale, which I have had for a long time in my mind, under the title of 'First Command' no suggestion of the Supernatural would have been found in it by any impartial reader, critical or otherwise. I will not consider here the origins of the feeling in which its actual title, 'The Shadow-Line,' occurred to my mind. Primarily the aim of this piece of writing was the presentation of certain facts which certainly were associated with the change from youth, care-free and fervent, to the more self-conscious and more poignant period of maturer life. Nobody can doubt that before the supreme trial of a whole generation I had an acute consciousness of the minute and insignificant character of my own obscure experience. There could be no question here of any parallelism. That notion never entered my head. But there was a feeling of identity, though with an enormous difference of scale – as of one single drop measured against the bitter and stormy immensity of an ocean. And this was very natural too. For when we begin to meditate on the meaning of our own past it seems to fill all the world in its profundity and its magnitude. This book was written in the last three months of the year 1916. Of all the subjects of which a writer of tales is more or less conscious within himself this is the only one I found it possible to attempt at the time. The depth and the nature of the mood with which I approached it is best expressed perhaps in the dedication which strikes me now as a most disproportionate thing – as another instance of the overwhelming greatness of our own emotion to ourselves.

This much having been said I may pass on now to a few remarks about the mere material of the story. As to locality it belongs to that part of the Eastern Seas from which I have carried away into my writing life the greatest number of suggestions. From my statement that I thought of this story for a long time under the title of 'First Command' the reader may guess that it is concerned with my personal experience. And as a matter of fact it *is* personal experience seen in perspective with the eye of the mind and coloured by that affection one can't help feeling for such events of one's life as one has no reason to be ashamed of. And that affection is as intense (I appeal here to universal experience) as the shame, and almost the anguish with which one remembers some unfortunate occurrences, down to mere mistakes in speech, that have been perpetrated by one in the past. The effect of perspective in memory is to make things loom large because the essentials stand out isolated from their surroundings of insignificant daily facts which have naturally faded out of one's mind. I remember that period of my sea-life with pleasure because begun inauspiciously it turned out in the end a success from a personal point of view, leaving a tangible proof in the terms of the letter the owners of the ship wrote to me two years afterwards when I resigned my command in order to come home. This resignation marked the beginning of another phase of my seaman's life, its terminal phase, if I may say so, which in its own way has coloured another portion of my writings. I didn't know then how near its end my sea-life was, and therefore I felt no sorrow except at parting with the ship. I was sorry also to break my connection with the firm which owned her and who were pleased to receive with friendly kindness and give their confidence to a man who had entered their service in an accidental manner and in very adverse circumstances. Without disparaging the

earnestness of my purpose I suspect now that luck had no
small part in the success of the trust reposed in me. And
one cannot help remembering with pleasure the time when
one's best efforts were seconded by a run of luck.

The words '*Worthy of my undying regard*,' selected by me
for the motto on the title page, are quoted from the text of
the book itself; and, though one of my critics surmised that
they applied to the ship, it is evident from the place where
they stand that they refer to the men of that ship's company: complete strangers to their new captain and yet who
stood by him so well during those twenty days that seemed
to have been passed on the brink of a slow and agonizing
destruction. And *that* is the greatest memory of all! For
surely it is a great thing to have commanded a handful of
men worthy of one's undying regard.

1920.   J. C.

THE SHADOW LINE

... – D'autres fois, calme plat, grand miroir
De mon désespoir.

BAUDELAIRE.

I

ONLY the young have such moments. I don't mean the very young. No. The very young have, properly speaking, no moments. It is the privilege of early youth to live in advance of its days in all the beautiful continuity of hope which knows no pauses and no introspection.

One closes behind one the little gate of mere boyishness – and enters an enchanted garden. Its very shades glow with promise. Every turn of the path has its seduction. And it isn't because it is an undiscovered country. One knows well enough that all mankind has streamed that way. It is the charm of universal experience from which one expects an uncommon or personal sensation – a bit of one's own.

One goes on recognizing the landmarks of the predecessors, excited, amused, taking the hard luck and the good luck together – the kicks and the halfpence, as the saying is – the picturesque common lot that holds so many possibilities for the deserving or perhaps for the lucky. Yes. One goes on. And the time, too, goes on – till one perceives ahead a shadow-line warning one that the region of early youth, too, must be left behind.

This is the period of life in which such moments of which I have spoken are likely to come. What moments? Why, the moments of boredom, of weariness, of dissatisfaction. Rash moments. I mean moments when the still young are inclined to commit rash actions, such as getting married suddenly or else throwing up a job for no reason.

This is not a marriage story. It wasn't so bad as that with
me. My action, rash as it was, had more the character of
divorce – almost of desertion. For no reason on which a
sensible person could put a finger I threw up my job –
chucked my berth – left the ship of which the worst that
could be said was that she was a steamship and therefore,
perhaps, not entitled to that blind loyalty which...
However, it's no use trying to put a gloss on what even at
the time I myself half suspected to be a caprice.

It was in an Eastern port. She was an Eastern ship,
inasmuch as then she belonged to that port. She traded
among dark islands on a blue reef-scarred sea, with the Red
Ensign over the taffrail and at her mast-head a house-flag,
also red, but with a green border and with a white crescent
in it. For an Arab owned her, and a Syed at that. Hence the
green border on the flag. He was the head of a great House
of Straits Arabs, but as loyal a subject of the complex
British Empire as you could find east of the Suez Canal.
World politics did not trouble him at all, but he had a great
occult power amongst his own people.

It was all one to us who owned the ship. He had to
employ white men in the shipping part of his business, and
many of those he so employed had never set eyes on him
from the first to the last day. I myself saw him but once,
quite accidentally on a wharf – an old, dark little man blind
in one eye, in a snowy robe and yellow slippers. He was
having his hand severely kissed by a crowd of Malay
pilgrims to whom he had done some favour, in the way
of food and money. His alms-giving, I have heard, was
most extensive, covering almost the whole Archipelago.
For isn't it said that 'The charitable man is the friend of
Allah'?

Excellent (and picturesque) Arab owner, about whom
one needed not to trouble one's head, a most excellent
Scottish ship – for she was that from the keel up – excellent
sea-boat, easy to keep clean, most handy in every way, and
if it had not been for her internal propulsion, worthy of any

man's love, I cherish to this day a profound respect for her memory. As to the kind of trade she was engaged in and the character of my shipmates, I could not have been happier if I had had the life and the men made to my order by a benevolent Enchanter.

And suddenly I left all this. I left it in that, to us, inconsequential manner in which a bird flies away from a comfortable branch. It was as though all unknowing I had heard a whisper or seen something. Well – perhaps! One day I was perfectly right and the next everything was gone – glamour, flavour, interest, contentment – everything. It was one of these moments, you know. The green sickness of late youth descended on me and carried me off. Carried me off that ship, I mean.

We were only four white men on board, with a large crew of Kalashes and two Malay petty officers. The Captain stared hard as if wondering what ailed me. But he was a sailor, and he, too, had been young at one time. Presently a smile came to lurk under his thick iron-grey moustache, and he observed that, of course, if I felt I must go he couldn't keep me by main force. And it was arranged that I should be paid off the next morning. As I was going out of the chart-room he added suddenly, in a peculiar, wistful tone, that he hoped I would find what I was so anxious to go and look for. A soft, cryptic utterance which seemed to reach deeper than any diamond-hard tool could have done. I do believe he understood my case.

But the second engineer attacked me differently. He was a sturdy young Scot, with a smooth face and light eyes. His honest red countenance emerged out of the engine-room companion and then the whole robust man, with shirt-sleeves turned up, wiping slowly the massive fore-arms with a lump of cotton-waste. And his light eyes expressed bitter distaste, as though our friendship had turned to ashes. He said weightily: 'Oh! Aye! I've been thinking it was about time for you to run away home and get married to some silly girl.'

It was tacitly understood in the port that John Nieven was a fierce mysogynist; and the absurd character of the sally convinced me that he meant to be nasty – very nasty – had meant to say the most crushing thing he could think of. My laugh sounded deprecatory. Nobody but a friend could be so angry as that. I became a little crestfallen. Our chief engineer also took a characteristic view of my action, but in a kindlier spirit.

He was young, too, but very thin, and with a mist of fluffy brown beard all round his haggard face. All day long, at sea or in harbour, he could be seen walking hastily up and down the after-deck, wearing an intense, spiritually rapt expression, which was caused by a perpetual consciousness of unpleasant physical sensations in his internal economy. For he was a confirmed dyspeptic. His view of my case was very simple. He said it was nothing but deranged liver. Of course! He suggested I should stay for another trip and meantime dose myself with a certain patent medicine in which his own belief was absolute. 'I'll tell you what I'll do. I'll buy you two bottles, out of my own pocket. There. I can't say fairer than that, can I?'

I believe he would have perpetrated the atrocity (or generosity) at the merest sign of weakening on my part. By that time, however, I was more discontented, disgusted, and dogged than ever. The past eighteen months, so full of new and varied experience, appeared a dreary, prosaic waste of days. I felt – how shall I express it? – that there was no truth to be got out of them.

What truth? I should have been hard put to it to explain. Probably, if pressed, I would have burst into tears simply. I was young enough for that.

Next day the Captain and I transacted our business in the Harbour Office. It was a lofty, big, cool, white room, where the screened light of day glowed serenely. Everybody in it – the officials, the public – were in white. Only the heavy polished desks gleamed darkly in a central avenue, and some papers lying on them were blue. Enormous punkahs sent from on high a gentle draught through that immaculate interior and upon our perspiring heads.

The official behind the desk we approached grinned amiably and kept it up till, in answer to his perfunctory question, 'Sign off and on again?' my Captain answered, 'No! Signing off for good.' And then his grin vanished in sudden solemnity. He did not look at me again till he handed me my papers with a sorrowful expression, as if they had been my passports for Hades.

While I was putting them away he murmured some question to the Captain, and I heard the latter answer good-humouredly:

'No. He leaves us to go home.'

'Oh!' the other exclaimed, nodding mournfully over my sad condition.

I didn't know him outside the official building, but he leaned forward over the desk to shake hands with me, compassionately, as one would with some poor devil going out to be hanged; and I am afraid I performed my part ungraciously, in the hardened manner of an impenitent criminal.

No homeward-bound mail-boat was due for three or four days. Being now a man without a ship, and having for a time broken my connection with the sea – become, in fact, a mere potential passenger – it would have been more appropriate perhaps if I had gone to stay at an hotel. There it was, too, within a stone's throw of the Harbour Office, low, but somehow palatial, displaying its white, pillared pavilions surrounded by trim grass plots. I would have felt a passenger indeed in there! I gave it a hostile glance and directed my steps towards the Officers' Sailors' Home.

I walked in the sunshine, disregarding it, and in the shade of the big trees on the Esplanade without enjoying it. The heat of the tropical East descended through the leafy boughs, enveloping my thinly clad body, clinging to my rebellious discontent, as if to rob it of its freedom.

The Officers' Home was a large bungalow with a wide verandah and a curiously suburban-looking little garden of bushes and a few trees between it and the street. That institution partook somewhat of the character of a residential club, but with a slightly Governmental flavour about it, because it was administered by the Harbour Office. Its manager was officially styled Chief Steward. He was an unhappy, wizened little man, who if put into a jockey's rig would have looked the part to perfection. But it was obvious that at some time or other in his life, in some capacity or other, he had been connected with the sea. Possibly in the comprehensive capacity of a failure.

I should have thought his employment a very easy one, but he used to affirm for some reason or other that his job would be the death of him some day. It was rather mysterious. Perhaps everything naturally was too much trouble for him. He certainly seemed to hate having people in the house.

On entering it I thought he must be feeling pleased. It was as still as a tomb. I could see no one in the living-rooms; and the verandah, too, was empty, except for a man at the far end dozing prone in a long chair. At the noise of my footsteps he opened one horribly fish-like eye. He was a stranger to me. I retreated from there, and, crossing the dining-room − a very bare apartment with a motionless punkah hanging over the centre table − I knocked at a door labelled in black letters: 'Chief Steward.'

The answer to my knock being a vexed and doleful plaint: 'Oh, dear! Oh, dear! What is it now?' I went in at once.

It was a strange room to find in the tropics. Twilight and stuffiness reigned in there. The fellow had hung enormously ample, dusty, cheap lace curtains over his windows, which were shut. Piles of cardboard boxes, such as milliners and dressmakers use in Europe, cumbered the corners; and by some means he had procured for himself the sort of furniture that might have come out of a respectable parlour in the East End of London – a horsehair sofa, arm-chairs of the same. I glimpsed grimy antimacassars scattered over that horrid upholstery, which was awe-inspiring, insomuch that one could not guess what mysterious accident, need, or fancy had collected it there. Its owner had taken off his tunic, and in white trousers and a thin short-sleeved singlet prowled behind the chair-backs nursing his meagre elbows.

An exclamation of dismay escaped him when he heard that I had come for a stay; but he could not deny that there were plenty of vacant rooms.

'Very well. Can you give me the one I had before?'

He emitted a faint moan from behind a pile of cardboard boxes on the table, which might have contained gloves or handkerchiefs or neckties. I wonder what the fellow did keep in them? There was a smell of decaying coral, or Oriental dust, of zoological specimens in that den of his. I could only see the top of his head and his unhappy eyes levelled at me over the barrier.

'It's only for a couple of days,' I said, intending to cheer him up.

'Perhaps you would like to pay in advance?' he suggested eagerly.

'Certainly not!' I burst out directly I could speak. 'Never heard of such a thing! This is the most infernal cheek...'

He had seized his head in both hands – a gesture of despair which checked my indignation.

'Oh, dear! Oh, dear! Don't fly out like this. I am asking everybody.'

'I don't believe it,' I said bluntly.

'Well, I am going to. And if you gentlemen all agree to pay in advance I could make Hamilton pay up too. He's always turning up ashore dead broke, and even when he has some money he won't settle his bills. I don't know what to do with him. He swears at me and tells me I can't chuck a white man out into the street here. So if you only would...'

I was amazed. Incredulous too. I suspected the fellow of gratuitous impertinence. I told him with marked emphasis that I would see him and Hamilton hanged first, and requested him to conduct me to my room with no more of his nonsense. He produced then a key from somewhere and led the way out of his lair, giving me a vicious sidelong look in passing.

'Any one I know staying here?' I asked him before he left my room.

He had recovered his usual pained impatient tone, and said that Captain Giles was there, back from a Solo Sea trip. Two other guests were staying also. He paused. And, of course, Hamilton, he added.

'Oh, yes! Hamilton,' I said, and the miserable creature took himself off with a final groan.

His impudence still rankled when I came into the dining-room at tiffin time. He was there on duty overlooking the Chinamen servants. The tiffin was laid on one end only of the long table, and the punkah was stirring the hot air lazily – mostly above a barren waste of polished wood.

We were four around the cloth. The dozing stranger from the chair was one. Both his eyes were partly opened now, but they did not seem to see anything. He was supine. The dignified person next him, with short side whiskers and a carefully scraped chin, was, of course, Hamilton. I have never seen any one so full of dignity for the station in life Providence had been pleased to place him in. I had been told that he regarded me as a rank outsider. He raised not only his eyes, but his eyebrows as well, at the sound I made pulling back my chair.

Captain Giles was at the head of the table. I exchanged a few words of greeting with him and sat down on his left. Stout and pale, with a great shiny dome of a bald forehead and prominent brown eyes, he might have been anything but a seaman. You would not have been surprised to learn that he was an architect. To me (I know how absurd it is) he looked like a churchwarden. He had the appearance of a man from whom you would expect sound advice, moral sentiments, with perhaps a platitude or two thrown in on occasion, not from a desire to dazzle, but from honest conviction.

Though very well known and appreciated in the shipping world, he had no regular employment. He did not want it. He had his own peculiar position. He was an expert. An expert in – how shall I say it? – in intricate navigation. He was supposed to know more about remote and imperfectly charted parts of the Archipelago than any man living. His brain must have been a perfect warehouse of reefs, positions, bearings, images of headlands, shapes of obscure coasts, aspects of innumerable islands, desert and otherwise. Any ship, for instance, bound on a trip to Palawan or somewhere that way would have Captain Giles on board, either in temporary command or 'to assist the master.' It was said that he had a retaining fee from a wealthy firm of Chinese steamship owners, in view of such services. Besides, he was always ready to relieve any man who wished to take a spell ashore for a time. No owner was ever known to object to an arrangement of that sort. For it seemed to be the established opinion at the port that Captain Giles was as good as the best, if not a little better. But in Hamilton's view he was an 'outsider.' I believe that for Hamilton the generalization 'outsider' covered the whole lot of us; though I suppose that he made some distinctions in his mind.

I didn't try to make conversation with Captain Giles, whom I had not seen more than twice in my life. But, of course, he knew who I was. After a while, inclining his big shiny head my way, he addressed me first in his friendly fashion. He presumed from seeing me there, he said, that I had come ashore for a couple of days' leave.

He was a low-voiced man. I spoke a little louder saying that: No – I had left the ship for good.

'A free man for a bit,' was his comment.

'I suppose I may call myself that – since eleven o'clock,' I said.

Hamilton had stopped eating at the sound of our voices. He laid down his knife and fork gently, got up, and muttering something about 'this infernal heat cutting one's appetite,' went out of the room. Almost immediately we heard him leave the house down the verandah steps.

On this Captain Giles remarked easily that the fellow had no doubt gone off to look after my old job. The Chief Steward, who had been leaning against the wall, brought his face of an unhappy goat nearer to the table and addressed us dolefully. His object was to unburden himself of his eternal grievance against Hamilton. The man kept him in hot water with the Harbour Office as to the state of his accounts. He wished to goodness he would get my job, though in truth what would it be? Temporary relief at best.

I said: 'You needn't worry. He won't get my job. My successor is on board already.'

He was surprised, and I believe his face fell a little at the news. Captain Giles gave a soft laugh. We got up and went out on the verandah, leaving the supine stranger to be dealt with by the Chinamen. The last thing I saw they had put a plate with a slice of pineapple on it before him and stood back to watch what would happen. But the experiment seemed a failure. He sat insensible.

It was imparted to me in a low voice by Captain Giles that this was an officer of some Rajah's yacht which had come into port to be dry-docked. Must have been 'seeing life' last night, he added, wrinkling his nose in an intimate, confidential way which pleased me vastly. For Captain Giles had prestige. He was credited with wonderful adventures and with some mysterious tragedy in his life. And no man had a word to say against him. He continued:

'I remember him first coming ashore here some years ago. Seems only the other day. He was a nice boy. Oh! these nice boys!'

I could not help laughing aloud. He looked startled, then joined in the laugh. 'No! No! I didn't mean that,' he cried. 'What I meant is that some of them do go soft mighty quick out here.'

Jocularly I suggested the beastly heat as the first cause. But Captain Giles disclosed himself possessed of a deeper philosophy. Things out East were made easy for white men. That was all right. The difficulty was to go on keeping white, and some of these nice boys did not know how. He gave me a searching look, and in a benevolent, heavy-uncle manner asked point blank:

'Why did you throw up your berth?'

I became angry all of a sudden; for you can understand how exasperating such a question was to a man who didn't know. I said to myself that I ought to shut up that moralist; and to him aloud I said with challenging politeness:

'Why...? Do you disapprove?'

He was too disconcerted to do more than mutter confusedly: 'I!...In a general way...' and then gave me up. But he retired in good order, under the cover of a heavily humorous remark that he, too, was getting soft, and that this was his time for taking his little siesta – when he was on shore. 'Very bad habit. Very bad habit.'

The simplicity of the man would have disarmed a touchiness even more youthful than mine. So when next day at tiffin he bent his head towards me and said that he had met my late Captain last evening, adding in an undertone: 'He's very sorry you left. He had never had a mate that suited him so well,' I answered him earnestly, without any affection, that I certainly hadn't been so comfortable in any ship or with any commander in all my sea-going days.

'Well – then,' he murmured.

'Haven't you heard, Captain Giles, that I intend to go home?'

'Yes,' he said benevolently. 'I have heard that sort of thing so often before.'

'What of that?' I cried. I thought he was the most dull, unimaginative man I had ever met. I don't know what more I would have said, but the much-belated Hamilton came in just then and took his usual seat. So I dropped into a mumble.

'Anyhow, you shall see it done this time.'

Hamilton, beautifully shaved, gave Captain Giles a curt nod, but didn't even condescend to raise his eyebrows at me; and when he spoke it was only to tell the Chief Steward that the food on his plate wasn't fit to be set before a gentleman. The individual addressed seemed much too unhappy to groan. He only cast his eyes up to the punkah and that was all.

Captain Giles and I got up from the table, and the stranger next to Hamilton followed our example, manœuvring himself to his feet with difficulty. He, poor fellow, not because he was hungry but I verily believe only to recover his self-respect, had tried to put some of that unworthy food into his mouth. But after dropping his fork twice and generally making a failure of it, he had sat still with an air of intense mortification combined with a ghastly glazed stare. Both Giles and I avoided looking his way at table.

On the verandah he stopped short on purpose to address to us anxiously a long remark which I failed to understand completely. It sounded like some horrible unknown language. But when Captain Giles, after only an instant for reflection, answered him with homely friendliness, 'Aye, to be sure. You are right there,' he appeared very much gratified indeed, and went away (pretty straight too) to seek a distant long chair.

'What was he trying to say?' I asked with disgust.

'I don't know. Mustn't be down too much on a fellow. He's feeling pretty wretched, you may be sure; and to-morrow he'll feel worse yet.'

Judging by the man's appearance it seemed impossible. I wondered what sort of complicated debauch had reduced him to that unspeakable condition. Captain Giles's benevolence was spoiled by a curious air of complacency which I disliked. I said with a little laugh:

'Well, he will have you to look after him.'

He made a deprecatory gesture, sat down, and took up a paper. I did the same. The papers were old and uninteresting, filled up mostly with dreary stereotyped descriptions of Queen Victoria's first jubilee celebrations. Probably we should have quickly fallen into a tropical afternoon doze if it had not been for Hamilton's voice raised in the dining-room. He was finishing his tiffin there. The big double doors stood wide open permanently, and he could not have had any idea how near to the doorway our chairs were placed. He was heard in a loud, supercilious tone answering some statement ventured by the Chief Steward.

'I am not going to be rushed into anything. They will be glad enough to get a gentleman I imagine. There is no hurry.'

A loud whispering from the steward succeeded and then again Hamilton was heard with even intenser scorn.

'What? That young ass who fancies himself for having been chief mate with Kent so long? . . . Preposterous.'

Giles and I looked at each other. Kent being the name of my late commander, Captain Giles's whisper, 'He's talking of you,' seemed to me sheer waste of breath. The Chief Steward must have stuck to his point whatever it was, because Hamilton was heard again more supercilious, if possible, and also very emphatic:

'Rubbish, my good man! One doesn't *compete* with a rank outsider like that. There's plenty of time.'

Then there was pushing of chairs, footsteps in the next room, and plaintive expostulations from the Steward, who was pursuing Hamilton, even out of doors through the main entrance.

'That's a very insulting sort of man,' remarked Captain Giles – superfluously, I thought. 'Very insulting. You haven't offended him in some way, have you?'

'Never spoke to him in my life,' I said grumpily. 'Can't imagine what he means by competing. He has been trying for my job after I left – and didn't get it. But that isn't exactly competition.'

Captain Giles balanced his big benevolent head thoughtfully. 'He didn't get it,' he repeated very slowly. 'No, not likely either, with Kent. Kent is no end sorry you left him. He gives you the name of a good seaman too.'

I flung away the paper I was still holding. I sat up, I slapped the table with my open palm. I wanted to know why he would keep harping on that, my absolutely private affair. It was exasperating, really.

Captain Giles silenced me by the perfect equanimity of his gaze. 'Nothing to be annoyed about,' he murmured reasonably, with an evident desire to soothe the childish irritation he had aroused. And he was really a man of an appearance so inoffensive that I tried to explain myself as much as I could. I told him that I did not want to hear any more about what was past and gone. It had been very nice while it lasted, but now it was done with I preferred not to talk about it or even think about it. I had made up my mind to go home.

He listened to the whole tirade in a particular, lending-the-ear attitude, as if trying to detect a false note in it somewhere; then straightened himself up and appeared to ponder sagaciously over the matter.

'Yes. You told me you meant to go home. Anything in view there?'

Instead of telling him that it was none of his business I said sullenly:

'Nothing that I know of.'

I had indeed considered that rather blank side of the situation I had created for myself by leaving suddenly my very satisfactory employment. And I was not very pleased with it. I had it on the tip of my tongue to say that common sense had nothing to do with my action, and that therefore it didn't deserve the interest Captain Giles seemed to be taking in it. But he was puffing at a short wooden pipe now, and looked so guileless, dense, and commonplace, that it seemed hardly worth while to puzzle him either with truth or sarcasm.

He blew a cloud of smoke, then surprised me by a very abrupt: 'Paid your passage money yet?'

Overcome by the shameless pertinacity of a man to whom it was rather difficult to be rude, I replied with exaggerated meekness that I had not done so yet. I thought there would be plenty of time to do that to-morrow.

And I was about to turn away, withdrawing my privacy from his fatuous, objectless attempts to test what sort of stuff it was made of, when he laid down his pipe in an extremely significant manner, you know, as if a critical moment had come, and leaned sideways over the table between us.

'Oh! You haven't yet!' He dropped his voice mysteriously. 'Well, then I think you ought to know that there's something going on here.'

I had never in my life felt more detached from all earthly goings on. Freed from the sea for a time, I preserved the sailor's consciousness of complete independence from all land affairs. How could they concern me? I gazed at Captain Giles's animation with scorn rather than with curiosity.

To his obviously preparatory question whether our steward had spoken to me that day I said he hadn't. And what's more he would have had precious little encouragement if he had tried to. I didn't want the fellow to speak to me at all.

Unrebuked by my petulance, Captain Giles, with an air of immense sagacity, began to tell me a minute tale about a Harbour Office peon. It was absolutely pointless. A peon was seen walking that morning on the verandah with a letter in his hand. It was in an official envelope. As the habit of these fellows is, he had shown it to the first white man he came across. That man was our friend in the armchair. He, as I knew, was not in a state to interest himself in any sublunary matters. He could only wave the peon away. The peon then wandered on along the verandah and came upon Captain Giles, who was there by an extraordinary chance....

At this point he stopped with a profound look. The letter, he continued, was addressed to the Chief Steward. Now what could Captain Ellis, the Master Attendant, want to write to the Steward for? The fellow went every morning, anyhow, to the Harbour Office with his report, for orders or what not. He hadn't been back more than an hour before there was an office peon chasing him with a note. Now what was that for?

And he began to speculate. It was not for this – and it could not be for that. As to that other thing it was unthinkable.

The fatuousness of all this made me stare. If the man had not been somehow a sympathetic personality I would have resented it like an insult. As it was, I felt only sorry for him. Something remarkably earnest in his gaze prevented me from laughing in his face. Neither did I yawn at him. I just stared.

His tone became a shade more mysterious. Directly the fellow (meaning the Steward) got that note he rushed for his hat and bolted out of the house. But it wasn't because the note called him to the Harbour Office. He didn't go there. He was not absent long enough for that. He came darting back in no time, flung his hat away, and raced about the dining-room moaning and slapping his forehead. All these exciting facts and manifestations had been observed by Captain Giles. He had, it seems, been meditating upon them ever since.

I began to pity him profoundly. And in a tone which I tried to make as little sarcastic as possible I said that I was glad he had found something to occupy his morning hours.

With his disarming simplicity he made me observe, as if it were a matter of some consequence, how strange it was that he should have spent the morning indoors at all. He generally was out before tiffin, visiting various offices, seeing his friends in the harbour, and so on. He had felt out of sorts somewhat on rising. Nothing much. Just enough to make him feel lazy.

All this with a sustained, holding stare which, in con-junction with the general inanity of the discourse, conveyed the impression of mild, dreary lunacy. And when he hitched his chair a little and dropped his voice to the low note of mystery, it flashed upon me that high professional reputation was not necessarily a guarantee of sound mind.

It never occurred to me then that I didn't know in what soundness of mind exactly consisted and what a delicate and, upon the whole, unimportant matter it was. With some idea of not hurting his feelings I blinked at him in an interested manner. But when he proceeded to ask me mysteriously whether I remembered what had passed just now between that Steward of ours and 'that man Hamilton,' I only grunted sour assent and turned away my head.

'Aye. But do you remember every word?' he insisted tactfully.

'I don't know. It's none of my business,' I snapped out, consigning, moreover, the Steward and Hamilton aloud to eternal perdition.

I meant to be very energetic and final, but Captain Giles continued to gaze at me thoughtfully. Nothing could stop him. He went on to point out that my personality was involved in that conversation. When I tried to preserve the semblance of unconcern he became positively cruel. I heard what the man had said? Yes? What did I think of it then? – he wanted to know.

Captain Giles's appearance excluding the suspicion of mere sly malice, I came to the conclusion that he was simply the most tactless idiot on earth. I almost despised myself for the weakness of attempting to enlighten his common understanding. I started to explain that I did not think anything whatever. Hamilton was not worth a thought. What such an offensive loafer... – 'Aye! that he is,' interjected Captain Giles – ...thought or said was below any decent man's contempt, and I did not propose to take the slightest notice of it.

This attitude seemed to me so simple and obvious that I was really astonished at Giles giving no sign of assent. Such perfect stupidity was almost interesting.

'What would you like me to do?' I asked laughing. 'I can't start a row with him because of the opinion he has formed of me. Of course, I've heard of the contemptuous way he alludes to me. But he doesn't intrude his contempt on my notice. He has never expressed it in my hearing. For even just now he didn't know we could hear him. I should only make myself ridiculous.'

That hopeless Giles went on puffing at his pipe moodily. All at once his face cleared, and he spoke.

'You missed my point.'

'Have I? I am very glad to hear it,' I said.

With increasing animation he stated again that I had missed his point. Entirely. And in a tone of growing self-conscious complacency he told me that few things escaped his attention, and he was rather used to think them out, and generally from his experience of life and men arrived at the right conclusion.

This bit of self-praise, of course, fitted excellently the laborious inanity of the whole conversation. The whole thing strengthened in me that obscure feeling of life being but a waste of days, which, half-unconsciously, had driven me out of a comfortable berth, away from men I liked, to flee from the menace of emptiness ... and to find inanity at the first turn. Here was a man of recognized character and achievement disclosed as an absurd and dreary chatterer. And it was probably like this everywhere – from east to west, from the bottom to the top of the social scale.

A great discouragement fell on me. A spiritual drowsiness. Giles's voice was going on complacently; the very voice of the universal hollow conceit. And I was no longer angry with it. There was nothing original, nothing new, startling, informing to expect from the world: no opportunities to find out something about oneself, no wisdom to acquire, no fun to enjoy. Everything was stupid and over-rated, even as Captain Giles was. So be it.

The name of Hamilton suddenly caught my ear and roused me up.

'I thought we had done with him,' I said, with the greatest possible distaste.

'Yes. But considering what we happened to hear just now I think you ought to do it.'

'Ought to do it?' I sat up bewildered. 'Do what?'

Captain Giles confronted me very much surprised.

'Why! Do what I have been advising you to try. You go and ask the Steward what was there in that letter from the Harbour Office. Ask him straight out.'

I remained speechless for a time. Here was something unexpected and original enough to be altogether incomprehensible. I murmured, astounded:

'But I thought it was Hamilton that you...'

'Exactly. Don't you let him. You do what I tell you. You tackle that Steward. You'll make him jump, I bet,' insisted Captain Giles, waving his smouldering pipe impressively at me. Then he took three rapid puffs at it.

His aspect of triumphant acuteness was indescribable. Yet the man remained a strangely sympathetic creature. Benevolence radiated from him ridiculously, mildly, impressively. It was irritating, too. But I pointed out coldly, as one who deals with the incomprehensible, that I didn't see any reason to expose myself to a snub from the fellow. He was a very unsatisfactory steward and a miserable wretch besides, but I would just as soon think of tweaking his nose.

'Tweaking his nose,' said Captain Giles in a scandalized tone. 'Much use it would be to you.'

That remark was so irrelevant that one could make no answer to it. But the sense of the absurdity was beginning at last to exercise its well-known fascination. I felt I must not let the man talk to me any more. I got up, observing curtly that he was too much for me – that I couldn't make him out.

Before I had time to move away he spoke again in a changed tone of obstinacy and puffing nervously at his pipe.

'Well – he's a – no account cuss – anyhow. You just – ask him. That's all.'

That new manner impressed me – or rather made me pause. But sanity asserting its sway at once I left the verandah after giving him a mirthless smile. In a few strides I found myself in the dining-room, now cleared and empty. But during that short time various thoughts occurred to me, such as: that Giles had been making fun of me, expecting some amusement at my expense; that I probably looked silly and gullible; that I knew very little of life. . . .

The door facing me across the dining-room flew open to my extreme surprise. It was the door inscribed with the word 'Steward' and the man himself ran out of his stuffy Philistinish lair in his absurd hunted animal manner, making for the garden door.

To this day I don't know what made me call after him: 'I say! Wait a minute.' Perhaps it was the sidelong glance he gave me; or possibly I was yet under the influence of Captain Giles's mysterious earnestness. Well, it was an impulse of some sort; an effect of that force somewhere within our lives which shapes them this way or that. For if these words had not escaped from my lips (my will had nothing to do with that) my existence would, to be sure, have been still a seaman's existence, but directed on now to me utterly inconceivable lines.

No. My will had nothing to do with it. Indeed, no sooner had I made that fateful noise than I became extremely sorry for it. Had the man stopped and faced me I would have had to retire in disorder. For I had no notion to carry out Captain Giles's idiotic joke, either at my own expense or at the expense of the Steward.

But here the old human instinct of the chase came into play. He pretended to be deaf, and I, without thinking a second about it, dashed along my own side of the dining table and cut him off at the very door.

'Why can't you answer when you are spoken to?' I asked roughly.

He leaned against the side of the door. He looked extremely wretched. Human nature is, I fear, not very nice right through. There are ugly spots in it. I found myself growing angry, and that, I believe, only because my quarry looked so woe-begone. Miserable beggar!

I went for him without more ado. 'I understand there was an official communication to the Home from the Harbour Office this morning. Is that so?'

Instead of telling me to mind my own business, as he might have done, he began to whine with an undertone of impudence. He couldn't see me anywhere this morning. He couldn't be expected to run all over the town after me.

'Who wants you to?' I cried. And then my eyes became opened to the inwardness of things and speeches the triviality of which had been so baffling and tiresome.

I told him I wanted to know what was in that letter. My sternness of tone and behaviour was only half assumed. Curiosity can be a very fierce sentiment – at times.

He took refuge in a silly, muttering sulkiness. It was nothing to me, he mumbled. I had told him I was going home. And since I was going home he didn't see why he should. . . .

That was the line of his argument, and it was irrelevant enough to be almost insulting. Insulting to one's intelligence, I mean.

In that twilight region between youth and maturity, in which I had my being then, one is peculiarly sensitive to that kind of insult. I am afraid my behaviour to the Steward became very rough indeed. But it wasn't in him to face out anything or anybody. Drug habit or solitary tippling, perhaps. And when I forgot myself so far as to swear at him he broke down and began to shriek.

I don't mean to say that he made a great outcry. It was a cynical shrieking confession, only faint – piteously faint. It wasn't very coherent either, but sufficiently so to strike me dumb at first. I turned my eyes from him in righteous indignation, and perceived Captain Giles in the verandah doorway surveying quietly the scene, his own handiwork, if I may express it in that way. His smouldering black pipe was very noticeable in his big, paternal fist. So, too, was the glitter of his heavy gold watch-chain across the breast of his white tunic. He exhaled an atmosphere of virtuous sagacity thick enough for any innocent soul to fly to confidently. I flew to him.

'You would never believe it,' I cried. 'It was a notification that a master is wanted for some ship. There's a command apparently going about and this fellow puts the thing in his pocket.'

The Steward screamed out in accents of loud despair, 'You will be the death of me!'

The mighty slap he gave his wretched forehead was very loud, too. But when I turned to look at him he was no longer there. He had rushed away somewhere out of sight. This sudden disappearance made me laugh.

This was the end of the incident – for me. Captain Giles, however, staring at the place where the Steward had been, began to haul at his gorgeous gold chain till at last the watch came up from the deep pocket like solid truth from a well. Solemnly he lowered it down again and only then said:

'Just three o'clock. You will be in time – if you don't lose any, that is.'

'In time for what?' I asked.

'Good Lord! For the Harbour Office. This must be looked into.'

Strictly speaking, he was right. But I've never had much taste for investigation, for showing people up and all that, no doubt, ethically meritorious kind of work. And my view of the episode was purely ethical. If any one had to be the death of the Steward I didn't see why it shouldn't be Captain Giles himself, a man of age and standing, and a permanent resident. Whereas I, in comparison, felt myself a mere bird of passage in that port. In fact, it might have been said that I had already broken off my connection. I muttered that I didn't think – it was nothing to me....

'Nothing!' repeated Captain Giles, giving some signs of quiet, deliberate indignation. 'Kent warned me you were a peculiar young fellow. You will tell me next that a command is nothing to you – and after all the trouble I've taken, too!'

'The trouble!' I murmured, uncomprehending. What trouble? All I could remember was being mystified and bored by his conversation for a solid hour after tiffin. And he called that taking a lot of trouble.

He was looking at me with self-complacency which would have been odious in any other man. All at once, as if a page of a book had been turned over disclosing a word which made plain all that had gone before, I perceived that this matter had also another than an ethical aspect.

And still I did not move. Captain Giles lost his patience a little. With an angry puff at his pipe he turned his back on my hesitation.

But it was not hesitation on my part. I had been, if I may express myself so, put out of gear mentally. But as soon as I had convinced myself that this stale, unprofitable world of my discontent contained such a thing as a command to be seized, I recovered my powers of locomotion.

It's a good step from the Officers' Home to the Harbour Office; but with the magic word 'Command' in my head I found myself suddenly on the quay as if transported there in the twinkling of an eye, before a portal of dressed white stone above a flight of shallow white steps.

All this seemed to glide towards me swiftly. The whole great roadstead to the right was just a mere flicker of blue, and the dim, cool hall swallowed me up out of the heat and glare of which I had not been aware till the very moment I passed in from it.

The broad inner staircase insinuated itself under my feet somehow. Command is a strong magic. The first human beings I perceived distinctly since I had parted with the indignant back of Captain Giles was the crew of the harbour steam-launch lounging on the spacious landing about the curtained archway of the shipping office.

It was there that my buoyancy abandoned me. The atmosphere of officialdom would kill anything that breathes the air of human endeavour, would extinguish hope and fear alike in the supremacy of paper and ink. I passed heavily under the curtain which the Malay coxswain of the harbour launch raised for me. There was nobody in the office except the clerks, writing in two industrious rows. But the head shipping-master hopped down from his elevation and hurried along on the thick mats to meet me in the broad central passage.

He had a Scottish name, but his complexion was of a rich olive hue, his short beard was jet black, and his eyes, also black, had a languishing expression. He asked confidentially:

'You want to see Him?'

All lightness of spirit and body having departed from me at the touch of officialdom, I looked at the scribe without animation and asked in my turn wearily:

'What do you think? Is it any use?'

'My goodness! He has asked for you twice to-day.'

This emphatic He was the supreme authority, the Marine Superintendent, the Harbour-Master – a very great person in the eyes of every single quill-driver in the room. But that was nothing to the opinion he had of his own greatness.

Captain Ellis looked upon himself as a sort of divine (pagan) emanation, the deputy-Neptune for the circumambient seas. If he did not actually rule the waves, he pretended to rule the fate of the mortals whose lives were cast upon the waters.

This uplifting illusion made him inquisitorial and peremptory, and as his temperament was choleric there were fellows who were actually afraid of him. He was redoubtable, not in virtue of his office, but because of his unwarrantable assumptions. I had never had anything to do with him before.

I said: 'Oh! He has asked for me twice. Then perhaps I had better go in.'

'You must! You must!'

The shipping-master led the way with a mincing gait round the whole system of desks to a tall and important-looking door, which he opened with a deferential action of the arm.

He stepped right in (but without letting go of the handle) and, after gazing down the room for a while, beckoned me in by a silent jerk of the head. Then he slipped out at once and shut the door after me most delicately.

Three lofty windows gave on to the harbour. There was nothing in them but the dark-blue sparkling sea and the paler luminous blue of the sky. My eye caught in the depths and distances of these blue tones the white speck of some big ship just arrived and about to anchor in the outer roadstead. A ship from home – after perhaps ninety days at sea. There is something touching about a ship coming in from sea and folding her white wings for a rest.

The next thing I saw was the top-knot of silver hair surmounting Captain Ellis's smooth red face, which would have been apoplectic if it hadn't had such a fresh appearance.

Our deputy-Neptune had no beard on his chin, and there was no trident to be seen standing in a corner any-where, like an umbrella. But his hand was holding a pen – the official pen, far mightier than the sword in making or marring the fortune of simple toiling men. He was looking over his shoulder at my advance.

When I had come well within range he saluted me by a nerve-shattering: 'Where have you been all this time?'

As it was no concern of his I did not take the slightest notice of the shot. I said simply that I had heard there was a master needed for some vessel, and being a sailing-ship man I thought I would apply...

He interrupted me. 'Why! Hang it! *You* are the right man for that job – if there had been twenty others after it. But no fear of that. They are all afraid to catch hold. That's what's the matter.'

He was very irritated. I said innocently: 'Are they, sir? I wonder why?'

'Why!' he fumed. 'Afraid of the sails. Afraid of a white crew. Too much trouble. Too much work. Too long out here. Easy life and deck-chairs more their mark. Here I sit with the Consul-General's cable before me, and the only man fit for the job not to be found anywhere. I began to think you were funking it too....'

'I haven't been long getting to the office,' I remarked calmly.

'You have a good name out here, though,' he growled savagely without looking at me.

'I am very glad to hear it from you, sir,' I said.

'Yes. But you are not on the spot when you are wanted. You know you weren't. That steward of yours wouldn't dare to neglect a message from this office. Where the devil did you hide yourself for the best part of the day?'

I only smiled kindly down on him, and he seemed to recollect himself, and asked me to take a seat. He explained that the master of a British ship having died in Bankok the Consul-General had cabled to him a request for a competent man to be sent out to take command.

Apparently, in his mind, I was the man from the first, though for the looks of the thing the notification addressed to the Sailors' Home was general. An agreement had already been prepared. He gave it to me to read, and when I handed it back to him with the remark that I accepted its terms, the deputy-Neptune signed it, stamped it with his own exalted hand, folded it in four (it was a sheet of blue foolscap), and presented it to me – a gift of extraordinary potency, for, as I put it in my pocket, my head swam a little.

'This is your appointment to the command,' he said with a certain gravity. 'An official appointment binding the owners to conditions which you have accepted. Now – when will you be ready to go?'

I said I would be ready that very day if necessary. He caught me at my word with great readiness. The steamer 'Melita' was leaving for Bankok that evening about seven. He would request her captain officially to give me a passage and wait for me till ten o'clock.

Then he rose from his office chair, and I got up too. My head swam, there was no doubt about it, and I felt a heaviness of limbs as if they had grown bigger since I had sat down on that chair. I made my bow.

A subtle change in Captain Ellis's manner became perceptible as though he had laid aside the trident of deputy-Neptune. In reality, it was only his official pen that he had dropped on getting up.

II

HE shook hands with me: 'Well, there you are, on your own, appointed officially under my responsibility.'

He was actually walking with me to the door. What a distance off it seemed! I moved like a man in bonds. But we reached it at last. I opened it with the sensation of dealing with mere dream-stuff, and then at the last moment the fellowship of seamen asserted itself, stronger than the difference of age and station. It asserted itself in Captain Ellis's voice.

'Good-bye – and good luck to you,' he said so heartily that I could only give him a grateful glance. Then I turned and went out, never to see him again in my life. I had not made three steps into the outer office when I heard behind my back a gruff, loud, authoritative voice, the voice of our deputy-Neptune.

It was addressing the head shipping-master, who, having let me in, had, apparently, remained hovering in the middle distance ever since.

'Mr R., let the harbour launch have steam up to take the Captain here on board the "Melita" at half-past nine tonight.'

I was amazed at the startled assent of R.'s 'Yes, sir.' He ran before me out on the landing. My new dignity sat yet so lightly on me that I was not aware that it was I, the Captain, the object of this last graciousness. It seemed as if all of a sudden a pair of wings had grown on my shoulders. I merely skimmed along the polished floor.

But R. was impressed.

'I say!' he exclaimed on the landing, while the Malay crew of the steam-launch standing by looked stonily at the man for whom they were going to be kept on duty so late, away from their gambling, from their girls, or their pure domestic joys. 'I say! His own launch. What have you done to him?'

His stare was full of respectful curiosity. I was quite confounded.

'Was it for me? I hadn't the slightest notion,' I stammered out.

He nodded many times. 'Yes. And the last person who had it before you was a Duke. So, there!'

I think he expected me to faint on the spot. But I was in too much of a hurry for emotional displays. My feelings were already in such a whirl that this staggering information did not seem to make the slightest difference. It fell into the seething cauldron of my brain, and I carried it off with me after a short but effusive passage of leave-taking with R.

The favour of the great throws an aureole round the fortunate object of its selection. That excellent man inquired whether he could do anything for me. He had known me only by sight, and he was well aware he would never see me again; I was, in common with the other seamen of the port, merely a subject for official writing, filling up of forms with all the artificial superiority of a man of pen and ink to the men who grapple with realities outside the consecrated walls of official buildings. What ghosts we must have been to him! Mere symbols to juggle with in books and heavy registers, without brains and muscles and perplexities; something hardly useful and decidedly inferior.

And he – the office hours being over – wanted to know if he could be of any use to me!

I ought, properly speaking – I ought to have been moved to tears. But I did not even think of it. It was only another miraculous manifestation of that day of miracles. I parted from him as if he had been a mere symbol. I floated down the staircase. I floated out of the official and imposing portal. I went on floating along.

I use that word rather than the word 'flew,' because I have a distinct impression that, though uplifted by my aroused youth, my movements were deliberate enough. To that mixed white, brown, and yellow portion of mankind, out abroad on their own affairs, I presented the appearance of a man walking rather sedately. And nothing in the way of abstraction could have equalled my deep detachment from the forms and colours of this world. It was, as it were, absolute.

And yet, suddenly, I recognized Hamilton. I recognized him without effort, without a shock, without a start. There he was, strolling towards the Harbour Office with his stiff, arrogant dignity. His red face made him noticeable at a distance. It flamed, over there, on the shady side of the street.

He had perceived me too. Something (unconscious exuberance of spirits perhaps) moved me to wave my hand to him elaborately. This lapse from good taste happened before I was aware that I was capable of it.

The impact of my impudence stopped him short, much as a bullet might have done. I verily believe he staggered,

though as far as I could see he didn't actually fall. I had gone
past in a moment and did not turn my head. I had forgotten
his existence.

The next ten minutes might have been ten seconds or ten
centuries for all my consciousness had to do with it. People
might have been falling dead around me, houses crumbling,
guns firing, I wouldn't have known. I was thinking: 'By Jove!
I have got it.' *It* being the command. It had come about in a
way utterly unforeseen in my modest day-dreams.

I perceived that my imagination had been running in
conventional channels and that my hopes had always been
drab stuff. I had envisaged a command as a result of a slow
course of promotion in the employ of some highly respectable firm. The reward of faithful service. Well, faithful
service was all right. One would naturally give that for
one's own sake, for the sake of the ship, for the love of
the life of one's choice; not for the sake of the reward.

There is something distasteful in the notion of a reward.

And now here I had my command, absolutely in my
pocket, in a way undeniable indeed, but most unexpected;
beyond my imaginings, outside all reasonable expectations,
and even notwithstanding the existence of some sort of
obscure intrigue to keep it away from me. It is true that the
intrigue was feeble, but it helped the feeling of wonder – as
if I had been specially destined for that ship I did not know,
by some power higher than the prosaic agencies of the
commercial world.

A strange sense of exultation began to creep into me. If
I had worked for that command ten years or more there
would have been nothing of the kind. I was a little frightened.

'Let us be calm,' I said to myself.

Outside the door of the Officers' Home the wretched
Steward seemed to be waiting for me. There was a broad
flight of a few steps, and he ran to and fro on the top of it as
if chained there. A distressed cur. He looked as though his
throat were too dry for him to bark.

I regret to say I stopped before going in. There had been a revolution in my moral nature. He waited opened-mouthed, breathless, while I looked at him for half a minute.

'And you thought you could keep me out of it,' I said scathingly.

'You said you were going home,' he squeaked miserably. 'You said so. You said so.'

'I wonder what Captain Ellis will have to say to that excuse,' I uttered slowly with a sinister meaning.

His lower jaw had been trembling all the time and his voice was like the bleating of a sick goat. 'You have given me away? You have done for me?'

Neither his distress nor yet the sheer absurdity of it was able to disarm me. It was the first instance of harm being attempted to be done to me – at any rate, the first I had ever found out. And I was still young enough, still too much on this side of the shadow-line, not to be surprised and indignant at such things.

I gazed at him inflexibly. Let the beggar suffer. He slapped his forehead and I passed in, pursued, into the dining-room, by his screech: 'I always said you'd be the death of me.'

This clamour not only overtook me, but went ahead as it were to the verandah and brought out Captain Giles.

He stood before me in the doorway in all the common-place solidity of his wisdom. The gold chain glittered on his breast. He clutched a smouldering pipe.

I extended my hand to him warmly and he seemed surprised, but did respond heartily enough in the end, with a faint smile of superior knowledge which cut my thanks short as if with a knife. I don't think that more than one word came out. And even for that one, judging by the temperature of my face, I had blushed as if for a bad action. Assuming a detached tone, I wondered how on earth he had managed to spot the little underhand game that had been going on.

He murmured complacently that there were but few things done in the town that he could not see the inside of. And as to this house, he had been using it off and on for nearly ten years. Nothing that went on in it could escape his great experience. It had been no trouble to him. No trouble at all.

Then in his quiet thick tone he wanted to know if I had complained formally of the Steward's action.

I said that I hadn't – though, indeed, it was not for want of opportunity. Captain Ellis had gone for me bald-headed in a most ridiculous fashion for being out of the way when wanted.

'Funny old gentleman,' interjected Captain Giles. 'What did you say to that?'

'I said simply that I came along the very moment I heard of his message. Nothing more. I didn't want to hurt the Steward. I would scorn to harm such an object. No. I made no complaint, but I believe he thinks I've done so. Let him think. He's got a fright that he won't forget in a hurry, for Captain Ellis would kick him out into the middle of Asia....'

'Wait a moment,' said Captain Giles, leaving me suddenly. I sat down feeling very tired, mostly in my head. Before I could start a train of thought he stood again before me, murmuring the excuse that he had to go and put the fellow's mind at ease.

I looked up with surprise. But in reality I was indifferent. He explained that he had found the Steward lying face downwards on the horsehair sofa. He was all right now.

'He would not have died of fright,' I said contemptuously.

'No. But he might have taken an overdose out of one of those little bottles he keeps in his room,' Captain Giles argued seriously. 'The confounded fool has tried to poison himself once – a couple of years ago.'

'Really,' I said without emotion. 'He doesn't seem very fit to live, anyhow.'

'As to that, it may be said of a good many.'

'Don't exaggerate like this!' I protested, laughing irritably. 'But I wonder what this part of the world would do if you were to leave off looking after it, Captain Giles? Here you have got me a command and saved the Steward's life in one afternoon. Though why you should have taken all that interest in either of us is more than I can understand.'

Captain Giles remained silent for a minute.

Then gravely:

'He's not a bad steward really. He can find a good cook, at any rate. And, what's more, he can keep him when found. I remember the cooks we had here before his time. . . .'

I must have made a movement of impatience, because he interrupted himself with an apology for keeping me yarning there, while no doubt I needed all my time to get ready.

What I really needed was to be alone for a bit. I seized this opening hastily. My bedroom was a quiet refuge in an apparently uninhabited wing of the building. Having absolutely nothing to do (for I had not unpacked my things), I sat down on the bed and abandoned myself to the influences of the hour. To the unexpected influences. . . .

And first I wondered at my state of mind. Why was I not more surprised? Why? Here I was, invested with a command in the twinkling of an eye, not in the common course of human affairs, but more as if by enchantment. I ought to have been lost in astonishment. But I wasn't. I was very much like people in fairy tales. Nothing ever astonishes them. When a fully appointed gala coach is produced out of a pumpkin to take her to a ball Cinderella does not exclaim. She gets in quietly and drives away to her high fortune.

Captain Ellis (a fierce sort of fairy) had produced a command out of a drawer almost as unexpectedly as in a fairy tale. But a command is an abstract idea, and it seemed a sort of 'lesser marvel' till it flashed upon me that it involved the concrete existence of a ship.

A ship! My ship! She was mine, more absolutely mine for possession and care than anything in the world; an object of responsibility and devotion. She was there waiting for me, spellbound, unable to move, to live, to get out into the world (till I came), like an enchanted princess. Her call had come to me as if from the clouds. I had never suspected her existence. I didn't know how she looked, I had barely heard her name, and yet we were indissolubly united for a certain portion of our future, to sink or swim together!

A sudden passion of anxious impatience rushed through my veins and gave me such a sense of the intensity of existence as I have never felt before or since. I discovered how much of a seaman I was, in heart, in mind, and, as it were, physically – a man exclusively of sea and ships; the sea the only world that counted, and the ships the test of manliness, of temperament, of courage and fidelity – and of love.

I had an exquisite moment. It was unique also. Jumping up from my seat, I paced up and down my room for a long time. But when I came into the dining-room I behaved with sufficient composure. I only couldn't eat anything at dinner.

Having declared my intention not to drive but to walk down to the quay, I must render the wretched Steward justice that he bestirred himself to find me some coolies for the luggage. They departed, carrying all my worldly possessions (except a little money I had in my pocket) slung from a long pole. Captain Giles volunteered to walk down with me.

We followed the sombre, shaded alley across the Esplanade. It was moderately cool there under the trees. Captain Giles remarked, with a sudden laugh: 'I know who's jolly thankful at having seen the last of you.'

I guess that he meant the Steward. The fellow had borne himself to me in a sulkily frightened manner at the last. I expressed my wonder that he should have tried to do me a bad turn for no reason at all.

'Don't you see that what he wanted was to get rid of our friend Hamilton by dodging him in front of you for that job? That would have removed him for good, see?'

'Heavens!' I exclaimed, feeling humiliated somehow. 'Can it be possible? What a fool he must be! That over-bearing, impudent loafer! Why! He couldn't...And yet he's nearly done it, I believe; for the Harbour Office was bound to send somebody.'

'Aye. A fool like our Steward can be dangerous some-times,' declared Captain Giles sententiously. 'Just because he is a fool,' he added, imparting further instruction in his complacent low tones. 'For,' he continued in the manner of a set demonstration, 'no sensible person would risk being kicked out of the only berth between himself and starvation just to get rid of a simple annoyance – a small worry. Would he now?'

'Well, no,' I conceded, restraining a desire to laugh at that something mysteriously earnest in delivering the con-clusions of his wisdom as though they were the product of prohibited operations. 'But that fellow looks as if he were rather crazy. He must be.'

'As to that, I believe everybody in the world is a little mad,' he announced quietly.

'You make no exceptions?' I inquired, just to hear his answer.

He kept silent for a little while, then got home in an effective manner.

'Why! Kent says that even of you.'

'Does he?' I retorted, extremely embittered all at once against my former captain. 'There's nothing of that in the written character from him which I've got in my pocket. Has he given you any instances of my lunacy?'

Captain Giles explained in a conciliating tone that it had been only a friendly remark in reference to my abrupt leaving the ship for no apparent reason.

I muttered grumpily: 'Oh! leaving his ship,' and mended my pace. He kept up by my side in the deep gloom of the avenue as if it were his conscientious duty to see me out of the colony as an undesirable character. He panted a little, which was rather pathetic in a way. But I was not moved. On the contrary. His discomfort gave me a sort of malicious pleasure.

Presently I relented, slowed down, and said:

'What I really wanted was to get a fresh grip. I felt it was time. Is that so very mad?'

He made no answer. We were issuing from the avenue. On the bridge over the canal a dark, irresolute figure seemed to be awaiting something or somebody.

It was a Malay policeman, barefooted, in his blue uniform. The silver band on his little round cap shone dimly in the light of the street lamp. He peered in our direction timidly.

Before we could come up to him he turned about and walked in front of us in the direction of the jetty. The distance was some hundred yards; and then I found my coolies squatting on their heels. They had kept the pole on their shoulders, and all my worldly goods, still tied to the pole, were resting on the ground between them. As far as the eye could reach along the quay there was not another soul abroad except the police peon, who saluted us.

It seems he had detained the coolies as suspicious characters, and had forbidden them the jetty. But at a sign from me he took off the embargo with alacrity. The two patient fellows, rising together with a faint grunt, trotted off along the planks, and I prepared to take my leave of Captain Giles, who stood there with an air as though his mission were drawing to a close. It could not be denied that he had done it all. And while I hesitated about an appropriate sentence he made himself heard:

'I expect you'll have your hands pretty full of tangled up business.'

I asked him what made him think so; and he answered that it was his general experience of the world. Ship a long time away from her port, owners inaccessible by cable, and the only man who could explain matters dead and buried.

'And you yourself new to the business in a way,' he concluded in a sort of unanswerable tone.

'Don't insist,' I said. 'I know it only too well. I only wish you could impart to me some small portion of your experience before I go. As it can't be done in ten minutes I had better not begin to ask you. There's that harbour-launch waiting for me too. But I won't feel really at peace till I have that ship of mine out in the Indian Ocean.'

He remarked casually that from Bankok to the Indian Ocean was a pretty long step. And this murmur, like a dim flash from a dark lantern, showed me for a moment the broad belt of islands and reefs between that unknown ship, which was mine, and the freedom of the great waters of the globe.

But I felt no apprehension. I was familiar enough with the Archipelago by that time. Extreme patience and extreme care would see me through the region of broken land, of faint airs of dead water to where I would feel at last my command swing on the great swell and list over to the great breath of regular winds, that would give her the feeling of a large, more intense life. The road would be long. All roads are long that lead towards one's heart's desire. But this road my mind's eye could see on a chart, professionally, with all its complications and difficulties, yet simple enough in a way. One is a seaman or one is not. And I had no doubt of being one.

The only part I was a stranger to was the Gulf of Siam. And I mentioned this to Captain Giles. Not that I was concerned very much. It belonged to the same region the nature of which I knew, into whose very soul I seemed to have looked during the last months of that existence with which I had broken now, suddenly, as one parts with some enchanting company.

'The Gulf...Ay! A funny piece of water that,' said Captain Giles.

Funny, in this connection, was a vague word. The whole thing sounded like an opinion uttered by a cautious person mindful of actions for slander.

I didn't inquire as to the nature of that funniness. There was really no time. But at the very last he volunteered a warning.

'Whatever you do keep to the east side of it. The west side is dangerous at this time of the year. Don't let anything tempt you over. You'll find nothing but trouble there.'

Though I could hardly imagine what could tempt me to involve my ship amongst the currents and reefs of the Malay shore, I thanked him for the advice.

He gripped my extended arm warmly, and the end of our acquaintance came suddenly in the words: 'Good night.'

That was all he said: 'Good night.' Nothing more. I don't know what I intended to say, but surprise made me swallow it, whatever it was. I choked slightly, and then exclaimed with a sort of nervous haste: 'Oh! Good night, Captain Giles, good night.'

His movements were always deliberate, but his back had receded some distance along the deserted quay before I collected myself enough to follow his example and made a half turn in the direction of the jetty.

Only my movements were not deliberate. I hurried down to the steps and leaped into the launch. Before I had fairly landed in her stern-sheets the slim little craft darted away from the jetty with a sudden swirl of her propeller and the hard, rapid puffing of the exhaust in her vaguely gleaming brass funnel amidships.

The misty churning at her stern was the only sound in the world. The shore lay plunged in the silence of the deepest slumber. I watched the town recede still and soundless in the hot night, till the abrupt hail, 'Steam-launch, ahoy!' made me spin round face forward. We were close to a white, ghostly steamer. Lights shone on her decks, in her portholes. And the same voice shouted from her: 'Is that our passenger?'

'It is,' I yelled.

Her crew had been obviously on the jump. I could hear them running about. The modern spirit of haste was loudly vocal in the orders to 'Heave away on the cable' – to 'Lower the side-ladder,' and in urgent requests to me to 'Come along, sir! We have been delayed three hours for you. . . . Our time is seven o'clock, you know!'

I stepped on the deck. I said 'No! I don't know.' The spirit of modern hurry was embodied in a thin, long-armed, long-legged man, with a closely clipped grey beard. His meagre hand was hot and dry. He declared feverishly:

'I am hanged if I would have waited another five minutes – harbour-master or no harbour-master.'

'That's your own business,' I said. 'I didn't ask you to wait for me.'

'I hope you don't expect any supper,' he burst out. 'This isn't a boarding-house afloat. You are the first passenger I ever had in my life and I hope to goodness you will be the last.'

I made no answer to this hospitable communication; and, indeed, he didn't wait for any, bolting away on to his bridge to get his ship under way.

For the four days he had me on board he did not depart from that half-hostile attitude. His ship having been delayed three hours on my account he couldn't forgive me for not being a more distinguished person. He was not exactly outspoken about it, but that feeling of annoyed wonder was peeping out perpetually in his talk.

He was absurd.

He was also a man of much experience, which he liked to trot out; but no greater contrast with Captain Giles could have been imagined. He would have amused me if I had wanted to be amused. But I did not want to be amused. I was like a lover looking forward to a meeting. Human hostility was nothing to me. I thought of my unknown ship. It was amusement enough, torment enough, occupation enough.

He perceived my state, for his wits were sufficiently sharp for that, and he poked sly fun at my preoccupation in the manner some nasty, cynical old men assume towards the dreams and illusions of youth. I, on my side, refrained from questioning him as to the appearance of my ship, though I knew that being in Bankok every month or so he must have known her by sight. I was not going to expose the ship, my ship! to some slighting reference.

He was the first really unsympathetic man I had ever come in contact with. My education was far from being finished, though I didn't know it. No! I didn't know it.

All I knew was that he disliked me and had some contempt for my person. Why? Apparently because his ship had been delayed three hours on my account. Who was I to have such a thing done for me? Such a thing had never been done for him. It was a sort of jealous indignation.

My expectation, mingled with fear, was wrought to its highest pitch. How slow had been the days of the passage and how soon they were over. One morning early, we crossed the bar, and while the sun was rising splendidly over the flat spaces of the land we steamed up the innumerable bends, passed under the shadow of the great gilt pagoda, and reached the outskirts of the town.

There it was, spread largely on both banks, the Oriental capital which had as yet suffered no white conqueror; an expanse of brown houses of bamboo, of mats, of leaves, of a vegetable-matter style of architecture, sprung out of the brown soil on the banks of the muddy river. It was amazing to think that in those miles of human habitations there was not probably half a dozen pounds of nails. Some of those houses of sticks and grass, like the nests of an aquatic race, clung to the low shores. Others seemed to grow out of the water; others again floated in long anchored rows in the very middle of the stream. Here and there in the distance, above the crowded mob of low, brown roof ridges, towered great piles of masonry, King's Palace, temples, gorgeous and dilapidated, crumbling under the vertical sunlight,

tremendous, overpowering, almost palpable, which seemed
to enter one's breast with the breath of one's nostrils and
soak into one's limbs through every pore of one's skin.

The ridiculous victim of jealousy had for some reason or
other to stop his engines just then. The steamer drifted
slowly up with the tide. Oblivious of my new surroundings
I walked the deck, in anxious, deadened abstraction, a
commingling of romantic reverie with a very practical
survey of my qualifications. For the time was approaching
for me to behold my command and to prove my worth in
the ultimate test of my profession.

Suddenly I heard myself called by that imbecile. He was
beckoning me to come up on his bridge.

I didn't care very much for that, but as it seemed that he
had something particular to say I went up the ladder.

He laid his hand on my shoulder and gave me a slight
turn, pointing with his other arm at the same time.

'There! That's your ship, Captain,' he said. I felt a thump
in my breast – only one, as if my heart had ceased to beat.
There were ten or more ships moored along the bank,
and the one he meant was partly hidden from my sight by
her next astern. He said: 'We'll drift abreast her in a
moment.'

What was his tone? Mocking? Threatening? Or only
indifferent? I could not tell. I suspected some malice in this
unexpected manifestation of interest.

He left me, and I leaned over the rail of the bridge
looking over the side. I dared not raise my eyes. Yet it had
to be done – and, indeed, I could not have helped myself.
I believe I trembled.

But directly my eyes had rested on my ship all my fear
vanished. It went off swiftly, like a bad dream. Only that a
dream leaves no shame behind it, and that I felt a momentary shame at my unworthy suspicions.

Yes, there she was. Her hull, her rigging filled my eye
with a great content. That feeling of life-emptiness which
had made me so restless for the last few months lost its

bitter plausibility, its evil influence, dissolved in a flow of joyous emotion.

At the first glance I saw that she was a high-class vessel, a harmonious creature in the lines of her fine body, in the proportioned tallness of her spars. Whatever her age and her history, she had preserved the stamp of her origin. She was one of those craft that in virtue of their design and complete finish will never look old. Amongst her companions moored to the bank, and all bigger than herself, she looked like a creature of high breed – an Arab steed in a string of cart-horses.

A voice behind me said in a nasty equivocal tone: 'I hope you are satisfied with her, Captain.' I did not even turn my head. It was the master of the steamer, and whatever he meant, whatever he thought of her, I knew that, like some rare women, she was one of those creatures whose mere existence is enough to awaken an unselfish delight. One feels that it is good to be in the world in which she has her being.

That illusion of life and character which charms one in men's finest handiwork radiated from her. An enormous bulk of teak-wood timber swung over her hatchway; lifeless matter, looking heavier and bigger than anything aboard of her. When they started lowering it the surge of the tackle sent a quiver through her from water-line to the trucks up the fine nerves of her rigging, as though she had shuddered at the weight. It seemed cruel to load her so. . . .

Half-an-hour later, putting my foot on her deck for the first time, I received the feeling of deep physical satisfaction. Nothing could equal the fullness of that moment, the ideal completeness of that emotional experience which had come to me without the preliminary toil and disenchantments of an obscure career.

My rapid glance ran over her, enveloped, appropriated the form concreting the abstract sentiment of my command. A lot of details perceptible to a seaman struck my eye vividly in that instant. For the rest, I saw her disengaged from the material conditions of her being. The shore to which she was moored was as if it did not exist. What were to me all the countries of the globe? In all the parts of the world washed by navigable waters our relation to each other would be the same – and more intimate than there are words to express in the language. Apart from that, every scene and episode would be a mere passing show. The very gang of yellow coolies busy about the main hatch was less substantial than the stuff dreams are made of. For who on earth would dream of Chinamen? . . .

I went aft, ascended the poop, where, under the awning, gleamed the brasses of the yacht-like fittings, the polished surfaces of the rails, the glass of the skylights. Right aft two seamen, busy cleaning the steering gear, with the reflected ripples of light running playfully up their bent backs, went on with their work, unaware of me and of the almost affectionate glance I threw at them in passing towards the companion-way of the cabin.

The doors stood wide open, the slide was pushed right back. The half-turn of the staircase cut off the view of the lobby. A low humming ascended from below, but it stopped abruptly at the sound of my descending footsteps.

III

THE first thing I saw down there was the upper part of a man's body projecting backwards, as it were, from one of the doors at the foot of the stairs. His eyes looked at me very wide and still. In one hand he held a dinner plate, in the other a cloth.

'I am your new captain,' I said quietly.

In a moment, in the twinkling of an eye, he had got rid of the plate and the cloth and jumped to open the cabin door. As soon as I passed into the saloon he vanished, but only to reappear instantly, buttoning up a jacket he had put on with the swiftness of a 'quick-change' artist.

'Where's the chief mate?' I asked.

'In the hold, I think, sir. I saw him go down the after-hatch ten minutes ago.'

'Tell him I am on board.'

The mahogany table under the skylight shone in the twilight like a dark pool of water. The sideboard, surmounted by a wide looking-glass in an ormolu frame, had a marble top. It bore a pair of silver-plated lamps and some other pieces – obviously a harbour display. The saloon itself was panelled in two kinds of wood in the excellent, simple taste prevailing when the ship was built.

I sat down in the arm-chair at the head of the table – the captain's chair, with a small tell-tale compass swung above it – a mute reminder of unremitting vigilance.

A succession of men had sat in that chair. I became aware of that thought suddenly, vividly, as though each had left a little of himself between the four walls of these ornate bulkheads; as if a sort of composite soul, the soul of command, had whispered suddenly to mine of long days at sea and of anxious moments.

'You, too!' it seemed to say, 'you, too, shall taste of that peace and that unrest in a searching intimacy with your own self – obscure as we were and as supreme in the face of all the winds and all the seas, in an immensity that receives no impress, preserves no memories, and keeps no reckoning of lives.'

Deep within the tarnished ormolu frame, in the hot half-light sifted through the awning, I saw my own face propped between my hands. And I stared back at myself with the perfect detachment of distance, rather with curiosity than with any other feeling, except of some sympathy for this latest representative of what for all intents and purposes was a dynasty; continuous not in blood, indeed, but in its experience, in its training, in its conception of duty, and in the blessed simplicity of its traditional point of view on life.

It struck me that this quietly staring man whom I was watching, both as if he were myself and somebody else, was not exactly a lonely figure. He had his place in a line of men whom he did not know, of whom he had never heard; but who were fashioned by the same influences, whose souls in relation to their humble life's work had no secrets for him.

Suddenly I perceived that there was another man in the saloon, standing a little on one side and looking intently at me. The chief mate. His long, red moustache determined the character of his physiognomy, which struck me as pugnacious in (strange to say) a ghastly sort of way.

How long had he been there looking at me, appraising me in my unguarded day-dreaming state? I would have been more disconcerted if, having the clock set in the top of the mirror-frame right in front of me, I had not noticed that its long hand had hardly moved at all.

I could not have been in that cabin more than two minutes altogether. Say three.... So he could not have been watching me more than a mere fraction of a minute, luckily. Still, I regretted the occurrence.

But I showed nothing of it as I rose leisurely (it had to be leisurely) and greeted him with perfect friendliness.

There was something reluctant and at the same time attentive in his bearing. His name was Burns. We left the cabin and went round the ship together. His face in the full light of day appeared very worn, meagre, even haggard. Somehow I had a delicacy as to looking too often at him; his eyes, on the contrary, remained fairly glued on my face. They were greenish and had an expectant expression.

He answered all my questions readily enough, but my ear seemed to catch a tone of unwillingness. The second officer, with three or four hands, was busy forward. The mate mentioned his name and I nodded to him in passing. He was very young. He struck me as rather a cub.

When we returned below I sat down on one end of a deep, semi-circular, or, rather, semi-oval settee, upholstered in red plush. It extended right across the whole after-end of the cabin. Mr Burns, motioned to sit down, dropped into one of the swivel-chairs round the table, and kept his eyes on me as persistently as ever, and with that strange air as if all this were make-believe and he expected me to get up, burst into a laugh, slap him on the back, and vanish from the cabin.

There was an odd stress in the situation which began to make me uncomfortable. I tried to react against this vague feeling.

'It's only my inexperience,' I thought.

In the face of that man, several years, I judged, older than myself, I became aware of what I had left already behind me – my youth. And that was indeed poor comfort. Youth is a fine thing, a mighty power – as long as one does not think of it. I felt I was becoming self-conscious. Almost against my will I assumed a moody gravity. I said: 'I see you have kept her in very good order, Mr Burns.'

Directly I had uttered these words I asked myself angrily why the deuce did I want to say that? Mr Burns in answer had only blinked at me. What on earth did he mean?

I fell back on a question which had been in my thoughts for a long time – the most natural question on the lips of any seaman whatever joining a ship. I voiced it (confound this self-consciousness) in a *dégagé* cheerful tone: 'I suppose she can travel – what?'

Now a question like this might have been answered normally, either in accents of apologetic sorrow or with a visibly suppressed pride, in a 'I don't want to boast, but you shall see' sort of tone. There are sailors, too, who would have been roughly outspoken: 'Lazy brute,' or openly delighted: 'She's a flyer.' Two ways, if four manners.

But Mr Burns found another way, a way of his own which had, at all events, the merit of saving his breath, if no other.

Again he did not say anything. He only frowned. And it was an angry frown. I waited. Nothing more came.

'What's the matter? . . . Can't you tell after being nearly two years in the ship?' I addressed him sharply.

He looked as startled for a moment as though he had discovered my presence only that very moment. But this passed off almost at once. He put on an air of indifference. But I suppose he thought it better to say something. He said that a ship needed, just like a man, the chance to show the best she could do, and that this ship had never had a chance since he had been on board of her. Not that he could remember. The last captain... He paused.

'Has he been so very unlucky?' I asked with frank incredulity. Mr Burns turned his eyes away from me. No, the late captain was not an unlucky man. One couldn't say that. But he had not seemed to want to make use of his luck.

Mr Burns – man of enigmatic moods – made this statement with an inanimate face and staring wilfully at the rudder-casing. The statement itself was obscurely suggestive. I asked quietly:

'Where did he die?'

'In this saloon. Just where you are sitting now,' answered Mr Burns.

I repressed a silly impulse to jump up; but upon the whole I was relieved to hear that he had not died in the bed which was now to be mine. I pointed out to the chief mate that what I really wanted to know was where he had buried his late captain.

Mr Burns said that it was at the entrance to the Gulf. A roomy grave; a sufficient answer. But the mate, overcoming visibly something within him – something like a curious reluctance to believe in my advent (as an irrevocable fact, at any rate), did not stop at that – though, indeed, he may have wished to do so.

As a compromise with his feelings, I believe, he addressed himself persistently to the rudder-casing, so that to me he had the appearance of a man talking in solitude, a little unconsciously, however.

His tale was that at seven bells in the forenoon watch he had all hands mustered on the quarter-deck and told them that they had better go down to say good-bye to the captain.

Those words, as if grudged to an intruding personage, were enough for me to evoke vividly that strange ceremony: The bare-footed, bare-headed seamen crowding shyly into that cabin, a small mob pressed against that sideboard, uncomfortable rather than moved, shirts open on sunburnt chests, weather-beaten faces, and all staring at the dying man with the same grave and expectant expression.

'Was he conscious?' I asked.

'He didn't speak, but he moved his eyes to look at them,' said the mate.

After waiting a moment Mr Burns motioned the crew to leave the cabin, but he detained the two eldest men to stay with the captain while he went on deck with his sextant to 'take the sun.' It was getting towards noon and he was anxious to obtain a good observation for latitude. When he returned below to put his sextant away he found that the two men had retreated out into the lobby. Through the open door he had a view of the captain lying easy against the pillows. He had 'passed away' while Mr Burns was taking his observation. As near noon as possible. He had hardly changed his position.

Mr Burns sighed, glanced at me inquisitively, as much as to say, 'Aren't you going yet?' and then turned his thoughts from his new captain back to the old, who, being dead, had no authority, was not in anybody's way, and was much easier to deal with.

Mr Burns dealt with him at some length. He was a peculiar man – of about sixty-five – iron grey, hardfaced, obstinate, and uncommunicative. He used to keep the ship loafing at sea for inscrutable reasons. Would come on deck at night sometimes, take some sail off her, God only knows why or wherefore, then go below, shut himself up in his cabin, and play on the violin for hours – till daybreak perhaps. In fact, he spent most of his time day or night

playing the violin. That was when the fit took him. Very
loud, too.

It came to this, that Mr Burns mustered his courage one
day and remonstrated earnestly with the captain. Neither
he nor the second mate could get a wink of sleep in their
watches below for the noise.... And how could they be
expected to keep awake while on duty? he pleaded. The
answer of that stern man was that if he and the second mate
didn't like the noise, they were welcome to pack up their
traps and walk over the side. When this alternative was
offered the ship happened to be 600 miles from the nearest
land.

Mr Burns at this point looked at me with an air of
curiosity. I began to think that my predecessor was a
remarkably peculiar old man.

But I had to hear stranger things yet. It came out that
this stern, grim, wind-tanned, rough, sea-salted, taciturn
sailor of sixty-five was not only an artist, but a lover as well.
In Haiphong, when they got there after a course of most
unprofitable peregrinations (during which the ship was
nearly lost twice), he got himself, in Mr Burns's own
words, 'mixed up' with some woman. Mr Burns had had
no personal knowledge of that affair, but positive evidence
of it existed in the shape of a photograph taken in
Haiphong. Mr Burns found it in one of the drawers in
the captain's room.

In due course I, too, saw that amazing human document
(I even threw it overboard later). There he sat with his
hands reposing on his knees, bald, squat, grey, bristly,
recalling a wild boar somehow; and by his side towered
an awful, mature, white female with rapacious nostrils and
a cheaply ill-omened stare in her enormous eyes. She was
disguised in some semi-oriental, vulgar, fancy costume.
She resembled a low-class medium or one of those
women who tell fortunes by cards for half-a-crown. And
yet she was striking. A professional sorceress from the
slums. It was incomprehensible. There was something

awful in the thought that she was the last reflection of the
world of passion for the fierce soul which seemed to look at
one out of the sardonically savage face of that old seaman.
However, I noticed that she was holding some musical
instrument – guitar or mandoline – in her hand. Perhaps
that was the secret of her sortilege.

For Mr Burns that photograph explained why the
unloaded ship was kept sweltering at anchor for three
weeks in a pestilential hot harbour without air. They lay
there and gasped. The captain, appearing now and then on
short visits, mumbled to Mr Burns unlikely tales about
some letters he was waiting for.

Suddenly, after vanishing for a week, he came on board
in the middle of the night and took the ship out to sea with
the first break of dawn. Daylight showed him looking wild
and ill. The mere getting clear of the land took two days,
and somehow or other they bumped slightly on a reef.
However, no leak developed, and the captain, growling
'no matter,' informed Mr Burns that he had made up his
mind to take the ship to Hong-Kong and dry-dock her
there.

At this Mr Burns was plunged into despair. For indeed,
to beat up to Hong-Kong against a fierce monsoon, with a
ship not sufficiently ballasted and with her supply of water
not completed, was an insane project.

But the captain growled peremptorily, 'Stick her at it,'
and Mr Burns, dismayed and enraged, stuck her at it, and
kept her at it, blowing away sails, straining the spars,
exhausting the crew – nearly maddened by the absolute
conviction that the attempt was impossible and was bound
to end in some catastrophe.

Meantime the captain, shut up in his cabin and wedged
in a corner of his settee against the crazy bounding of the
ship, played the violin – or, at any rate, made continuous
noise on it.

When he appeared on deck he would not speak and
not always answer when spoken to. It was obvious that he

was ill in some mysterious manner, and beginning to break up.

As the days went by the sounds of the violin became less and less loud, till at last only a feeble scratching would meet Mr Burns's ear as he stood in the saloon listening outside the door of the captain's state-room.

One afternoon in perfect desperation he burst into that room and made such a scene, tearing his hair and shouting such horrid imprecations that he cowed the contemptuous spirit of the sick man. The watertanks were low, they had not gained 50 miles in a fortnight. She would never reach Hong-Kong.

It was like fighting desperately towards destruction for the ship and the men. This was evident without argument. Mr Burns, losing all restraint, put his face close to his captain's and fairly yelled: 'You, sir, are going out of the world. But I can't wait till you are dead before I put the helm up. You must do it yourself. You must do it now!'

The man on the couch snarled in contempt: 'So I am going out of the world – am I?'

'Yes, sir – you haven't many days left in it,' said Mr Burns, calming down. 'One can see it by your face.'

'My face, eh? ... Well, put the helm up and be damned to you.'

Burns flew on deck, got the ship before the wind, then came down again, composed but resolute.

'I've shaped a course for Pulo Condor, sir,' he said. 'When we make it, if you are still with us, you'll tell me into what port you wish me to take the ship and I'll do it.'

The old man gave him a look of savage spite, and said these atrocious words in deadly, slow tones:

'If I had my wish, neither the ship nor any of you would ever reach a port. And I hope you won't.'

Mr Burns was profoundly shocked. I believe he was positively frightened at the time. It seems, however, that he managed to produce such an effective laugh that it was the old man's turn to be frightened. He shrank within himself and turned his back on him.

'And his head was not gone then,' Mr Burns assured me excitedly. 'He meant every word of it.'

Such was practically the late captain's last speech. No connected sentence passed his lips afterwards. That night he used the last of his strength to throw his fiddle over the side. No one had actually seen him in the act, but after his death Mr Burns couldn't find the thing anywhere. The empty case was very much in evidence, but the fiddle was clearly not in the ship. And where else could it have gone to but overboard?

'Threw his violin overboard!' I exclaimed.

'He did,' cried Mr Burns excitedly. 'And it's my belief he would have tried to take the ship down with him if it had been in human power. He never meant her to see home again. He wouldn't write to his owners, he never wrote to his old wife either – he wasn't going to. He had made up his mind to cut adrift from everything. That's what it was. He didn't care for business, or freights, or for making a passage – or anything. He meant to have gone wandering about the world till he lost her with all hands.'

Mr Burns looked like a man who had escaped great danger. For a little he would have exclaimed: 'If it hadn't been for me!' And the transparent innocence of his indignant eyes was underlined quaintly by the arrogant pair of moustaches which he proceeded to twist, and as if extend, horizontally.

I might have smiled if I had not been busy with my own sensations, which were not those of Mr Burns. I was already the man in command. My sensations could not be like those of any other man on board. In that community I stood, like a king in his country, in a class all by myself. I mean an hereditary king, not a mere elected head of a state. I was brought there to rule by an agency as remote from the people and as inscrutable almost to them as the Grace of God.

And like a member of a dynasty, feeling a semi-mystical bond with the dead, I was profoundly shocked by my immediate predecessor.

That man had been in all essentials but his age just such another man as myself. Yet the end of his life was a complete act of treason, the betrayal of a tradition which seemed to me as imperative as any guide on earth could be. It appeared that even at sea a man could become the victim of evil spirits. I felt on my face the breath of unknown powers that shape our destinies.

Not to let the silence last too long I asked Mr Burns if he had written to his captain's wife. He shook his head. He had written to nobody.

In a moment he became sombre. He never thought of writing. It took him all his time to watch incessantly the loading of the ship by a rascally Chinese stevedore. In this Mr Burns gave me the first glimpse of the real chief mate's soul which dwelt uneasily in his body.

He mused, then hastened on with gloomy force.

'Yes! The captain died as near noon as possible. I looked through his papers in the afternoon. I read the service over him at sunset and then I stuck the ship's head north and brought her in here. I – brought – her – in.'

He struck the table with his fist.

'She would hardly have come in by herself,' I observed. 'But why didn't you make for Singapore instead?'

His eyes wavered. 'The nearest port,' he muttered sullenly.

I had framed the question in perfect innocence, but this answer (the difference in distance was insignificant) and his manner offered me a clue to the simple truth. He took the ship to a port where he expected to be confirmed in his temporary command from lack of a qualified master to put over his head. Whereas Singapore, he surmised justly, would be full of qualified men.

But his naïve reasoning forgot to take into account the telegraph cable reposing on the bottom of the very Gulf up which he had turned that ship which he imagined himself to have saved from destruction. Hence the bitter flavour of our interview. I tasted it more and more distinctly – and it was less and less to my taste.

'Look here, Mr Burns,' I began, very firmly. 'You may as well understand that I did not run after this command. It was pushed in my way. I've accepted it. I am here to take the ship home first of all, and you may be sure that I shall see to it that every one of you on board here does his duty to that end. This is all I have to say – for the present.'

He was on his feet by this time, but instead of taking his dismissal he remained with trembling, indignant lips, and looking at me hard as though, really, after this, there was nothing for me to do in common decency but to vanish from his outraged sight. Like all very simple emotional states this was moving. I felt sorry for him – almost sympathetic, till (seeing that I did not vanish) he spoke in a tone of forced restraint.

'If I hadn't a wife and a child at home you may be sure, sir, I would have asked you to let me go the very minute you came on board.'

I answered him with a matter-of-course calmness as though some remote third person were in question.

'And I, Mr Burns, would not have let you go. You have signed the ship's articles as chief officer, and till they are terminated at the final port of discharge I shall expect you to attend to your duty and give me the benefit of your experience to the best of your ability.'

Stony incredulity lingered in his eyes; but it broke down before my friendly attitude. With a slight upward toss of his arms (I got to know that gesture well afterwards) he bolted out of the cabin.

We might have saved ourselves that little passage of harmless sparring. Before many days had elapsed it was Mr Burns who was pleading with me anxiously not to leave him behind; while I could only return him but doubtful answers. The whole thing took on a somewhat tragic complexion.

And this horrible problem was only an extraneous episode, a mere complication in the general problem of how to get that ship – which was mine with her appurtenances and her men, with her body and her spirit now slumbering in that pestilential river – how to get her out to sea.

Mr Burns, while still acting captain, had hastened to sign a charter-party which in an ideal world without guile would have been an excellent document. Directly I ran my eye over it I foresaw trouble ahead unless the people of the other part were quite exceptionally fair-minded and open to argument.

Mr Burns, to whom I imparted my fears, chose to take great umbrage at them. He looked at me with that usual incredulous stare, and said bitterly:

'I suppose, sir, you want to make out I've acted like a fool?'

I told him, with my systematic kindliness which always seemed to augment his surprise, that I did not want to make out anything. I would leave that to the future.

And, sure enough, the future brought in a lot of trouble. There were days when I used to remember Captain Giles with nothing short of abhorrence. His confounded acuteness had let me in for this job; while his prophecy that I 'would have my hands full' coming true, made it appear as if done on purpose to play an evil joke on my young innocence.

Yes. I had my hands full of complications which were most valuable as 'experience.' People have a great opinion of the advantages of experience. But in that connection experience means always something disagreeable as opposed to the charm and innocence of illusions.

I must say I was losing mine rapidly. But on these instructive complications I must not enlarge more than to say that they could all be resumed in the one word: Delay.

A mankind which has invented the proverb, 'Time is money,' will understand my vexation. The word 'Delay' entered the secret chamber of my brain, resounded there

like a tolling bell which maddens the ear, affected all my
senses, took on a black colouring, a bitter taste, a deadly
meaning.

'I am really sorry to see you worried like this. Indeed,
I am...'

It was the only humane speech I used to hear at that
time. And it came from a doctor, appropriately enough.

A doctor is humane by definition. But that man was so
in reality. His speech was not professional. I was not ill. But
other people were, and that was the reason of his visiting
the ship.

He was the doctor of our Legation and, of course, of the
Consulate too. He looked after the ship's health, which
generally was poor, and trembling, as it were, on the verge
of a break-up. Yes. The men ailed. And thus time was not
only money, but life as well.

I had never seen such a steady ship's company. As the
doctor remarked to me: 'You seem to have a most respectable lot of seamen.' Not only were they consistently sober,
but they did not even want to go ashore. Care was taken to
expose them as little as possible to the sun. They were
employed on light work under the awnings. And the
humane doctor commended me.

'Your arrangements appear to me to be very judicious,
my dear Captain.'

It is difficult to express how much that pronouncement
comforted me. The doctor's round full face framed in a
light-coloured whisker was the perfection of a dignified
amenity. He was the only human being in the world who
seemed to take the slightest interest in me. He would generally sit in the cabin for half-an-hour or so at every visit.

I said to him one day:

'I suppose the only thing now is to take care of them as
you are doing, till I can get the ship to sea?'

He inclined his head, shutting his eyes under the large
spectacles, and murmured:

'The sea... undoubtedly.'

The first member of the crew fairly knocked over was the steward – the first man to whom I had spoken on board. He was taken ashore (with choleraic symptoms) and died there at the end of a week. Then, while I was still under the startling impression of this first home-thrust of the climate, Mr Burns gave up and went to bed in a raging fever without saying a word to anybody.

I believe he had partly fretted himself into that illness; the climate did the rest with the swiftness of an invisible monster ambushed in the air, in the water, in the mud of the river bank. Mr Burns was a predestined victim.

I discovered him lying on his back, glaring sullenly and radiating heat on one like a small furnace. He would hardly answer my questions, and only grumbled: Couldn't a man take an afternoon off duty with a bad headache – for once?

That evening, as I sat in the saloon after dinner, I could hear him muttering continuously in his room. Ransome, who was clearing the table, said to me:

'I am afraid, sir, I won't be able to give the mate all the attention he's likely to need. I will have to be forward in the galley a great part of my time.'

Ransome was the cook. The mate had pointed him out to me the first day, standing on the deck, his arms crossed on his broad chest, gazing on the river.

Even at a distance his well-proportioned figure, something thoroughly sailor-like in his poise, made him noticeable. On nearer view the intelligent, quiet eyes, a well-bred face, the disciplined independence of his manner made up an attractive personality. When, in addition, Mr Burns told me that he was the best seaman in the ship, I expressed my surprise that in his earliest prime and of such appearance he should sign on as cook on board a ship.

'It's his heart,' Mr Burns had said. 'There's something wrong with it. He mustn't exert himself too much or he may drop dead suddenly.'

And he was the only one the climate had not touched – perhaps because, carrying a deadly enemy in his breast, he had schooled himself into a systematic control of feelings and movements. When one was in the secret this was apparent in his manner. After the poor steward died, and as he could not be replaced by a white man in this Oriental port, Ransome had volunteered to do the double work.

'I can do it all right, sir, as long as I go about it quietly,' he had assured me.

But obviously he couldn't be expected to take up sick-nursing in addition. Moreover, the doctor peremptorily ordered Mr Burns ashore.

With a seaman on each side holding him up under the arms, the mate went over the gangway more sullen than ever. We built him up with pillows in the gharry, and he made an effort to say brokenly:

'Now – you've got – what you wanted – got me out of – the ship.'

'You were never more mistaken in your life, Mr Burns,' I said quietly, duly smiling at him; and the trap drove off to a sort of sanatorium, a pavilion of bricks which the doctor had in the grounds of his residence.

I visited Mr Burns regularly. After the first few days, when he didn't know anybody, he received me as if I had come either to gloat over a crushed enemy or else to curry favour with a deeply-wronged person. It was either one or the other, just as it happened according to his fantastic sick-room moods. Whichever it was, he managed to convey it to me even during the period when he appeared almost too weak to talk. I treated him to my invariable kindliness.

Then one day, suddenly, a surge of downright panic burst through all this craziness.

If I left him behind in this deadly place he would die. He felt it, he was certain of it. But I wouldn't have the heart to leave him ashore. He had a wife and child in Sydney.

He produced his wasted fore-arms from under the sheet which covered him and clasped his fleshless claws. He would die! He would die here. . . .

He absolutely managed to sit up, but only for a moment, and when he fell back I really thought that he would die there and then. I called to the Bengali dispenser, and hastened away from the room.

Next day he upset me thoroughly by renewing his entreaties. I returned an evasive answer, and left him the picture of ghastly despair. The day after I went in with reluctance, and he attacked me at once in a much stronger voice and with an abundance of argument which was quite startling. He presented his case with a sort of crazy vigour, and asked me finally how would I like to have a man's death on my conscience? He wanted me to promise that I would not sail without him.

I said that I really must consult the doctor first. He cried out at that. The doctor! Never! That would be a death sentence.

The effort had exhausted him. He closed his eyes, but went on rambling in a low voice. I had hated him from the start. The late captain had hated him too. Had wished him dead. Had wished all hands dead. . . .

'What do you want to stand in with that wicked corpse for, sir? He'll have you too,' he ended, blinking his glazed eyes vacantly.

'Mr Burns,' I cried, very much discomposed, 'what on earth are you talking about?'

He seemed to come to himself, though he was too weak to start.

'I don't know,' he said languidly. 'But don't ask that doctor, sir. You and I are sailors. Don't ask him, sir. Some day perhaps you will have a wife and child yourself.'

And again he pleaded for the promise that I would not leave him behind. I had the firmness of mind not to give it to him. Afterwards this sternness seemed criminal; for my mind was made up. That prostrated man, with hardly strength enough to breathe and ravaged by a passion of fear, was irresistible. And, besides, he had happened to hit on the right words. He and I were sailors. That was a claim, for I had no other family. As to the wife-and-child (some day) argument it had no force. It sounded merely bizarre.

I could imagine no claim that would be stronger and more absorbing than the claim of that ship, of these men snared in the river by silly commercial complications, as if in some poisonous trap.

However, I had nearly fought my way out. Out to sea. The sea – which was pure, safe, and friendly. Three days more.

That thought sustained and carried me on my way back to the ship. In the saloon the doctor's voice greeted me, and his large form followed his voice, issuing out of the star-board spare cabin where the ship's medicine chest was kept securely lashed in the bed-place.

Finding that I was not on board he had gone in there, he said, to inspect the supply of drugs, bandages, and so on. Everything was completed and in order.

I thanked him; I had just been thinking of asking him to do that very thing, as in a couple of days, as he knew, we were going to sea, where all our troubles of every sort would be over at last.

He listened gravely and made no answer. But when I opened to him my mind as to Mr Burns he sat down by my side, and, laying his hand on my knee amicably, begged me to think what it was I was exposing myself to.

The man was just strong enough to bear being moved and no more. But he couldn't stand a return of the fever. I had before me a passage of sixty days perhaps, beginning with intricate navigation and ending probably with a lot of bad weather. Could I run the risk of having to go through it single-handed, with no chief officer and with a second quite a youth? . . .

He might have added that it was my first command too. He did probably think of that fact, for he checked himself. It was very present to my mind.

He advised me earnestly to cable to Singapore for a chief officer, even if I had to delay my sailing for a week.

'Not a day,' I said. The very thought gave me the shivers. The hands seemed fairly fit, all of them, and this was the time to get them away. Once at sea I was not afraid of facing anything. The sea was now the only remedy for all my troubles.

The doctor's glasses were directed at me like two lamps searching the genuineness of my resolution. He opened his lips as if to argue further, but shut them again without saying anything. I had a vision of poor Burns so vivid in his exhaustion, helplessness, and anguish, that it moved me more than the reality I had come away from only an hour before. It was purged from the drawbacks of his personality, and I could not resist it.

'Look here,' I said. 'Unless you tell me officially that the man must not be moved I'll make arrangements to have him brought on board to-morrow, and shall take the ship out of the river next morning, even if I have to anchor outside the bar for a couple of days to get her ready for sea.'

'Oh! I'll make all the arrangements myself,' said the doctor at once. 'I spoke as I did only as a friend – as a well-wisher, and that sort of thing.'

He rose in his dignified simplicity and gave me a warm handshake, rather solemnly, I thought. But he was as good as his word. When Mr Burns appeared at the gangway carried on a stretcher, the doctor himself walked by its side. The programme had been altered in so far that this transportation had been left to the last moment, on the very morning of our departure.

It was barely an hour after sunrise. The doctor waved his big arm to me from the shore and walked back at once to his trap, which had followed him empty to the river-side. Mr Burns, carried across the quarter-deck, had the appearance of being absolutely lifeless. Ransome went down to settle him in his cabin. I had to remain on deck to look after the ship, for the tug had got hold of our tow-rope already.

The splash of our shore-fasts falling in the water produced a complete change of feeling in me. It was like the imperfect relief of awakening from a nightmare. But when the ship's head swung down the river away from that town, Oriental and squalid, I missed the expected elation of that striven-for moment. What there was, undoubtedly, was a relaxation of tension which translated itself into a sense of weariness after an inglorious fight.

About mid-day we anchored a mile outside the bar. The afternoon was busy for all hands. Watching the work from the poop, where I remained all the time, I detected in it some of the languor of the six weeks spent in the steaming heat of the river. The first breeze would blow that away. Now the calm was complete. I judged that the second officer – a callow youth with an unpromising face – was not, to put it mildly, of that invaluable stuff from which a commander's right hand is made. But I was glad to catch along the main deck a few smiles on those seamen's faces at which I had hardly had time to have a good look as yet. Having thrown off the mortal coil of shore affairs, I felt myself familiar with them and yet a little strange, like a long-lost wanderer among his kin.

Ransome flitted continually to and fro between the galley and the cabin. It was a pleasure to look at him. The man positively had grace. He alone of all the crew had not had a day's illness in port. But with the knowledge of that uneasy heart within his breast I could detect the restraint he put on the natural sailor-like agility of his movements. It was as though he had something very fragile or very explosive to carry about his person and was all the time aware of it.

I had occasion to address him once or twice. He answered me in his pleasant quiet voice and with a faint, slightly wistful smile. Mr Burns appeared to be resting. He seemed fairly comfortable.

After sunset I came out on deck again to meet only a still void. The thin, featureless crust of the coast could not be distinguished. The darkness had risen around the ship like a mysterious emanation from the dumb and lonely waters.

I leaned on the rail and turned my ear to the shadows of the night. Not a sound. My command might have been a planet flying vertiginously on its appointed path in a space of infinite silence. I clung to the rail as if my sense of balance were leaving me for good. How absurd. I hailed nervously.

'On deck there!'

The immediate answer, 'Yes, sir,' broke the spell. The anchor-watch man ran up the poop ladder smartly. I told him to report at once the slightest sign of a breeze coming.

Going below I looked in on Mr Burns. In fact, I could not avoid seeing him, for his door stood open. The man was so wasted that, in that white cabin, under a white sheet, and with his diminished head sunk in the white pillow, his red moustaches captured one's eyes exclusively, like something artificial – a pair of moustaches from a shop exhibited there in the harsh light of the bulkhead-lamp without a shade.

While I stared with a sort of wonder he asserted himself by opening his eyes and even moving them in my direction. A minute stir.

'Dead calm, Mr Burns,' I said resignedly.

In an unexpectedly distinct voice Mr Burns began a rambling speech. Its tone was very strange, not as if affected by his illness, but as if of a different nature. It sounded unearthly. As to the matter, I seemed to make out that it was the fault of the 'old man' – the late captain – ambushed down there under the sea with some evil intention. It was a weird story.

I listened to the end; then stepping into the cabin I laid my hand on the mate's forehead. It was cool. He was light-headed only from extreme weakness. Suddenly he seemed to become aware of me, and in his own voice – of course, very feeble – he asked regretfully:

'Is there no chance at all to get under way, sir?'

'What's the good of letting go our hold of the ground only to drift, Mr Burns?' I answered.

He sighed, and I left him to his immobility. His hold on life was as slender as his hold on sanity. I was oppressed by my lonely responsibilities. I went into my cabin to seek relief in a few hours' sleep, but almost before I closed my eyes the man on deck came down reporting a light breeze. Enough to get under way with, he said.

And it was no more than just enough. I ordered the windlass manned, the sails loosed, and the topsails set. But by the time I had cast the ship I could hardly feel any breath of wind. Nevertheless, I trimmed the yards and put everything on her. I was not going to give up the attempt.

IV

WITH her anchor at the bow and clothed in canvas to her very trucks, my command seemed to stand as motionless as a model ship set on the gleams and shadows of polished marble. It was impossible to distinguish land from water in the enigmatical tranquillity of the immense forces of the world. A sudden impatience possessed me.

'Won't she answer the helm at all?' I said irritably to the man whose strong brown hands grasping the spokes of the wheel stood out lighted on the darkness; like a symbol of mankind's claim to the direction of its own fate.

He answered me:

'Yes, sir. She's coming-to slowly.'

'Let her head come up to south.'

'Aye, aye, sir.'

I paced the poop. There was not a sound but that of my footsteps, till the man spoke again.

'She is at south now, sir.'

I felt a slight tightness of the chest before I gave out the first course of my first command to the silent night, heavy with dew and sparkling with stars. There was a finality in the act committing me to the endless vigilance of my lonely task.

'Steady her head at that,' I said at last. 'The course is south.'

'South, sir,' echoed the man.

I sent below the second mate and his watch and remained in charge, walking the deck through the chill, somnolent hours that precede the dawn.

Slight puffs came and went, and whenever they were strong enough to wake up the black water the murmur alongside ran through my very heart in a delicate crescendo of delight and died away swiftly. I was bitterly tired. The very stars seemed weary of waiting for daybreak. It came at last with a mother-of-pearl sheen at the zenith, such as I had never seen before in the tropics, unglowing, almost grey, with a strange reminder of high latitudes.

The voice of the look-out man hailed from forward:

'Land on the port bow, sir.'

'All right.'

Leaning on the rail I never even raised my eyes. The motion of the ship was imperceptible. Presently Ransome brought me the cup of morning coffee. After I drunk it I looked ahead, and in the still streak of very bright pale orange light I saw the land profiled flatly as if cut out of black paper and seeming to float on the water as light as cork. But the rising sun turned it into mere dark vapour, a doubtful, massive shadow trembling in the hot glare.

The watch finished washing decks. I went below and stopped at Mr Burns's door (he could not bear to have it shut), but hesitated to speak to him till he moved his eyes. I gave him the news.

'Sighted Cape Liant at daylight. About fifteen miles.'

He moved his lips then, but I heard no sound till I put my ear down, and caught the peevish comment: 'This is crawling. . . . No luck.'

'Better luck than standing still, anyhow,' I pointed out resignedly, and left him to whatever thoughts or fancies haunted his hopeless prostration.

Later that morning, when relieved by my second officer, I threw myself on my couch and for some three hours or so I really found oblivion. It was so perfect that on waking up I wondered where I was. Then came the immense relief of the thought: on board my ship! At sea! At sea!

Through the port-holes I beheld an unruffled, sun-smitten horizon. The horizon of a windless day. But its spaciousness alone was enough to give me a sense of a fortunate escape, a momentary exultation of freedom.

I stepped out into the saloon with my heart lighter than it had been for days. Ransome was at the sideboard preparing to lay the table for the first sea dinner of the passage. He turned his head, and something in his eyes checked my modest elation.

Instinctively I asked, 'What is it now?' not expecting in the least the answer I got. It was given with that sort of contained serenity which was characteristic of the man.

'I am afraid we haven't left all sickness behind us, sir.'

'We haven't! What's the matter?'

He told me then that two of our men had been taken bad with fever in the night. One of them was burning and the other was shivering, but he thought that it was pretty much the same thing. I thought so too. I felt shocked by the news.

'One burning, the other shivering, you say? No. We haven't left the sickness behind. Do they look very ill?'

'Middling bad, sir.' Ransome's eyes gazed steadily into mine. We exchanged smiles. Ramsome's a little wistful, as usual, mine no doubt grim enough, to correspond with my secret exasperation.

I asked:

'Was there any wind at all this morning?'

'Can hardly say that, sir. We've moved all the time, though. The land ahead seems a little nearer.'

That was it. A little nearer. Whereas if we had only had a little more wind, only a very little more, we might, we should, have been abreast of Liant by this time and increasing our distance from that contaminated shore. And it was not only the distance. It seemed to me that a stronger breeze would have blown away the infection which clung to the ship. It obviously did cling to the ship. Two men. One burning, one shivering. I felt a distinct reluctance to go and look at them. What was the good? Poison is poison. Tropical fever is tropical fever. But that it should have stretched its claw after us over the sea seemed to me an extraordinary and unfair licence. I could hardly believe that it could be anything worse than the last desperate pluck of the evil from which we were escaping into the clean breath of the sea. If only that breath had been a little stronger. However, there was the quinine against the fever. I went into the spare cabin where the medicine chest was kept to prepare two doses. I opened it full of faith as a man opens a miraculous shrine. The upper part was inhabited by a collection of bottles, all square-shouldered and as like each other as peas. Under that orderly array there were two drawers, stuffed as full of things as one could imagine – paper packages, bandages, cardboard boxes officially labelled. The lower of the two, in one of its compartments, contained our provision of quinine.

There were five bottles, all round and all of a size. One was about a third full. The other four remained still wrapped up in paper and sealed. But I did not expect to see an envelope lying on top of them. A square envelope, belonging, in fact, to the ship's stationery.

It lay so that I could see it was not closed down, and on picking it up and turning it over I perceived that it was addressed to myself. It contained a half-sheet of notepaper, which I unfolded with a queer sense of dealing with the uncanny, but without any excitement as people meet and do extraordinary things in a dream.

'My dear Captain,' it began, but I ran to the signature. The writer was the doctor. The date was that of the day on which, returning from my visit to Mr Burns in the hospital, I had found the excellent doctor waiting for me in the cabin; and when he told me that he had been putting in time inspecting the medicine chest for me. How bizarre! While expecting me to come in at any moment he had been amusing himself by writing me a letter, and then as I came in had hastened to stuff it into the medicine chest drawer. A rather incredible proceeding. I turned to the text in wonder.

In a large, hurried, but legible hand the good, sympathetic man for some reason, either of kindness or more likely impelled by the irresistible desire to express his opinion, with which he didn't want to damp my hopes before, was warning me not to put my trust in the beneficial effects of a change from land to sea. 'I didn't want to add to your worries by discouraging your hopes,' he wrote. 'I am afraid that, medically speaking, the end of your troubles is not yet.' In short, he expected me to have to fight a probable return of tropical illness. Fortunately I had a good provision of quinine. I should put my trust in that, and administer it steadily, when the ship's health would certainly improve.

I crumpled up the letter and rammed it into my pocket. Ransome carried off two big doses to the men forward. As to myself, I did not go on deck as yet. I went instead to the door of Mr Burns's room, and gave him that news too.

It was impossible to say the effect it had on him. At first I thought that he was speechless. His head lay sunk in the pillow. He moved his lips enough, however, to assure me that he was getting much stronger; a statement shockingly untrue on the face of it.

That afternoon I took my watch as a matter of course. A great over-heated stillness enveloped the ship and seemed to hold her motionless in a flaming ambience composed in two shades of blue. Faint, hot puffs eddied nervelessly from her sails. And yet she moved. She must have. For, as the sun was setting, we had drawn abreast of Cape Liant and dropped it behind us: an ominous retreating shadow in the last gleams of twilight.

In the evening, under the crude glare of his lamp, Mr Burns seemed to have come more to the surface of his bedding. It was as if a depressing hand had been lifted off him. He answered my few words by a comparatively long, connected speech. He asserted himself strongly. If he escaped being smothered by this stagnant heat, he said, he was confident that in a very few days he would be able to come up on deck and help me.

While he was speaking I trembled lest this effort of energy should leave him lifeless before my eyes. But I cannot deny that there was something comforting in his willingness. I made a suitable reply, but pointed out to him that the only thing that could really help us was wind – a fair wind.

He rolled his head impatiently on the pillow. And it was not comforting in the least to hear him begin to mutter crazily about the late captain, that old man buried in latitude 8° 20', right in our way – ambushed at the entrance of the Gulf.

'Are you still thinking of your late captain, Mr Burns?' I said. 'I imagine the dead feel no animosity against the living. They care nothing for them.'

'You don't know that one,' he breathed out feebly.

'No. I didn't know him, and he didn't know me. And so he can't have any grievance against me, anyway.'

'Yes. But there's all the rest of us on board,' he insisted.

I felt the inexpugnable strength of common sense being insidiously menaced by this gruesome, by this insane delusion. And I said:

'You mustn't talk so much. You will tire yourself.'

'And there is the ship herself,' he persisted in a whisper.

'Now, not a word more,' I said, stepping in and laying my hand on his cool forehead. It proved to me that this atrocious absurdity was rooted in the man himself and not in the disease, which, apparently, had emptied him of every power, mental and physical, except that one fixed idea.

I avoided giving Mr Burns any opening for conversation for the next few days. I merely used to throw him a hasty, cheery word when passing his door. I believe that if he had

had the strength he would have called out after me more than once. But he hadn't the strength. Ransome, however, observed to me one afternoon that the mate 'seemed to be picking up wonderfully.'

'Did he talk any nonsense to you of late?' I asked casually.

'No, sir.' Ransome was startled by the direct question; but, after a pause, he added equably: 'He told me this morning, sir, that he was sorry he had to bury our late captain right in the ship's way, as one may say, out of the Gulf.'

'Isn't this nonsense enough for you?' I asked, looking confidently at the intelligent, quiet face on which the secret uneasiness in the man's breast had thrown a transparent veil of care.

Ransome didn't know. He had not given a thought to the matter. And with a faint smile he flitted away from me on his never-ending duties, with his usual guarded activity.

Two more days passed. We had advanced a little way – a very little way – into the larger space of the Gulf of Siam. Seizing eagerly upon the elation of the first command thrown into my lap, by the agency of Captain Giles, I had yet an uneasy feeling that such luck as this has got perhaps to be paid for in some way. I had held, professionally, a review of my chances. I was competent enough for that. At least, I thought so. I had a general sense of my preparedness which only a man pursuing a calling he loves can know. That feeling seemed to me the most natural thing in the world. As natural as breathing. I imagined I could not have lived without it.

I don't know what I expected. Perhaps nothing else than that special intensity of existence which is the quintessence of youthful aspirations. Whatever I expected I did not expect to be beset by hurricanes. I knew better than that. In the Gulf of Siam there are no hurricanes. But neither did I expect to find myself bound hand and foot to the hopeless extent which was revealed to me as the days went on.

Not that the evil spell held us always motionless. Mysterious currents drifted us here and there, with a stealthy power made manifest by the changing vistas of the islands fringing the east shore of the Gulf. And there were winds too, fitful and deceitful. They raised hopes only to dash them into the bitterest disappointment, promises of advance ending in lost ground, expiring in sighs, dying into dumb stillness in which the currents had it all their own way – their own inimical way.

The Island of Koh-ring, a great, black, upheaved ridge amongst a lot of tiny islets, lying upon the glassy water like a triton amongst minnows, seemed to be the centre of the fatal circle. It seemed impossible to get away from it. Day after day it remained in sight. More than once, in a favourable breeze, I would take its bearing in the fast ebbing twilight, thinking that it was for the last time. Vain hope. A night of fitful airs would undo the gains of temporary favour, and the rising sun would throw out the black relief of Koh-ring, looking more barren, inhospitable, and grim than ever.

'It's like being bewitched, upon my word,' I said once to Mr Burns, from my usual position in the doorway.

He was sitting up in his bed-place. He was progressing towards the world of living men; if he could hardly have been said to have rejoined it yet. He nodded to me his frail and bony head in a wisely mysterious assent.

'Oh, yes, I know what you mean,' I said. 'But you cannot expect me to believe that a dead man has the power to put out of joint the meteorology of this part of the world. Though indeed it seems to have gone utterly wrong. The land and sea breezes have got broken up into small pieces. We cannot depend upon them for five minutes together.'

'It won't be very long now before I can come up on deck,' muttered Mr Burns, 'and then we shall see.'

Whether he meant this for a promise to grapple with supernatural evil I couldn't tell. At any rate, it wasn't the kind of assistance I needed. On the other hand, I had been living on deck practically night and day so as to take advantage of every chance to get my ship a little more to the southward. The mate, I could see, was extremely weak yet, and not quite rid of his delusion, which to me appeared but a symptom of his disease. At all events, the hopefulness of an invalid was not to be discouraged. I said:

'You will be most welcome there, I am sure, Mr Burns. If you go on improving at this rate you'll be presently one of the healthiest men in the ship.'

This pleased him, but his extreme emaciation converted his self-satisfied smile into a ghastly exhibition of long teeth under the red moustache.

'Aren't the fellows improving, sir?' he asked soberly, with an extremely sensible expression of anxiety on his face.

I answered him only with a vague gesture and went away from the door. The fact was that disease played with us capriciously very much as the winds did. It would go from one man to another with a lighter or heavier touch, which always left its mark behind, staggering some, knocking others over for a time, leaving this one, returning to another, so that all of them had now an invalidish aspect and a hunted, apprehensive look in their eyes; while Ransome and I, the only two completely untouched, went amongst them assiduously distributing quinine. It was a double fight. The adverse weather held us in front and the disease pressed on our rear. I must say that the men were very good. The constant toil of trimming the yards they faced willingly. But all spring was out of their limbs, and as I looked at them from the poop I could not keep from my mind the dreadful impression that they were moving in poisoned air.

Down below, in his cabin, Mr Burns had advanced so far as not only to be able to sit up, but even to draw up his legs. Clasping them with bony arms, like an animated skeleton, he emitted deep, impatient sighs.

'The great thing to do, sir,' he would tell me on every occasion, when I gave him the chance, 'the great thing is to get the ship past 8° 20′ of latitude. Once she's past that we're all right.'

At first I used only to smile at him, though, God knows, I had not much heart left for smiles. But at last I lost my patience.

'Oh, yes. The latitude 8° 20′. That's where you buried your late captain, isn't it?' Then with severity: 'Don't you think, Mr Burns, it's about time you dropped all that nonsense?'

He rolled at me his deep-sunken eyes in a glance of invincible obstinacy. But for the rest, he only muttered, just loud enough for me to hear, something about 'Not surprised ... find ... play us some beastly trick yet ...'

Such passages as this were not exactly wholesome for my resolution. The stress of adversity was beginning to tell on me. At the same time I felt a contempt for that obscure weakness of my soul. I said to myself disdainfully that it should take much more than that to affect in the smallest degree my fortitude.

I didn't know then how soon and from what unexpected direction it would be attacked.

It was the very next day. The sun had risen clear of the southern shoulder of Koh-ring, which still hung, like an evil attendant, on our port quarter. It was intensely hateful to my sight. During the night we had been heading all round the compass, trimming the yards again and again, to what I fear must have been for the most part imaginary puffs of air. Then just about sunrise we got for an hour an inexplicable, steady breeze, right in our teeth. There was no sense in it. It fitted neither with the season of the year, nor with the secular experience of seamen as recorded in books, nor with the aspect of the sky. Only purposeful malevolence could account for it. It sent us travelling at a great pace away from our proper course; and if we had been out on pleasure sailing bent it would have been a delightful breeze, with the awakened sparkle of the sea, with the sense of motion and a feeling of unwonted freshness. Then all at once, as if disdaining to carry farther the sorry jest, it dropped and died out completely in less than five minutes. The ship's head swung where it listed; the stilled sea took on the polish of a steel plate in the calm.

I went below, not because I meant to take some rest, but simply because I couldn't bear to look at it just then. The indefatigable Ransome was busy in the saloon. It had become a regular practice with him to give me an informal health report in the morning. He turned away from the sideboard with his usual pleasant, quiet gaze. No shadow rested on his intelligent forehead.

'There are a good many of them middling bad this morning, sir,' he said in a calm tone.

'What? All knocked out?'

'Only two actually in their bunks, sir, but . . .'

'It's the last night that has done for them. We have had to pull and haul all the blessed time.'

'I heard, sir. I had a mind to come out and help only, you know. . . .'

'Certainly not. You mustn't. . . . The fellows lie at night about the decks, too. It isn't good for them.'

Ransome assented. But men couldn't be looked after like children. Moreover, one could hardly blame them for trying for such coolness and such air as there was to be found on deck. He himself, of course, knew better.

He was, indeed, a reasonable man. Yet it would have been hard to say that the others were not. The last few days had been for us like the ordeal of the fiery furnace. One really couldn't quarrel with their common, imprudent humanity making the best of the moments of relief, when the night brought in the illusion of coolness and the starlight twinkled through the heavy, dew-laden air. Moreover, most of them were so weakened that hardly anything could be done without everybody that could totter mustering on the braces. No, it was no use remonstrating with them. But I fully believed that quinine was of very great use indeed.

I believed in it. I pinned my faith to it. It would save the men, the ship, break the spell by its medicinal virtue, make time of no account, the weather but a passing worry, and, like a magic powder working against mysterious malefices, secure the first passage of my first command against the evil powers of calms and pestilence. I looked upon it as more precious than gold, and unlike gold, of which there ever hardly seems to be enough anywhere, the ship had a sufficient store of it. I went in to get it with the purpose of weighing out doses. I stretched my hand with the feeling of a man reaching for an unfailing panacea, took up a fresh bottle and unrolled the wrapper, noticing as I did so that the ends, both top and bottom, had come unsealed. . . .

But why record all the swift steps of the appalling discovery. You have guessed the truth already. There was the wrapper, the bottle, and the white powder inside, some sort of powder! But it wasn't quinine. One look at it was quite enough. I remember that at the very moment of picking up the bottle, before I even dealt with the wrapper, the weight of the object I had in my hand gave me an instant of premonition. Quinine is as light as feathers; and my nerves must have been exasperated into an extraordinary sensibility. I let the bottle smash itself on the floor. The stuff, whatever it was, felt gritty under the sole of my shoe. I snatched up the next bottle and then the next. The weight alone told the tale. One after another they fell, breaking at my feet, not because I threw them down in my dismay, but slipping through my fingers as if this disclosure were too much for my strength.

It is a fact that the very greatness of a mental shock helps one to bear up against it, by producing a sort of temporary insensibility. I came out of the state-room stunned, as if something heavy had dropped on my head. From the other side of the saloon, across the table, Ransome, with a duster in his hand, stared open-mouthed. I don't think that I looked wild. It is quite possible that I appeared to be in a hurry because I was instinctively hastening up on deck.

An example of this training become instinct. The difficulties, the dangers, the problems of a ship at sea must be met on deck.

To this fact, as it were of nature, I responded instinctively; which may be taken as a proof that for a moment I must have been robbed of my reason.

I was certainly off my balance, a prey to impulse, for at the bottom of the stairs I turned and flung myself at the doorway of Mr Burns's cabin. The wildness of his aspect checked my mental disorder. He was sitting up in his bunk, his body looking immensely long, his head drooping a little sideways, with affected complacency. He flourished, in his trembling hand, on the end of a fore-arm no thicker than a stout walking-stick, a shining pair of scissors which he tried before my very eyes to jab at his throat.

I was to a certain extent horrified; but it was rather a secondary sort of effect, not really strong enough to make me yell at him in such a manner as: 'Stop!' ... 'Heavens!' ... 'What are you doing?'

In reality he was simply overtaxing his returning strength in a shaky attempt to clip off the thick growth of his red beard. A large towel was spread over his lap, and a shower of stiff hairs, like bits of copper wire, was descending on it at every snip of the scissors.

He turned to me his face grotesque beyond the fantasies of mad dreams, one cheek all bushy as if with a swollen flame, the other denuded and sunken, with the untouched long moustache on that side asserting itself, lonely and fierce. And while he stared thunderstruck, with the gaping scissors on his fingers, I shouted my discovery at him fiendishly, in six words, without comment.

V

I HEARD the clatter of the scissors escaping from his hand, noted the perilous heave of his whole person over the edge of the bunk after them, and then, returning to my first purpose, pursued my course on to the deck. The sparkle of the sea filled my eyes. It was gorgeous and barren, monotonous and without hope under the empty curve of the sky. The sails hung motionless and slack, the very folds of their sagging surfaces moved no more than carved granite. The impetuosity of my advent made the man at the helm start slightly. A block aloft squeaked incomprehensibly, for what on earth could have made it do so? It was a whistling note like a bird's. For a long, long time I faced an empty world, steeped in an infinity of silence, through which the sunshine poured and flowed for some mysterious purpose. Then I heard Ransome's voice at my elbow.

'I have put Mr Burns back to bed, sir.'

'You have.'

'Well, sir, he got out, all of a sudden, but when he let go of the edge of the bunk he fell down. He isn't light-headed, though, it seems to me.'

'No,' I said dully, without looking at Ransome. He waited for a moment, then, cautiously as if not to give offence: 'I don't think we need lose much of that stuff, sir,' he said, 'I can sweep it up, every bit of it almost, and then we could sift the glass out. I will go about it at once. It will not make the breakfast late, not ten minutes.'

'Oh, yes,' I said bitterly. 'Let the breakfast wait, sweep up every bit of it, and then throw the damned lot overboard!'

The profound silence returned, and when I looked over my shoulder Ransome – the intelligent, serene Ransome – had vanished from my side. The intense loneliness of the sea acted like poison on my brain. When I turned my eyes to the ship, I had a morbid vision of her as a floating grave. Who hasn't heard of ships found drifting, haphazard, with their crews all dead? I looked at the seaman at the helm, I had an impulse to speak to him, and, indeed, his face took on an expectant cast as if he had guessed my intention. But in the end I went below, thinking I would be alone with the greatness of my trouble for a little while. But through his open door Mr Burns saw me come down, and addressed me grumpily: 'Well, sir?'

I went in. 'It isn't well at all,' I said.

Mr Burns, re-established in his bed-place, was conceal-ing his hirsute cheek in the palm of his hand.

'That confounded fellow has taken away the scissors from me,' were the next words he said.

The tension I was suffering from was so great that it was perhaps just as well that Mr Burns had started on this grievance. He seemed very sore about it and grumbled, 'Does he think I am mad, or what?'

'I don't think so, Mr Burns,' I said. I looked upon him at that moment as a model of self-possession. I even con-ceived on that account a sort of admiration for that man, who had (apart from the intense materiality of what was left of his beard) come as near to being a disembodied spirit as any man can do and live. I noticed the preternatural sharpness of the ridge of his nose, the deep cavities of his temples, and I envied him. He was so reduced that he would probably die very soon. Enviable man! So near extinction – while I had to bear within me a tumult of suffering vitality, doubt, confusion, self-reproach, and an indefinite reluctance to meet the horrid logic of the situa-tion. I could not help muttering: 'I feel as if I were going mad myself.'

Mr Burns glared spectrally, but otherwise wonderfully composed.

'I always thought he would play us some deadly trick,' he said, with a peculiar emphasis on the *he*.

It gave me a mental shock, but I had neither the mind, nor the heart, nor the spirit to argue with him. My form of sickness was indifference. The creeping paralysis of a hope-less outlook. So I only gazed at him. Mr Burns broke into further speech.

'Eh? What? No! You won't believe it? Well, how do you account for this? How do you think it could have happened?'

'Happened?' I repeated dully. 'Why, yes, how in the name of the infernal powers did this thing happen?'

Indeed, on thinking it out, it seemed incomprehensible that it should just be like this: the bottles emptied, refilled, rewrapped, and replaced. A sort of plot, a sinister attempt to deceive, a thing resembling sly vengeance – but for what? – or else a fiendish joke. But Mr Burns was in possession of a theory. It was simple, and he uttered it solemnly in a hollow voice.

'I suppose they have given him about fifteen pounds in Haiphong for that little lot.'

'Mr Burns!' I cried.

He nodded grotesquely over his raised legs, like two broomsticks in the pyjamas, with enormous bare feet at the end.

'Why not? The stuff is pretty expensive in this part of the world, and they were very short of it in Tonkin. And what did he care? You have not known him. I have, and I have defied him. He feared neither God, nor devil, nor man, nor wind, nor sea, nor his own conscience. And I believe he hated everybody and everything. But I think he was afraid to die. I believe I am the only man who ever stood up to him. I faced him in that cabin where you live now, when he was sick, and I cowed him then. He thought I was going to twist his neck for him. If he had had his way we would have been beating up against the North-East monsoon, as long as he lived and afterwards too, for ages and ages. Acting the Flying Dutchman in the China Sea! Ha! Ha!'

'But why should he replace the bottles like this?' ... I began.

'Why shouldn't he? Why should he want to throw the bottles away? They fit the drawer. They belong to the medicine chest.'

'And they were wrapped up,' I cried.

'Well, the wrappers were there. Did it from habit, I suppose, and as to refilling, there is always a lot of stuff they send in paper parcels that burst after a time. And then, who can tell? I suppose you didn't taste it, sir? But of course, you are sure...'

'No,' I said. 'I didn't taste it. It is all overboard now.'

Behind me, a soft, cultivated voice said: 'I have tasted it. It seemed a mixture of all sorts, sweetish, saltish, very horrible.'

Ransome, stepping out of the pantry, had been listening for some time, as it was very excusable in him to do.

'A dirty trick,' said Mr Burns. 'I always said he would.'

The magnitude of my indignation was unbounded. And the kind, sympathetic doctor too. The only sympathetic man I ever knew... instead of writing that warning letter, the very refinement of sympathy, why didn't the man make a proper inspection? But, as a matter of fact, it was hardly fair to blame the doctor. The fittings were in order and the medicine chest is an officially arranged affair. There was nothing really to arouse the slightest suspicion. The person I could never forgive was myself. Nothing should ever be taken for granted. The seed of everlasting remorse was sown in my breast.

'I feel it's all my fault,' I exclaimed, 'mine, and nobody else's. That's how I feel. I shall never forgive myself.'

'That's very foolish, sir,' said Mr Burns fiercely.

And after this effort he fell back exhausted on his bed. He closed his eyes, he panted; this affair, this abominable surprise had shaken him up too. As I turned away I perceived Ransome looking at me blankly. He appreciated what it meant, but he managed to produce his pleasant, wistful smile. Then he stepped back into his pantry, and I rushed up on deck again to see whether there was any wind, any breath under the sky, any stir of the air, any sign of hope. The deadly stillness met me again. Nothing was changed except that there was a different man at the wheel. He looked ill. His whole figure drooped, and he seemed rather to cling to the spokes than hold them with a controlling grip. I said to him:

'You are not fit to be here.'

'I can manage, sir,' he said feebly.

As a matter of fact, there was nothing for him to do. The ship had no steerage way. She lay with her head to the westward, the everlasting Koh-ring visible over the stern, with a few small islets, black spots in the great blaze, swimming before my troubled eyes. And but for those bits of land there was no speck on the sky, no speck on the water, no shape of vapour, no wisp of smoke, no sail, no boat, no stir of humanity, no sign of life, nothing!

The first question was, what to do? What could one do? The first thing to do obviously was to tell the men. I did it that very day. I wasn't going to let the knowledge simply get about. I would face them. They were assembled on the quarter-deck for the purpose. Just before I stepped out to speak to them I discovered that life could hold terrible moments. No confessed criminal had ever been so oppressed by his sense of guilt. This is why, perhaps, my face was set hard and my voice curt and unemotional while I made my declaration that I could do nothing more for the sick, in the way of drugs. As to such care as could be given them they knew they had had it.

I would have held them justified in tearing me limb from limb. The silence which followed upon my words was almost harder to bear than the angriest uproar. I was crushed by the infinite depth of its reproach. But, as a matter of fact, I was mistaken. In a voice which I had great difficulty in keeping firm, I went on: 'I suppose, men, you have understood what I have said, and you know what it means.'

A voice or two were heard: 'Yes, sir. . . . We understand.'

They had kept silent simply because they thought that they were not called to say anything; and when I told them that I intended to run into Singapore and that the best chance for the ship and the men was in the efforts all of us, sick and well, must make to get her along out of this, I received the encouragement of a low assenting murmur and of a louder voice exclaiming: 'Surely there is a way out of this blamed hole.'

*   *   *

Here is an extract from the notes I wrote at the time:

We have lost Koh-ring at last. For many days now I don't think I have been two hours below altogether. I remain on deck, of course, night and day, and the nights and the days wheel over us in succession, whether long or short, who can say? All sense of time is lost in the monotony of expectation, of hope, and of desire – which is only one: Get the ship to the southward! Get the ship to the southward! The effect is curiously mechanical; the sun climbs and descends, the night swings over our heads as if somebody below the horizon were turning a crank. It is the pettiest, the most aimless! . . . and all through that miserable performance I go on, tramping, tramping the deck. How many miles have I walked on the poop of that ship! A stubborn pilgrimage of sheer restlessness, diversified by short excursions below to look upon Mr Burns. I don't know whether it is an illusion, but he seems to become more substantial from day to day. He doesn't say much, for, indeed, the situation doesn't lend itself to idle remarks. I notice this even with the men as I watch them moving or sitting about the decks. They don't talk to each other. It strikes me that if there exist an invisible ear catching the whispers of the earth, it will find this ship the most silent spot on it. . . .

No, Mr Burns has not much to say to me. He sits in his bunk with his beard gone, his moustaches flaming, and with an air of silent determination on his chalky physiognomy. Ransome tells me he devours all the food that is given him to the last scrap, but that, apparently, he sleeps very little. Even at night, when I go below to fill my pipe, I notice that, though dozing flat on his back, he still looks very determined. From the side glance he gives me when awake it seems as though he were annoyed at being interrupted in some arduous mental operation; and as I emerge on deck the ordered arrangement of the stars meets my eye, unclouded, infinitely wearisome. There they are: stars, sun, sea, light, darkness, space, great waters; the formidable Work of the Seven Days, into which mankind seems to have blundered unbidden. Or else decoyed. Even as I have been decoyed into this awful, this death-haunted command . . .

The only spot of light in the ship at night was that of the compass-lamps, lighting up the faces of the succeeding helmsmen; for the rest we were lost in the darkness, I walking the poop and the men lying about the decks. They were all so reduced by sickness that no watches could be kept. Those who were able to walk remained all the time on duty, lying about in the shadows of the main deck, till my voice raised for an order would bring them to their enfeebled feet, a tottering little group, moving patiently about the ship, with hardly a murmur, a whisper amongst them all. And every time I had to raise my voice it was with a pang of remorse and pity.

Then about four o'clock in the morning a light would gleam forward in the galley. The unfailing Ransome with the uneasy heart, immune, serene, and active, was getting ready the early coffee for the men. Presently he would bring me a cup up on the poop, and it was then that I allowed myself to drop into my deck chair for a couple of hours of real sleep. No doubt I must have been snatching short dozes when leaning against the rail for a moment in sheer exhaustion; but, honestly, I was not aware of them, except in the painful form of convulsive starts that seemed to come on me even while I walked. From about five, however, until after seven I would sleep openly under the fading stars.

I would say to the helmsman, 'Call me at need,' and drop into that chair and close my eyes, feeling that there was no more sleep for me on earth. And then I would know nothing till, some time between seven and eight, I would feel a touch on my shoulder and look up at Ransome's face, with its faint, wistful smile and friendly, grey eyes, as though he were tenderly amused at my slumbers. Occasionally the second mate would come up and relieve me at early coffee time. But it didn't really matter. Generally it was dead calm, or else faint airs so changing and fugitive that it really wasn't worth while to touch a brace for them. If the air steadied at all the seaman at the helm could be trusted for a warning shout, 'Ship's all aback, sir!' which like a trumpet-call would make me spring a foot above the deck. Those were the words which it seemed to me would have made me spring up from eternal sleep. But this was not often. I have never met since such breathless sunrises. And if the second mate happened to be there (he had generally one day in three free of fever) I would find him sitting on the skylight half-senseless, as it were, and with an idiotic gaze fastened on some object near by – a rope, a cleat, a belaying pin, a ringbolt.

That young man was rather troublesome. He remained cubbish in his sufferings. He seemed to have become completely imbecile; and when the return of fever drove him to his cabin below the next thing would be that we would miss him from there. The first time it happened Ransome and I were very much alarmed. We started a quiet search and ultimately Ransome discovered him curled up in the sail-locker, which opened into the lobby by a sliding-door. When remonstrated with, he muttered sulkily, 'It's cool in there.' That wasn't true. It was only dark there.

The fundamental defects of his face were not improved by its uniform livid hue. It was not so with many of the men. The wastage of ill-health seemed to idealize the general character of the features, bringing out the unsuspected nobility of some, the strength of others, and in one case revealing an essentially comic aspect. He was a short, gingery, active man with a nose and chin of the Punch type, and whom his shipmates called 'Frenchy.' I don't know why. He may have been a Frenchman, but I have never heard him utter a single word in French.

To see him coming aft to the wheel comforted one. The blue dungaree trousers turned up the calf, one leg a little higher than the other, the clean check shirt, the white canvas cap, evidently made by himself, made up a whole peculiar smartness, and the persistent jauntiness of his gait, even, poor fellow, when he couldn't help tottering, told of his invincible spirit. There was also a man called Gambril.

He was the only grizzled person in the ship. His face was of an austere type. But if I remember all their faces, wasting tragically before my eyes, most of their names have vanished from my memory.

The words that passed between us were few and puerile in regard of the situation. I had to force myself to look them in the face. I expected to meet reproachful glances. There were none. The expression of suffering in their eyes was indeed hard enough to bear. But that they couldn't help. For the rest, I ask myself whether it was the temper of their souls or the sympathy of their imagination that made them so wonderful, so worthy of my undying regard.

For myself, neither my soul was highly tempered, nor my imagination properly under control. There were moments when I felt, not only that I would go mad, but that I had gone mad already; so that I dared not open my lips for fear of betraying myself by some insane shriek. Luckily I had only orders to give, and an order has a steadying influence upon him who has to give it. Moreover, the seaman, the officer of the watch, in me was sufficiently sane. I was like a mad carpenter making a box. Were he ever so convinced that he was King of Jerusalem, the box he would make would be a sane box. What I feared was a shrill note escaping me involuntarily and upsetting my balance. Luckily, again, there was no necessity to raise one's voice. The brooding stillness of the world seemed sensitive to the slightest sound like a whispering gallery. The conversational tone would almost carry a word from one end of the ship to the other. The terrible thing was that the only voice that I ever heard was my own. At night especially it reverberated very lonely amongst the planes of the unstirring sails.

Mr Burns, still keeping to his bed with that air of secret determination, was moved to grumble at many things. Our interviews were short five-minute affairs, but fairly frequent. I was everlastingly diving down below to get a light, though I did not consume much tobacco at that time. The pipe was always going out; for in truth my mind was not composed enough to enable me to get a decent smoke. Likewise, for most of the time during the twenty-four hours I could have struck matches on deck and held them aloft till the flame burnt my fingers. But I always used to run below. It was a change. It was the only break in the incessant strain; and, of course, Mr Burns through the open door could see me come in and go out every time.

With his knees gathered up under his chin and staring with his greenish eyes over them, he was a weird figure, and with my knowledge of the crazy notion in his head, not a very attractive one for me. Still, I had to speak to him now and then, and one day he complained that the ship was very silent. For hours and hours, he said, he was lying there, not hearing a sound, till he did not know what to do with himself.

'When Ransome happens to be forward in his galley everything's so still that one might think everybody in the ship was dead,' he grumbled. 'The only voice I do hear sometimes is yours, sir, and that isn't enough to cheer me up. What's the matter with the men? Isn't there one left that can sing out at the ropes?'

'Not one, Mr Burns,' I said. 'There is no breath to spare on board this ship for that. Are you aware that there are times when I can't muster more than three hands to do anything?'

He asked swiftly but fearfully:

'Nobody dead yet, sir?'

'No.'

'It wouldn't do,' Mr Burns declared forcibly. 'Mustn't let him. If he gets hold of one he will get them all.'

I cried out angrily at this. I believe I even swore at the disturbing effect of these words. They attacked all the self-possession that was left to me. In my endless vigil in the face of the enemy I had been haunted by grue-some images enough. I had had visions of a ship drifting in calms and swinging in light airs, with all her crew dying slowly about her decks. Such things had been known to happen.

Mr Burns met my outburst by a mysterious silence.

'Look here,' I said. 'You don't believe yourself what you say. You can't. It's impossible. It isn't the sort of thing I have a right to expect from you. My position's bad enough without being worried by your silly fancies.'

He remained unmoved. On account of the way in which the light fell on his head I could not be sure whether he had smiled faintly or not. I changed my tone.

'Listen,' I said. 'It's getting so desperate that I had thought for a moment, since we can't make our way south, whether I wouldn't try to steer west and make an attempt to reach the mail-boat track. We could always get some quinine from her, at least. What do you think?'

He cried out: 'No, no, no. Don't do that, sir. You mustn't for a moment give up facing that old ruffian. If you do he will get the upper hand of us.'

I left him. He was impossible. It was like a case of possession. His protest, however, was essentially quite sound. As a matter of fact, my notion of heading out west on the chance of sighting a problematical steamer could not bear calm examination. On the side where we were we had enough wind, at least from time to time, to struggle on towards the south. Enough, at least, to keep hope alive. But suppose that I had used those capricious gusts of wind to sail away to the westward, into some region where there was not a breath of air for days on end, what then? Perhaps my appalling vision of a ship floating with a dead crew would become a reality for the discovery weeks afterwards by some horror-stricken mariners.

That afternoon Ransome brought me up a cup of tea, and while waiting there, tray in hand, he remarked in the exactly right tone of sympathy:

'You are holding out well, sir.'

'Yes,' I said. 'You and I seem to have been forgotten.'

'Forgotten, sir?'

'Yes, by the fever-devil who has got on board this ship,' I said.

Ransome gave me one of his attractive, intelligent, quick glances and went away with the tray. It occurred to me that I had been talking somewhat in Mr Burns's manner. It annoyed me. Yet often in darker moments I forgot myself into an attitude towards our troubles more fit for a contest against a living enemy.

Yes. The fever-devil had not laid his hand yet either on Ransome or on me. But he might at any time. It was one of those thoughts one had to fight down, keep at arm's length at any cost. It was unbearable to contemplate the possibility of Ransome, the housekeeper of the ship, being laid low. And what would happen to my command if I got knocked over, with Mr Burns too weak to stand without holding on to his bed-place and the second mate reduced to a state of permanent imbecility? It was impossible to imagine, or, rather, it was only too easy to imagine.

I was alone on the poop. The ship having no steerage way, I had sent the helmsman away to sit down or lie down somewhere in the shade. The men's strength was so reduced that all unnecessary calls on it had to be avoided. It was the austere Gambril with the grizzly beard. He went away readily enough, but he was so weakened by repeated bouts of fever, poor fellow, that in order to get down the poop ladder he had to turn sideways and hang on with both hands to the brass rail. It was just simply heart-breaking to watch. Yet he was neither very much worse nor much better than most of the half-dozen miserable victims I could muster up on deck.

It was a terribly lifeless afternoon. For several days in succession low clouds had appeared in the distance, white masses with dark convolutions resting on the water, motionless, almost solid, and yet all the time changing their aspects subtly. Towards evening they vanished as a rule. But this day they awaited the setting sun, which glowed and smouldered sulkily amongst them before it sank down. The punctual and wearisome stars reappeared over our mast-heads, but the air remained stagnant and oppressive.

The unfailing Ransome lighted the binnacle lamps and glided, all shadowy, up to me.

'Will you go down and try to eat something, sir?' he suggested.

His low voice startled me. I had been standing looking out over the rail, saying nothing, feeling nothing, not even the weariness of my limbs, overcome by the evil spell.

'Ransome,' I asked abruptly, 'how long have I been on deck? I am losing the notion of time.'

'Fourteen days, sir,' he said. 'It was a fortnight last Monday since we left the anchorage.'

His equable voice sounded mournful somehow. He waited a bit, then added: 'It's the first time that it looks as if we were to have some rain.'

I noticed then the broad shadow on the horizon extinguishing the low stars completely, while those overhead, when I looked up, seemed to shine down on us through a veil of smoke.

How it got there, how it had crept up so high, I couldn't say. It had an ominous appearance. The air did not stir. At a renewed invitation from Ransome I did go down into the cabin to – in his own words – 'try and eat something.' I don't know that the trial was very successful. I suppose at that period I did exist on food in the usual way; but the memory is now that in those days life was sustained on invincible anguish, as a sort of infernal stimulant exciting and consuming at the same time.

It's the only period of my life in which I attempted to keep a diary. No, not the only one. Years later, in conditions of moral isolation, I did put down on paper the thoughts and events of a score of days. But this was the first time. I don't remember how it came about or how the pocket-book and the pencil came into my hands. It's inconceivable that

I should have looked for them on purpose. I suppose they saved me from the crazy trick of talking to myself.

Strangely enough, in both cases I took to that sort of thing in circumstances in which I did not expect, in colloquial phrase, 'to come out of it.' Neither could I expect the record to outlast me. This shows that it was purely a personal need for intimate relief and not a call of egotism.

Here I must give another sample of it, a few detached lines, now looking very ghostly to my own eyes, out of the part scribbled that very evening:

* * *

There is something going on in the sky like a decomposition, like a corruption of the air, which remains as still as ever. After all, mere clouds, which may or may not hold wind or rain. Strange that it should trouble me so. I feel as if all my sins had found me out. But I suppose the trouble is that the ship is still lying motionless, not under command; and that I have nothing to do to keep my imagination from running wild amongst the disastrous images of the worst that may befall us. What's going to happen? Probably nothing. Or anything. It may be a furious squall coming, butt-end foremost. And on deck there are five men with the vitality and the strength of, say, two. We may have all our sails blown away. Every stitch of canvas has been on her since we broke ground at the mouth of the Mei-nam, fifteen days ago . . . or fifteen centuries. It seems to me that all my life before that momentous day is infinitely remote, a fading memory of light-hearted youth, something on the other side of a shadow. Yes, sails may very well be blown away. And that would be like a death sentence on the men. We haven't strength enough on board to bend another suit; incredible thought, but it is true. Or we may even get dismasted. Ships have been dismasted in squalls simply because they weren't handled quick enough, and we have no power to whirl the yards around. It's like being bound hand and foot preparatory to having one's throat cut. And what appals me most of all is that I shrink from going on deck to face it. It's due to the ship, it's due to the men who are there on deck – some of them, ready to put out the last remnant of their strength at a word from me. And I am shrinking from it. From the mere vision. My first command. Now I understand that strange sense of insecurity in my past. I always suspected that I might be no good. And here is proof positive, I am shirking it, I am no good.

* * *

At that moment, or, perhaps, the moment after, I became aware of Ransome standing in the cabin. Something in his expression startled me. It had a meaning which I could not make out. I exclaimed:

'Somebody's dead.'

It was his turn to look startled.

'Dead? Not that I know of, sir. I have been in the forecastle only ten minutes ago and there was no dead man there then.'

'You did give me a scare,' I said.

His voice was extremely pleasant to listen to. He explained that he had come down below to close Mr Burns's port in case it should come on to rain. He did not know that I was in the cabin, he added.

'How does it look outside?' I asked him.

'Very black indeed, sir. There is something in it for certain.'

'In what quarter?'

'All round, sir.'

I repeated idly: 'All round. For certain,' with my elbows on the table.

Ransome lingered in the cabin as if he had something to do there, but hesitated about doing it. I said suddenly:

'You think I ought to be on deck?'

He answered at once but without any particular emphasis or accent: 'I do, sir.'

I got to my feet briskly, and he made way for me to go out. As I passed through the lobby I heard Mr Burns's voice saying:

'Shut the door of my room, will you, steward?' And Ransome's rather surprised: 'Certainly, sir.'

I thought that all my feelings had been dulled into complete indifference. But I found it as trying as ever to be on deck. The impenetrable blackness beset the ship so

close that it seemed that by thrusting one's hand over
the side one could touch some unearthly substance. There
was in it an effect of inconceivable terror and of inexpressible mystery. The few stars overhead shed a dim
light upon the ship alone, with no gleams of any kind
upon the water, in detached shafts piercing an atmosphere
which had turned to soot. It was something I had never
seen before, giving no hint of the direction from which
any change would come, the closing in of a menace from
all sides.

There was still no man at the helm. The immobility of
all things was perfect. If the air had turned black, the sea,
for all I knew, might have turned solid. It was no good
looking in any direction, watching for any sign, speculat-
ing upon the nearness of the moment. When the time
came the blackness would overwhelm silently the bit
of starlight falling upon the ship, and the end of all
things would come without a sigh, stir, or murmur of any
kind, and all our hearts would cease to beat like run-down
clocks.

It was impossible to shake off that sense of finality. The
quietness that came over me was like a foretaste of
annihilation. It gave me a sort of comfort, as though my
soul had become suddenly reconciled to an eternity of blind
stillness.

The seaman's instinct alone survived whole in my moral
dissolution. I descended the ladder to the quarter-deck.
The starlight seemed to die out before reaching that spot,
but when I asked quietly, 'Are you there, men?' my eyes
made out shadowy forms starting up around me, very few,
very indistinct; and a voice spoke: 'All here, sir.' Another
amended anxiously:

'All that are any good for anything, sir.'

Both voices were very quiet and unringing; without any
special character of readiness or discouragement. Very
matter-of-fact voices.

'We must try to haul this mainsail close up,' I said.

The shadows swayed away from me without a word. Those men were the ghosts of themselves, and their weight on a rope could be no more than the weight of a bunch of ghosts. Indeed, if ever a sail was hauled up by sheer spiritual strength it must have been that sail, for, properly speaking, there was not muscle enough for the task in the whole ship, let alone the miserable lot of us on deck. Of course, I took the lead in the work myself. They wandered feebly after me from rope to rope, stumbling and panting. They toiled like Titans. We were an hour at it at least, and all the time the black universe made no sound. When the last leech-line was made fast, my eyes, accustomed to the darkness, made out the shapes of exhausted men drooping over the rails, collapsed on hatches. One hung over the after-capstan, sobbing for breath; and I stood amongst them like a tower of strength, impervious to disease and feeling only the sickness of my soul. I waited for some time, fighting against the weight of my sins, against my sense of unworthiness, and then I said:

'Now, men, we'll go aft and square the mainyard. That's about all we can do for the ship; and for the rest she must take her chance.'

VI

As we all went up it occurred to me that there ought to be a man at the helm. I raised my voice not much above a whisper, and, noiselessly, an uncomplaining spirit in a fever-wasted body appeared in the light aft, the head with hollow eyes illuminated against the blackness which had swallowed up our world – and the universe. The bare fore-arm extended over the upper spokes seemed to shine with a light of its own. I murmured to that luminous appearance:

'Keep the helm right amidships.'

It answered in a tone of patient suffering:

'Right amidships, sir.'

Then I descended to the quarter-deck. It was impossible to tell whence the blow would come. To look round the ship was to look into a bottomless, black pit. The eye lost itself in inconceivable depths. I wanted to ascertain whether the ropes had been picked up off the deck. One could only do that by feeling with one's feet. In my cautious progress I came against a man in whom I recognized Ransome. He possessed an unimpaired physical solidity which was manifest to me at the contact. He was leaning against the quarter-deck capstan and kept silent. It was like a revelation. He was the collapsed figure sobbing for breath I had noticed before we went on the poop.

'You have been helping with the mainsail!' I exclaimed in a low tone.

'Yes, sir,' sounded his quiet voice.

'Man! What were you thinking of? You mustn't do that sort of thing.'

After a pause he assented. 'I suppose I mustn't.' Then after another short silence he added: 'I am all right now,' quickly, between the tell-tale gasps.

I could neither hear nor see anybody else; but when I spoke up, answering sad murmurs filled the quarter-deck, and its shadows seemed to shift here and there. I ordered all the halyards laid down on deck clear for running.

'I'll see to that, sir,' volunteered Ransome in his natural, pleasant tone, which comforted one and aroused one's compassion too, somehow.

That man ought to have been in his bed, resting, and my plain duty was to send him there. But perhaps he would not have obeyed me. I had not the strength of mind to try. All I said was:

'Go about it quietly, Ransome.'

Returning on the poop I approached Gambril. His face, set with hollow shadows in the light, looked awful, finally silenced. I asked him how he felt, but hardly expected an answer. Therefore I was astonished at his comparative loquacity.

'Them shakes leaves me as weak as a kitten, sir,' he said, preserving finely that air of unconsciousness as to anything but his business a helmsman should never lose. 'And before I can pick up my strength that there hot fit comes along and knocks me over again.'

He sighed. There was no complaint in his tone, but the bare words were enough to give me a horrible pang of self-reproach. It held me dumb for a time. When the torment-ing sensation had passed off I asked:

'Do you feel strong enough to prevent the rudder taking charge if she gets sternway on her? It wouldn't do to get something smashed about the steering-gear now. We've enough difficulties to cope with as it is.'

He answered with just a shade of weariness that he was strong enough to hang on. He could promise me that she shouldn't take the wheel out of his hands. More he couldn't say.

At that moment Ransome appeared quite close to me, stepping out of the darkness into visibility suddenly, as if just created with his composed face and pleasant voice.

Every rope on deck, he said, was laid down clear for running, as far as one could make certain by feeling. It was impossible to see anything. Frenchy had stationed himself forward. He said he had a jump or two left in him yet.

Here a faint smile altered for an instant the clear, firm design of Ransome's lips. With his serious, clear, grey eyes, his serene temperament, he was a priceless man altogether. Soul as firm as the muscles of his body.

He was the only man on board (except me, but I had to preserve my liberty of movement) who had a sufficiency of muscular strength to trust to. For a moment I thought I had better ask him to take the wheel. But the dreadful know-ledge of the enemy he had to carry about him made me hesitate. In my ignorance of physiology it occurred to me that he might die suddenly, from excitement, at a critical moment.

While this gruesome fear restrained the ready words on the tip of my tongue, Ransome stepped back two paces and vanished from my sight.

At once an uneasiness possessed me, as if some support had been withdrawn. I moved forward too, outside the circle of light, into the darkness that stood in front of me like a wall. In one stride I had penetrated it. Such must have been the darkness before creation. It had closed behind me. I knew I was invisible to the man at the helm. Neither could I see anything. He was alone, I was alone, every man was alone where he stood. And every form was gone too, spar, sail, fittings, rails; everything was blotted out in the dreadful smoothness of that absolute night.

A flash of lightning would have been a relief – I mean physically. I would have prayed for it if it hadn't been for my shrinking apprehension of the thunder. In the tension of silence I was suffering from, it seemed to me that the first crash must turn me into dust.

And thunder was, most likely, what would happen next. Stiff all over and hardly breathing, I waited with a horribly strained expectation. Nothing happened. It was maddening. But a dull, growing ache in the lower part of my face made me aware that I had been grinding my teeth madly enough, for God knows how long.

It's extraordinary I should not have heard myself doing it; but I hadn't. By an effort which absorbed all my faculties I managed to keep my jaw still. It required much attention, and while thus engaged I became bothered by curious, irregular sounds of faint tapping on the deck. They could be heard single, in pairs, in groups. While I wondered at this mysterious devilry, I received a slight blow under the left eye and felt an enormous tear run down my cheek. Raindrops. Enormous. Forerunners of something. Tap. Tap. Tap. . . .

I turned about, and, addressing Gambril earnestly, entreated him to 'hang on to the wheel.' But I could hardly speak from emotion. The fatal moment had come. I held my breath. The tapping had stopped as unexpectedly as it had begun, and there was a renewed moment of intolerable suspense; something like an additional turn of the racking screw. I don't suppose I would have ever screamed, but I remember my conviction that there was nothing else for it but to scream.

Suddenly – how am I to convey it? Well, suddenly the darkness turned into water. This is the only suitable figure. A heavy shower, a downpour, comes along, making a noise. You hear its approach on the sea, in the air too, I verily believe. But this was different. With no preliminary whisper or rustle, without a splash, and even without the ghost of impact, I became instantaneously soaked to the skin. Not a very difficult matter, since I was wearing only my sleeping suit. My hair got full of water in an instant, water streamed on my skin, it filled my nose, my ears, my eyes. In a fraction of a second I swallowed quite a lot of it.

As to Gambril, he was fairly choked. He coughed pitifully, the broken cough of a sick man; and I beheld him as one sees a fish in an aquarium by the light of an electric bulb, an elusive, phosphorescent shape. Only he did not glide away. But something else happened. Both binnacle lamps went out. I suppose the water forced itself into them, though I wouldn't have thought that possible, for they fitted into the cowl perfectly.

The last gleam of light in the universe had gone, pursued by a low exclamation of dismay from Gambril. I groped for him and seized his arm. How startlingly wasted it was.

'Never mind,' I said. 'You don't want the light. All you need to do is to keep the wind, when it comes, at the back of your head. You understand?'

'Aye, aye, sir.... But I should like to have a light,' he added nervously.

All that time the ship lay as steady as a rock. The noise of the water pouring off the sails and spars, flowing over the break of the poop, had stopped short. The poop scuppers gurgled and sobbed for a little while longer, and then perfect silence, joined to perfect immobility, proclaimed the yet unbroken spell of our helplessness, poised on the edge of some violent issue, lurking in the dark.

I started forward restlessly. I did not need my sight to pace the poop of my ill-starred first command with perfect assurance. Every square foot of her decks was impressed indelibly on my brain, to the very grain and knots of the planks. Yet, all of a sudden, I fell clean over something, landing full length on my hands and face.

It was something big and alive. Not a dog – more like a sheep, rather. But there were no animals in the ship. How could an animal.... It was an added and fantastic horror which I could not resist. The hair of my head stirred even as I picked myself up, awfully scared; not as a man is scared while his judgment, his reason still try to resist, but completely, boundlessly and, as it were, innocently scared – like a little child.

I could see It – that Thing! The darkness, of which so much had just turned into water, had thinned down a little. There It was! But I did not hit upon the notion of Mr Burns issuing out of the companion on all fours till he attempted to stand up, and even then the idea of a bear crossed my mind first.

He growled like one when I seized him round the body. He had buttoned himself up into an enormous winter overcoat of some woolly material, the weight of which was too much for his reduced state. I could hardly feel the incredibly thin lath of his body, lost within the thick stuff, but his growl had depth and substance: Confounded dumb ship with a craven, tip-toeing crowd. Why couldn't they stamp and go with a brace? Wasn't there one God-forsaken lubber in the lot fit to raise a yell on a rope?

'Skulking's no good, sir,' he attacked me directly. 'You can't slink past the old murderous ruffian. It isn't the way. You must go for him boldly – as I did. Boldness is what you want. Show him that you don't care for any of his damned tricks. Kick up a jolly old row.'

'Good God, Mr Burns,' I said angrily. 'What on earth are you up to? What do you mean by coming up on deck in this state?'

'Just that! Boldness. The only way to scare the old bullying rascal.'

I pushed him, still growling, against the rail. 'Hold on to it,' I said roughly. I did not know what to do with him. I left him in a hurry, to go to Gambril, who had called faintly that he believed there was some wind aloft. Indeed, my own ears had caught a feeble flutter of wet canvas, high up overhead, the jingle of a slack chain sheet....

These were eerie, disturbing, alarming sounds in the dead stillness of the air around me. All the instances I had heard of topmasts being whipped out of a ship while there was not wind enough on her deck to blow out a match rushed into my memory.

'I can't see the upper sails, sir,' declared Gambril shakily.

'Don't move the helm. You'll be all right,' I said confidently.

The poor man's nerve was gone. I was not in much better case. It was the moment of breaking strain and was relieved by the abrupt sensation of the ship moving forward as if of herself under my feet. I heard plainly the soughing of the wind aloft, the low cracks of the upper spars taking the strain, long before I could feel the least draught on my face turned aft, anxious and sightless like the face of a blind man.

Suddenly a louder sounding note filled our ears, the darkness started streaming against our bodies, chilling them exceedingly. Both of us, Gambril and I, shivered violently in our clinging, soaked garments of thin cotton. I said to him:

'You are all right now, my man. All you've got to do is to keep the wind at the back of your head. Surely you are up to that. A child could steer this ship in smooth water.'

He muttered: 'Aye! A healthy child.' And I felt ashamed of having been passed over by the fever which had been preying on every man's strength but mine, in order that my remorse might be the more bitter, the feeling of unworthiness more poignant, and the sense of responsibility heavier to bear.

The ship had gathered great way on her almost at once on the calm water. I felt her slipping through it with no other noise but a mysterious rustle alongside. Otherwise she had no motion at all, neither lift nor roll. It was a disheartening steadiness which had lasted for eighteen days now; for never, never had we had wind enough in that time to raise the slightest run of the sea. The breeze freshened suddenly. I thought it was high time to get Mr Burns off the deck. He worried me. I looked upon him as a lunatic who would be very likely to start roaming over the ship and break a limb or fall overboard.

I was truly glad to find he had remained holding on where I had left him, sensibly enough. He was, however, muttering to himself ominously.

This was discouraging. I remarked in a matter-of-fact tone:

'We have never had so much wind as this since we left the roads.'

'There's some heart in it too,' he growled judiciously. It was a remark of a perfectly sane seaman. But he added immediately: 'It was about time I should come on deck. I've been nursing my strength for this – just for this. Do you see it, sir?'

I said I did, and proceeded to hint that it would be advisable for him to go below now and take a rest.

His answer was an indignant: 'Go below! Not if I know it, sir.'

Very cheerful! He was a horrible nuisance. And all at once he started to argue. I could feel his crazy excitement in the dark.

'You don't know how to go about it, sir. How could you? All this whispering and tip-toeing is no good. You can't hope to slink past a cunning, wideawake, evil brute like he was. You never heard him talk. Enough to make your hair stand on end. No! No! He wasn't mad. He was no more mad than I am. He was just downright wicked. Wicked so as to frighten most people. I will tell you what he was. He was nothing less than a thief and a murderer at heart. And do you think he's any different now because he's dead? Not he! His carcass lies a hundred fathom under, but he's just the same . . . in latitude 8° 20′ North.'

He snorted defiantly. I noted with weary resignation that the breeze had got lighter while he raved. He was at it again.

'I ought to have thrown the beggar out of the ship over the rail like a dog. It was only on account of the men. . . . Fancy having to read the Burial Service over a brute like that! . . . "Our departed brother" . . . I could have laughed. That was what he couldn't bear. I suppose I am the only man that ever stood up to laugh at him. When he got sick it used to scare that . . . brother . . . Brother . . . Departed . . . Sooner call a shark brother.'

The breeze had let go so suddenly that the way of the ship brought the wet sails heavily against the mast. The spell of deadly stillness had caught us up again. There seemed to be no escape.

'Hallo!' exclaimed Mr Burns in a startled voice. 'Calm again!'

I addressed him as though he had been sane.

'This is the sort of thing we've been having for seventeen days, Mr Burns,' I said with intense bitterness. 'A puff, then a calm, and in a moment, you'll see, she'll be swinging on her heel with her head away from her course to the devil somewhere.'

He caught at the word. 'The old dodging Devil,' he screamed piercingly, and burst into such a loud laugh as I had never heard before. It was a provoking, mocking peal, with a hair-raising, screeching over-note of defiance. I stepped back utterly confounded.

Instantly there was a stir on the quarter-deck, murmurs of dismay. A distressed voice cried out in the dark below us: 'Who's that gone crazy, now?'

Perhaps they thought it was their captain! Rush is not the word that could be applied to the utmost speed the poor fellows were up to; but in an amazing short time every man in the ship able to walk upright had found his way on to the poop.

I shouted to them: 'It's the mate. Lay hold of him, a couple of you. . . .'

I expected this performance to end in a ghastly sort of fight. But Mr Burns cut his derisive screeching dead short and turned upon them fiercely, yelling:

'Aha! Dog-gone ye! You've found your tongues — have ye? I thought you were dumb. Well, then — laugh! Laugh — I tell you. Now then — all together. One, two, three — laugh!'

A moment of silence ensued, of silence so profound that you could have heard a pin drop on the deck. Then Ransome's unperturbed voice uttered pleasantly the words:

'I think he has fainted, sir —' The little motionless knot of men stirred, with low murmurs of relief. 'I've got him under the arms. Get hold of his legs, someone.'

Yes. It was a relief. He was silenced for a time — for a time. I could not have stood another peal of that insane screeching. I was sure of it; and just then Gambril, the austere Gambril treated us to another vocal performance. He began to sing out for relief. His voice wailed pitifully in the darkness: 'Come aft, somebody! I can't stand this. Here she'll be off again directly and I can't. . . .'

I dashed aft myself meeting on my way a hard gust of wind whose approach Gambril's ear had detected from afar and which filled the sails on the main in a series of muffled reports mingled with the low plaint of the spars. I was just in time to seize the wheel while Frenchy, who had followed me, caught up the collapsing Gambril. He hauled him out of the way, admonished him to lie still where he was, and then stepped up to relieve me, asking calmly:

'How am I to steer her, sir?'

'Dead before it, for the present. I'll get you a light in a moment.'

But going forward I met Ransome bringing up the spare binnacle lamp. That man noticed everything, attended to everything, shed comfort around him as he moved. As he passed me he remarked in a soothing tone that the stars were coming out. They were. The breeze was sweeping clear the sooty sky, breaking through the indolent silence of the sea.

The barrier of awful stillness which had encompassed us for so many days as though we had been accursed was broken. I felt that. I let myself fall on to the skylight seat. A faint white ridge of foam, thin, very thin, broke alongside. The first for ages – for ages. I could have cheered, if it hadn't been for the sense of guilt which clung to all my thoughts secretly. Ransome stood before me.

'What about the mate?' I asked anxiously. 'Still unconscious?'

'Well, sir – it's funny.' Ransome was evidently puzzled. 'He hasn't spoken a word, and his eyes are shut. But it looks to me more like sound sleep than anything else.'

I accepted this view as the least troublesome of any, or at any rate, least disturbing. Dead faint or deep slumber, Mr Burns had to be left to himself for the present. Ransome remarked suddenly:

'I believe you want a coat, sir.'

'I believe I do,' I sighed out.

But I did not move. What I felt I wanted were new limbs. My arms and legs seemed utterly useless, fairly worn out. They didn't even ache. But I stood up all the same to put on the coat when Ransome brought it up. And when he suggested that he had better now 'take Gambril forward,' I said:

'All right. I'll help you to get him down on the main deck.'

I found that I was quite able to help, too. We raised Gambril up between us. He tried to help himself along like a man, but all the time he was inquiring piteously:

'You won't let me go when we come to the ladder? You won't let me go when we come to the ladder?'

The breeze kept on freshening and blew true, true to a hair. At daylight by careful manipulation of the helm we got the foreyards to run square by themselves (the water keeping smooth) and then went about hauling the ropes tight. Of the four men I had with me at night, I could see now only two. I didn't inquire as to the others. They had given in. For a time only I hoped.

Our various tasks forward occupied us for hours, the two men with me moved so slowly and had to rest so often. One of them remarked that 'every blamed thing in the ship felt about a hundred times heavier than its proper weight.' This was the only complaint uttered. I don't know what we should have done without Ransome. He worked with us, silent too, with a little smile frozen on his lips. From time to time I murmured to him: 'Go steady' – 'Take it easy, Ransome' – and received a quick glance in reply.

When we had done all we could do to make things safe, he disappeared into his galley. Some time afterwards, going forward for a look round, I caught sight of him through the open door. He sat upright on the locker in front of the stove, with his head leaning back against the bulkhead. His eyes were closed; his capable hands held open the front of his thin cotton shirt, baring tragically his powerful chest, which heaved in painful and laboured gasps. He didn't hear me.

I retreated quietly and went straight on to the poop to relieve Frenchy, who by that time was beginning to look very sick. He gave me the course with great formality and tried to go off with a jaunty step, but reeled widely twice before getting out of my sight.

And then I remained all alone aft, steering my ship, which ran before the wind with a buoyant lift now and then, and even rolling a little. Presently Ransome appeared before me with a tray. The sight of food made me ravenous all at once. He took the wheel while I sat down on the after grating to eat my breakfast.

'This breeze seems to have done for our crowd,' he murmured. 'It just laid them low – all hands.'

'Yes,' I said. 'I suppose you and I are the only two fit men in the ship.'

'Frenchy says there's still a jump left in him. I don't know. It can't be much,' continued Ransome with his wistful smile. 'Good little man that. But suppose, sir, that this wind flies round when we are close to the land – what are we going to do with her?'

'If the wind shifts round heavily after we close in with the land she will either run ashore or get dismasted or both. We won't be able to do anything with her. She's running away with us now. All we can do is to steer her. She's a ship without a crew.'

'Yes. All laid low,' repeated Ransome quietly. 'I do give them a look-in forward every now and then, but it's precious little I can do for them.'

'I, and the ship, and everyone on board of her, are very much indebted to you, Ransome,' I said warmly.

He made as though he had not heard me, and steered in silence till I was ready to relieve him. He surrendered the wheel, picked up the tray, and for a parting shot informed me that Mr Burns was awake and seemed to have a mind to come up on deck.

'I don't know how to prevent him, sir. I can't very well stop down below all the time.'

It was clear that he couldn't. And sure enough Mr Burns came on deck dragging himself painfully aft in his enormous overcoat. I beheld him with a natural dread. To have him around and raving about the wiles of a dead man while I had to steer a wildly rushing ship full of dying men was a rather dreadful prospect.

But his first remarks were quite sensible in meaning and tone. Apparently he had no recollection of the night scene. And if he had he didn't betray himself once. Neither did he talk very much. He sat on the skylight looking desperately ill at first, but that strong breeze, before which the last remnant of my crew had wilted down, seemed to blow a fresh stock of vigour into his frame with every gust. One could almost see the process.

By way of sanity test I alluded on purpose to the late captain. I was delighted to find that Mr Burns did not display undue interest in the subject. He ran over the old tale of that savage ruffian's iniquities with a certain vindictive gusto and then concluded unexpectedly:

'I do believe, sir, that his brain began to go a year or more before he died.'

A wonderful recovery. I could hardly spare it as much admiration as it deserved, for I had to give all my mind to the steering.

In comparison with the hopeless languor of the preceding days this was dizzy speed. Two ridges of foam streamed from the ship's bows; the wind sang in a strenuous note which under other circumstances would have expressed to me all the joy of life. Whenever the hauled-up mainsail started trying to slat and bang itself to pieces in its gear, Mr Burns would look at me apprehensively.

'What would you have me do, Mr Burns? We can neither furl it nor set it. I only wish the old thing would thrash itself to pieces and be done with it. This beastly racket confuses me.'

Mr Burns wrung his hands, and cried out suddenly:

'How will you get the ship into harbour, sir, without men to handle her?'

And I couldn't tell him.

Well – it did get done about forty hours afterwards. By the exorcising virtue of Mr Burns's awful laugh, the malicious spectre had been laid, the evil spell broken, the curse removed. We were now in the hands of a kind and energetic Providence. It was rushing us on....

I shall never forget the last night, dark, windy, and starry. I steered. Mr Burns, after having obtained from me a solemn promise to give him a kick if anything happened, went frankly to sleep on the deck close to the binnacle. Convalescents need sleep. Ransome, his back propped against the mizzenmast and a blanket over his legs, remained perfectly still, but I don't suppose he closed his eyes for a moment. That embodiment of jauntiness, Frenchy, still under the delusion that there was 'a jump' left in him, had insisted on joining us; but mindful of discipline, had laid himself down as far on the forepart of the poop as he could get, alongside the bucket-rack.

And I steered, too tired for anxiety, too tired for connected thought. I had moments of grim exultation and then my heart would sink awfully at the thought of that forecastle at the other end of the dark deck, full of fever-stricken men – some of them dying. By my fault. But never mind. Remorse must wait. I had to steer.

In the small hours the breeze weakened, then failed altogether. About five it returned, gentle enough, enabling us to head for the roadstead. Daybreak found Mr Burns sitting wedged up with coils of rope on the stern-grating, and from the depth of his overcoat steering the ship with very white bony hands; while Ransome and I rushed along the decks letting go all the sheets and halliards by the run. We dashed next up on to the forecastle head. The perspiration of labour and sheer nervousness simply poured off our heads as we toiled to get the anchors cock-billed. I dared not look at Ransome as we worked side by side. We exchanged curt words; I could hear him panting close to me and I avoided turning my eyes his way for fear of seeing him fall down and expire in the act of putting out his strength – for what? Indeed for some distinct ideal.

The consummate seaman in him was aroused. He needed no directions. He knew what to do. Every effort, every movement was an act of consistent heroism. It was not for me to look at a man thus inspired.

At last all was ready, and I heard him say, 'Hadn't I better go down and open the compressors now, sir?'

'Yes. Do,' I said. And even then I did not glance his way. After a time his voice came up from the main deck:

'When you like, sir. All clear on the windlass here.'

I made a sign to Mr Burns to put the helm down and then I let both anchors go one after another, leaving the ship to take as much cable as she wanted. She took the best part of them both before she brought up. The loose sails coming aback ceased their maddening racket above my head. A perfect stillness reigned in the ship. And while I stood forward feeling a little giddy in that sudden peace, I caught faintly a moan or two and the incoherent mutterings of the sick in the forecastle.

As we had a signal for medical assistance flying on the mizzen it is a fact that before the ship was fairly at rest three steam-launches from various men-of-war arrived alongside; and at least five naval surgeons clambered on board. They stood in a knot gazing up and down the empty main deck, then looked aloft – where not a man could be seen either.

I went towards them – a solitary figure in a blue and grey striped sleeping suit and a pipe-clayed cork helmet on its head. Their disgust was extreme. They had expected surgical cases. Each one had brought his carving tools with him. But they soon got over their little disappointment. In less than five minutes one of the steam-launches was rushing shorewards to order a big boat and some hospital people for the removal of the crew. The big steam-pinnace went off to her ship to bring over a few bluejackets to furl my sails for me.

One of the surgeons had remained on board. He came out of the forecastle looking impenetrable, and noticed my inquiring gaze.

'There's nobody dead in there, if that's what you want to know,' he said deliberately. Then added in a tone of wonder: 'The whole crew!'

'And very bad?'

'And very bad,' he repeated. His eyes were roaming all over the ship. 'Heavens! What's that?'

'That,' I said, glancing aft, 'is Mr Burns, my chief officer.'

Mr Burns with his moribund head nodding on the stalk of his lean neck was a sight for any one to exclaim at. The surgeon asked:

'Is he going to the hospital too?'

'Oh, no,' I said jocosely. 'Mr Burns can't go on shore till the mainmast goes. I am very proud of him. He's my only convalescent.'

'You look...' began the doctor, staring at me. But I interrupted him angrily:

'I am not ill.'

'No.... You look queer.'

'Well, you see, I have been seventeen days on deck.'

'Seventeen!... But you must have slept.'

'I suppose I must have. I don't know. But I'm certain that I didn't sleep for the last forty hours.'

'Phew!... You will be going ashore presently, I suppose?'

'As soon as ever I can. There's no end of business waiting for me there.'

The surgeon released my hand, which he had taken while we talked, pulled out his pocket-book, wrote in it rapidly, tore out the page, and offered it to me.

'I strongly advise you to get this prescription made up for yourself ashore. Unless I am much mistaken, you will need it this evening.'

'What is it, then?' I asked with suspicion.

'Sleeping draught,' answered the surgeon curtly; and moving with an air of interest towards Mr Burns, he engaged him in conversation.

As I went below to dress to go ashore, Ransome followed me. He begged my pardon; he wished, too, to be sent ashore and paid off.

I looked at him in surprise. He was waiting for my answer with an air of anxiety.

'You don't mean to leave the ship!' I cried out.

'I do really, sir. I want to go and be quiet somewhere. Anywhere. The hospital will do.'

'But, Ransome,' I said, 'I hate the idea of parting with you.'

'I must go,' he broke in. 'I have a right!' He gasped and a look of almost savage determination passed over his face. For an instant he was another being. And I saw under the worth and the comeliness of the man the humble reality of things. Life was a boon to him – this precarious hard life – and he was thoroughly alarmed about himself.

'Of course I shall pay you off if you wish it,' I hastened to say. 'Only I must ask you to remain on board till this afternoon. I can't leave Mr Burns absolutely by himself in the ship for hours.'

He softened at once and assured me with a smile and in his natural pleasant voice that he understood that very well.

When I returned on deck everything was ready for the removal of the men. It was the last ordeal of that episode which had been maturing and tempering my character – though I did not know it.

It was awful. They passed under my eyes one after another – each of them an embodied reproach of the bitterest kind, till I felt a sort of revolt wake up in me. Poor Frenchy had gone suddenly under. He was carried past me insensible, his comic face horribly flushed and as if swollen, breathing stertorously. He looked more like Mr Punch than ever; a disgracefully intoxicated Mr Punch.

The austere Gambril, on the contrary, had improved temporarily. He insisted on walking on his own feet to the rail – of course with assistance on each side of him. But he gave way to a sudden panic at the moment of being swung over the side and began to wail pitifully:

'Don't let them drop me, sir. Don't let them drop me, sir!' While I kept on shouting to him in most soothing accents: 'All right, Gambril. They won't! They won't!'

It was no doubt very ridiculous. The bluejackets on our deck were grinning quietly, while even Ransome himself (much to the fore in lending a hand) had to enlarge his wistful smile for a fleeting moment.

I left for the shore in the steam-pinnace, and on looking back beheld Mr Burns actually standing up by the taffrail, still in his enormous woolly overcoat. The bright sunlight brought out his weirdness amazingly. He looked like a frightful and elaborate scarecrow set up on the poop of a death-stricken ship, to keep the seabirds from the corpses.

Our story had got about already in town and everybody on shore was most kind. The marine office let me off the port dues, and as there happened to be a shipwrecked crew staying in the Home I had no difficulty in obtaining as many men as I wanted. But when I inquired if I could see Captain Ellis for a moment I was told in accents of pity for my ignorance that our deputy-Neptune had retired and gone home on a pension about three weeks after I left the port. So I suppose that my appointment was the last act, outside the daily routine, of his official life.

It is strange how on coming ashore I was struck by the springy step, the lively eyes, the strong vitality of everyone I met. It impressed me enormously. And amongst those I met there was Captain Giles of course. It would have been very extraordinary if I had not met him. A prolonged stroll in the business part of the town was the regular employment of all his mornings when he was ashore.

I caught the glitter of the gold watch-chain across his chest ever so far away. He radiated benevolence.

'What is it I hear?' he queried with a 'kind uncle' smile, after shaking hands. 'Twenty-one days from Bankok?'

'Is this all you've heard?' I said. 'You must come to tiffin with me. I want you to know exactly what you have let me in for.'

He hesitated for almost a minute.

'Well – I will,' he decided condescendingly at last.

We turned into the hotel. I found to my surprise that I could eat quite a lot. Then over the cleared table-cloth I unfolded to Captain Giles all the story since I took command in all its professional and emotional aspects, while he smoked patiently the big cigar I had given him.

Then he observed sagely:

'You must feel jolly well tired by this time.'

'No,' I said. 'Not tired. But I'll tell you, Captain Giles, how I feel. I feel old. And I must be. All of you on shore look to me just a lot of skittish youngsters that have never known a care in the world.'

He didn't smile. He looked insufferably exemplary. He declared:

'That will pass. But you do look older – it's a fact.'

'Aha!' I said.

'No! No! The truth is that one must not make too much of anything in life, good or bad.'

'Live at half-speed,' I murmured perversely. 'Not everybody can do that.'

'You'll be glad enough presently if you can keep going even at that rate,' he retorted with his air of conscious virtue. 'And there's another thing: a man should stand up to his bad luck, to his mistakes, to his conscience, and all that sort of thing. Why – what else would you have to fight against?'

I kept silent. I don't know what he saw in my face, but he asked abruptly:

'Why – you aren't faint-hearted?'

'God only knows, Captain Giles,' was my sincere answer.

'That's all right,' he said calmly. 'You will learn soon how not to be faint-hearted. A man has got to learn everything – and that's what so many of those youngsters don't understand.'

'Well, I am no longer a youngster.'

'No,' he conceded. 'Are you leaving soon?'

'I am going on board directly,' I said. 'I shall pick up one of my anchors and heave in to half-cable on the other as soon as my new crew comes on board and I shall be off at daylight to-morrow.'

'You will?' grunted Captain Giles approvingly. 'That's the way. You'll do.'

'What did you expect? That I would want to take a week ashore for a rest?' I said, irritated by his tone. 'There's no rest for me till she's out in the Indian Ocean, and not much of it even then.'

He puffed at the cigar moodily, as if transformed.

'Yes, that's what it amounts to,' he said in a musing tone. It was as if a ponderous curtain had rolled up disclosing an unexpected Captain Giles. But it was only for a moment, merely the time to let him add: 'Precious little rest in life for anybody. Better not think of it.'

We rose, left the hotel, and parted from each other in the street with a warm handshake, just as he began to interest me for the first time in our intercourse.

The first thing I saw when I got back to the ship was Ransome on the quarter-deck sitting quietly on his neatly lashed sea-chest.

I beckoned him to follow me into the saloon, where I sat down to write a letter of recommendation for him to a man I knew on shore.

When finished I pushed it across the table. 'It may be of some good to you when you leave the hospital.'

He took it, put it in his pocket. His eyes were looking away from me – nowhere. His face was anxiously set.

'How are you feeling now?' I asked.

'I don't feel bad now, sir,' he answered stiffly. 'But I am afraid of its coming on. . . .' The wistful smile came back on his lips for a moment. 'I – I am in a blue funk about my heart, sir.'

I approached him with extended hand. His eyes, not looking at me, had a strained expression. He was like a man listening for a warning call.

'Won't you shake hands, Ransome?' I said gently.

He exclaimed, flushed up dusky red, gave my hand a hard wrench – and next moment, left alone in the cabin,

I listened to him going up the companion stairs cautiously, step by step, in mortal fear of starting into sudden anger our common enemy it was his hard fate to carry consciously within his faithful breast.

ABOUT THE INTRODUCER

MARTIN SEYMOUR-SMITH has written on a wide range of literary subjects. His works include studies of Thomas Hardy and Robert Graves.

This book is set in CASLON, designed and engraved by William
Caslon of WILLIAM CASLON & SON, Letter-Founders in
London, around 1740. In England at the beginning of
the eighteenth century, Dutch type was probably
more widely used than English. The rise
of William Caslon put a stop to the
importation of Dutch types
and so changed the his-
tory of English
typecutting.